Ere Roosevelt Came

"A compelling addition to the canon of Pan-African creative writing from the 1930s. The engaging, informative essays by the editors show how Ali brought to life core themes of African American literature for readers in colonial Africa."
—Stephanie Newell, George M. Bodman Professor of English,
Yale University

"Ali's creative intellectual productivity was a major force in early-twentieth-century Pan-Africanism. The introductory material by Alex Lubin and Marina Bilbija offer essential tools for today's readers to appreciate this extraordinary, yet previously inaccessible, novel and its author. Reading this text through the multi-continental circuits of both its author's travels and the novel's protagonists, we recalibrate our own grid of Pan-African literary productivity."
—Dr. Leslie James, Queen Mary University of London

"Bilbija and Lubin have made an outstanding contribution to literary Pan-Africanism by reintroducing the obscure Pan-African novel of Duse Mohamed Ali. This once influential Pan-Africanist … introduced Islam and the history of Africa to members of [Marcus Garvey's] UNIA. His novel and the accompanying essays make a welcome addition to the field."
—Rey Bowen, University of Chichester

"In recovering this daringly speculative serial novel by Duse Mohamed Ali, Lubin and Bilbija have excavated a landmark of literary Pan-Africanism while capturing the vibrancy of transatlantic Black periodical networks in the 1930s."
—Brent Hayes Edwards, author of *The Practice of Diaspora:
Literature, Translation, and the Rise of Black Internationalism*

Black Critique

Series editors: Anthony Bogues and Bedour Alagraa

Throughout the twentieth century and until today, anti-racist, radical decolonisation struggles have attempted to create new forms of thought. Figures from Ida B. Wells to W.E.B. Du Bois and Steve Biko, from Claudia Jones to Walter Rodney and Amílcar Cabral produced work which drew from the historical experiences of Africa and the African diaspora. They drew inspiration from the Haitian revolution, radical Black abolitionist thought and practice, and other currents that marked the contours of a Black radical intellectual and political tradition.

The Black Critique series operates squarely within this tradition of ideas and political struggles. It includes books which foreground this rich and complex history. At a time when there is a deep desire for change, Black radicalism is one of the most underexplored traditions that can drive emancipatory change today. This series highlights these critical ideas from anywhere in the Black world, creating a new history of radical thought for our times.

Also available:

Against Racial Capitalism:
Selected Writings
Neville Alexander
Edited by Salim Vally and Enver Motala

Moving Against the System:
The 1968 Congress of Black Writers and
the Making of Global Consciousness
Edited and with an Introduction by
David Austin

Revolutionary Movements in
Sub-Saharan Africa:
An Untold Story
Edited by Pascal Bianchini, Ndongo
Samba Sylla and Leo Zeilig

Anarchism and the Black Revolution:
The Definitive Edition
Lorenzo Kom'boa Ervin

After the Postcolonial Caribbean:
Memory, Imagination, Hope
Brian Meeks

A Certain Amount of Madness:
The Life, Politics and Legacies of Thomas
Sankara
Edited by Amber Murrey

Of Black Study
Joshua Myers

On Racial Capitalism, Black Internation-
alism, and Cultures of Resistance
Cedric J. Robinson
Edited by H.L.T. Quan

Black Minded:
The Political Philosophy of Malcolm X
Michael Sawyer

Red International and Black Caribbean
Communists in New York City,
Mexico and the West Indies, 1919–1939
Margaret Stevens

The Point is to Change the World:
Selected Writings of Andaiye
Edited by Alissa Trotz

Ere Roosevelt Came

A Record of the Adventures of the Man in the Cloak

A Pan-African Novel of the Global 1930s

Duse Mohamed Ali

Edited by Marina Bilbija and Alex Lubin

First published 2024 by Pluto Press
New Wing, Somerset House, Strand, London WC2R 1LA
and Pluto Press, Inc.
1930 Village Center Circle, 3-834, Las Vegas, NV 89134

www.plutobooks.com

British Library Cataloguing in Publication Data
A catalogue record for this book is available from the British Library

ISBN   978 0 7453 4860 5   Paperback
ISBN   978 0 7453 4862 9   PDF
ISBN   978 0 7453 4861 2   EPUB

This book is printed on paper suitable for recycling and made from fully managed and sustained forest sources. Logging, pulping and manufacturing processes are expected to conform to the environmental standards of the country of origin.

Typeset by Stanford DTP Services, Northampton, England

Simultaneously printed in the United Kingdom and United States of America

Duse Mohamed Ali, circa 1911. Unknown photographer, from *In the Land of the Pharaohs: A Short History of Egypt*, by Duse Mohamed Ali (London, Stanley Paul & Co.) Public Domain, https://commons.wikimedia.org/w/index.php?curid=93119668

Contents

Duse Mohamed Ali and the Cultures of Pan-Africanism

Alex Lubin

Throughout the first three decades of the twentieth century, an enigmatic thinker, activist, and artist helped define the contours of the Pan-African world. Duse Mohamed Ali[1] is a foundational figure in Pan-African movements due to his active political, religious, and literary life, including his role as the editor of the influential London-based newspaper *African Times and Orient Review (ATOR)*, which was published from July 1912 to December 1920. Ali launched *ATOR* before World War I, at a time when he forecast a rising tide of global colonialism and racism. As he wrote in the inaugural issue, "The recent Universal Races Congress, convened in the Metropolis of the *Anglo-Saxon world*, clearly demonstrated that there was ample need for a Pan-Oriental, Pan-African journal at the seat of the British Empire, which would lay the aims, desires, and intentions of the Black, Brown, and Yellow races—within and without the empire—at the throne of Caesar."[2] Ali understood there to be an "Anglo-Saxon world," or a white world order that was being remade in the early decades of the twentieth century in the crucible of imperial warfare, overseas colonialism, and racist violence in the metropoles. Ali saw the need to create something like an Afro-Oriental analogue to the Anglo-Saxon world that could challenge global racism and colonialism. Within these contexts, Ali believed, like his contemporary, W.E.B. Du Bois, that "the problem of the twentieth century is the problem of the color line—the relation of the darker to the lighter races of men in Asia and Africa, in America and the islands of the sea," and he committed

---

1   This is how Ali presented his name in *The Comet*, where he published the novel. In other publications, Ali presents his first name as "Dusé."
2   Cited in Alex Lubin, *Geographies of Liberation: The Making of an Afro-Arab Political Imaginary* (Chapel Hill: University of North Carolina Press, 2016), 59; italics added.

to conjuring an Afro-Asian world, rooted to extant cultures of global Black resistance.[3]

Duse Mohamed Ali understood more than many of his contemporaries that the early twentieth century represented a new historical conjuncture. He was keenly aware of the crises precipitated by global warfare and colonialism, including the rising tide of fascism and the limits of Black leadership when divorced from the Black masses. The post–World War I dissolution of old empires and the formation of an international order rooted to the nation-state would forever alter the lives of those who lived through the transition from subjecthood to national citizenship. The Afro-Oriental world that Ali desired, however, was not readily available to him; it had to be created, often in cultural and social formations. Thus, Ali was part of the vanguard of an emergent cultural and political formation—Afro-Asia—that was constituted by disparate experiences and geographies of racial, colonial, and imperial violence. While Ali became a representative of what Cedric Robinson has called a "Pan-African commonwealth,"[4] it is crucial that we understand that this formation was merely emergent within new geopolitical conjunctures and had not yet crystalized into a legible resource for political power, as it would following World War II.

Ali found himself at the epicenter of the emergent cultures of resistance that constituted early Pan-Africanism because of the ways he encountered

---

3   W.E.B. Du Bois, *The Souls of Black Folk* (New York: New American Library, 1982 [1903]), 54.
4   In his essay "In Search of a Pan-African Commonwealth," which originally appeared in *Social Identities*, Cedric Robinson offers criticism of Pan-African formations that are rooted in the nation-state and that, therefore, reproduce forms of bourgeois leadership that undermine Black mass movements. Instead, he identifies revolutionary Pan-Africanism as that form of imagined community that works against the nation-state, that resists identitarian categories as its rationale, and that provides belonging to the many.

> Drawing on the cultural Pan-Africanism embedded in the revolutionary Pan-Africanism employed and articulated by James Padmore, Nkrumah, Nyerere, Cabral, Fanon and more frequently and significantly the anonymous Black masses which confronted slavery, colonialism, and imperialism on the ground in Africa and the Diaspora, the Pan-African Commonwealth must seek to fulfill Sekou Toure's (1974) recognition that 'Since revolutionary Pan-Africanism basically refers to an Africa of Peoples, it is in its interest to uphold the primacy of peoples as against States.' In such a conspiracy with other supranational forces, Pan-Africanism would continue its sojourn toward its more faint signification: in prehistory, Africa was the origins of us all. (52)

Cedric J. Robinson and Ruth Wilson Gilmore, "In Search of a Pan-African Commonwealth," in *Cedric J. Robinson: On Racial Capitalism, Black Internationalism, and Cultures of Resistance*, edited by H.L.T. Quan (London: Pluto Press, 2019), 45–53.

the contradictions and crises of the modern, Anglo-Saxon world. During a lifetime of migration, he experienced the tumultuous waves of imperial transformation, experienced the birth of new nation-states, and assumed new identities to survive and exist within new geopolitical contexts. Along the way, he became one of the most significant contributors to the Anglo-Saxon world's antithesis—a vibrant Pan-African imaginary forged in Black cultures of resistance, including manifestos, conferences, and varied cultural formations, as well as novels like *Ere Roosevelt Came*.

The outline of Duse Mohamed Ali's biography is, by now, relatively well known even as biographers have faced challenges identifying the archival evidence to validate Ali's self-representation.[5] The chasm between Ali's various self-representations and the archive is due in part to the inability of imperial archives to account for the lives of colonized and minoritized people as well as Ali's propensity to overstate, if not to fabricate, identities drawing on his considerable talents as an actor and orator (he founded the Hull Shakespeare Society in 1903).[6] That said, the aims of recounting Ali's life narrative here are not so much to prove the veracity of his self-fashioning, but instead to suggest that the person who became Duse Mohamed Ali, the editor of *ATOR*, *The Comet*, and the author of *Ere Roosevelt Came*, was very much the outcome of the collision of imperialism and racism—the Anglo-Saxon world—with Pan-Africanism. As his biography attests, Ali was conscripted to the project of European modernity, even as he tried to fashion its undertow in an Afro-Asian political imaginary.[7]

5 British officials and historians have questioned the veracity of Ali's origin story. Ian Duffield's 1971 dissertation on Ali raised questions about Ali's autobiography and speculated that Ali may have been from the United States. Ian Duffield, *Duse Mohamed Ali and the development of Pan-Africanism, 1866-1945*. Dissertation completed at Edinburgh University, 1971. Recently, Jacob S. Dorman has also suggested that Ali may have been an American actor assuming various identities to escape racist persecution and to expand economic opportunities. See, for example, Jacob S. Dorman, "'Western Civilization through Eastern Spectacles': Duse Mohamed Ali, Black Orientalist Imposture, and Black Internationalism," *The Journal of African American History* 108, no. 1 (Winter 2023): 23–49. For our purposes, Ali's "roots" are far less consequential than his "routes."
6 "Pan-African Campaigner Duse Mohamed Ali's Hull Honour," https://www.bbc.com/news/uk-england-humber-43033986, accessed February 21, 2023.
7 In using the word "conscripted" to discuss Ali's relationship to European modernity, I draw on Stuart Hall's insights about how Jamaican colonial subjects were "conscripts of modernity," by which Hall meant to invoke the unwilling ways that colonial subjects are required to acculturate to colonial norms to gain legitimacy as modern subjects. See, for example, Stuart Hall, "Conscripts of Modernity," in *Familiar Stranger: A Life Between Two Islands* (Durham, NC: Duke University Press, 2017). Of course, Hall's notion of

Ali published his autobiography, *Leaves from an Active Life*, in his Nigerian newspaper *The Comet* in 1937–38.[8] *Leaves* details Ali's personal development as well as how the world transformed in profound ways during his lifetime. Ali reports his birthyear as 1866 to Sudanese and Egyptian parents, during the years that Egypt was under the dynastic rule or Muhamad Ali (which united what would become Sudanese and Egyptian territory). Having neither Sudanese nor Egyptian documents to authenticate his birth and possessing no British official papers to mark his inclusion as a British colonial subject, Ali crafted a plausible story of the archival absences concerning his ancestry. He claimed that the midwife who attended his birth kept no paperwork and therefore there was no birth certificate. To explain why he had not learned Arabic as a child, despite having resided in Egypt for the first seven years of his life, Ali writes that his parents sent him to a boarding school in the United Kingdom, and that as a seven-year-old, a French military official (with the name Dusé) working in Egypt had adopted him and moved him to England. Eventually, after World War I, Ali sought a British passport by virtue of Egypt's status as a British protectorate. Yet Ali's lack of birth certificate made it difficult to prove either Egyptian or British belonging. World War I had not only redrawn the map of the world; it had also revised the criteria by which people claimed national belonging. No longer a subject of an empire, Ali and many other refugees of war had to become legible within nations to which they never physically belonged.

A telling example of how the new global order created in the aftermath of World War I impacted Ali's belongings can be found in his struggle to obtain a British passport during a moment when Egypt was a British protectorate. To prove that he was Egyptian, Ali enlisted the assistance of British acquaintances who knew that he was involved in Turkish solidarity work in London following the war. Such work, Ali believed, linked him to the former Ottoman Empire and therefore made plausible his claim to Egypt, which was then a British protectorate. In his petition to Britain authorities for the passport, Ali asked a British Foreign Service official named Aubrey Herbert to write a letter on his behalf. Herbert had worked with Ali in an organization Ali formed in Britain called the Anglo-Ottoman Society, which

---

conscription draws on an intellectual genealogy that includes scholars such as Talal Asad and David Scott.

8   Ali's autobiography was republished by Mustafa Abdekwahid, *Duse Mohamed Ali (1866–1945): The Autobiography of a Pioneer Pan African and Afro-Asian Activist, Compiled with an Introduction by Mustafa Abdelwahid* (Trenton, NJ: The Red Sea Press, 2011).

was intended to facilitate trade relations between the United Kingdom and Turkey. Herbert could, Ali believed, convince British authorities that Ali identified as a Muslim and that Ali presented himself as Egyptian in public venues. Yet Herbert's letter of support offered little help. Herbert wrote to British authorities:

> There is a Negro called Dusé Mohamed. He is by way of being an Ottoman subject, though actually I believe he may be American born, and does not talk either Turkish or Arabic, but he is, or calls himself, Mohammeden. In the past he was quite useful at Moslem meetings, when a number of people used always to try and make anti-Government speeches. He is anxious to go to West Africa for trade purposes and has been refused a [British] passport.[9]

British immigration officials could not verify Ali's Egyptian ancestry or belonging, and as Herbert's letter attests, Ali's complex identities were collapsed into the signifier "a Negro." As a result of the confusion of locating archival evidence to prove Ali's Egyptian belonging, the British authorities refused Ali's passport petition. In an era of European imperial expansion and transition over much of the African continent, Ali became something of a refugee without a country.

Ali was uniquely situated to understand the global contradictions precipitated by the end of World War I—not only because he experienced its accompanying statelessness as shown in his struggle to obtain a passport, but also because he had observed how the making of the liberal international global order produced refugees. He was an attendee at the 1911 Universal Races Congress, an influential forum in which Western understandings of racial difference and national belonging were discussed in the service of drawing new global boundaries organized by nations rather than empires. The Congress was convened in London by Gustav Spiller and Felix Adler and was intended to address "the problem of contact of European with other developed types of civilization. . . . The object of the congress will be to discuss in the light of science and the modern conscience, the general relations subsisting between the peoples of the West and those of the East, between so-called coloured peoples, with a view to encouraging between them a fuller understanding, the most friendly feelings, and a heartier coop-

---

9 Quoted in Lubin, *Geographies of Liberation*, 49.

eration."[10] The Congress was one among several international conferences that helped enshrine liberal understandings of how to regard minority and colonized communities in the formation of nation-states. Ali had hoped to be an official attendee at the Congress, yet he had little standing in such prominent company. Instead of addressing the Congress as an invited speaker, as did W.E.B. Du Bois, Ali performed the third act of *Othello* at the Congress, offering entertainment to the dignitaries in attendance.

Ali's experience attending the Universal Races Congress encouraged him to consider creating a publication venue to articulate the aspirations not only of Black subjects in the UK and its empire, but also of Arab and Islamic people who faced similar forms of exclusion and hostility as him. In this way, Ali saw the need to shift Pan-African consciousness beyond the Atlantic world, and to incorporate Asian and Arab geographies. Ali had befriended advocates for Egyptian nationalism in London and frequently attended political meetings organized to advocate for Egyptian independence. He was also an active member of London's Islamic Society, where he met religious mentors as well as anti-colonial activists.

In 1912, Ali made his signal contribution to the nascent imaginary of Afro-Asian politics by founding *African Times and Orient Review*. As he indicated in the first issue of the newspaper, "Herein will be found the views of the coloured man, whether African or Oriental from the Pillars of Hercules to the Golden Horn, from the Ganges to the Euphrates, from the Nile to the Potomac, and from the Mississippi to the American East, West, North or South, wherever the Oriental or African may found a congregated habitation from thence shall our information spring."[11] *ATOR* offered readers a road map of an Afro-Asian world, one that knit together information and news from across Afro-Asian geographies. In addition to convening writers from across a global map of colonized spaces, Ali attracted a cadre of African and Arab diasporic writers—including a young Jamaican in the UK named Marcus Garvey, who published his first article in *ATOR*.

World War I was a turning point not only for Ali but also for global Black politics. The liberal international order that was established following the Treaty of Versailles and the formation of the League of Nations created new political entities, nation-states, and colonial arrangements, inspiring emergent political imaginaries from which people like Duse Mohamed Ali created resistant cultures. Within the post–World War I conjuncture flour-

---

10   Lubin, 53.
11   Lubin, 48.

ished the powerful countercurrent of Pan-Africanism, which had formed before the war but crystalized into several mass movements afterward. If the creation of the liberal international order was an attempt by the European imperial powers to divide the world into geopolitical territory still under the political ambit of the Atlantic powers, the Pan-African movements were entirely different constructions of the modern world that sutured together a polity that centered the African world as well as its values, beliefs, and diaspora. While he was often cast aside and asunder by the tides of liberal internationalism, Duse Mohamed Ali found belonging and buoyancy in the currents of global Pan-Africanism between the world wars, what we refer to as "the global 1930s."

The politics of Pan-Africanism were diverse; although they had been launched prior to World War I, the global war inspired a flourishing of movements across the Black diaspora. Ali drew inspiration from varied Pan-African social and cultural formations that emerged to make sense of the global crisis precipitated by the formation of an Anglo-Saxon world order. Across the Black world, cultures of Black resistance emerged to contest the racist violence of Jim Crow segregation in the metropoles and the ravages of imperial warfare and colonialism across the African and Asian continents. Ali and his contemporaries understood that imperial warfare and colonial plunder were dialectically related to racist violence in European and American metropoles, a dialectic that Du Bois had referred to as "the anarchy of empire."[12] The constellation of politics organized under the banner of Pan-Africanism were responses to conjunctures in particular geopolitical locations; Ali's genius would be in recognizing how these Pan-African movements could harmonize under the banner of the Afro-Oriental world.

Ali was influenced and inspired by the Pan-African Congresses, the Universal Negro Improvement Association (UNIA), and the Négritude movement, but he could be critical of how these movements had too often lionized charismatic Black leaders, often in ways that hid the activism of the Black masses. A Pan-African commonwealth had been built by the Black global masses; following World War I, however, Ali saw how some Black leaders were complicit with emergent fascism and colonialism within the Anglo-Saxon world. In *Ere Roosevelt Came*, therefore, Ali lampoons Pan-African leaders while elevating the agency of Black masses.

---

12 W.E.B. Du Bois, *Darkwater: Voices from within the Veil* (New York: Harcourt, Brace, and Howe, 1920), 276.

Pan-African politics were not inevitable responses to racism and colonialism; rather, they were attempts to formulate cultures of resistance to these forces at particular historical conjunctures and in specific geographical spaces. Pan-African movements especially coalesced in the wake of World War I as a new geopolitical order enshrined in the League of Nations charter called for "self-determination" as a rubric for international governance. The unit of political recognition in postwar international governance was the nation-state, a political entity that replaced empires and their territorial possessions in the world order. The League of Nations reproduced many of the Eurocentric assumptions of the previous world order; it replaced brute-force colonialism with a liberal rhetoric of self-government, but in doing so it enshrined a hierarchy of territories that were fit and unfit for self-rule. This hierarchy was a difference structured in race and racisms. A system of mandates and trusteeships were created after World War I to foster European tutelage over still-developing, and presumably unfit, African nations. If the war was a conjunctural moment for Europe and the West, it was a different kind of conjunctural moment for the Black world, which was interpolated into a new world order in which they were regarded as unfit for self-government. The Black cultures of resistance that emerged within the postwar conjunctures were internationalist and formed under the banner of Pan-Africanism. The cultures of Pan-Africanism, as we will see, had to be created through political meetings, literary texts, journalism, aesthetic practices, and more. In other words, the emergent politics of Pan-Africanism were formed in narration.[13]

Following World War I, W.E.B. Du Bois organized the inaugural Pan-African Congress. Du Bois recognized the need for African anti-colonial struggle to work alongside anti-racist struggle in European and American

---

13 I mean to invoke here Benedict Anderson's insight that print capitalism helped from the imagined community of the nation-state. Similarly, Pan-Africanism, while not a nation-state, is nevertheless an imagined community constituted by print and other cultures of resistance across disparate geographies. The Pan-African commonwealth, however, is not based in a singular language or cultural formation; unlike the European nationalisms that are the subject of Anderson's *Imagined Communities*, the Pan-African commonwealth is structured in differences across geopolitical spaces. They are articulated, therefore, not through a singular language but via translation. As Brent Hayes Edwards has argued in *The Practice of Diaspora*, Black diasporic community is formed as *decalage*, or an (incomplete) assemblage of texts across different sociolinguistic spaces. See, for example, Benedict Anderson, *Imagined Communities* (London: Verso Books, 2016); and Brent Hayes Edwards, *The Practice of Diaspora: Literature, Translation, and the Rise of Black Internationalism* (Cambridge, MA: Harvard University Press, 2003).

metropoles. Specially, the Pan-African Congresses were formed to challenge the Anglo-Saxon world's colonialism in African territory following the dissolution of European empires. Du Bois rejected the formation of European trusteeships that had been enshrined in the League of Nations and organized conferences among Afro-diasporic anti-colonial leaders to theorize an anti-colonial response. The inaugural Pan-African Congress was organized in 1919 in Paris, and included fifty-seven participants from across Africa, the Caribbean, and the United States. Conference attendees demanded political self-determination and reparations for Black peoples across African and New World territories. The Pan-African Congress was a means for anti-colonial leaders in African territories to form local anti-colonial movements. For example, a contingent of political activists, from what was then called British West Africa, formed the National Congress of British West Africa at the inaugural Pan-African Congress. The second Pan-African Congress was convened across London, Paris, and Brussels in 1921, with more than a hundred delegates. The second congress crystalized demands for political independence across Africa. The congress also theorized the global color line as means to unite an "imagined community" among Afro-descended peoples not only in Africa but also in the United States. The 1927 Congress (the fourth) was convened in New York and focused explicitly on the relationship of lynching and Jim Crow to the global color line.[14]

Although the Pan-African Congresses were important venues to imagine the global color line and to set the terms for the struggle ahead, it could be faulted for privileging an educated vanguard at the expense of working-class activists. The Pan-African Congresses did not have offices across the Afro-Asian world, and its leaders could be disdainful of alternative Pan-African movements, such as Marcus Garvey's UNIA, which they accused of being overly concerned with economic development and too little with developing anti-imperialist and anti-racist fronts.

Inspired by the African emigration movements of figures like Chief Sam, the Black self-improvement movement of Booker T. Washington, and the cultural politics of Black history found in the Negro Historical Society, Marcus Garvey's UNIA formulated a Pan-African movement focused on Black economic entrepreneurship and Black emigration back to the

---

14   See, for example, George Padmore (ed), *History of the Pan-African Congress: Colonial and Coloured Unity, a Programme of Action* (London: Hammersmith Bookshop, 1963); and Hakim Adi, *Pan-Africanism: A History* (London: Bloomsbury Academic, 2018).

"homeland." The UNIA first opened in Jamaica then moved to New York amid the Great Migration. Committed to Afrocentrism, the ability of New World Black people to build their own cultural and economic institutions, the UNIA formed several business enterprises, including the Black Star line to transport African Americans in their "return" voyage to the African continent. The UNIA also launched a line of Black-owned laundry and grocery stores.

If Du Bois's Pan-African Congresses were mostly intellectual projects that theorized the politics of anti-colonialism, Garvey's UNIA was a political and cultural formation from below—one that organized the Black masses in the United States and the Caribbean, and eventually in Africa, around a politics of Black nationalism and racial consciousness. The UNIA became the largest Pan-African organization in history, and included women as organizers, nurses, newspaper editors, and mechanics.

Garvey developed a global racial consciousness via the publication of his popular newspaper *Negro World*. Foreshadowing Benedict Anderson's insights in *Imagined Communities*, Garvey—who had been an assistant at Duse Mohamed Ali's publication *ATOR*—understood the importance of print cultures and news media to forge national consciousness. After the launch of the UNIA and the success of his outlet *Negro World*, Garvey would turn the tables by hiring Ali to serve as an African correspondent to the newspaper.

Garvey's success coincided with the so-called New Negro Movement or Harlem Renaissance. These were cultural movements with innovations in sound and writing, inspired by the migration of more than half a million Black people from the southern United States to northern US metropoles following World War I. An additional hundred thousand migrants entered the United States from the Caribbean, many of whom formed the intellectual, artistic, and political vanguard of the New Negro Movement. The Garvey movement capitalized on the multiethnic migration of Black peoples to the United States by fostering a vibrant print culture to match the literary and artistic flourishing of the Harlem Renaissance. Not only its main political organ, *Negro World*, but also several additional newspapers were fostered in the era of the UNIA, including *The Liberator, The Emancipator, The Voice, The New Negro*, and others.[15]

---

15   See, for example, Todd Vogel, *The Black Press: New Literary and Historical Essays* (New Brunswick, NJ: Rutgers University Press, 2001).

The UNIA helped foster a vibrant literary culture and helped translate older diasporic Afro-Asian movements into its emergent culture of Pan-Africanism. For example, members of the UNIA, including Duse Mohamed Ali, were influential in translating "eastern" forms of Islam to New World contexts. Ali, for example, toured much of the East Coast of the United States as an Islamic orator, and in the US he hosted South Asian, Ahmadiyya Muslims he had befriended while living in the United Kingdom. These tours inspired the formation of Black American religious movements inspired by Pan-Africanism, including Noble Drew Ali's Moorish Science Temple, and eventually the Nation of Islam.

While the Pan-African Congresses helped build an anti-imperialist and anti-racist front across the Black world, and Garvey's UNIA fostered a cultural politics of Black nationalism and economic self-determination, the French Négritude movement sought to create a Black world aesthetic, a culture of Pan-African resistance that reframed the Anglo-Saxon world from the vantage point of Black geographies—especially francophone ones. Based primarily in France and its colonies, particularly in the Caribbean, the Négritude movement, like the other Pan-African movements, responded to the crisis of the post–World War I era. Colonialism had driven the forced migration of thousands of African and Caribbean people to France, where they found themselves treated with racism, while also enlisting in the French war effort in World War I. Around 135,000 African soldiers fought for France in the war, with around 800,000 workers and soldiers pitching in from French colonies.[16] The contradictions of being enlisted in a project of French nationalism to save the world for democracy while facing racism and colonialism called into question the relationship between the colonies and the metropole.

A francophone Pan-African front was created in the wake of the war, and it was constituted in and by print culture and visual art. Among the cultural formations that contributed to the making of these resistant politics were the newspaper *La Paria*, which committed to "the liberation of the oppressed from the forces of domination, and the realization of love and fraternity."[17] The Martiniquais writer René Maran's novel *Batouala* (1921) helped expose the contradictions of French colonialism amid a war for self-determination.

---

16   Adi, *Pan-Africanism*.
17   Adi. Also see G. D. Camara, "Faces of Blackness: The Creation of the New Negro and Négritude Movements in Harlem and Paris," *Journal of Black Studies 51*, no. 8 (2020): 846–64.

The monthly journal of the Ligue Universelle, *Les Continents*, was edited by Kojo Tovalou Houénou, who was born in present-day Benin. The journal demanded citizenship rights for French colonial citizens. The collective politics of Négritude articulated a Black nationalism similar to Garvey's.

Duse Mohamed Ali was inspired by each of the Pan-African movements he saw flourishing in the wake of World War I, and *ATOR* was a precursor to the many Black world newspapers that would be launched by postwar Pan-African movements. At the same time, however, Ali also witnessed how, ascendant fascism within the Anglo-Saxon world complicated the politics of anti-fascism by Western-based Pan-African movements as several fascist movements gained traction after the war, especially in Italy under the leadership of Benito Mussolini and in Germany under the leadership of Adolf Hitler. Within the United States, fascist movements coalesced under the banner of the Ku Klux Klan as well as under other movements like that of Father Coughlin's, who established a nativist, antisemitic organization that lent rhetorical support to European fascism and challenged the rights of Black migrants in Detroit, where his popular radio show was located. Other forms of fascism in the United States emerged in the Red Summer of 1919, in which dozens of anti-Black race riots took place across the United States, targeting Black soldiers and businesspeople. In 1921, the middle-class Black community in the Greenwood area of Tulsa, Oklahoma, was targeted by white rioters who were threatened by the success of the so-called Black Wall Street. The violence directed at Black people in Tulsa led to an estimate of three hundred deaths.[18] Ali would feature Tulsa in *Ere Roosevelt Came* as the city where a secret organization of Black airmen began training to confront global fascism and white supremacy.

While European fascism and anti-Black racism within the United States drew Black masses to Pan-African politics, so too did the ascendance of US overseas imperialism just before and after World War I. In 1912, US-backed forces defeated Afro-Cuban nationalists. Three years later, the US launched what would become a nineteen-year occupation of Haiti. And by 1929 the United States had formed partnerships with an elite Americo-Liberian political leadership to grant land to the Firestone Tire and Rubber company in

18   On the Tulsa race riot, see Scott Ellsworth and John Hope Franklin, *Death in a Promised Land: The Tulsa Race Riot of 1921* (Baton Rouge: Louisiana State University, 1982). Also see Cameron McWhirter, *Red Summer: The Summer of 1919 and the Awakening of Black America* (New York: Henry Holt & Co., 2011).

what would launch decades of Western corporate-military partnerships to undermine Liberian sovereignty.

Within the context of ascendant domestic and international fascism, as well as of US imperialism across Black geographies, several Pan-African leaders within the West had contradictory relationships to these fascist and imperialist projects. As Cedric Robinson has written, "Blacks had to contend with the spectacle of their most influential 'race' leaders as collaborators" in US imperial projects over Black global territory. Robinson continues:

> The diffidence of leaders like Washington in the Haitian affair; the role of figures like Du Bois in the opposition to and the destruction of the UNIA organization and programme; Du Bois' collaboration with the War Department during the First World War . . . ; the collusion of Black leaders with the Liberian elite's use of forced labour, had all produced a deep resentment towards a stratum whose greed and self-deceptions led it to identification with American imperialism at home and Black ruling-class oligarchies abroad.[19]

Some postwar Black leaders failed to vociferously attack the imposition of US colonial forces in places like Haiti (in 1915). For example, several Black luminaries accepted roles in the US occupation forces in Haiti, including Robert Russa Moton, who was president of Tuskegee Institute. Booker T. Washington lent support to US occupying forces and conveyed his sentiments that Haiti was, as Brenda Gayle Plummer notes, a "backward country."[20] Although Du Bois opposed the US occupation of Haiti, NAACP board member James Weldon Johnson was initially ambivalent about the occupation, yet eventually criticized US policy there. Similarly, Lemuel Livingston, who had been the US consul in Haiti, was initially supportive of intervention and occupation but eventually became critical when he saw the limits of the US presence and its negative impacts on the Haitian people. Eventually, as Plummer and Robinson argue, the occupation of Haiti became a touchstone for Black politics in the United States, one that helped coalesce a Pan-African perspective calling for solidarity across global Black geographies.

---

19   Robinson, "Fascism and the Response of Black Radical Theorists," in *Cedric J. Robinson*, 134.
20   Brenda Gayle Plummer, "The Afro-American Response to the Occupation of Haiti, 1915-1934," *Phylon (1960-)* 43, no. 2 (1982): 125–43.

Duse Mohamed Ali lived in the United States during much of the 1920s and then in West Africa during the 1930s; he was therefore on the front lines of these complex currents of US and European fascism and the contradictory alliances drawn by Western-based Pan-African leaders. Yet for Ali the possibilities of Pan-Africanism were reflected not in Black leadership but in the ways in which movements for Pan-Africanism created new geopolitical imaginaries for the many. In 1921, Ali had stopped publishing *ATOR* and moved to the United States, where he reunited with Marcus Garvey and joined the UNIA. Garvey hired Ali to head the Africa section of the UNIA's newspaper, *Negro World*. Ali's experience in the UK and North Africa made him the ideal candidate to serve as the UNIA's foreign secretary; in this capacity he drafted the UNIA's 1922 petition to the League of Nations requesting that German colonies in Africa be ceded to the UNIA for the formation of a diasporic Black nation-state.

By 1924, however, Ali terminated his formal work in the Garvey movement and moved to Detroit, where he helped introduce some of the South Asian Muslims he had met in the UK to Garveyites, with the belief that the Garvey movement could be more successful in Islamic countries if its members better understood the faith. In this way, Ali sought to expand Garvey's Pan-Africanism beyond the Black Atlantic. In Detroit, Ali established a Muslim Society and invited the Indian Ahmadiyya Muslim leader Muhammed Sadiq to lead it. These relationships between Pan-Africanists and Pan-Islamicists in Detroit were important, and although it is not clear to what extent Ali was involved, they helped inspire the growth of Black American Islamic organizations like the Moorish Science Temple and the Nation of Islam. Furthermore, from the time Ali lived in the UK to his involvement with Black Muslim communities in the United States, his engagement with Pan-Islamic movements oriented his notion of the Pan-African commonwealth beyond the Atlantic world, to include Arab and Asian publics as well.[21]

In 1931, Duse Mohamed Ali moved to Lagos, Nigeria, where he followed a business opportunity in the cocoa business, but ultimately found success publishing another newspaper based in Lagos, called *The Comet*. It was from here that Ali published a serialized version of his autobiography, and the novel *Ere Roosevelt Came: A Record of the Adventures of the Man in the Cloak*. In some ways, *Ere Roosevelt Came* is a retrospective of the previous

---

21 See, for example, Kambiz GhaneaBassiri, *A History of Islam in America: From the New World to the New World Order* (Cambridge: Cambridge University Press, 2010).

decade of Ali's life in America, where he witnessed how the ruptures of World War I produced an emergent cultural formation called Pan-Africanism that seemed to help him make sense of his place in the world as a former refugee and as someone who was frequently illegible in the spaces he considered home. The novel is also a record of US global power and fascism. Ali had witnessed the complicated relationship of US-based Black leadership to US imperialism and fascism and offers criticism in *Ere Roosevelt Came*. This helps explain, perhaps, why in the book Ali lodges harsh criticism of Black leaders like Marcus Garvey and W.E.B. Du Bois and lionizes the self-agency of the Black soldiers who organize in secret in the wake of the Red Summer.

Ere Roosevelt Came marks the conjuncture between the world wars by forecasting possible futures of a world undergoing transformation. As indicated previously, Duse Mohamed Ali was both participant and witness to massive geopolitical change on a planetary scale, and he was uniquely situated to understand and respond to the contradictions of his moment. *Ere Roosevelt Came* offers an example of the Pan-African cultures of resistance that would inform Ali's understanding of the global conjuncture; in this way, the book can be read as a history of the present as well as a forecast of a new world in the making.

Reading *Ere Roosevelt Came* as a Pan-African Novel par Excellence

Marina Bilbija

In February 1934, *The Comet*, a West African newsmagazine published out of Lagos, began serializing a novel about African America entitled *Ere Roosevelt Came: A Record of the Adventures of the Man in the Cloak*. Its subtitle hinted at its genre classification (loosely identifying it as an adventure tale) while its title grounded its storylines in recent US history—"ere" Franklin Delano Roosevelt's presidency and the New Deal. Equal parts roman à clef, spy novel, and reportage, *Ere Roosevelt Came* narrates a white supremacist organization's plot to overthrow the US government and the courageous efforts of a secret African American society to foil them and ultimately redeem the promises of US democracy. Notably, the white supremacists (who in the novel sometimes call themselves the Invisible State, and other times the Invisible Empire) are aided in their sinister plans by a cabal of Japanese and Russian agents who, though not ideologically aligned with this Ku Klux Klan–inspired organization, seek any internal lever for destabilizing the United States. Thus, by the end of the novel, the secret Black society's elite aviation unit, "the All Black Airline" finds itself squaring off with both the Invisible Empire's and Russian fighter jets. On the outcome of this spectacular air battle hinges not only the survival of the US's Black community but also US democracy writ large. Moreover, given that the Russian and Invisible Empire alliance's actions in the US have seismic effects on the economies and political institutions of the entire world, the All Black Airline's actions will ultimately determine the course of the new world war and decide which power will ascend to global hegemony.

Although the majority of *Ere Roosevelt Came*'s action takes place within the borders of the US, it is not difficult to extrapolate the implications of a novel depicting the rising tide of white supremacy and prophesying a new catastrophic world war for *The Comet*'s West African readers. In the year in which this novel was serialized, both African-owned newspapers and those from the metropole were filled with discussion of a looming world war, reports on lynching in the US, and opinion pieces on the consequences of the fissures within the League of Nations. *Ere Roosevelt Came*'s installments appeared serially each week alongside with *The Comet*'s sundry other news and cultural items—many of which covered the same global events listed above. Therefore, it would have been hard to miss the parallels between the novel's fictional American catastrophes and the economic and political crises at home (in Nigeria) and worldwide.

This 2024 edition of *Ere Roosevelt Came* marks not only its first appearance between covers, but also its first publication outside of West Africa. While this is not a lost, hitherto unknown text, it has been inaccessible to modern readers. Occasional bibliographic references to *Ere Roosevelt Came* found in scholarship on its author, Duse Mohamed Ali (and occasionally on Marcus Garvey), demonstrate a selective awareness of its existence, but the dearth of research on this fascinating Pan-African novel speaks to the missing "infrastructures," to borrow Bridget Fielder and Jonathan Senchyne's formulation, for its study.[1] Furthermore, the fact that until now, the only way to access this novel was on microfilm, copies of which can only be found in select research libraries, has meant that no one could teach *Ere Roosevelt Came* in courses on the Black global 1930s, interwar Pan-Africanism, or colonial Nigerian history and literature. We hope that this critical, portable edition of *Ere Roosevelt Came* will be of interest to students and researchers of Black Internationalism, Pan-Africanism, postcolonialism, colonial Nigerian and West African literary history and literature, as well as to those working in the fields of Anglophone modernism and the global Anglophone. However, as Fielder usefully reminds us elsewhere, the work of recovery extends beyond locating lost, completely unknown texts, or reprinting neglected and out-of-print texts to developing specific *practices* that "reimagine criteria for textual valuation as preconditions for recovery work."[2] Geared toward "shifting the parameters for evaluating recovered texts," these recovery practices "implicitly demand a reassessment of the larger disciplinary body itself."[3]

Following Fielder, I wish to suggest that the recovery of *Ere Roosevelt Came* requires revisiting and conceptualizing the very frameworks within which we read and study this 1934 work. Editing this novel has highlighted the

---

1   See Brigitte Fielder and Jonathan Senchyne, eds., *Against a Sharp White Background: Infrastructures of African American Print* (Madison: University of Wisconsin Press, 2019).
2   Brigitte Fielder, "Recovery," *American Periodicals: A Journal of History & Criticism* 30, no. 1 (2020): 18.
3   Fielder, "Recovery."

inadequacy of recovery projects conceived along national lines for literary works produced by itinerant Black artists like Ali. In fact, national literary frameworks obstruct access to and distort the works of stateless authors and texts conceived at the cusp of multiple literary traditions. *Ere Roosevelt Came*, written by a Sudanese Egyptian Pan-Africanist, published in Nigeria, and set in the US, is a case in point. This 1934 novel has been eclipsed from both Nigerian and African American literary history due to a combination of factors. First, its author, Duse Mohamed Ali (who also happened to be the editor of *The Comet*), was not Nigerian himself. During Ali's lifetime, his émigré status did not prevent either him or *The Comet* from becoming fixtures in the interwar Lagos publishing scene. It did, however, contribute to their uneven incorporation into Nigerian literary history in the decades following his death—the period, incidentally, of Nigerian decolonial and postcolonial nation building.

Second, Ali's decision to market *The Comet* as an Anglophone *West African* newsmagazine with an eye to regional advertisers and readers beyond Nigeria has presented additional impediments to classifying this journal along national lines.[4] As Nigerian historian Fred I. A. Omu has observed, *The Comet*'s identity in the Nigerian publishing market—or, in today's parlance, "brand"—was, from the onset, wrapped up in its cosmopolitan and Pan-African outlooks.[5] Sometimes these features identified Ali's journal as a node in an international network of Black journals and journalists, and at other times they contextualized *The Comet*'s wide-lens approach to local issues. The fact that *The Comet* was characterized as Lagos's "cosmopolitan" and "Pan-African" journal while also being acknowledged by peer journals and editors as a mainstay of Nigerian publishing, speaks to the heterogeneity of West African publishing outlets and the protean frameworks within which its cultural workers were defining their projects and affiliations.[6] Moreover, as Stephanie Newell and Karin Barber remind us, the colonial West African press was, from its beginnings, deeply attentive to

---

4   For a thoughtful discussion of Ali's editorial policies, see Stephanie Newell, *Newsprint Literature and Local Literary Creativity in West Africa, 1900s–1960s* (Woodbridge, Suffolk: James Currey/Boydell & Brewer, 2023).

5   Fred I. A. Omu, *Press and Politics in Nigeria, 1880–1937* (Atlantic Highlands, NJ: Humanities Press, 1978).

6   According to historian Ian Duffield, *The Comet* was one of the longest continuously published journals in the history of colonial Nigerian journalism. See Ian Duffield, "Duse Mohamed Ali and the Development of Pan-Africanism, 1866–1945, Vol. 2" (unpublished dissertation, Edinburgh University, 1971), 743.

news and events from the wider region and the rest of the African continent, as well as occurrences across different parts of the British empire (beyond both Africa and the metropole) and the US.[7]

Whether we consider *The Comet*'s activities and content in their own time period or examine the magazine's place in the longer history of Lagos publishing, where itinerant and émigré Black journalists abound, we are confronted with the discontinuities between the broad range of identities and scales of affiliation avowed by the inhabitants of colonial Nigeria and more contemporary conceptions of Nigerianness. Tóyìn Fálolá, Matthew Heaton, Rebecca Jones, Wale Adebanwi, Karin Barber, and Stephanie Newell have shown how the meanings of Nigerianness, West Africanness, Africanness and Pan-Africanism were in constant flux in the colonial era, arguing that national frameworks flatten a host of regional, local, and ethnic formations and flatten linguistic as well as cultural differences.[8] Adebanwi contends that privileging the scale of the nation obscures the role of the late-colonial Nigerian press in producing and disseminating multiple different narratives of what we might now categorize as "Nigerianness."[9] In the years leading up to decolonization, these competing narratives pivoted on an aspirational, yet-to-be realized "grand narrative" of the Nigerian nation. Rebecca Jones pushes Adebanwi's periodization back to the 1920s and 1930s (the period in which Ali's novel was set and published) explaining how the interwar period proliferated "ideas about particular kinds of 'nations' or other forms of collective identity that writers and their readers might want to establish, which did not always correspond with the colony of Nigeria."[10] These scholars teach us to use the term "Nigerian" loosely when referring to people, texts, and cultural phenomena in earlier periods of the country's history.

---

7 See Karin Barber, "Popular Arts in Africa," *The African Studies Review* 30, no. 3 (1987): 1–78; Stephanie Newell, "'Paracolonial' Networks: Some Speculations on Local Readerships in Colonial West Africa," *Interventions: International Journal of Postcolonial Studies* 3, no. 3 (2001): 336–54, Stephanie Newell, "Local Cosmopolitans in Colonial West Africa," *Journal of Commonwealth Literature* 46, no. 1 (2011): 103–17.

8 See Wale Adebanwi, *Nation as Grand Narrative: The Nigerian Press and the Politics of Meaning* (Rochester, NY: University of Rochester Press, 2016); Toyin Falola and Matthew M. Heaton, *A History of Nigeria* (Cambridge: Cambridge University Press, 2008); Rebecca Jones, *At the Crossroads: Nigerian Travel Writing and Literary Culture in Yoruba and English* (Suffolk and Rochester: Boydell & Brewer, 2019).

9 See also Wale Adebanwi, "The City, Hegemony and Ethno-Spatial Politics: The Press and the Struggle for Lagos in Colonial Nigeria," *Nationalism and Ethnic Politics* 9, no. 4 (2004): 25–51.

10 Jones, 20.

Conversely, the fact that the novel was never published in the US explains why it is largely absent from discussions of African American literary Pan-Africanism too, despite its many thematic and generic overlaps with Schuyler's Afro-topian fiction, African American pulps, and the African American romans à clef from the 1930s. Finally, the classification issues that complicate *Ere Roosevelt Came*'s recovery into either African American or colonial Nigerian literary history cannot be disentangled from questions of access and preservation. Until now, the only way to read this novel was on microfilm at a handful of research libraries across the world. Print copies of *The Comet* are even harder to find.

This chapter addresses the question of *Ere Roosevelt Came*'s classification by considering its place at the *intersection* of different Black literary and print cultures. Moreover, I wish to suggest that we approach *The Comet*'s serialization of *Ere Roosevelt Came* as a Pan-African literary event, and consequently a crossover event in the literary histories of colonial Nigeria and African America. Doing so reveals a Pan-African and Black Internationalist print infrastructure that connected Ali's novel to genres of Black utopian fiction and a crop of romans à clef coming out of 1930s African America. It also illuminates a host of formal and thematic links between this serial novel published in 1930s Nigeria and George S. Schuyler's Afro-topian *Pittsburgh Courier* fiction: *Black Empire* (1936–38) and the *Ethiopian Stories* (1935–39) on the one hand, and Claude McKay's *Amiable with Big Teeth* (1941) on the other.[11] While each of the subsequent individual reprints of McKay's, Schuyler's, and Ali's texts benefits researchers of African American literary studies and Black Internationalism, bringing these texts into relation highlights the shared reference points, inter-texts and cultural narratives of the global Black 1930s.

ERE ROOSEVELT CAME'S NIGERIAN PUBLICATION CONTEXTS

To understand how a novel about African American airmen came to be part of the weekly reading material of Anglophone Nigeria throughout most of 1934, we must take into consideration first Ali's long career as a cultural broker between West Africa and African America, and second, the

---

11   In *Ethiopian Stories*, Robert A. Hill collected two different novellas by George S. Schuyler previously serialized in the *Pittsburgh Courier*: "The Ethiopian Murder Mystery: A Story of Love and International Intrigue" (1935–1936) and "Revolt in Ethiopia: A Tale of Black Insurrection Against Italian Imperialism" (1938–1939). Schuyler published the latter under one of his many pseudonyms, "Rachel Call."

broader migration patterns of Black artists, print workers, and activists in the interwar period.

Ali's decision to publish a novel about African American airmen defending the US from a coordinated attack from the Ku Klux Klan, Soviet Russia, and Japan in a Lagos journal marks the culmination of his decades-long career as an intermediary between West Africa and African America. As my coeditor Alex Lubin explains in his essay, Ali's work at the *African Times and Orient Review* dovetailed with his efforts to establish a Pan-African economic cooperative between African America and West Africa in particular. This was the motivation behind his first visit to Nigeria and Ghana in 1920. Throughout his US sojourn, which took place between 1921 and 1931, Ali urged African Americans to emigrate to West Africa and fund Pan-African business ventures.[12] He did so both on behalf of the Universal Negro Improvement Association (UNIA), with whom he worked closely in the early years of that decade, as well as on behalf of West African businessmen. To this end, Ali even launched a Pan-African business journal, *Africa*, in 1928, which he was ultimately unable to sustain.[13]

In a way, *The Comet* itself was a byproduct of Ali's unrealized dream of a West African and African American cooperative, which brought him, for the second time, to West Africa in 1931.[14] After this venture failed, Ali reverted to his other vocation (and, paradoxically, a more reliable revenue stream): journalism, and founded *The Comet*, where he eventually serialized *Ere Roosevelt Came*. Like his earlier, unsuccessful business endeavor, *The Comet* was advertised as a regional, or paracolonial project, to borrow Stephanie Newell's term.[15] When its first issue was published on July 22,

---

12 For a detailed discussion of Ali's business ventures and how they intersected with his cultural Pan-African initiatives, see Ian Duffield, "The Business Activities of Dusé Mohammed Ali: An Example of the Economic Dimension of Pan-Africanism, 1912–1945," *Journal of the Historical Society of Nigeria* (1969): 571–600. See also Duffield's earlier mentioned unpublished dissertation "Duse Mohamed Ali and the Development of Pan-Africanism 1866–1945."

13 For a discussion of Ali's unsuccessful attempts to start a Pan-African business journal in the US, see chapter 7, vol. 2 of Duffield's aforementioned dissertation.

14 For a more detailed discussion of the circumstances of Ali's emigration to West Africa, and his settlement in Nigeria, see chapter 8, vol. 2 of Duffield's dissertation.

15 Stephanie Newell has coined this term to describe new West African regional networks between Ghana, Nigeria, and Sierra Leone which emerged "alongside and beyond the British presence in the region, as a consequence of the British presence but not as its direct product" (350). See Stephanie Newell, "'Paracolonial' Networks," 336–54.

1933, Ali introduced it as "West Africa's first newsmagazine."[16] Although, as I have already suggested, Ali's decision to identify his new venture as a West African magazine reflected his ambitions to attract advertisers and readers beyond Nigeria, it also spoke to Ali's penchant for approaching local issues from a regional standpoint. Thus, in the October 7, 1933, issue, Ali doubled down on his journal's West African frameworks and reminded his readers that "our object is to deal with the larger issues affecting West Africa rather than the minor issues of Nigerian politics."[17] For Stephanie Newell, Ali's efforts to extract himself from the purportedly "minor" local political struggles in Lagos and Nigeria indicate the distinctions between his "editorial project in Nigeria" and that of his colleagues in the Nigerian anti-colonial press.[18] Newell observes that "rather than adopting the bold nationalism of Azikiwe and other radical anticolonial editors in the 1930s, Ali's editorial project in Nigeria was to cultivate the exchange of ideas, in English, between people on a global scale while recognising the degeneration of 'civilisation' in Europe and the regenerative political energy and intellectual vitality to be found among local intellectuals in the colonies."[19] But if we reread *The Comet*'s mission statement in the context of *Ere Roosevelt Came*'s international plots, we gain a better understanding of Ali's preoccupation with what he called "the larger issues affecting West Africa." The implications of the journal's international focus crystalize when the novel's sole African character calls for a global approach to different local attacks on Blacks, thus identifying a common thread between his oppression in different parts of Africa, the Americas, and Europe.

It is important to note here that when Ali framed *The Comet*'s purview along regional lines beyond the putatively "minor issues of Nigerian politics," he was claiming his place as the designated expert on foreign affairs, a reputation for which he had honed both in the Lagos press, as a contributor to the *Lagos Daily Times* and *Nigerian Daily Telegraph* (1931–33), and in various foreign Black papers published in London and New York. Older members of the English-speaking Nigerian public were already acquainted with Ali— even if only by reputation. In the 1910s, papers like the *Lagos Daily Standard* advertised and reprinted selections from his London-based *African Times and Orient Review*; in the early 1920s, West African readers who were able

---

16   Duse Mohamed Ali, "Ourselves," *The Comet*, July 23, 1933, 3.

17   Duse Mohamed Ali, "Men and Matters," *The Comet*, October 7, 1933, 3.

18   Stephanie Newell, *Newsprint Literature and Local Literary Creativity in West Africa, 1900s–1960s* (Woodbridge, Suffolk: James Currey/Boydell & Brewer, 2023), 45.

19   Newell, 45.

to get their hands on the suppressed *Negro World* would have encountered his name in that paper's "Foreign Affairs" column.

I point to Ali's niche in the Lagos publishing scene prior to *The Comet's* founding in order to demonstrate that even though *Ere Roosevelt Came* is somewhat of an oddity when viewed from the perspective of Nigerian literary history, it is less so when considered in the context of the Lagos press more broadly, and *The Comet's* literary output in particular. It is unlikely that any of the paper's readers would have been surprised by *Ere Roosevelt Came's* foreign setting and characters, given that most of the literary texts published in this magazine were either written by foreign writers or set in foreign locations. The only difference between *Ere Roosevelt Came* and the sundry other literary texts that had previously appeared in *The Comet* was that it focused on African America. (*The Comet's* previous fictional works had been set in different parts of the British Empire and ancient Egypt.)

The Comet's history speaks to the shifting place of regionally focused and Pan-African publications in Nigerian literary history. By 1934, the year that it serialized *Ere Roosevelt Came*, *The Comet* was selling four thousand copies weekly, but as Stephanie Newell notes, its number of readers was closer to 16,000.[20] This was the year that *The Comet's* sales peaked. While its circulation numbers dropped to three thousand sold copies a week in 1938 (likely due to Nnamdi Azikiwe's launch of his iconic *West African Pilot* the year prior). *The Comet* nevertheless remained one of the most popular Nigerian Anglophone journals.[21] Its success can be gleaned from its development into a franchise and its absorption by Nnamdi Azikiwe's Zik Press conglomerate. First came the additional midweek edition, and then the daily one. The magazine continued evolving under a new, Nigerian-born editor and new management after Ali's death in 1944. A year before his death, Ali sold *The Comet* to the Zik Press, where it was rebranded as a daily paper, now retitled *The Daily Comet*, and relocated from Lagos to Kano.

It is fitting that *The Comet* lived on at the Zik Press given that the latter's founder and publisher, Azikiwe was himself an itinerant Black journalist with Pan-African leanings like Ali, albeit one with roots in Nigeria. Azikiwe was also the second author in 1930s Nigeria (after Ali) to publish a long-form text set in the US; Azikiwe's autobiography, *My Odyssey*, was serialized in the

---

20   See Stephanie Newell, "Local Authors, Ephemeral Texts: Anglo-Scribes and Anglo-Literates in West African Newspapers," in *Routledge Handbook of African Popular Culture*, edited by Grace A. Musila (London: Routledge, 2022), 56–73.
21   Duffield, "Duse Mohamed Ali and the Development of Pan-Africanism 1866–1945," 743.

West African Pilot in 1938. Many of its chapters focused on his time in the America, where Azikiwe pursued an undergraduate and multiple graduate degrees. (Incidentally, the period that Azikiwe spent in the US roughly corresponds to the timeline of Ali's novel.) I point to Azikiwe's American period because it highlights the shifting status of the US in the West African imaginary, revealing how African intellectuals studying abroad were slowly turning to the North America, and not just automatically going to Britain.

Once we consider that the editors of *two* major Anglophone Nigerian journals: *The Comet* and the *West African Pilot* had, prior to establishing them, edited and/or contributed to Black journals in multiple other Black communities, Ali looks less like an outlier in the West African publishing world and the intellectual history of British West Africa. Similarly, once we acknowledge that the publication contexts of both *Ere Roosevelt Came* and the journal in which it was published were not exceptions in the history of either 1930s Nigerian publishing or Black publishing globally, we become more attuned to itinerant early twentieth-century Black print workers, artists, and activists as repeating figures in the intellectual history of the Black Atlantic.

ERE ROOSEVELT CAME AS A GENRE OF LITERARY PAN-AFRICANISM

Ere Roosevelt Came's Pan-African frameworks cohered at the cusp of two differently articulated visions of Pan-Africanism: Nigerian and African American. Examining Ali's negotiation between the two intradiagetically, and within the physical layout of *The Comet*, highlights the points of convergence between this literary Pan-Africanist text and its African American counterparts such as George Schuyler's Afro-topian stories, while also revealing their divergences.[22]

Robert A. Hill has defined literary Pan-Africanism as a "genre" of Black imaginative writing that encompasses "literary history, textual analysis, and commentaries" and weaves together the themes of different Black commu-

---

22   For critical discussions of Schuyler's Empire, see Yogita Goyal, "Black Nationalist Hokum: George Schuyler's Transnational Critique," *African American Review* 47, no. 1 (2014): 21–36; Brooks E. Hefner, "Signifying Genre: George S. Schuyler and the Vagaries of Black Pulp," *Modernism/modernity* 26, no. 3 (2019): 483–504; Etsuko Taketani, "Colored Empires in the 1930s: Black Internationalism, the US Black Press, and George Samuel Schuyler," *American Literature* 82, no. 1 (2010): 121–49; Mark C. Thompson, "The God of Love: Fascism in George S. Schuyler's Black Empire, *CLA Journal* 48, no. 2 (2004): 183–99.

nities in the Americas and Africa while grounding them in their particular historical contexts.[23] As cases in point, Hill lists a cluster of stories and novellas that George Schuyler originally wrote for the *Pittsburgh Courier* in the late 1930s (notably, a few years *after* Ali's *Ere Roosevelt Came*). Furthermore, he identifies political and aesthetic throughlines between Schuyler's fictional responses to the Italian occupation of Ethiopia and J. A. Rogers's political journalism animated by the same set of historical events. Consequently, for Hill "literary Pan-Africanism," becomes a shorthand for a wide range of interwar African American and Caribbean texts addressing Mussolini's occupation of Ethiopia directly or obliquely.[24] Conversely, Christel L. Temple has operationalized this term to describe the inverse dynamic: African literary engagement with African America.[25]

---

23   Quoted in Robert A. Hill, "Ethiopian Stories: George S. Schuyler and Literary Pan-Africanism in the 1930s," *Comparative Studies of South Asia, Africa and the Middle East* 14, no. 2 (1994): 68.

24   For analyses of the link between literary Pan-Africanism in the US and the invasion of Ethiopia, see Neelam Srivastava, "Harlem's Ethiopia: Literary Pan-Africanism and the Italian Invasion," in *Italian Colonialism and Resistances to Empire, 1930–1970* (London: Palgrave Macmillan, 2018), 101–46. For discussions of literary Pan-Africanism in the Caribbean, see Kersuze Simeon-Jones, "Literary Pan-Africanism in Caribbean Literature," in *Routledge Handbook of Pan-Africanism*, edited by Reiland Rabaka (London: Routledge, 2020), 418–32. For considerations of literary Pan-Africanism in African literary traditions, see Alice Aterianus-Owanga, "A Pan-African Space in Cape Town? The Chimurenga Archive of Pan-African Festivals," *Journal of African Cultural Studies* 32, no. 3 (2020): 251–69; Ruth Bush, "Publishing Francophone African Literature in Translation: Towards a Relational Account of Postcolonial Book History," in *Intimate Enemies: Translation in Francophone Contexts*, edited by Claire Bisdorff and Kathryn Batchelor (Liverpool: Liverpool University Press, 2013), 49–68; Zamda R. Geuza and Kate Wallis, "New Cartographies for World Literary Space: Locating Pan-African Publishing and Prizing," in *African Literatures as World Literature*, edited by Alexander Fyfe and Madhu Krishnan (Dublin, London, and New York: Bloomsbury Press, 2022), 153–82; Tsitsi Jaji, *Africa in Stereo: Modernism, Music, and Pan-African Solidarity* (Oxford and New York: Oxford University Press, 2014). Babacar M'Baye, "Literary Pan-Africanism in African Epics: The Legends of Chaka Zulu and Sundiata Keita," in *Routledge Handbook of Pan-Africanism*, edited by Reiland Rabaka (London: Routledge, 2020), 401–17; Francis B. Nyamnjoh and Katleho Shoro, "Language, Mobility, African Writers and Pan-Africanism," *African Communication Research* 4, no. 1 (2011): 35–62; Oyeniyi Okunoye, "Pan-Africanism and Globalized Black Identity in the Poetry of Kofi Anyidoho and Kwadwo Opokwu-Agyemang," *Ariel: A Review of International English Literature* 40, no. 1 (2009); Christopher E. W. Ouma, "Es' kia Mphahlele, Chemchemi and Pan-African Literary Publics," *Foundational African Writers: Peter Abrahams, Noni Jabavu, Sibusiso Nyembezi and Es'kia Mphahlele*, edited by Bhekizizwe Peterson, Khwezi Mkhize, and Makhosazana Xaba (Johannesburg: Wits University Press, 2022), 301.

25   For a lengthier discussion of literary Pan-Africanism and its definitions, see Anne Adams, "Literary Pan-Africanism," in *Africa and Its Significant Others: Forty Years of*

In *Ere Roosevelt Came*, we find a third articulation of literary Pan-Africanism that touches on different aspects of Temple's and Hill's definitions but is also distinct from them. Like the texts that Temple and Hill analyze, *Ere Roosevelt Came* features a pivotal encounter between African Americans and Africans that awakens both parties to their common predicaments as Black subjects. Only in Ali's novel, this scene yields a categorical rejection of fantasies of return to Africa. Notably, this stance signaled a major shift in Ali's own attitudes on the African prospects for disenfranchised Black people in the Caribbean in the US. Ten years prior, during his time in the US, Ali had been a vocal enthusiast for emigration campaigns to West Africa. The fact that he changed his mind on this matter once he himself had migrated to Lagos reveals how much Ali's own conceptions of the political programs and aims of Pan-Africanism were informed by his sojourns among different Black communities.

To understand the choices and political desires of *Ere Roosevelt Came*'s African American protagonists and its sole African character, we must take into account the novel's African publication context and its projected Nigeria readership. Doing so clarifies the distinctions between Ali's and Schuyler's representations of Africa. Moreover, it explains why Africa is ghosted from the main plots of a novel serialized in Nigeria but foregrounded in Schuyler's *Pittsburgh Courier* fiction. It is not surprising that *Ere Roosevelt Came* rejects the political and economic feasibility of mass emigration to Africa given that these campaigns were not welcomed by either the British colonial authorities or Nigerians. While Nigerian Garveyites embraced the UNIA's emphasis on self-reliance and race pride, they were much less enthusiastic about any of its "Back to Africa" rhetoric. Aspects of Garveyism that suggested the possibility of African American paternalism were either ignored as inapplicable to Nigerian contexts or directly opposed.[26] Appositely, the specter of Com-

---

Intercultural Entanglement, edited by Isabel Hoving, Frans-Willem Korsten, and Ernst Van Alphen, 135–50 (Amsterdam: Rodopi, 2003); Christel N. Temple, *Literary Pan-Africanism: History, Contexts, and Criticism* (Durham, NC: Carolina Academic Press, 2005).

26 For discussions of the UNIA's reception in Nigeria and British West Africa, see Olufunke Adeboye, "Visionaries of a 'New Order': Young Elites in the Politics of Colonial Western Nigeria," *AAU: African Studies Review* 1, no. 3 (2004): 118–53; Hakim Adi, "Amy Ashwood Garvey and the Nigerian Progress Union," In Judith Ann-Marie Byfield, LaRay Denzer, and Anthea Morrison, *Gendering the African Diaspora: Women, Culture and Historical Change in the Caribbean and Nigerian Hinterland* (Bloomington: Indiana University Press, 2010), 199–219; Robert A. Hill and Marcus Garvey, *The Marcus Garvey and Universal Negro Improvement Association Papers, Vol. IX: Africa for the Africans June 1921—December 1922* (Berkeley: University of California Press, 1983); K. A. B.

munism in the US that Black writers like Schuyler and McKay addressed in their works looked different (though not necessarily less problematic) from the perspective of British-ruled West Africa. Since *Ere Roosevelt Came* was set in the US, these West African contexts were not addressed head-on. Rather, Ali engaged with them indirectly via an unnamed, wandering African character who makes a memorable appearance in chapter 13.

Although there is only one African character in the novel, and although he only features in one scene, he nevertheless plays a critical role in galvanizing the political energies of his African American counterparts. He does this by explicating to them the global dimensions of their struggle. He materializes seemingly out of nowhere, and takes the stage just as the convenors have begun to despair at their inability to reach a consensus. He breaks their stalemate, insisting that the only way forward is to "awake and strike"—to go to war with their assailants. Riffing on Claude McKay's famous poem "If We Must Die," he intones: "If we must die, let us die sword in hand—our faces to the foe—covering ourselves with glory as we fall; so shall our names be graven eternally upon the hearts of mother Africa's sons!"[27]

The African is able to cut through the internecine divisions of the African American community because his message clarifies the disastrous consequences for Black people should the Invisible Empire prevail. Moreover, his success in unifying the crowd stems from his arguments about the ubiquity of their struggle. He is the first character in the novel to explicitly articulate the links between anti-Black violence in the US and the persecution and dispossession of people of African descent worldwide. In support of his call to arms, Ali's exiled African character enlists various historical precedents when Black revolutionary forces successfully defeated their white attackers:

the black Haitians threw off the Frenchmen's yoke! The half-caste Cubans bravely won their liberty! The Basutos of Africa stood up well-armed against the invaders of their lands, and they are free! Are we men? Nature demands the sacrifice of blood—the fittest only can survive! kill or be

Jones-Quartey, "The Moulding of Azikiwe," *Transition* 15 (1964): 50–53; Jabez Ayodele Langley, "Garveyism and African Nationalism," *Race* 11, no. 2 (1969): 157–72; Rina L. Okonkwo, "The Garvey Movement in British West Africa," *The Journal of African History* 21, no. 1 (1980): 105–17; and Rina L. Okonkwo, "The Garvey Movement in Nigeria," *Calabar Historical Journal* 11 (1978): 98–113; Rhoda Reddock, "Amy Ashwood Garvey: Global Pan-African Feminist," in *The Pan-African Pantheon*, edited by Adekeye Adebajo (Manchester: Manchester University Press, 2021), 131–43.
27   Duse Mohamed Ali, *Ere Roosevelt Came*, 81.

killed is Nature's unalterable law! If we are men—true men—and worthy of our noble heritage, let us awake and strike![28]

This list of historical Black revolutions serves two purposes. It is, of course, a reminder of the triumphs of Black revolutionaries worldwide. But insofar as it appears within a speech about the continuing oppression of Black people everywhere, it also underlines the global scale of the problem under consideration at this African American convention.

From the perspective of the African speaker, the Invisible Empire's pogroms in the US are not instances of American exceptionalism, but rather a local manifestation of a global and transhistorical war against Black people. This explains why he experiences the war against the Invisible Empire as his war too, and why he heads to the convention in the first place. When he is shot in an ambush attack by the Invisible Empire, his battle cry proves to be both prophecy and a future creed for those who survive.

The African character's participation in an African American convention—not to mention his decisive role in catalyzing its battle plan against the Invisible Empire—signpost the relevance of the events unfolding in African America to Black people in the Caribbean, Europe, and Africa, and vice versa. Indeed, his call for action is predicated on the thesis that "there is no place in all this world for the Blackman."[29] This is how he begins his speech before launching into an overview of his own experiences of exile. His speech is worth quoting at length because of its sweeping representation of precarity and exile as the defining characteristics of Black modernity:

I've sailed the seven seas. I left my home to seek education among the so-called civilized to assist my people. I got that education and returned to the homeland to find myself a misfit in the land of my fathers—a Europeanized African! Every worth-while job was in the hands of our masters and while they played golf and tennis and gambled in their clubs, my people did their work on starvation pay. I saw my people illtreated because their skins were black! They called us savages or half-civilized monkeys because we wore the clothes of civilization. I stood up to defend my people! I was jailed as an agitator. I left the homeland in disgust and went to Europe. I starved and walked the streets of Christendom at night because I had no bed to lay upon. Then I got a chance to go to sea, working in the bowels

---

28   Ali, *Ere Roosevelt Came*, 81.
29   Ali, 80.

of the shop—a stroker: I, the descendent of a thousand kings, tended fires till the pains of my hands and strained muscles, bereft my eyes of sleep. My sorry plight made me weep tears of blood and I became the butt and ridicule of those unfeeling brutes dressed in the trappings of a brief authority! I travelled far and was hardened in the process. There was no place for me in Europe, for I am black! There was no place for me in Africa for I was black! In East Africa, where the Portugese are lords, they jailed me because I wore a chain of gold and dared to trod the pavements where the white men walked. In South Africa it was the same. On board ship I was brutalized by the Nordics in command. I came to America. Someone was killed in Harlem. I was taken to the Police Station on suspicion, where I was unmercifully beaten upon the head with rubber hose to wrest a false confession from me for a crime I had no knowledge of.[30]

Even though the African is narrating this litany of injustices as if they were all experienced by a single wandering Black man, his account is better understood as a composite, synchronic, and diachronic representation of the oppression of Black people worldwide. When, in the same breath, he utters: "There was no place for me in Europe, for I am black! There was no place for me in Africa, for I was black!" he identifies exile as the universal Black predicament.

Not only do the African's ruminations on exile as the universal condition of Black people reveal the limitations of national solutions to global problems; they also throw the proverbial wrench into Hatbry's "Back to Africa" schemes. One of the implications of his harrowing speech is that a return to Africa cannot improve the condition of the returnees. To illustrate that Africa does not occupy an autonomous space outside the global economy that oppresses and exiles Black people, the speaker lists his tribulations in East Africa, "where the Portuguese are lords," as well as in South Africa, where things are "the same."[31] At different points in the text, both the narrator and other characters reach this conclusion too. When, at the end of the novel, Napoleon Hatbry (Ali's Garvey character militating for a mass exodus to Africa) is accused of treason after being discovered receiving Russian funds, his downfall becomes metonymic of the end of the dream of return to Africa. Even as the other characters, including the white ally Doctor Detritcher, concur that Hatbry only colluded with Russia to try to

---

30 Ali, *Ere Roosevelt Came*, 80–81.
31 Ali, 81.

save his people from genocide (unlike the white nationalist Colonel Blood who joins the Russians in order to better execute his genocidal plan), they all agree that Hatbry's political program has become obsolete.

This scene depicting an exiled African persuading his rapt African American audience that their threat of extermination in the US is "but a local phase of a world problem" gains additional connotations when we consider that it was written for a West African readership.[32] After all, the soon-to-be-martyred African is addressing two audiences: the novel's fictional African American crowd, and *The Comet's* real-world West African readers. Since his call to arms is predicated on the global Black condition, rather than on the particularities of anti-Black violence in the US, it is equally directed to West Africans as to African Americans. By printing this novel in installments, week in and week out, for five months in *The Comet's* pages, Ali embedded a continuing African American story into *The Comet's* weekly news cycle. The novel's Pan-Africanist frameworks emerged dynamically and serially through the circulation of an African American story in a West African print ecology.

READING *ERE ROOSEVELT CAME* IN *THE COMET*

Reading *Ere Roosevelt Came* in *The Comet* reveals a host of intratextual connections between the political messages of the magazine's news columns and those of its novel about African America.[33] The resonances between the magazine's fiction and news grounded the novel's more fantastical plots in reality. Thus, Ali's running political commentary on foreign affairs in the weekly "About It and About" column supplied readers not only with real historical referents for the novel's storylines, but also with interpretative frameworks for understanding the ramifications and potential outcomes of its intradiagetic fictional crises.

In this edition, we have reproduced facsimiles of pages from different numbers of *The Comet* to illustrate how this novelization of the events that shook 1920s African America (including Garvey's meeting with the KKK, arrest and deportation, and the Tulsa bombings) was framed in and by a Nigerian magazine. Take, for instance, Appendix 17 featuring an excerpt

---

32   I take this phrase, originally articulated by W.E.B Du Bois, from Robin D. G. Kelley's article "'But a Local Phase of a World Problem': Black History's Global Vision, 1883–1950," *Journal of American History* (1999): 1045–77.

33   My use of the term "intratextual" here is consistent with Katy Chiles's definition in "Within and without Raced Nations: Intratextuality, Martin Delany, and Blake; or the Huts of America," *American Literature* 80, no. 2 (2008): 323–52.

from Ali's "About It and About" column from the Saturday, May 26, 1934, number of *The Comet*, which also included chapter 13 of *Ere Roosevelt Came*. That week's subtitle, "Dictators, Colonies and Disarmament," listed the political issues driving *Ere Roosevelt Came*'s plot. In the novel, by contrast, the effects of Germany's disarmament and the ascent of dictatorships on various colonies were relegated to exposition sections, with the spotlight placed on the US. Nevertheless, as the novel's narrator repeatedly points out in his long expository sections, no place on earth would remain safe from either the threats of dictatorship or dictatorship's logical conclusion: total war. Not coincidentally, in later chapters, *Ere Roosevelt Came*'s chief antagonist, Colonel Blood, the "Emperor" of the Invisible State, explicitly states his desire to turn the US into a dictatorship and install himself as its dictator.

The column's apocalyptic prophecy that the "insane armament race" between world powers would lead to "the utter destruction of civilization," might as well have been a spoiler for the last chapters of *Ere Roosevelt Came*. Drawing on an article by Sir Philip Gibbs, Ali's news column outlines the catastrophic consequences of new disarmament policies, arguing that fantasies of disarming enemies and defensively arming oneself are but two sides of the same coin. Citing Gibbs again, Ali argues that disarmament would only "result in rivers of human blood amongst the innocent and the most helpless of the world's populations."[34] Although Gibbs does not explicitly state that colonized peoples could arguably be considered to comprise a large segment of "the most helpless of the world's populations," this is Ali's conclusion that can be inferred from the subtitle of his column, "Dictators, Colonies and Disarmament."[35]

As we can see, the predictions of Ali's news column resonated with the novel's central problematic. The sections of the article that interrogated the promises of socialism in particular were especially germane to the themes of chapter 13 of *Ere Roosevelt Came*, printed on the recto page. In his discussion of the dangers of fascism in Europe, Ali explained that socialism posed another, related threat to people in Britain and elsewhere, insofar as it avowed a dictatorship too. His main critique of the dangers posed by the socialists in Britain centered on the repercussions of its failure. Appositely, on the next page, *Ere Roosevelt Came*'s African American protagonist Hewitt Browne modeled the "proper" response to the lure of socialists. He is depicted collecting intelligence from Russian spies who are trying to recruit

---

34   Quoted in Ali, "About It and About," *The Comet*, May 26, 1934, 10.
35   Ali, "About It and About," 10.

him to their side, but instead of colluding with them, Browne relays this information to the US government. Ali's arguments against socialism in Britain proffered in the article on the opposite page offer an extradiegetic justification for Browne's actions, reframing them as a safeguard against fascism and not merely as a sign of fealty to the US.

Interestingly enough, Ali's reservations about Socialists have less to do with any ideological premises than with his fear of the catastrophic backlash to experiments with socialism. These fears were not entirely unfounded given the fate of the Weimar Republic, whose downfall was still fresh in the minds of *The Comet*'s readers in 1934. According to Ali, socialism's destabilizing effect on British institutions and labor would only play into the populist fearmongering of the Fascists. Thus, in Britain, "the socialist scheme" would "very probably provoke anger, resonance, and national disease occasioned by unemployment admitting of Mosley's intervention to readjust economic condition on Germanic lines."[36] In the novel, Ali creates a fictional scenario in which socialist interventions into US politics unleash and support fascism. *Ere Roosevelt Came*'s denouement thus reads like a simulation of the outcomes projected in Ali's May 26 column. There, Ali represents Soviet agents funding the Invisible Empire, in the process of which they endanger the Black working class and intelligentsia alike—and by the end of the novel, the entire world.

The combined anti-Fascist and anti-communist message that limns chapter 13 of *Ere Roosevelt Came* to Ali's editorial on the neighboring page might not, at first glance, come across as a matter of concern for Pan-Africanists per se. However, the linkages between the political challenges faced by the novel's African American protagonists and the global political crises that loom large in the everyday lives of Nigerians brought the stakes of these scenarios for Black people worldwide into high relief. The vulnerability of colonial populations in the next world war was a frequent topic in *The Comet*, censorship laws notwithstanding. Seen from this light, *Ere Roosevelt Came*'s fantasy of an underground Black organization arming itself with not only guns but also fighter jets, and secretly training an elite aviation unit for war, had additional purchase for Nigerian readers.

ERE ROOSEVELT CAME AS A PAN-AFRICAN NOVEL WITH A KEY

Ere Roosevelt Came is a curious hybrid between a Pan-African novel with a key and various pulp fiction genres. Approaching it as such helps illumi-

---

36 Ali, "About It and About," 10.

nate Ali's thematic and formal negotiations between the African American world depicted in Ali's novel and the political and cultural contexts of his West African readers. Ali signposted the text's generic hybridity, its curious braiding of history and fantasy, and its US frameworks from the outset in the novel's title: *Ere Roosevelt Came: A Record of the Adventures of the Man in the Cloak.* This nod to President Roosevelt located the text's plot in recent history, and linked its story (however tenuously) to a living historical figure. (Based on the title alone, one might mistakenly assume that the novel dealt with the life of President Roosevelt!) The appearance of the word "record" in the subtitle, further reinforced the idea that the novel had some grounding in the historical record. But parts of that same subtitle also linked it to fantastical genres of writing ("adventures," "man in the cloak.")

By the time they had finished reading *Ere Roosevelt Came*'s first installment, *The Comet*'s readers could easily deduce that they were dealing with a roman à clef, a genre that is "dedicated to the embedding of sociohistorical facts but that nevertheless resists the tyranny of 'actual' history," and is therefore "able to offer a more empowering speculative history."[37]

Clearly Ali anticipated its reception as a roman à clef, given that he prefaced the inaugural installment (and subsequently each one after it) with a disclaimer stating that "the characters in this story are entirely fictitious and do not represent any living persons."[38] While this note ostensibly shielded Ali from censure and libel charges, its inclusion also underlined the likeliness of readers confusing "living persons" with "the characters in this story." In other words, it incited the very speculation it purported to forestall. The fact that Ali appended a disclaimer like this to a novel set in the US reveals that he was working from the assumption that his West African readers were familiar enough with recent American history, and knowledgeable enough about the characteristics of the most prominent African American leaders, to catch his winking references to Garvey and Du Bois in the names and descriptions of the characters Napoleon Hatbry and Dr. Reginald de Bologne De Woode.

Of course, the novel's central plot and many of its characters *were* fictional. But Ali had also packed into *Ere Roosevelt Came* a decade's worth of real, historical events ranging from the Tulsa bombings to the Red Scare, and from Marcus Garvey's meeting with the Klan to his later arrest follow-

---

37 Jean-Christophe Cloutier, *Shadow Archives: The Lifecycles of African American Literature* (New York: Columbia University Press, 2019), 97.

38 Ali, "Ere Roosevelt Came," *The Comet*, February 24, 1934, 10.

ing fraud charges. To complicate things further, Ali had represented all those historical events as if they had happened within a much shorter time span, rearranging in the process their chronology and effects.

The narrative strategies I am describing here will sound familiar to contemporary readers of *Amiable with Big Teeth*, Claude McKay's recently discovered 1941 unpublished novel about the African American response to Mussolini's occupation of Ethiopia and the Communist Party's concomitant interferences into this diasporic alliance. To be sure, McKay is the superior novelist; *Amiable with Big Teeth* is also noticeably more satirical than *Ere Roosevelt Came*. But there is also an uncanny family resemblance, so to speak, between these two texts. Both are historical novels about the recent past—although in Ali's case the focus is on a series of catastrophes rather than on a single crisis. Both are, as I have already noted, Black romans à clef written in a speculative mode. By introducing counterfactual plots and elements into accounts of the recent past, Ali and McKay revisit crises in different Black locales and highlight their imbrication. As Jean-Christophe Cloutier has observed, McKay "contextualizes historical knowledge regarding important facets of African American life by creating correspondences between the local and the global" in the text of the novel.[39] As I explained in the previous section, Ali amplified the parallels between local and global political problems represented in the novel by printing installments of his "African American novel" alongside news articles on international political crises and reports on Nigerian occurrences.

The generic and thematic correspondences between *Ere Roosevelt Came* and *Amiable with Big Teeth* extend beyond their categorization as romans à clef. Both Ali and McKay draw on conventions of popular fiction in the denouement of their novels' plots. Both depict secret Black societies, conspiracies orchestrated by foreign spies, and detection plots. Attending to *Ere Roosevelt Came*'s pulp influences brings into high relief its similarities with yet another interwar Black novel: George Schyler's *Black Empire*. We can think of Ali's novel as sitting somewhere in the middle of what we might call a Pan-African sensationalist fiction continuum between *Amiable with Big Teeth*'s more muted and selective iteration of the genre, and George Schuyler's more bombastic Afro-topian fiction on the other. In their introduction to *Amiable with Big Teeth*, Cloutier and Edwards acknowledge the parallels between Schuyler's Ethiopian stories from the *Pittsburg Courier* and McKay's novel, while also noting that the latter is "less concerned with fantasy and

---

39 Cloutier, *Shadow Archives*, 115.

much more framed as a caustic, even overtly polemical, depiction of the complex Harlem political landscape in the mid-1930s as it shifted in the shadow of international events."[40] *Ere Roosevelt Came* shares *Amiable with Big Teeth*'s polemical approach. It too revisits the rifts in African American political leadership through the lens of both global Black struggles and international political tensions. Only McKay is looking back to the late 1930s, while Ali focuses on the 1920s and early 1930s.

Ali also shares Schuyler's interest in the racialized horizons of expectations built into pulps. Both writers subvert the hierarchies of racial dystopia pulps and aviation fiction by rewriting the scripts of rugged white heroism. Brooks E. Hefner's arguments about Schuyler's "inversions and perversions of the systems of genre that characterized most pulp production" can thus also be extended to *Ere Roosevelt Came*'s experiments with genre fiction, although the ways in which they invert and pervert these conventions vary.[41] Whereas Schuyler's *Black Empire* serials "challenge[d] the pulp conventions that figure heroes as white individuals and villains as shadowy nonwhite conspiracies," Ali's novel satirizes the white genius figure, revealing the alleged genius at the helm of the Invisible Empire to be ideologically incoherent and easily duped by his Russian sponsor.[42] Hefner notes how Schuyler's pulps also place ideological pressure on the very concept of charismatic leadership, a concern that animates both Ali and Schuyler's texts.[43]

For a pulpy novel full of speeches and narratorial exposition, *Ere Roosevelt Came* is uncharacteristically skeptical of political charisma. The fact that this critique of charismatic leaders appears in a text that pays homage to the pulps is all the more striking. Ali's warnings about the dangers of charisma punctuate the novel's narration. Indeed, the narrator not only condemns the white nationalist leader's ambitions to become a dictator, but he also satirizes the Garvey figure's dreams of empire and dictatorship. The characters best equipped to lead the African American community are those who know how to facilitate and work with others rather than those who give the most electrifying speeches and exude personal magnetism. For instance,

---

40 Jean-Christophe Cloutier and Brent Hayes Edwards. "Introduction," In Claude McKay, *Amiable with Big Teeth* (New York: Penguin Books, 2017), xvii.

41 Brooks E. Hefner, "Signifying Genre: George S. Schuyler and the Vagaries of Black Pulp," *Modernism/modernity* 26, no. 3 (September 2019): 498.

42 Hefner, 498.

43 For a discussion of the characteristics of Black pulps, see Brooks E. Hefner, *Black Pulp: Genre Fiction in the Shadow of Jim Crow* (Minneapolis: University of Minnesota Press, 2021).

Smithson, the millionaire sponsor of the secret African American organization often acts as one of its strategists too, but he is not their leader. In fact, he never becomes the public face of any African American group since he passes as white from the novel's opening to its conclusion. By contrast, the icons of Black leadership: Hatbry and De Woode (W.E.B. Du Bois and Marcus Garvey) prove to be woefully ill-equipped to face the challenges of the contemporary moment and are easily swayed by foreign powers.

There is one crucial difference between Ali's roman à clef about crises in African American leadership and McKay's and Schuyler's. Ali was serializing a roman à clef about African America to readers in West Africa. Insofar as this was a novel with a key about foreign Black figures and events, *Ere Roosevelt Came* interpellated its West African readers as part of a transatlantic Black community with shared references and inside jokes. While contemporary readers might find the novel's ending disappointing or too conservative for a Pan-African story, one cannot discount the Pan-African premise on which the story relies: that Black readers in one location (Nigeria) would be sufficiently versed in the recent history of another Black community (African America) to understand its various allusions and inside jokes. Following Sean Latham's argument that a roman à clef requires "the introduction of a key that lies beyond the diegesis itself," a Pan-African roman à clef relies on the introduction of a key that lies outside its diegesis but also beyond the reader's national and imperial contexts.[44]

A Pan-African novel with a key presumes a reading community *in the know*, so to speak, that transcends national and possibly imperial boundaries. Or, at the very least, it requires a reading community willing to learn to be in the know. *Ere Roosevelt Came*'s success as a *Pan-African* roman à clef hinged on *The Comet*'s readers possessing the "key" to decoding the text's allusions to historical African American and American figures and events. Consequently, Ali's earlier-mentioned disclaimer can be understood as an invitation to readers to detect connections between "living persons" and "characters in this story," and to thus keep in mind the grounding of this (admittedly fantastical) novel in the historical record. Given *The Comet*'s dedicated coverage of news from African America, Ali's inclusion of a continuing story about recent events affecting Black Americans on its pages amplified attention to current US news too. In sum, the novel's placement in *The Comet* required, honed, and rewarded Pan-African literacy.

---

44   Sean Latham, *The Art of Scandal: Modernism, Libel Law, and the Roman à Clef* (New York: Oxford University Press, 2009), 9.

Because we have little information about this novel's reception history, it is unclear to what extent *The Comet*'s readers were in possession of this Pan-African key. But if anyone could predict West Africa's knowledge of African American politics and history, it was Duse Mohamed Ali. As Lubin explains in chapter 1, Ali was a veteran Pan-African editor who had spent his entire life mediating between different Black collectives (and sometimes Arab, Asian, and Muslim ones too). He had done so in print arenas and speaking engagements across Britain, the US, and West Africa. Therefore, Ali probably had a better understanding of how much globally dispersed Black publics knew of each other's histories and predicaments more than any Black journalist and intellectual of this period. Very few of Ali's contemporaries had lived in all these locations and among so many different Black communities for sustained periods of time, or written for and edited Black newspaper on three continents.

Insofar as *Ere Roosevelt Came*'s Pan-African frameworks cohered through its West African publishing context—that is, through the weekly juxtaposition of a novel about African America with texts about local, regional, and international news in a Lagos-based magazine—it cannot be classified as a precursor to later generation of Pan-African romans à clef such as Peter Abrahams's *A Wreath for Udomo* (1956) and Ousmane Sembène's *The Last of the Empire* (1981) from the decolonial and postcolonial periods. The distinctions between these later novels and Ali's extend from their generic and stylistic features to their themes and political imaginaries. Whereas Abrahams and Sembène's later novels chronicle the complicated processes and challenges of decolonization, *Ere Roosevelt Came* bypasses the question of sovereignty altogether (in African America at least).

As I noted earlier, Ali's novel has more in common thematically and formally with the Black romans à clef about and from 1930s African America, and with genres of literary Pan-Africanism produced in the US. In the 1930s, a number of African American writers were experimenting with the genre of the Black roman à clef. Two years before Ali began serializing *Ere Roosevelt Came* in Lagos, the African American writer and literary critic Wallace Thurman had published *Infants of the Spring*, a satirical "novel with a key" about the bygone Harlem Renaissance. Thurman's friend and fellow writer Richard Bruce Nugent had concurrently been at work on a parallel fictional account of roughly the same events and figures featured in *Infants of the Spring*. Schuyler and McKay's novels with their sly references to historical figures and events can be considered to be a part of a continuum of 1930s and 1940s novels that looked back to both the promises of the 1920s (indexed by the Harlem Renaissance, the rise of both Garvey and Black communists) as well as the horrors and disappointments (Tulsa, the Great Depression, Garvey's fall and the internecine fighting between Black leaders, an impending world war). *Ere Roosevelt Came*'s publication history is in and of itself an indication of Black artists, texts, and ideas traveling across the interwar Black world.

The fact that all the texts listed in this chapter draw heavily on conventions of genre fiction and emphasize plot and detection (whether of mysteries or encoded historical figures) over character development suggests that popular literary forms are an important avenue of study for scholars of Pan-Africanism and Black Internationalism. As critics such as Alexander Bain, André M. Carrington, and Yogita Goyal have shown, this connection between popular literary forms and Black internationalist political imaginaries is sustained across multiple conjunctures in African American literary history, whether we look back to the 1920s to W.E.B. Du Bois's *Dark Princess*, the 1900s to Pauline Hopkins's *Of One Blood*, or the late 1850s to Martin Delany's *Blake, or the Huts of America*.[45] It is also significant that the bulk of this writing originally appeared in serial format, in so far as it indicates that their installments always accompanied news items and were thus embedded in the day-to-day political realities of their original readers. Situating *Ere Roosevelt Came* in this longer history of Black speculative newspaper fiction thus highlights the linkages between popular literary forms and political crises.

CODA: AVENUES FOR FUTURE RESEARCH

One of the aims of this chapter—and indeed of the edition as a whole—has been to facilitate comparative studies of interwar and midcentury Pan-African literature. Yet there is a tension between our efforts to republish *Ere Roosevelt Came* as a discrete text that centers the work of Ali the author and connects the novel to other Afro-topian novels and Black romans à clef from and about the 1930s and our desire to highlight Ali's legacy as a Pan-Africanist journalist and *editor*. As discussed earlier, in his dual capacity as *Ere Roosevelt Came*'s author and as the editor of the journal in which it was published, Ali had creative control over not only the novel's contents but

---

45   See Alexander M. Bain, "Shocks Americana!: George Schuyler Serializes Black Internationalism," *American Literary History* 19, no. 4 (2007): 937–63; André M. Carrington, *Speculative Blackness: The Future of Race in Science Fiction* (Minneapolis: University of Minnesota Press, 2016); Yogita Goyal, "Black Nationalist Hokum: George Schuyler's Transnational Critique." *African American Review* 47, no. 1 (2014): 21–36.

also its formatting and placement in relation to *The Comet*'s other texts. In other words, he decided where to end and resume each installment and had a hand in creating extradiegetic connections (whether intentionally or accidentally) between the themes and concerns of any given installment and the various other neighboring texts in *The Comet*.

While the primary aim of extracting *Ere Roosevelt Came*'s serial installments from *The Comet* and collating them into a single book is to make it accessible and portable, we also appreciate that this new format produces a different interface inasmuch as it removes the intertextual connections between the novel's themes of Black self-reliance, liberation, and a coming world war and those of the articles on local, regional, and international news that appeared alongside each of *Ere Roosevelt Came*'s installments in *The Comet*. A bound edition cannot recreate the gamut of intratextual connections between items published in *The Comet* between February and July 1934 (the length of the novel's serialization). We have attempted to address this limitation built into our remediation project by appending a selection of facsimiles of pages from *The Comet* to the novel. These appendices are designed to provide glimpses into this West African magazine's print ecology and to illuminate the material and historical contexts of *The Comet*'s original printing of *Ere Roosevelt Came*.

At the same time, we see these selections from *The Comet* as entry points into a West African magazine archive that deserves more scholarly attention. In other words, we hope that this edition of *Ere Roosevelt Came* will spark more interest in *The Comet*, leading future scholars to explore its other contents beyond Ali's 1934 novel. Some of this research on the *Comet* is already underway, as attested by Stephanie Newell's recent and forthcoming chapters on the place of *The Comet*'s literary texts in West African and Nigerian literary history.[46] Newell thus draws attention to Ali's tendency to articulate his journal's Pan-African frameworks with more vaguely defined cosmopolitan and Anglophile ones. One of the consequences of the magazine's centrifugal impulse was its elision of local writing. As I have argued elsewhere, comparative studies of *The Comet* and the *West African Pilot* would provide more insight into the role of itinerant editors in Nigeria's late-colonial press and politics. Studying these two archives together further

---

46 Newell, "Local Authors, Ephemeral Texts," 56–73. Newell has devoted a chapter of her forthcoming book on Nigerian periodical culture to *The Comet*. See *Newsprint Literature and Local Literary Creativity in West Africa, 1900s–1960s* (Woodbridge, Suffolk: James Currey/Boydell & Brewer, 2023).

illuminates both the overlaps and divergences between Azikiwe's international Black networks and Ali's, consequently shining a light on a range of different, and sometimes antithetical, political and cultural frameworks through which late-colonial Nigeria engaged with Pan-Africanism. In her 2018 article on the figure of the flying newspaperman in the *West African Pilot* and *Daily Comet*, historian Leslie James examines *The Comet*'s afterlife at the Zik Press, and analyzes the political contexts that launched these fantastical flying figures as regular features of the Nigerian press.[47]

James's essay is additionally useful to future researchers of *The Comet* insofar as it engages with the later iteration of the *Daily Comet*, published after Ali's death. As I have noted elsewhere, considering *The Comet*'s run before and after its entry into the Zik Press and attending to the *Daily Comet*'s recalibration raises a host of questions about the journal's classifications.[48] Should scholars approach *The Comet* and its later Wednesday edition and daily paper as the same journal, or should they classify each as a distinct publication? To what extent is the iteration of the *Daily Comet* that was being published after Ali's death the same journal as the one Ali edited? These are just a few directions in which we hope to point readers.

Finally, we hope that our efforts to restore this text to the library of literary Pan-Africanism will revitalize the study of not only *The Comet* but also its editor (and *Ere Roosevelt Came*'s author) as an important Pan-African thinker whose legacy limned multiple Black literary and print traditions.

BIBLIOGRAPHY

Adams, Anne. "Literary Pan-Africanism." In *Africa and Its Significant Others: Forty Years of Intercultural Entanglement*, edited by Isabel Hoving, Frans-Willem Korsten, and Ernst Van Alphen, 135–50. Amsterdam: Rodopi, 2003.

Adebanwi, Wale. "The City, Hegemony and Ethno-Spatial Politics: The Press and the Struggle for Lagos in Colonial Nigeria." *Nationalism and Ethnic Politics* 9, no. 4 (2004): 25–51.

——. *Nation as Grand Narrative: The Nigerian Press and the Politics of Meaning.* Rochester, NY: University of Rochester Press, 2016.

---

47 See Leslie James, "The Flying Newspapermen and the Time-Space of Late Colonial Nigeria," *Comparative Studies in Society and History* 60, no. 3 (2018): 569–98.

48 See Marina Bilbija, "'Not a Newspaper in the Ordinary Sense of the Term': The Geopolitics of the Newspaper/Magazine Divide in the Nigerian *Comet*," *The Edinburgh Companion to Colonial Periodicals*, edited by Caroline Davis, David Finkelstein, and David Johnson (Edinburgh: Edinburgh University Press, forthcoming).

Adi, Hakim. "Amy Ashwood Garvey and the Nigerian Progress Union." In Judith Ann-Marie Byfield, LaRay Denzer, and Anthea Morrison, *Gendering the African Diaspora: Women, Culture and Historical Change in the Caribbean and Nigerian Hinterland*, 199–219. Bloomington: Indiana University Press, 2010.

Adeboye, Olufunke. "Visionaries of a 'New Order': Young Elites in the Politics of Colonial Western Nigeria." *AAU: African Studies Review* 1, no. 3 (2004): 118–53.

Ali, Duse Mohamed. "About It and About." *The Comet*, May 26, 1934, 10.

——. "Ere Roosevelt Came." *The Comet*, February 24, 1934, 10.

——. "Men and Matters." *The Comet*, October 7, 1933, 5.

——. "Ourselves." *The Comet*, July 23, 1933, 3.

Aterianus-Owanga, Alice. "A Pan-African Space in Cape Town? The Chimurenga Archive of Pan-African Festivals." *Journal of African Cultural Studies* 32, no. 3 (2020): 251–69.

Bain, Alexander M. "Shocks Americana!: George Schuyler Serializes Black Internationalism." *American Literary History* 19, no. 4 (2007): 937–63.

Barber, Karin. "Popular Arts in Africa." *The African Studies Review* 30, no. 3 (1987): 1–78.

Bilbija, Marina. "'Not a Newspaper in the Ordinary Sense of the Term': The Geopolitics of the Newspaper/Magazine Divide in the Nigerian Comet." In *The Edinburgh Companion to Colonial Periodicals*, edited by Caroline Davis, David Finkelstein, and David Johnson Edinburgh: Edinburgh University Press, forthcoming.

Bush, Ruth. "Publishing Francophone African Literature in Translation: Towards a Relational Account of Postcolonial Book History." In *Intimate Enemies: Translation in Francophone Contexts*, edited by Claire Bisdorff and Kathryn Batchelor, 49–68. Liverpool: Liverpool University Press, 2013.

Carrington, André M. *Speculative Blackness: The Future of Race in Science Fiction*. Minneapolis: University of Minnesota Press, 2016.

Chiles, Katy. "Within and without Raced Nations: Intratextuality, Martin Delany, and Blake; or the Huts of America." *American Literature* 80, no. 2 (2008): 323–52.

Cloutier, Jean-Christophe. "*Amiable with Big Teeth*: The Case of Claude McKay's Last Novel." *Modernism/modernity* 20, no. 3 (2013): 557–76.

——. *Shadow Archives: The Lifecycles of African American Literature*. New York: Columbia University Press, 2019.

Cloutier, Jean-Christophe, and Brent Hayes Edwards. "Introduction." *Amiable with Big Teeth*. New York: Penguin, 2017.

Duffield, Ian. "The Business Activities of Dusé Mohammed Ali: An Example of the Economic Dimension of Pan-Africanism, 1912–1945." *Journal of the Historical Society of Nigeria* (1969): 571–600.

——. "Duse Mohamed Ali and the Development of Pan-Africanism 1866–1945." Diss. University of Edinburgh, 1971.

Falola, Toyin and Matthew M. Heaton, *A History of Nigeria*. Cambridge: Cambridge University Press, 2008.

Fielder, Brigitte. "Recovery." *American Periodicals: A Journal of History & Criticism* 30, no. 1 (2020): 18–21.

Fielder, Brigitte, and Jonathan Senchyne, eds. *Against a Sharp White Background: Infrastructures of African American Print.* Madison: University of Wisconsin Press, 2019.

Geuza, Zamda R and Kate Wallis. "New Cartographies for World Literary Space: Locating Pan-African Publishing and Prizing." In *African Literatures as World Literature,* edited by Alexander Fyfe and Madhu Krishnan, 153–82. Dublin, London, and New York: Bloomsbury Press, 2022.

Goyal, Yogita. "Black Nationalist Hokum: George Schuyler's Transnational Critique." *African American Review* 47, no. 1 (2014): 21–36.

——. *Romance, Diaspora, and Black Atlantic Literature.* Cambridge: Cambridge University Press, 2010.

Hill, Robert A. "Ethiopian Stories: George S. Schuyler and Literary Pan-Africanism in the 1930s." *Comparative Studies of South Asia, Africa and the Middle East* 14, no. 2 (1994): 67–85.

Hill, Robert A., and Marcus Garvey. *The Marcus Garvey and Universal Negro Improvement Association Papers, Vol. IX: Africa for the Africans June 1921—December 1922.* Berkeley: University of California Press, 1983.

Hefner, Brooks E. *Black Pulp: Genre Fiction in the Shadow of Jim Crow.* Minneapolis and London: University of Minnesota Press, 2021.

——. "Signifying Genre: George S. Schuyler and the Vagaries of Black Pulp." *Modernism/modernity* 26, no. 3 (2019): 483–504.

Jaji, Tsitsi. *Africa in Stereo: Modernism, Music, and Pan-African Solidarity.* Oxford and New York: Oxford University Press, 2014.

James, Leslie, "The Flying Newspapermen and the Time-Space of Late Colonial Nigeria." *Comparative Studies in Society and History* 60, no. 3 (2018): 569–98.

Jones, Rebecca. *At the Crossroads: Nigerian Travel Writing and Literary Culture in Yoruba and English.* Woodbridge, Suffolk: James Currey/Boydell & Brewer, 2019.

Jones-Quartey, K. A. B. "The Moulding of Azikiwe." *Transition* 15 (1964): 50–53.

Kelley, Robin D. G. "'But a Local Phase of a World Problem': Black History's Global Vision, 1883–1950." *Journal of American History* (1999): 1045–77.

Langley, Jabez Ayodele. "Garveyism and African Nationalism." *Race* 11, no. 2 (1969): 157–72.

Latham, Sean. *The Art of Scandal: Modernism, Libel Law, and the Roman à Clef.* New York: Oxford University Press, 2009.

M'Baye, Babacar. "Literary Pan-Africanism in African Epics: The Legends of Chaka Zulu and Sundiata Keita." In *Routledge Handbook of Pan-Africanism,* edited by Reiland Rabaka, 401–1. London: Routledge, 2020.

Newell, Stephanie. "Local Authors, Ephemeral Texts: Anglo-Scribes and Anglo-Literates in West African Newspapers." In *Routledge Handbook of African Popular Culture,* edited by Grace A. Musila, 56–73. London: Routledge, 2022.

——. "Local Cosmopolitans in Colonial West Africa." *Journal of Commonwealth Literature* 46, no. 1 (2011): 103–17.

——. *Newsprint Literature and Local Literary Creativity in West Africa, 1900s–1960s.* Woodbridge, Suffolk: James Currey/Boydell & Brewer, 2023.

——. "'Paracolonial' Networks: Some Speculations on Local Readerships in Colonial West Africa." *Interventions: International Journal of Postcolonial Studies* 3, no. 3 (2001): 336–54.

Nyamnjoh, Francis B., and Katleho Shoro. "Language, Mobility, African Writers and Pan-Africanism." *African Communication Research* 4, no. 1 (2011): 35–62.

Okonkwo, Rina L. "The Garvey Movement in British West Africa." *The Journal of African History* 21, no. 1 (1980): 105–17.

——. "The Garvey Movement in Nigeria." *Calabar Historical Journal* 11 (1978): 98–113.

Okunoye, Oyeniyi. "Pan-Africanism and Globalized Black Identity in the Poetry of Kofi Anyidoho and Kwadwo Opokwu-Agyemang." *Ariel: A Review of International English Literature* 40, no. 1 (2009).

Omu, Fred I. A. *Press and Politics in Nigeria, 1880–1937.* Atlantic Highlands, NJ: Humanities Press, 1978.

Ouma, Christopher E. W. "Es' kia Mphahlele, Chemchemi and Pan-African Literary Publics." *Foundational African Writers: Peter Abrahams, Noni Jabavu, Sibusiso Nyembezi and Es'kia Mphahlele,* edited by Bhekizizwe Peterson, Khwezi Mkhize, and Makhosazana Xaba, 301. Johannesburg: Wits University Press, 2022.

Reddock, Rhoda. "Amy Ashwood Garvey: Global Pan-African Feminist." In *The Pan-African Pantheon,* edited by Adekeye Adebajo, 131–43. Manchester: Manchester University Press, 2021.

Simeon-Jones, Kersuze. "Literary Pan-Africanism in Caribbean Literature." In *Routledge Handbook of Pan-Africanism,* edited by Reiland Rabaka, 418–32. London: Routledge 2020.

Srivastava, Neelam. "Harlem's Ethiopia: Literary Pan-Africanism and the Italian Invasion." In *Italian Colonialism and Resistances to Empire, 1930–1970,* 101–46. London: Palgrave Macmillan, 2018.

Taketani, Etsuko. "Colored Empires in the 1930s: Black Internationalism, the US Black Press, and George Samuel Schuyler." *American Literature* 82, no. 1 (2010): 121–49.

Temple, Christel N. "The History of Literary Pan-Africanism: Overview/Survey Essay." *Routledge Handbook of Pan-Africanism,* edited by Reiland Rabaka, 387–400. London: Routledge, 2020.

——. *Literary Pan-Africanism: History, Contexts, and Criticism.* Durham, NC: Carolina Academic Press, 2005.

Thompson, Mark C. "The God of Love: Fascism in George S. Schuyler's Black Empire, *CLA Journal* 48, no. 2 (2004): 183–99.

Ere Roosevelt Came: A Record of the Adventures of the Man in the Cloak

The original text of *Ere Roosevelt Came: A Record of the Adventures of the Man in the Cloak* was serialized between February 24 and October 13, 1934, in *The Comet* magazine, published out of Lagos, Nigeria. In *The Comet*, each serial installment was printed with two prefatory notes, the first of which ("All rights reserved") established copyright, the second ("The characters in this story are entirely fictitious and do not represent any living persons") protecting the author from defamation accusations. The editors of this new, bound edition of the novel have removed recurring disclaimers to avoid repetition. For the same purposes we have omitted the recurring notice "to be continued next week" at the end of each installment. Other minor corrections and edits of typographical errors and misspellings have been entered into the original text for clarity. In some instances, we have preserved the original formatting and orthographic conventions. In a few places, the original printing of the newsprint is indecipherable, and we note instances where we have had to decipher the intended words based on semi-legible characters and/ or contextual clues. We have preserved the British spelling conventions of the original text, and have corrected occasional American interpolations to conform with the rest of the text (for instance, in the original, titles like Mr, Mrs, and Miss sometimes appear without a period, in concordance with British usage, and at other times, they are followed with a period, as they would in US use). To ensure uniformity, all titles follow British conventions.

The editing criteria for the appendices is different than it is for the novel. In the appendices we have left unedited all typos. This is because the appendices consist of archival material that place different demands and expectations on readers than a novel.

A NOTE ON THE SPELLING OF THE AUTHOR'S NAME

At different points in his life and across different publishing outlets, the author of this novel varied in the spelling of his first name, alternating between "Duse" and "Dusé." Furthermore, his full name sometimes appeared with the suffix "effendi," a common indicator of "a man of property, authority, or education in an eastern Mediterranean country." Misspellings of "Mohamed" abound both in printed and private documents, as illustrated by the materials included as appendices to this edition. The present-day editors' decision to refer to the author as "Duse Mohamed Ali" (rather than "Dusé Mohamed Ali") is consistent with Ali's own orthographic practices both in the original text of the novel and its magazine paratexts in *The Comet* magazine, of which he was the editor. As the scanned facsimiles of *The Comet* show, Ali's name appears without diacritical marks throughout the serial installments of the 1934 printing of *Ere Roosevelt Came*. This is true of all invocations of his name in *The Comet* as a whole.

NOTE ON THE MYSTERY OF A POTENTIAL MISSING CHAPTER AND THE NUMBERING OF CHAPTERS

The extant serialized version of the novel that our critical edition draws upon includes two different Chapters XX, but is missing a Chapter VII. Whether Ali printed a Chapter VII or misnumbered his installments is inconclusive at this moment. Since Chapter VIII (published in the April 14 issue) seamlessly resumes the narration of the events that occurred in Chapter VI (published on March 31), there seems to be no gap between them. In other words, there appears to be no missing text. However, it is difficult to verify this since the April 7, 1934 issue of *The Comet* in which the elusive Chapter VII would have appeared is marked as missing from the microfilm reels held at the British Library (copies of which can be found at a few other libraries across the world). The fact that we have not been able to find physical copies of this missing number either introduces the possibility that perhaps this number was never published. But we also do not want to discount the exciting possibility that there is a missing chapter of this novel somewhere out there, after all (and a missing April 7, 1934 issue of *The Comet*.) We thus wish to use this opportunity to invite scholars of West African print culture and Duse Mohamed Ali to join us in our continued search for these texts.

ERE ROOSEVELT CAME.

A Record of the Adventures of
THE MAN IN THE CLOAK

BY DUSE MOHAMED ALI

PROLOGUE.

On a lonely country road some five miles from the suburbs of a well-known Southern town, there stood a little distance from the roadway, an artistically designed bungalow-cottage of white stucco nestling among a cluster of mimosa trees. A well-kept lawn and flower garden stretched down to the neatly trimmed shrubs that fenced the cottage from the road.

Within the cottage was every evidence of taste and luxury serving as an index to the character of the occupant.

On a small wooden bedstead covered with snowy linens a charming boy, some twelve years of age, lay fast asleep.

The perfumed-laden breezes that floated through the open window blew the boy's flaxen curls about in tangled negligence. At the foot of the dainty bed the mother stood gazing with tear-dimmed eyes upon her only child.

Surpassingly beautiful she was in face and figure, with cheeks like the pomegranate, full ripe cupid lips aquiline nose, long raven tresses with the slightest semblance of a wave and wondrous long-lashed eyes peeped forth from beneath a pair of arching brows, whose sable depths suggested the mystic and alluring beauty of a starlit moonless night.

Silently she wept and her tears like priceless pearls chased each other down her cheeks to find a resting-place within the ample folds of her rose-colored dressing gown.

Her tears were arrested by the sound of familiar footsteps upon the gravel path. With a dainty gossamer trifle of lace she dried her eyes. Her mouth assumed an unaccustomed sternness and throwing back her head she passed from the cozy bedroom closing the door silently behind her. She crossed the narrow hall and entering the living room of the cottage faced the tall blond man who had just stepped upon the threshold. There was a smile upon his lips that seemed to freeze at her approach.

"Hello?" he cried surprisedly. "What's the racket?"

"Sit down," she answered curtly, and going to the piano she took up the "Southern Leader," turning over its pages until she found the Society Column; she placed her thumb upon the portrait of a woman laconically asking: "What does this mean?"

The man appeared agitated as he took the sheet.

"What do you mean?" he asked somewhat lamely.

"You well know what I mean. Are you engaged to Miss Trumphey-Havers as the "Leader" says?"

"What right have you to ask?" he sternly inquired, casting the paper on the floor.

"By a mother's rights right—a wife's right—if there's any justice in heaven"—

"A wife?" he interrupted ironically.

"I said, wife! Let us understand each other if we can. I was a girl of bare sixteen when you approached my mother with lying words upon your lips." He was about to interrupt but her eyes shot fire. She raised her hand commandingly and he shrugged his shoulders and sat down. "You coaxed, you begged, you bribed and finally you threatened. You were the boss of the State; we were humble folks; we were helpless. You determined to seduce me—even as your father's cousin seduced my own mother,—leaving her to wash and cook and slave to bring me up."

"But I did not leave you to slave," he interrupted. "I built this house for you and gave you an allowance."

"Yes," she cried excitedly, "and promised, even swore, that you would never marry while I lived; that you would even marry me did the law of the State permit."

"Hold on a minute!" he exclaimed. "I ruined myself giving you fine dresses and jewelry—there was no end to your demands. I mean to be President, and I've got to have the money: I must marry money."

"And I may go to hell with the child—your child—is there a God," she cried in anguish: "while you marry money and the reigning beauty of the South? But you have another guess coming; I mean to see this woman's mother tomorrow and tell her the whole rotten story!"

"You'll do what?" he asked rising from his chair and approaching her with clenched fists. "You'll do what? Say that again! Do you think I'd let any nigger woman wreck my plans? You're crazy."

"It's the only weapon I have, and I am going to use it." She had barely uttered the words when he struck her to the floor.

"You brute!" she cried. "You blond beast!"

"That will do!" he exclaimed excitedly as he stood over her panting with suppresses rage.

"Do your damnedest!" she shrieked. "You dirty coward!" She was in the act of rising when he struck her once, twice, thrice and silenced her.

The noise had awakened the boy who stood open-eyed peeping through the half closed door. The child but dimly realised the scene before him. He wanted to rescue his mother but he feared the demon that possessed his father. So he drew back silently into the gloom, weeping quietly.

The woman lay unconscious on the floor. The man turned to go, he paused- and, looking down upon the prostrate form, whispered half aloud, "Why not? Dead men tell no tales." He knelt over the woman and taking a small knife from his pocket, touched the spring. A blade flew open which he thrust deep into the jugular vein of the woman's neck.

The blood spurted in his face. "Damn!" he exclaimed. He then wiped the knife, his hands and face upon the woman's dressing gown.

He rose and went to the front door a second time.

"Ah!" he cried, "the brat. He may have seen."

Crossing to the child's room he opened the door and switched on the light. The boy had wandered into the night.

CHAPTER I.

Thirty-five Years After.

"You mean?"

"That we shall have the world at our feet and the darker races within our grasp." And the long lean ascetic figure with the pale cadaverous face leaned back in his comfortable arm chair and stretched his lanky legs half across the small apartment. He tightly clenched his bony fingers as though he crushed an invisible and imaginary enemy in a death-like grip. The first speaker a short blond with steel-grey eyes, puffed nervously at his cigar awhile and then ventured hesitatingly, "Have you, ah, realized, O, Emperor of our Invisible State, that the black, the brown, and the yellow people represent more than two thirds of the human race?" Through half closed lids the "Emperor" bent his brows upon the questioner.

Leisurely he drew the ample folds of his hooded gown-like cape about his sinuous form. The lines that furrowed his clean shaved face assumed a sternness as his lips curled contemptuously beneath his hawklike nose; and assuming a studied air of mystery, he leaned forward placing his hand familiarly but patronizingly upon the other's shoulder the better to impress him.

"I raised you to a seat among the noble and EXALTED THREE he said, because your zeal had won you that reward. The lower council and the vulgar herd who do our bidding may not be trusted with our deepest aims. Using the term justice and morality they lynch and burn at our command, the better to enable us effectively to disguise our real intent. Two thirds of mankind gathers force against us. These as you say are the black, the brown and the yellow, whilst they increase our birth rate fails. Should they unite before we white men sink our differences and combine, we—whose heritage is to rule the earth—will soon become their slaves."

The "Emperor" again settled himself comfortably in his chair and resting his face upon his palm he searched the stolid countenance of his auditor. The blond man thoughtfully gazed upward at the ceiling. He made rings of smoke to aid his thoughts. "What of the Negroes here?" he asked.

A demonic expression momentarily flitted across the face of the "Emperor." "Ah!" he exclaimed. "That is our first problem. The Negroes have become too arrogant. They call themselves citizens! These pests must be removed!"

"But how?" inquired the other.

"We must make a hell for them! Burn, lynch, destroy them root and branch."

"They are fifteen million strong—how can we accomplish it?"

"The economic weapon must be used," the "Emperor," rejoined. "Burn their farms, their homes, their churches and schools. Take away their employment—already six hundred thousand Negro infants die annually from mal-nutrition—our doctors have the orders to remove the source of increase from their women wherever they can be forced or persuaded to go upon the operating table—and there are other means. These United States were wrested from the savage Redskins by our stern forefathers. This is a White man's land. It is our heritage!"

There was concentrated hate in the very utterance of this self-imposed minister of destruction: He was about to proceed with his malediction when, first one, then another bell rang to the number of seven. The self-styled "Emperor" and his companion drew their white hoods over their heads and in the semi-darkness, two pairs of gleaming eyes appeared to be the only evidence of life.

A ghost-like apparition silently emerged from behind a heavy curtained door.

"Speak!" the Emperor commanded,

"The Number Three"

"The word?"

"All White!"

"How deep?"

"From sole to crown outward. From skin to heart inward!"

The two seated figures stood up and joined hands with the new arrival. The three then cried out in concert;—"True to the cause till Death!—"

"On the Flaming Cross we swear!"

The three seated themselves and the "Emperor" inquired of the late arrival: "What news Triumvirate?"

"I have found the man we want," he answered; "a mulatto whom the Governor of X—has paroled to me. This Negro has been a gambler and a degenerate; he was educated at one of our colleges. His crime was forgery. He loves ease and luxury at the expense of others and will sell his soul for money."

"He shall have money if he does our bidding", the Emperor said, "or else" he concluded grimly. "A handy tree a hempen necktie and a cremation! Eh, Triumvirate?" He croaked mirthlessly at the jest he made and the portly Triumvirate, to gain the Emperor's favour, laughed long and loud. The blond remained calm, silent and frigid.

"When does this nigger report for duty?" asked the "Emperor."

"Tonight at ten; you will receive him?"

"Yes."

"Here?"

"Yes. He must not even guess the locality of this place. Blind-fold and take him on a joy-ride around the city, then bind and bring him to our presence. The Negro is superstitious and fears the supernatural. Every act when dealing with him must be nerve-racking. The traitor who betrays his own people must be watched with care, and he must have an advance lesson of our strength and power. He must be bound to us through fear." The Emperor pressed a button with his foot; a door in the opposite wall flew open and a towering skeleton stood forth a flaming cross in its right hand. This was the signal which usually ended conferences of the Three. They all stood upon their feet and each stretched forth his right hand towards the figure of Death, crying aloud:—"In the presence of an ever present Death, we swear our loyalty on the Flaming Cross!"

Slowly the skeleton retreated to its place. The illuminated cross was dimmed. The room was plunged in inky darkness and the three hooded figures left the apartment by separate doors.

CHAPTER II.

On a vacant plot just off Seventh Avenue, Harlem, New York, a very sable and by no means prepossessing demagogue was holding forth to a fairly large and nondescript gathering of Negroes on the disabilities of his people.

"Men and women of the Negro race," he cried. "We are more enslaved today than our forefathers were in the days of slavery! They lynch us and burn us and disgrace our daughters and there is no redress. Your leaders are no good! Your preachers are only concerned about fat collections on Sundays and they fail to raise their voices in defence of the rights of the helpless minions, who groan under a system of tyranny which is galling to men who call themselves men! We are subjects not citizens! We pay taxes and we have no representation. Every low class foreigner who comes to this country from Europe has a voice in the affairs of this nation except the Negro! The time has come for us to demand! We are fifteen millions strong; Let us get up and demand our rights and if liberty is denied us in this country to which our forefathers were brought against their will, let us return to Africa our Motherland."

At the mention of Africa members of the crowd uttered rather audibly, "We ain lost nothin' in Africa—wat we gwine to do chasin' monkeys and dodging snakes?" There was general laughter at the latter witticism, whilst others—obvious partisans of the speaker—called out; "Let us hear Napoleon Hatbry speak!—he knows wat he's talkin' about!" Voices were raised in alternation for and against the speaker who ineffectually tried to make himself heard.

Ultimately the meeting resolved itself into a series of free fights and the crowd was dispersed by the active intervention of the police.

Hatbry was quickly surrounded by a group of his followers who hustled him away from the danger zone.

A rather stout blond man who listened attentively to the speaker from the fringe of the crowd now followed the Leader and his bodyguard at a discreet distance. They passed through Seventh Avenue and turned into One Hundred and Forty Second Street and walked toward Eight Avenue where Hatbry, now being safe from molestation, halted with his companions who shook his hand effusively and departed their several ways whilst the Leader quickly ascended to the entrance to a block of flats. The blond man who had followed on the opposite side of the street walked towards Eighth Avenue from whence he watched the parting Negroes and having satisfied himself that he was unobserved retraced his steps, crossed the street, and entered the flats to find the habitation of Hatbry which he discovered after reading the names on the mail boxes in the entrance hall.

Leisurely presenting himself at the door of Hatbry's flat he rang the bell and was reluctantly admitted and ushered into a tiny sitting room by a tall vicious looking dark-skinned woman of undoubted African origin.

"What's your business with Mr Hatbry?" she inquired. "And what's your name?"

"Mr Hatbry does not know me," the blond man replied. "My name is Smith, no, I am not a detective—just a businessman and a bit of a politician interested in Hatbry's work."

The woman sniffed suspiciously. "I don't know how any white man can be interested in the work of Mr Hatbry," she rejoined. "White men interested in our work want to ruin the work as a rule." She laid considerable emphasis on the word "interested" which caused Smith to smile.

"Ah well," he replied, "things are not always what they seem. You must not be too suspicious."

"We Negroes have a lot cause to be—especially of your kind," was the ungracious rejoinder. "Anyhow I'll see if Mr Hatbry has time to talk to you. Sit down!" was her curt conclusion as she bustled out of the room leaving Mr Smith to his reflections. The small apartment in which he sat was so greatly overcrowded with a miscellaneous collection of spurious antiques that it was difficult to find a pathway to a seat without knocking over the cheap and gaudy bric-a-brac that seemed to find a malicious pleasure in resting perilously on the brink of destruction.

Mr Smith, with an awed feeling of amusement, was in the act of methodically contemplating this travesty of "The old Curiosity Shop" when Hatbry entered and awkwardly bowed to his visitor who, in rising to his feet to acknowledge the welcome, knocked over a cheap vivid green china vase with a villainous splash of red, which was intended to simulate a rose.

"I am so sorry!" the visitor cried in genuine concern as he stooped to pick up the scattered fragments of the "priceless" object, and in so doing almost upset a nude statue of a lacquer negress that held up a battered lamp in her extended right hand. Hatbry deftly caught the falling wooden lady and standing her once more in an upright position proceeded to place the visitor at his ease.

"So very awkward of me," began Mr Smith.

"It is nothing, really of no matter; don't worry about it, please. Will you sit down?"

Mr Smith sat down as requested and the Leader, having carefully negotiated a rather perilous path to a neighboring chair said: "I think you wanted to speak with me, Mr—"

"Smith!"

"Yes; Mr Smith."

"To be brief. I have listened to your talks at odd times for several months— no doubt you saw me in the crowd."

"I saw you" Hatbry rejoined "you always appeared interested."

"Yes, I was, and am, interested—very interested—in your work, now see here, I can help you: listen! He whispered in Hatbry's ear who looked astonished and turning his full gaze upon his visitor remarked, "Is that really a fact?"

"Absolutely," Mr Smith replied. "It is not known to my friends, but there it is. I'll tell you the simple story someday."

"I shall be very glad to hear it. This is quite a surprise."

"Well as I observed, I am interested in your work and I can materially assist. I have some inside information which will be of service to the cause." He leaned over again and whispered in Hatbry's ear.

"Good God!" Hatbry exclaimed. "Is it possible?"

"Yes, quite possible, they don't suspect the statement I first made; that's part of the game."

"I see, I see," reflected Hatbry. "You're a wonderful man, Mr Smith."

"Not at all—accident, fate, what you will. Now I think you understand." He took a note book from his pocket and wrote on one of the pages.

"Here," he said, "is a phone number you can call should you want me urgently. You must not give your full name. "Napoleon" will be sufficient; understand?"

"Yes," answered Hatbry, absently. "Napoleon is the name I shall give."

"And I trust that you will go forth to conquer as your namesake did. I shall be glad to help. But remember, there must be no Waterloos!"

"No, no Waterloo's," laughed Hatbry. "No Waterloos!"

"Well I must be going," cried Smith, looking at his wrist watch as he rose to his feet. "I will see you one day this week; goodbye." They shook hands and Hatbry saw Smith to the door. He stood for a moment at the open door watching Smith descend the stairs; then rubbing his chin reflectively he shut himself in, and as he gingerly picked his way through his "art" labyrinth he encountered a white marble statuette of Napoleon the Great which gave him pause. Suddenly, a wide smile overspread his homely countenance as he gazed at the Little Corporal. "No Waterloo for me, Mr Napoleon!" he exclaimed; "No Waterloo!"

CHAPTER III.

A taxi cab drew up at the curb. A young man of colour alighted. He was clean shaved and very much dressed in a suit of grey checks that shouted aloud, green socks with terra cotta stripes and scarf to match; patent-leather shoes that fitted snugly encased his feet causing him to step with caution. He might easily have been mistaken for a Sicilian or other Negroid Southern European. He held the door open for "Emperor" to descend. The latter was enveloped in a voluminous black military cloak. The coloured man paid the fare, after ostentatiously displaying a huge roll of "green backs" which brought a sarcastic smile to the face of his companion.

The taxi drove away, and the "Emperor" wrapping his ample cloak about his lanky form, pulling his black slouched hat well over his eyes, proceeded at a slow pace along the brightly lit South State Street in the wake of a bois-terous group of gaily clad Chicago Negroes who were out for a "hot time" in the cabarets of the windy city.

"Say Jones, I think we will follow that bunch of howling niggers," remarked the "Emperor" to his companion. "I want to see what they are up to."

"Alright Colonel, we'll keep right up with them," answered Jones, in gleeful anticipation of the high time he intended to have.

Jones had passed through an initiation of blood and fire. The minions of the Invisible State had performed the bidding of their "Emperor" with a thoroughness that left a mass of bruises and burns upon the body of Jones which he would carry to his grave. They had certainly given him complete and unmistakable evidence of their power. Among other things they had branded him in the small of the back with a cross which he had not discov-ered. He only knew he had been branded with a red hot instrument and that despite the ministrations of the Surgeon-general of the Invisible State which had lasted for ten days, he was still sore and found it extremely difficult either to lay comfortably in a bed or to successfully conjugate the verb to sit. Nev-ertheless as Jones' motto was: "To hell with yesterday! What's doing to-day?" his penchant for enjoying the *Now* not only carried him though a trying physical ordeal which few stronger men could have survived, but being well supplied with funds, his favorite bootlegger administered a soothing balm that assisted Jones to revel in his own peculiar brand of philosophy and, in some measure, allay his physical discomfort. When, therefore, the

"Emperor" suggested following "the bunch," he sensed their objective with an uncanny accuracy.

He knew the psychology, temperament and varying types of his race, and he felt convinced that "the bunch" which proceeded him was not bound for a prayer meeting. Hence, having already undergone a six months term of his sentence in jail and a ten days term of torture at the hands of members of the Invisible State, each step they took caused his spirits to rise in anticipation of the orgy of frolic for which his soul had yearned. Still following the hilarious bunch, they crossed Thirty-Fifth Street arriving at the "Sun Shine Inn"—a hostelry which had for its motto:

"Enjoy Your Self from Nite till Lunch:

"Our Dances get the worst of the bunch."

The unpretentious entrance was well guarded by observers whose business it was to pass the word along to the floor manager should any too inquisitive visitor or unknown detective break in upon the privacy of the revellers. When, therefore, Jones and the "Emperor" entered, the word was quickly passed on that a "split" had arrived which resulted in a sudden plunge into a decorum so unexpected and unknown that the awkwardness produced was more pronouncedly suspicious than a continuation of the somewhat lewd performance which preceded the "Emperor's" entrance, who had seated himself in an obscure corner, the better to observe the antics of the heterogeneous throng.

The frigidity of a cold douche had enveloped the gathering: the laugh died at its birth, whispers succeeded boisterous vulgarity and even the trap-drummer had lost his cunning, nerve and dexterity, and first one couple, then another, departed from the place which had suddenly become dull and "pepless" to the "pep-hunters." Jones, who meant to enjoy himself, saw that disaster was impending. He whispered in the "Emperor's" ear and then descended from the little gallery overlooking the dance floor and approached the sorely troubled manager.

There was a whispered consultation. Jones produced and reduced his bank roll by ten dollars. Gradually the manager's serious countenance assumed a smile, then a broad grin that took complete possession of his sable face, until nothing remained but two small twinkling eyes, and a red-rimmed cavity fenced about with a double row of gold-shot ivories.

"I got you!" was his response to Jones, and then he cried in stentorian tones: "Let the dance go on!"

The crowd took its cue from the orchestra, giving vent to its pent up feelings as the trap-drummer proceeded to out-do his accustomed "stuff" to the vocal out-bursts and approving plaudits of the motley throng.

Jones was in the thick of it. He meant to liven things up a bit. "Is this a morgue!" he cried, elbowing his way to the center of the floor. "No! no!" yelled the crowd.

"From nite till lunch!" shouted the floor manager.

"From nite till lunch!" echoed the assembly in chorus.

"Clear the floor for the Charleston," cried the manager.

"Clear the floor!" And Jones took up his stand in the middle of the room as the orchestra broke out in syncopated measure to the wobbling contortions of Jones.

Round upon round of applause greeted the performer who after some fifteen minutes of simian gymnastics, tottered exhaustedly to a vacant seat amid the vociferous plaudits of the revellers.

Some ten or twelve men, white and black, sprang to their feet, magically producing flasks of doubtful spirit to revive the wasted energies of the prostrate Jones. The dancers once more hurried to the floor.

The waiters shouted their orders. The "Emperor" from his perch sardonically looked down upon the scene. A very dark girl of prepossessing comeliness who had supped rather unwisely at the synthetic front was assisted to a space among the dancers by her white companion. They turned about unsteadily to the sensuous pulsating of the drums and then, losing her balance, she fell to the floor dragging her companion with her.

The 'fun' grew fast and furious.

The now resuscitated Jones out of bravado, seized a woman of the other group and entered energetically into the gyration of the "Black Bottom." The "Emperor" saw and silently fumed. He said nothing but registered a silent vow to administer condign punishment to Jones for this flaunting desecration of the person of this fair denizen of the underworld. He looked away. His sight and feelings were outraged. His eagle glance rested on another pair, a debonair Nordic and a none too comely Negress who atoned for her lack of beauty with a rhythmic grace which suggested the poetic excellence of motion.

Pandemonium reigned. The dance continued. "Black Bottom" succeeded. "Two Step" and "Two Step" yielded to "Fish Tail" with occasional "Charleston" interpolations. The dancers were tireless. The waiters continued to yell their orders and the hip flask went upon its merry round of vitalizing force to the enlivening and humorous directions of the floor manager.

The gin-laden women, who took a short respite from the dance climbed immodestly and wantonly about the necks of their amorous men in sensuous abandon. Many of these were young girls in, or just out of, their teens; not a few had passed through high school and college, and had now become initiates or extremely "freshmen" in the college of vice and degradation. An ebullient coloured Doctor sat at a table with a group of flappers who ostentatiously exchanged dainty boxes of cocaine which was sniffed with hilarious enjoyment.

The prelude to the "Charleston" sounded and the most young and vivacious of this group tearing off her evening wrap—she wore very little else—dashed into the centre of the room and climbed upon a table, to the unstinted applause of the audience. Seizing her brief skirt she lifted it high above her rolled stockings, shook the tangles from her wooly head, dashing with mad abandon into the intricate movements of the measureless.

"Some gal," came a voice. "Go to it sugar!" cried the floor manager.

"She's knockin'—she's knockin' em all! Some steps!" were the exclamations from various parts of the room.

The dance grew more wild and furious. The gathering was wrought up to the highest pitch of excitement. An elderly and much more painted venu fell from her chair in a drunken stupor, whilst a degenerate dragged off a beautiful but half intoxicated neophyte to his lair, who wept contritely on his shoulder, as the pair made an undignified exit.

The clock struck three. The "Emperor" beckoned Jones, who rejoined him and carefully replaced the cloak upon the great one's shoulders.

"You've got remarkable recuperative powers" remarked the "Emperor."

"Yes Colonel?"

"You would have fetched a tidy price before the Civil war," he continued. And turning once more to gaze at the subject of the degrading orgy, he asked, "What do you think of it, Jones?" Jones thought for a moment and then replied. "A celebrated Englishman once wrote: 'If Christ should visit Chicago.'"

"Yes," drawled the "Emperor" reflectively, as they passed out into the morning air. "But Stead got drowned and didn't see black Chicago."

CHAPTER IV.

A select dinner party was being held at Norman Towers, the palatial residence of Montague Smithson, the successful stockbroker whose firm dealt in guilt edge securities. There was no doubt of the firm's guilt, but its political pull was too strong for its guilt to bring it to a Justice who, in the case of the firm at least, had effectively mislaid her blinkers and her balances. The balances were entirely in favour of the Smithson and Company Inc., in the shape of solid cash deposits with their bankers.

Smithson was a mystery to his associates. He was never known to encourage a discussion on his antecedents. Whenever some super-inquisitive being referred to his ancestry, he would stick out his chest, which success had forced down to the region just about his waist line, smile blandly, stroke his blond silken ringlets, and reply: "My people come over with the Mayflower, like some of the other puritanical buccaneers. It has never been clear to me, whether they stowed away or travelled steerage." At which there would be general laughter and Smithson, or "Monty," as he was familiarly termed, would then adroitly turn the conversation into other channels. He had married Virginia Hillyarde, a famous Southern belle of an impeccable but impoverished family, which traced its lineage through a long line of Elizabethan aristocratic adventurers back to the Norman Conquest. It is true that the bar-sinister did appear on the coat-of-arms of the family, but the responsible philanderer being no less a person than a Plantagenet King, who could do no wrong, the Lady Hillyarde's moral lapse could hardly be accounted a sin. Of course, in slave time, the Hillyardes had been rather fond of their female slaves and the royal blood of Plantagenet—via the Hillyardes—had filtered through the veins of a numerous company of log cabin dwellers passing throughout the length and breadth of old Virginia. Thus the Hillyarde name, the Hillyarde blood, which was fast disappearing through the failure of the Caucasian line, was being perpetuated by the despised half-cast Negro who could claim kinship with the proud Virginia Hillyarde and her spend-thrift brother—the sole remnants of that "untainted stock."

By his marriage with Virginia Hillyarde, Smithson had brought the best bride that money could procure; but even she could not penetrate the veil that hid his past. To her oft repeated inquiry as to his family connections, he would answer, that he had married her because he possessed the wealth which supplied the luxuries necessary to her very existence. All things being, therefore, equal, it was quite unseemly of him to boast about the decayed roots of his family tree, seeing that her own ancestral tree transcended all that grew in the New World, and was sufficiently widespreading to cover them both. Finally she gave up asking, accepted the money he lavished upon her, enjoyed her pleasures to the full, without neglecting her magnificent homes nor the maternal care of her infant son.

Dinner parties at Norman Towers were by no means unusual, but on this occasion the dinner assumed an unwonted importance because of the diversity of the guests. Colonel Blood, the "Emperor" of the Invisible State, had been invited to meet Doctor Detritcher, the famous sociologist whose rubicund countenance reminded one of the traditional Santa Claus, and Algernon Hillyarde had brought his fiancée, Henriette Swanson, for presentation to his sister—the fifteenth girl to whom he had become engaged within the short space of three years. The young lady possessed some beauty and considerable natural distinction. Dark, after the accepted Spanish type, of medium height and slender proportions, with large lustrous brown eyes that were wont to assume a dreamy unfathomable character when in repose, and a startled expression when was suddenly addressed. She was the kind of girl who would attract attention in any company, especially after one had taken the second glance, her personality was so compelling that few persons could resist a second look at dainty little "Ette", as she was familiarly called by her associates.

The dinner with its wearisome courses had ended and Ette, being the only lady present other than the hostess, was ushered into the spacious reception room by Virginia with her brother Algernon in close attendance. Doctor Detritcher was discussing the ever present question of racial relations and the Negro problem in the United States. He held the opinion that the Negro was in America to stay and that repression would have a tendency to aggravate rather than solve the question, to which Colonel Blood dissented.

"The Negro" said the "Emperor," is a superior class of monkey no doubt, but a monkey just the same. To grant him the privileges of the white man would ultimately result in a condition of chaos that would be unprintably appalling."

"I fear," rejoined the Doctor, "that you have overdrawn the picture; you have overlooked the fact that this very despised Negro was the originator if there is anything original of our present civilization. We all admit the European civilization had its birth in Greece, but few of us stop to consider that Greece owed her cultural attainments to ancient Egypt which was undoubtedly the cradle of all civilizations as we know them; and we have it on the authority of Herodotus that the ancient Egyptians were black—black—what we call or miscall Negroes and—"

"Good God Doctor!" interrupted the Colonel, rising hastily from his chair, "You'll next be telling us that the nigger is our superior! I never expected to hear any red-blooded white man talk as you do. Why, if I thought I'd owed my culture to niggers, I'd go right out now and blow my brains out!"

The high pitched tones of the Colonel reverberated through the mansion bringing Algeron Hillyarde back to the dining room. "Well," remarked the Doctor, when he had recovered from the Colonel's outburst, "Truth, she may be denied her heritage for a time, but she usually comes into her own."

"What's the big idea?" asked Hillyarde.

"The Doctor, here" answered the Colonel, reseating himself, "wants us to believe that all our culture is the product of the niggers."

"Our jazz, he means, perhaps," said Hillyarde laughingly.

"I do not mean our jazz," responded the Doctor reflectively passing his fingers through his snowy beard. "Although, I must admit that in the matter of native American music, we have very little to boast about other than the music of the Negro."

"Come, come," cried Hillyarde, dropping comfortably into a chair. "Surely we have other Native music; the drums of the Indians for instance." There was sarcasm in Hillyarde's reference to the Indian drums.

Smithson, who refrained from joining in the conversation, glared contemptuously at his brother-in-law, but said nothing.

"Well I suppose the Doctor will be telling us that his nigger pets taught the Indian to use the drum," was the Colonel's bitter comment.

"That, Colonel, is precisely what I was about to say," was the ready response of the Doctor. "I suppose you have not troubled to read Professor Werner's book on the Negro and the discovery of America?"

"Did the Negro beat Columbus to it?" sneered Hillyarde.

"The facts certainly point that way," the Doctor coolly replied.

"Columbus was himself dependent upon the assistance of Negro navigators. Moreover, it must be born in mind that Columbus himself, like most Italians, was very probably negroid."

"At this rate the Doctor will very soon be telling us that we all belong to the Negro race", was the ironic remark of the Colonel.

"Which would be very near the truth," the Doctor blandly replied.

Hillyarde roared. The Colonel rose from his seat and walked towards the reception room to convey the information to Virginia, that Doctor Detritcher was planning to introduce mixed marriages and place the American Negro on terms of social equality with the white man. Virginia held up her hands in horror at the bare suggestion and turning to Henriette, said: "If such a thing ever comes to pass, I'm very much afraid I should start a little shooting on my own account."

"Who would you shoot?" Ette inquired innocently, turning her large dark eyes upon Virginia.

"Why a few niggers of course! Who else you think?" asked Virginia turning questioningly to Henriette, "you surely could not dream of any white woman marrying a nigger?"

"Worse things than that might happen to a white woman!" Ette answered with some spirit. "White men don't appear to be so particular if we may judge by the mulattoes one sees." Ette was astonished at her own boldness and the Colonel was about to reply when Smithson entered the room with Hillyarde and the Doctor. Before the Colonel could speak, Virginia sprang to her feet, crying: "Say, Doctor, here's a disciple for you! Miss Swanson says she wouldn't mind marrying a nigger!"

"She said what?" asked Hillyarde heatedly. "Did you say that Ette?"

"I did not say that," Ette answered evenly, "or rather, not quite that. I merely said that I did not consider it such a terrible thing, seeing that white men were not greatly—ah—shall we say repulsed?—shocked, would be a better word—perhaps—by their illicit amors with black women."

"It would have the moral merit of regularity at least," said the Doctor smiling.

"There!" exclaimed Virginia. "What did I say? The Doctor's disciple!"

"The devil's disciple," muttered the Colonel irritably.

"You astonish me Ette! In fact, quite disgust me by such talk!" was Hillyarde's rebuke. "No Southern gentleman could tolerate such views from his future wife. You have completely lost your sense," he concluded rudely.

"And no gentleman, Southern or other, would use such language to a lady," sneered Ette rising. Then, sweetly to Virginia, "thank you very much for a pleasant evening Mrs Smithson. I think I will go now." She moved toward the door without deigning a glance in Hillyarde's direction. And as Virginia followed, Ette turned and bowed to the men. "Good night gentlemen," she said unaffectedly. Then looking up into Virginia's face she asked: "Would you mind if your servant called a taxi?"

The Doctor jumped to his feet. "Can I see you home in my car?" he asked.

"Thank you very much—yes."

Smithson's disdainful gaze encountered that of the chagrined Hillyarde.

"I'll see you home Miss Swanson," the latter cried somewhat ungraciously, rising from his seat.

"I have already accepted the Doctor's offer. Thank you," was Ette's smiling reply. She dug her nails deep in her palms to repress her emotion and hurried upstairs after Virginia to procure her wraps. The Doctor bade the others goodnight and was joined by Smithson in the hall. Hillyarde shrugged his shoulders and turning sulkily seated himself beside the Colonel. Smithson remained silent. Virginia descended with her guest, who left on the Doctor's arm.

"Damn these new women!" was Hillyarde's ejaculation as the hall door closed.

"My sentiments exactly," the Colonel commented.

"And the niggers," he concluded.

"Quite a gentlemanly exhibition," murmured Smithson, as he returned to the room with his wife.

CHAPTER V.

"So this is nigger heaven, eh, Jones?" remarked the Colonel, as they looked down upon the overdressed throng of seething coloured humanity that paraded up and down Seventh Avenue, New York, like the king's daughter—"All glorious without."

"Yes Colonel, this is Negro heaven," corrected Jones, emphasizing the word Negro.

Jones had become rather resentful of the Colonel's studied use of the term "Nigger" whenever the great man referred to the group to which he, Jones, belonged. He knew he was a very unworthy representative of his race, but whilst he did not believe that the Negro was, or would ever be any good he was not unmindful of the affront which the "Emperor" seemed bent on placing upon the Negro through him. And he was convinced that the Colonel wanted to humble any small vestige of pride that remained to him.

On this particular summer evening, Jones had made a "date" with a very alluring "high stepping yaller," as he termed his amorita, but the Colonel's demand upon his time had caused him to lose the date and very possibly the girl as well. Hence, he was, to say the least, "sore" in the extreme. And the unnecessary stress the "Emperor" laid on the word "nigger" tended to increase that soreness, so in replying to the Colonel's sarcasm, he turned and glared pointedly at his employer when emphasizing the word Negro.

"I said nigger!" was Colonel Blood's corrective rejoinder. "And nigger is the word I'm using Jones. I want you to remember that from now on, unless you'd like to have your hide treated to a further dose of corrective respect by your masters!"

"Masters!" ejaculated Jones, pulling vigorously at his cigarette.

"Yes, masters!" the Colonel grimly replied. "We own you body and soul, Jones. And the sooner you realize that fact the better it will be for all concerned—especially you."

Jones moved about uneasily in his seat, but made no reply.

"You don't seem to take kindly to the warning, 'Nigger', the Colonel drawled. "Moreover, I expect an answer when I condescend to use precious words on 'Niggers'—throw that cigarette away!"

"Alright Colonel," Jones replied, throwing his lighted cigarette through the window upon the hat of a passing West Indian Negro.

"What in hell yo' mean by throwin' yo' cigarette on me new pannermab, man!" shouted the irate West Indian, as he stepped into the Avenue and looked up at the open window.

Jones leaned forward and was about to vent his spleen upon the head of the offended passerby, when the Colonel pulled him back.

"Damn you!" he exclaimed, "do you want to involve me in a nigger-town street brawl?"

"Beg pardon, Colonel" came Jones' humble response, as he resumed his seat. The West Indian having received no encouragement to wrangle, because of his failure to locate the individual who had shown such utter contempt for his immaculate cranial adornment, was about to continue his promenade when he was nearly run over by the automobile of a well known coloured Harlem Physician who laughingly disappeared in a cloud of dust to the further discomfiture of the Sable Beau Brummel from the Isles of the Sea.

"Who was the overdressed 'Nigger' in that expensive car that just went by?" the Colonel asked.

"That's Doctor Jennison, the prominent Harlem Physician", Jones answered somewhat sulkily.

"Umph" the Colonel grunted, ignoring Jones' sulkiness. "Makes a lot of money I guess?"

Jones glanced covertly at the "Emperor", and started to do some hard thinking.

"Yes, Colonel, they say he makes twenty-five thousand a year."

"Married?"

"Divorced his wife, sir. She helped him through college. Old woman now, and as black as he is, with no education to speak of. The Doctor's gotten a bit ashamed of her as he got on in the world. He wants a high yaller—college gal—but he is too much like a sack of coal for the most of them. They use up his "good time" money and when he steps on the gas they quit him cold. They say he's runnin down a near-white gal in Boston, with a name like a movie star."

"How do the niggers live? Where do they get the money to dress like that?" The Colonel asked the questions as he drew the window curtain to partly conceal him, and leaned forward the better to observe the passing show.

Jones told his friends that he had rented the front room the pair occupied as a place of observation, as a Real Estate Office, but it was seldom opened during the day. The drawers of the expensive office desks were, however, abundantly stocked with cards and poker chips.

"There's a fortune in dresses and jewelry down there," said the Colonel as he watched the Seventh Avenue fashion show. "Where do they get the money."

"Oh," responded Jones, "Some of them work for the money and put it all on their backs, when they ain't runnin' an expensive pimp—the women I mean—and most of them make a weekly pay off to the Jew peddlers in fine raiment."

"And what do they do when they run a pimp?" the Colonel asked.

"They work some, and if they're pretty, they're white men, good an plenty, an' rich one's at that who will put up some side money for a high stepping' brown skin."

Jones was delighted to have a sly dig at the morals of the Colonel's group.

"You don't mean to tell me that white men frequent Harlem to consort with nigger harlots," the Colonel cried with some show of surprise.

"Well sir," replied Jones reflectively. "They are runnin' true to form, look at me. My mother didn't treat me to no high yaller face. Look down the Avenue, Colonel, and see how many black people there is. There ain't no real black people left in the United States. I don't guess it's the fault of us Negroes—beg pardon, Colonel. Niggers! Niggers! I mean."

Jones was almost tearfully apologetic "My father was a white man," he concluded. "And down in Georgia the nigger woman's got no come back."

The statement was bold in view of the "Emperor's" warning. The challenge was also obvious although somewhat softened by the manner of its delivery. Jones was not a coward. He had mixed with the underworld too much for that. Many a time when caught in the act of stacking a deck of cards or in putting over a pair of loaded dice, he had to be handy with gun and razor to escape with his life. Even the recent grilling he had received at the hands of the members of the Invisible State was almost forgotten until he was reminded by the Colonel. He understood the Nordic psychology and being possessed of a nimble wit, he meant to use that knowledge by assuming an air of abject humility in all his future dealings with the "Emperor." He was earning "easy money" and being a "good timer," he did not intend to spoil his good fortune by interjecting personal pique or personal pride. He was out for a "killing" and the Colonel had the "bones" (money). Henceforth he meant to be the most humble and abject "good nigger" that ever came up from the South. It was the line of least resistance. The college-bred Afro-American, he knew, was a joke to the average white American and having taken the "Emperor's" measure, he felt convinced that the great man had been delivered into his hands. So he intended hereafter to wallow in the slime of humility and the honey of inferiority should flow from his lips. Colonel Blood was, therefore, puzzled by Jones' sudden change of manner. Naturally, he attributed the newly assumed and soft humble demeanor of Jones to be due to the warning he had uttered as well as to the inferiority complex which he firmly believed all Negroes possessed. The firm hand and the big stick had always been the sovereign remedy for "nigger" impudence, he reflected. He was flattered by the slime of Jones, but he felt that the nigger had no right to an opinion, so he remarked rather curtly.

"I didn't ask your opinion, Jones, nor about your family connections."

"I ain't got no opinion, Colonel. I was trying to answer your question."

"So they put all their earnings on their backs, eh, Jones, but the men; what about them?"

"Well Colonel, the men does the same thing with what's left over from supplying the women. Some of them who call themselves thrifty are buying homes. They starve themselves, take in all sorts of roomers to make up the payments on the notes, but eventually the Jew gets them—houses, furniture or clothes; The Earth is The Lord's and the fullness thereof belongs to the Jew."

"Then you don't think they'd hold out very long if they had no jobs?"

"Just about ten days, Colonel; by that time the niggers fine clothes and jewelry would be in the care of the eternal Jew—if he'd take them—and then, real starvation, an' that ain't maybe so, neither."

"In ten days, eh," reflected the "Emperor." "What are the nigger preachers doing for their people, Jones?"

"The nigger preacher, Colonel, is the last thing God ever let live. When they ain't graftin' on politics they're graftin' on the poor saps who listen to their shoutin an' Bible punchin'. They don't care how the congregation gets the money so long as they get the kale (cash) on Sunday. They're great on buyin second hand churches that are always in debt. If they weren't in debt all the time the niggers they preach to wouldn't part with a dime. The church has just naturally got to stay in debt, but the preacher can always have a clear title to his house and send his children to college. His is the sure-thing-land flowing with milk and honey. It's the poor washerwoman that keeps the preacher in idleness an' chicken dinners that has to live on coffee dregs an' frozen pork chops all week; she has a lean time. On Sunday she will strut with the best o' them to the tune of "Onward Christian Soldiers," an' go hungry Monday—Hot Damn! If that ain't Napoleon Hatbry struttin' his stuff up the Avenue!"

"Where?" asked the Colonel, rising.

"See that ugly bag o' coal in the blue 'See-the-sucker' suit, on the other side of the Avenue, with a crowd o' men an' women followin?—that's him!

"Yes," cried the "Emperor," "I see him. Where do you think he's going?"

"He holds a meeting every night on a vacant lot up the Avenue—that's where he's going now, I guess."

"What do you think of him, Jones?"

"Well, I don't know. He's a bit out o' my class, Colonel. Either he's doing some good or he's gotten hold of a new kind of graft, because of the way the preachers hate him. An' the nigger preacher can hate good an' plenty, when you try to spoil his graft."

"What do the niggers think of the other fellow, De Woods?"

"He's a popular joke—sort o' despised an' rejected of men: the high priest of education an culture that don't bring in a dime. The pool rooms an' gamblin' halls is full of that sort. So is the cabarets an' buffet flats."

"You don't appear to believe in nigger education?"

"What's the use, Colonel? My gran' father didn't know the letter A, from a load of manure, an' he got himself a farm an' made money. He sent me to college an' mortgaged the farm to do it. I came out o' school full o' hope an' ambition, but useless as an earner. No white man wanted me in his office, only as a messenger. I tried waiting, and portering, an' the Pullman service, for a while. The work was hard, the pay small, an' I quit. The old man lost his farm an' died, an' I—well, there was easy money at pimpin' and gamblin', an' I ended up in the "pen." That's what I got out o' college. There is plenty o' them waiting an' portering now—there's one Harvard graduate who's a policeman in Boston. You don't want no college education to porter an' wait table an' police. We niggers ain't doing a thing but dream. As for our mis-leaders, there ain't one that's any good—Booker T. Washington was the only one who was worth his salt an' he's dead."

"I ain't no prophet, Colonel, an' my education hasn't been much good to me, but the day is comin' when these folks o' mine will get a shock[1] that's

---

1   This word is difficult to read in original.

gwine to wake 'em up some. When that day comes, there won't be enough lamp-posts in the U. S. A. on which to hang our bogus leaders."

"So you think the niggers are going to get a shock, eh Jones?"

"Sure thing! I ain't no moralist; but them months I spent in jail did give me time to do some thinking. I'm just an'-out-an' out good timer. Just you look down in the Avenue on them Japs, Colonel, they're struttin' their peacock stuff, an' they borrowed the feathers! It won't do, Colonel—it jest naturally won't do! Look at that black gal over there, with the paradise feathers in her hat. She's wearing a rainbow dress with a cotton row glide, an' as much flour on her face as would start a small baker shop. An' that high yaller with the stilt heel shoes, four sizes too small; look at her Colonel—She is twelve bucks (dollars) a week waitress, dressed like a millionaire's daughter. An' them two dudes followin' her in their palm beach foolishness, an' hair as slick a skatin' rink. O, hell!—beg pardon, Colonel—it makes me sick!"

Jones sat down and drew a packet of cigarettes from his pocket and placed one between his lips. He was about to light up when his glance met that of the "Emperor". He was in the act of throwing the cigarette away when the Colonel indulgently said: "Alright Jones, you can smoke." Jones sighed. He had scored one point.

"O, thank you, Colonel, thank you sir," he humbly replied and lit up.

It must not be too hastily assumed that Jones was quite incapable of forming a correct estimate of his race. Nor should it be understood that he was merely covering the Colonel with slime. He said that his jail term had made him think, and his expressed opinions proved that he had also become critical. His was not constructive criticisms perhaps, but it was both healthy and timely. He had seen the world from the vantage point of the college graduate as well as from his underworld contacts, and his education assisted him to an appreciation of values. Granted a fair measure of opportunity he might have been an ornament to his race; as it was, the Afro-American had nothing in the way of business to offer him and his encounter with the spiked Nordic fence of progress had proved unpleasingly painful, shattering any ambitious illusions he may have possessed. His trend of sociological thought in so far as it affected the Afro-American, naturally appealed to the warped outlook of the Colonel, who regarded "Educated niggers" not only with contempt and suspicion, but with an unreasoning hate which was all but consuming. He, however, quickly realized that there might be considerable advantage in having a nigger devoted to his cause who was at once educated and docile. And, as Jones, in his new assumption of humility appeared to fill this requirement, the Colonel proceeded to shed his austerity, becoming almost urbane in his demeanor.

"Well Jones," he cried familiarly, rising and looking at his watch, "it's close to nine, I guess I'd better be moving on—"

There were several loud blasts from motor horns in the Avenue and a loud crash resulting from a collision, intermingled with shouts, imprecations and shrieks. The Colonel turned to the window and Jones jumped to his feet and looked out.

"Some mix up," said Jones.

"An opportune time for me to pass out unobserved," remarked the Colonel. He was about to turn from the window when his wandering gaze was arrested. "What in the heck is he doing on Seventh Avenue on foot at that hour?" The Colonel reflected, rubbing his smoothly shaven chin. "Say Jones", he exclaimed quickly, 'See that rather stout blond man over there?"

"Where, Colonel?"

"The one standing near the hind wheel of the wrecked car—there!'

"Yes, sir—with his hat in his hand?"

"Yes, look at him well, do you think you'd know him again?"

"Sure thing, Colonel."

"Alright – goodnight, Jones."

"Goodnight, Colonel."

CHAPTER VI.

"What's wrong with Miss Swanson today?" was the frequent question passed around the Boston Book Store of Brown Simpkins and Brown. The query that began with shop girls reached over and took in the office returning to the shop to overwhelm the regular customers. It was one of the regulars who put the question to the manageress. A wealthy woman who had always taken a keen interest in "dainty Miss Swanson," and would not accept the service of anyone else in the establishment.

"I really don't know, Mrs Wetherall," the manageress replied. "I fear she is in love or something.'

"It looks as though she has fallen out with love," commented Mrs Wetherall. "The poor dear girl seems quite distraught. You know how I depend upon her to select my books. Today she appears to have completely lost interest in everything. I hope there is nothing serious."

"I don't suppose there is anything serious. She seemed alright this morning when we opened up. But about ten o'clock she became suddenly gloomy. Not a word beyond "yes or no" could anyone get from her and she is usually cute as a rule—everybody likes her, she's so sweet."

"I do hope she will be alright in a day or two. I shall be in again next week—goodbye!"

"Goodbye Mrs Wetherall," cried the manageress as she bowed the lady out. "There," she said addressing one of the girls. "If Miss Swanson doesn't pull herself together soon, we shall be losing all of our regulars, that's the fourth complaint today." She did not wait for an answer but bustled into the office to report the matter to the senior partner.

Meanwhile the subject of all this concern was gazing into space quite oblivious to her surroundings. Now and then a tear would momentarily dim her eyes, falling unheeded down the front of her neat black satin dress. Occasionally she would press her powder puff into service turning to smile wanly when addressed.

Finally she straightened herself up and rushing up to the manageress said: "Miss Perkins, I really must go home. I am not at all well."

"Why didn't you say you wanted to go home, Miss Swanson? Get your things and run off at once. Take a good rest—a day, two days, a week if you like." Miss Perkins got Ette's wraps, sent one of the girls to phone for a cab and escorted her to the door with many cheering words.

Ette arrived home and rushed to the room of her maiden aunt, to whom she explained all that had taken place at the Smithson's party. Relating how Hillyarde, notwithstanding his ungallant conduct, had requested her to meet him that night at the Commonwealth Hotel, and she hated to do so, because she knew instinctively that there would be a scene, and she loathed scenes.

"But you love him," was her aunt's reply.

"I am not sure that I do," answered Ette, doubtfully. "At least not now."

"But you must remember he belongs to one of the first families of Virginia."

"First families fiddlesticks!" Ette exclaimed. "I am heartily tired of hearing about these first families."

"But blood will tell, my dear child," the aunt responded proudly. "Look at your own case. Anyone who looks at you knows at a glance that you're a real blue blood."

"Yes, and as soon as they know that—oh, I have a headache, I'm off to bed to be ready for the ordeal." And she bounced out of the room. "Ah," said the aunt, with a sigh. "Young people have changed." She arose from the couch, shook up the pillows and returning, curled herself up and went to sleep.

In the meantime Ette, having had her sleep, awoke and refreshing herself with a cup of tea, dressed carefully and went off to the Commonwealth to dine with Hillyarde who had selected a quiet corner in the spacious dining room.

The dinner was a rather silent affair. Both Ette and Hillyarde were busy with their thoughts. Towards the end Hillyarde brightened, having secretly helped himself to frequent doses of pre-Volstead joy from his hip-pocket. The table was cleared, black coffee was served and Ette steeled herself for what was soon to follow.

"Well?" came the first remark from Hillyarde. "Have you nothing to say, are you still running loose over niggers?"

"I don't understand your remark" was Ette's curt reply.

"My meaning is quite plain," he said. "You were upholding the Doctor in his mad views about Negro equality, but I am still in love with you, and I don't think we want to fuss over what's past. I suppose your feelings haven't undergone a change because we had a slight misunderstanding? You know Shakespeare says: 'The course of true love never did run smooth!'" His tones were conciliatory, almost abject. He had a plan which he meant to put into immediate execution.

She had dared to voice sentiments about the Negro, which did not meet his approval, and he considered himself insulted by the public affront which she, a shop girl, without wealth or family connections, had put upon him by leaving his brother-in-law's house with Doctor Detritcher. He had thought the matter out carefully and intended to break with her. But before doing so, he meant to be revenged by compromising her. Already he had checked in at the hotel and his name appeared on the register as "Algernon Hillyarde and wife." His better nature or what there was of it, rebelled against the mean act he contemplated. But his hip-flask assisted him to justify the contemptible crime he planned to commit.

Ette's dark eyes were turned searchingly upon him. She did not answer him and her searching gaze embarrassed him. "Don't you think this place a little too public for your love making?" she asked after a while.

Her remark gave him the opening he sought.

"I admit it's a bit public, and we have much to say to each other, dearest, sweetheart, Ette!" He possessed a musical voice and knew how to use it to advantage. The hot blood surged through his veins and suffused his face.

"Come," he said rising to his feet. "I think we'll have a private sitting-room; as you say, it's too public here."

He hustled Ette into her coat before she had time to demur, and as he assisted her he squeezed her arm playfully. He hurried to the desk, secured his key and, declining the attention of the ubiquitous bell-boy, returned quickly to Ette, took her arm and ascended to the room he had secured on the second floor.

"Why, this is a bedroom!" Ette exclaimed in surprise, as Hillyarde bustled her in and locked the door.

"Yes," he replied adroitly. "The best I could do, you're quite safe, nobody knows you are here. It'll be quite alright."

He led her to a couch and seated himself beside her. Cautiously he placed his arm around her waist and kissed her gently on the neck. Ette turned and looked at him questioningly.

"I've been doing all the talking," he said, "It's your turn—shoot!"

"You say you love me—do you?" She put the question firmly as she removed his hand from her waist.

"Can you doubt it?" he asked evasively.

"You do not answer my question," was her rejoinder.

"Why, sure I do!" his arm stole around her waist again.

"Don't do that," she pleaded. "I wish to talk—to settle things definitely. It was not kind to bring me to this room."

Hillyarde was about to protest. Ette removed his arm from her waist with a firmness that could not be mistaken. "You had better restrain yourself," she said, "and hear what I have to say."

"Alright," he replied sulkily. "Get on with it."

"I am just a shop girl," she said.

"That's ancient history," he interrupted. "Try something more up-to-the-minute."

"You belong to an aristocratic family," she continued without heeding the interruption.

"What of that?" he asked impatiently. "Didn't I introduce you to my people? And wasn't everything peaches until you showed me up before everybody, with your pro-nigger ideas?"

"And suppose I was a nigger, as you term it, would you still carry out your promise of marriage?" This was blurted out desperately, but with obvious determination.

"You! You! . . . a nigger?" he asked in surprise.

"The term is yours," she corrected. "I am a coloured woman if you like. A few drops of African blood makes me what you call a nigger, which is hardly a fitting term to apply to your future wife," Ette spoke in sincerity. She was not ashamed of her African blood. It was there unbidden and she made the best of it. It is true she had not previously mentioned it to Hillyarde. She had thought little about the matter. She never meant to sail under false colours. The discussion at the Smithson's had, however decided her to put the matter to the test on the first convenient occasion, by disclosing her birth and parentage. Hillyarde was dazed and nonplussed. He stood upon his feet and strode around the room gazing fixedly at Ette each time he reached the couch on which she sat. After a while he entered the bathroom, emptied the contents of his hip flask into a glass and drank it at a gulp. Returning to the room he proceeded to remove Ette's coat.

"What are you going to do?" she asked.

"Sleep with you!" he exclaimed with brutal frankness, as he roughly pulled the coat away and dragged her from the couch putting his strong arms about her as he moved towards the bed.

Suddenly Ette realized that she was not only in grave danger but had to deal with a designing brute, bent upon taking the only worthwhile thing she possessed. A revulsion of feeling took possession of her. A struggle ensued. She pleaded, bit, scratched, doing her utmost to protect her honour. "Is this the way Southern gentlemen perform a promise of marriage?", she cried disjointedly amid her struggles to be free.

"Southern gentlemen don't marry nigger women," he responded sarcastically. "They make concubines of them, as I was going to make of you!"

The struggle continued, the frail dressing-table fell with a crash and the broken mirror littered the floor.

Ette seemed endowed with super-human strength; she wondered in a vague way how long that strength would last. She thrust her fingers desperately into Hillyarde's eyes as the pair fell upon the bed and rolled over. "Damn you, I'll pay you for this!" he cried. "You can't escape me!" And as his hot alcoholic breath brushed her cheeks and he raised his hands to his injured eyes, releasing her for a moment from his tenacious grasp, she arose quickly to her feet and seizing the telephone receiver, cried: "Murder!" With difficulty Hillyarde—who had struck his head when falling on the bed—reached out and grasped the back of Ette's flimsy garments, tearing them from neck to waist, reducing her body to a condition of nudity. She continued to shriek as he bore her bodily to the bed again. The unusual noise attracted the attention of the guests in neighboring rooms. They gathered in the passages in whispering groups. A few of these called the office. The manager, the house detective, a porter and a group of excited bellboys in their wake, reached the door and rapped loudly. The shrieks continued interspersed with oaths. The door was broken in and the manager entered the room followed by some of the less timid guests who, with the house detective's aid, rescued Ette, throwing a counterpane about her to cover her nakedness as she fell fainting in the arms of Mrs Wetherall, who was on a visit to a friend in a neighboring room. Looking at the face of Ette, she cried in surprise: "Why, it's Miss Swanson of the book shop! There is some mystery here."

"I think you are mistaken" the manager interjected. "The name on the register is—"

"Mind your own damn business," Hillyarde interrupted hastily. "Or I'll see to it that you do!"

"How shocking!" exclaimed Mrs Wetherall. "Come somebody, help me with this poor girl to two—hundred—and—five!"

"Some wreck, by heck!" commented a facetious guest on the conditions of the room.

"Come along with me," said the house detective to Hillyarde, displaying his badge.

CHAPTER VII.[2]

Hillyarde's dastardly conspiracy in the hotel had prostrated Ette. She had found a sincere friend in Mrs Weatherall to whom she had imparted the whole unfortunate story. She had withheld nothing, not ever her parentage, and Mrs Weatherall had volunteered to assist in every way possible. She supplied a specialist and paid a visit to Ette's employers, arranging with them to permit her to resume her work when she had recovered from the shock.

In the meantime, Ette's aunt was mystified and chagrined at what she was pleased to term the absurd and utopian ideas which the young woman held. She could not understand how a girl like Ette could throw away the brilliant chance of becoming the mistress of a blue-blooded Virginian. She would like to see Ette married. But if she did marry, her aunt's selection would be a professional man of Ette's particular shade of colour, not simon-pure Negro, which thought almost produced an apoplectic seizure. Doctor Jennison had made many journeys from Harlem to Ette, but the dear old lady had endeavoured to discourage his visits and when she discovered that Ette did not seriously object to the Doctor's attentions she frigidly declined to see him, retiring to her room on his subsequent visits rather than be contaminated by his sable presence. She said that he reminded her so much of a baboon, and that his presence absolutely nauseated her.

While confined to her room Ette found ample time to do a little stock-taking. It gradually dawned upon her that her preconceived notions of social

---

2 No chapter VII was found. See editorial note at the beginning of the book.

equality in America was just so much humbug. That few white men would be prepared to stake social position on the altar of love, and those of them who would be prepared to enter a legitimate union with a negro woman, would be members of a semi-illiterate class without the slightest vestige of refinement. What could she do with a such a life partner? With her, marriage was a serious undertaking. Her education, her pride and natural refinement, precluded her from committing a misalliance. She regarded the poor half-educated white man with the same abhorrence, where marriage was concerned, as the average educated white man would regard a cotton-field Afro-American woman from the South. She had been reared in the belief that her white blood was a passport to any society. She had been advised, should her Negro associations result in ostracism, she had only to cross the line and become white. She was too proud to sail under false colours as had been abundantly proved by her confession to Hillyarde. Besides, she knew her people quite well and even if she had the inclination to "pass" for a white woman she was quite certain to encounter one of her race somewhere at sometime and her subterfuge would be discovered with resultant humiliation. The dread of discovery would outweigh any personal social advantage. As she lay on her bedroom couch turning these things over in her mind, it suddenly dawned upon her that she never really loved Hillyarde and that there were a number of ardent suitors among her own group from whom she might make suitable selection. Her aunt was growing feeble, and with advancing years the old woman had daily become more difficult to manage. Disagreements were frequent and this latest happening would only lead to further bickerings and a possible rupture. She hated scenes and she was not then in a mental or physical condition to entertain the prospect of a daily breakfast and dinner recrimination. It would be as well to marry and end it all. There was the Harlem Doctor: he was out of the question and could not be considered. He had not treated his divorced wife with the consideration she deserved, after she had slaved at the wash-tub and the kitchen stove, making every possible sacrifice to supply the means for his medical education. Moreover, not only had success turned his head but he was excessively vulgar.

Ette passed over the other suitors in review, dispatching one after the other, until Hewitt Browne's vision appeared.

She always retained a sneaking fondness for this man. He was a successful lawyer, graduated from Harvard Law School, who proved his merit by winning a number of difficult criminal cases in the Boston Courts. The Judges and his white confreres held him in high esteem and, but for the fact that he was a Negro, there would have been no limit to his advancement. His high and noble qualities were admired by all and Ette possessed a penchant for him. He had proposed marriage on several occasions and she had thought seriously about accepting him until one evening when returning from the theatre they encountered two Frenchmen, one of whom whispered to his companion who turned his gaze upon them and laughingly exclaimed: "Cafe au lait!" to which witticism they both laughed. The mild ridicule of the Frenchman was somewhat of a shock to Ette, who was rarely seen in public with Browne thereafter. In the meanwhile Hillyarde had appeared upon the scene and Ette saw very little of the lawyer. Now that her thoughts reverted to him, she began to think seriously of accepting him should he again offer marriage. While her thoughts were centered on him the door bell rang and after a few moments, a neighbour, who usually came to the house each day to assist with the domestic duties, entered the room to inform Ette that Lawyer Browne had called.

"Where is he?" asked the invalid.

"He is in the parlour," was the reply.

"Ask him to wait—I'll come to him in a few moments."

The woman departed on her errand and Ette slipped on a dressing-gown, arranged her hair, powdered her face, and went to the parlour.

Browne rose to his feet at her entrance.

"How changed you are," he cried, smiling and extending his hand.

"I'm so glad to see you!" she exclaimed cordially. "I thought you had quite forgotten the existence of poor little me."

"Oh dear no," he replied. "I only heard this morning you were ill, and just as soon as I got my cases over I drove over to see you."

"That was very kind and sweet of you. I was just thinking about you when the bell rang."

"Didn't your heart give one little bump when you heard the bell?"

Ette thought for a moment, then answered. "I don't think it did bump, but somehow I seemed to sense you were the visitor."

"That was awfully sweet of you. Let me see; it's been about four months since I last saw you. I called many times, both in person and over the wire, but you were so elusive, I never seemed to catch you. However, I find you at last."

"How are cases?" she asked, taking a seat.

"Pretty good," he replied. "I'm having a little more work than I can manage just now, only two days ago I was forced to take young Jenkins in with me."

"Jenkins?—oh yes I know, Bob's son! How does he shape?"

"Too early to determine that," he replied. "What has been the trouble with you, Ette?"

"Oh, just a nervous breakdown. I shall be alright in a week or so. The Doctor says I'm getting on famously."

'That's very nice—very nice," he cried smiling. "I shall be very glad to see you out and about again. Boston doesn't seem quite right without your engaging presence."

"Now, no flatteries, please!—how are politics?"

"Up and down. They wanted me to run for the Assembly but I turned it down—no time—but I must tell you this—the Communists have been working on me with telegrams and letters and visits—"

"What for?—do tell me!"

"It appears as though something serious is brewing—looks like war—"

"War!——"

"Yes, so it seems; and they want to mix our people up with it."

"But how?"

"Well, you know quite well the white supremacy gang—the "Silver Shirts"—have become very active of late and our people have been suffering all over the country. Farms have been burned, crops destroyed and there had been a new outbreak of lynchings and burnings not only in the South but in the West and the North."

"Yes, I have heard something about it—but what of the Communists?"

"It seems that they are using this unrest and persecution to induce us to join them, and they have picked on me to turn the trick for them."

"Well?"

"I have had enough fighting to last me for all eternity. You don't know the hell we had in France! All the same, something has got to be done. Things can't continue as they are—the worm will turn one day!"

"Yes, but what can we do?" Ette asked in concern.

"I think a little retaliation might make the Invisible Empire reconsider its position."

"I am not convinced that it would," answered Ette thoughtfully. "Revenge is sweet, but is it expedient? There are some good whites in the country who would see justice done to us."

"I admit there are a few, but they have no power. The party upon whom we have depended, to which we have been loyal all these years—was more concerned about enforcing the Eighteenth Amendment than the Fourteenth and Fifteenth. A drinkless nation was considered more important than the lives of the weakest section of the population—oh, it makes me quite sick!

Even their dogs receive greater consideration than we do. There is hardly a man or woman in the United States who would willfully permit a dog to be wantonly[3] killed—they have got a Society for the Protection of Animals!— there is no society for the protection of Negroes! I tell you Ette, I'm sick, and I'm not alone! All those boys who were out with us in France "to make the world safe for democracy" are not only sick of the whole rotten business, but they'd welcome a chance to have a go at their persecutors in this Land of the Free!"

"But what can we do?" asked Ette helplessly. "If we started anything, we should only get the worst of it in the end. They have the money the guns and everything. There would be a massacre—oh, it's too terrible to contemplate! The horror of it all!"

"Better to die with your face to the foe, than to be shot down like a rat in a hole, or be lynched and burned without a dog's chance to fight back."

"I can't help thinking somehow, that God will take care of this situation and He, I'm sure, will see that Truth and Justice will prevail."

"With all due respect, Ette, this is old stuff! God is not troubled about us while we sit around whining about our oppression. We must be men; die like men or live like men!"

Browne's words were hot words, bitter words. So Ette endeavoured to calm him. "But the Jews—the Italians," she said, "they have also suffered. Look at Germany. The Jews are still suffering."

"Not now!" he answered hotly. "The Jews own the earth and the fulness thereof! They did suffer in the long ago; they will survive the German expulsion; trouble taught them sense; they got together and pooled their money and helped each other. Now, they are buying up America and a large slice of the other parts of the earth. Some are returning to the Holy Land. We don't trust each other, hence, we get nowhere. As for the Italians, so recent as 1909, Americans crowded them off the sidewalks calling them "Wops" and "Dagoes." They started a little killing and the Americans began to sit up and take notice. The war came and they joined up with the Allies. When the war ended Mussolini began telling the world a thing or two and the world and America began to respect Italians. Some became bankers, others bootleggers, gangsters, Congressmen, Mayors and Magistrates. They are no longer Wops and Dagoes! The Nordic only understands force and that's the only thing that will get us anywhere!"

---

3 Original text is distorted.

Ette admired the energy and earnestness of Browne, although she was not in complete agreement with his theories. There was, however, a manliness, a stern determination that she had not previously noted. Here was a man indeed! Gradually her heart warmed up to him, and with that warmth was born that motherly protection which is the heritage of all women.

Calling up all her forces of persuasion, she began calmly: "All that you have said is perfectly true, but don't you think that these things will right themselves? Let us be rational. I do not believe that the Abolitionists were any more sincere than the Prohibitionists. Both movements were born of hysteria, emanating from a Puritan background charged with false values. The English with their matured experience emancipated their slaves more comprehensively than the Americans. The slaves represented real property to the planters. The government granted compensation and did not make the mistake of shedding blood with its resultant bitterness. The foreigner entering America must pass a period of probation before he becomes a citizen. The English when manumitting their slaves, did not thrust a full-fledged citizenship upon them, for which they were unfitted, as were our ancestors. They erected certain safeguards, such as education and property qualification—"

"But the systems were different!" hastily interjected Browne.

"Pray, hear me to the end," Ette answered.

"I'm so sorry! Please go on."

"I admit the English system differs from ours, but that does not materially alter the facts. I have cited the case of the foreign immigrant. Then there is the Red Indian. These people were and are, at least as ripe for citizenship as our fathers were. Our fathers did have closer contacts, in some instances, with the masters than the isolated Indians, but for all that they possessed no true concept of the responsibilities of citizenship; consequently, ignorance resulted in absurd Negro legislation and the pride of the planters rose in rebellion and the Negro of the South was disenfranchised and his infantile efforts in post-Emancipation days have been cited as a proof of his intellectual incapacity."

"You surprise me, Ette!" exclaimed Browne enthusiastically. "I never thought of it quite in that way. All the same, I think you will agree that something drastic must be done to remedy the evil."

"I'm not so sure," was Ette's answer. "I'm not a drifter. Something must be done, I admit, but we must be sure of pursuing the right course. These people who are approaching you to help them can mean us no real good.

They will only use us to serve their ends, should they succeed our lot will probably be worse than it is at present."

"What course do you suggest, Ette?"

"As a citizen of this Republic, I should say your duty is to discover all you can about the intentions of these people. Pretend to agree and draw them out. You know how to accomplish this better than I can tell you. Then inform the Government."

"You surely would not have me turn informer!—spy—stool—pigeon."

"Would not that be better than turn traitor?" was Ette's rejoinder.

"Traitor!" Browne exclaimed. "Ette, you surprise me!"

"What other name could I give it?" she calmly answered.

Browne reflected for a few moments. He rose to his feet and went to the window and looked into the street. Then he turned and gazed at Ette long and searchingly. "You are a wonderful woman," he answered simply.

"Not at all," Ette replied. "I'm merely using common sense. Our trouble is we want things to move too quickly. We have been emancipated about three quarters of a century. In the face of opposition and discouragement, we have accomplished big things—we will accomplish bigger things yet! We need real honest-to-goodness leaders who can think straight. Straight thinking is better than straight shooting. Had the diplomats of Europe done some straight thinking, the world would not be in such a mess today."

Browne was still standing with his back to the window, his hands thrust deep in his jacket pockets. Ette rose from her seat and went up to him, placing her hands upon his shoulders she looked up into his face. "Hewitt," she said, "I admire you immensely. You have the making of a leader, the real kind of leader, I mean. Don't be carried away by your emotions, I want you to be a real man. You can, you must, help our people! The thing worth having is worth waiting for."

He took his hands from his pockets and placed them gently about Ette's waist. "Have I not been patient about the thing which is worth having?" He looked down into her eyes with a grave yearning. He felt like taking her to his breast and kissing her, but previous experience of Ette had taught him caution. So he refrained with an effort.

"Well?" he asked.

"I have said, things that worth having are worth waiting for. One must be sure of the worthiness. I have expressed my view. Think the matter over and act. Then come to me again and we shall see."

"Can you not see how necessary you are to me?" he asked.

"It may be so," she replied, disengaging herself.

"I am far from well at present. Go to the work in hand and see me again in a month—"

"A month, a whole month," he cried.

"I did not say you were not to communicate with me—there's the telephone and the mail; be content."

"Thank you so much Ette, thank you." He took his hat from the table and extended his hand. "Goodbye, dear," he said, and turning went from the room without another word.

Ette went to the window and pulled the curtain aside. Browne saw her as he entered his car. He kissed his hand to her and she returned the salutation, waving her hand to him as the car passed on.

CHAPTER VIII.

The Grand Council of the Invisible Empire met in secret conclave. Much had happened since their last meeting.

Jones had been dispatched to various sections of the country, particularly in the South, to report upon the activities of the Negroes. Each of Jones' visits produced a crop of lynchings, burnings and ejectments from the several communities of the professional and successful Negro farming groups, until the Negroes, upon comparing notes, arrived at the conclusion that Jones, who was a stranger, but had successfully wormed himself into the good graces of each community with his ingratiating manner and his exhibition of wealth, must have been directly responsible for the epidemic of misfortune which had quickly followed on his heels. This conclusion was borne out by a statement in Hatbry's paper in which he claimed that the Invisible State had employed Negroes to spy on each other.

Protective committees were formed among these groups who armed themselves as best they could against the common enemy which descended upon them like a veritable thief in the night.

Meanwhile the Communists had also become busy among the Negroes of the South enrolling many and stirring up those who hesitated to join them openly. They had also engineered strikes among the workers throughout the land. Machinery had been ruthlessly smashed and many factories were forced to close their doors, almost bringing the industries of the South to a halt.

Japanese spies had not been idle. Many were employed in the houses of the rich as house-servants or chauffeurs. The Invisible Empire had found it impossible to eject them from the county because their employers could not be brought to believe that they were a menace to the Government, until a couple of them had been caught; one in the act of photographing some secret plans in the possession of a Government Naval Constructor, and the other who had somehow gained access to important documents in the War Department. The latter was traced to his lodging by the Secret Service and his information seized before he had time to get it to a place of safety or to transmit it to Japan.

Riot and bloodshed were the order of the day. Robbery with murder assumed alarming proportions and the rich migrated to the continent of Europe by the thousands. There were "Hunger Marches" on the Capitol and raids upon the Chain Stores in almost every State.

War was rumoured with the Soviet Government of Russia, and Japan appeared to threaten reprisals over the arrest of many of her Nationals as suspected spies.

Thus the secret conclave of the Invisible Empire on this fateful occasion possessed considerable significance of its members. Moreover, the carefully guarded secrets of the Supreme Council of Three had come into the possession of Hatbry and his followers who were broadcasting the activities of the Emperor and his minions. And, as previously stated, it was from this source that the first hint came to the Negroes as to the activities of Jones and his connection with the Invisible State. The Council sat around three sides of the large table occupying the centre of the room. Each member was covered from head to heel in a long enveloping gown through which the eyes alone were visible. At the head of the table were three vacant chairs for the Triumvirate. A gavel of solid gold rested on the table before the Emperor's chair. A large electrically illuminated cross stood in the centre of the table. Otherwise the room was plunged in impenetrable gloom.

The twelve members of the Supreme Council were engaged in whispered conversation when a gong sounded thrice. Conversation was instantly suspended and the twelve rose to their feet and bowed their heads.

The gong was once more sounded and the hooded Emperor, flanked on either side by the other members of the Triumvirate slowly entered and took up their places at the head of the table. The gong sounded again and each one thrust forth his right hand towards the cross.

"The word?" commanded the Emperor.

"White!" they shouted in chorus.

"How deep?" he asked.

"From head to toe, outward! To the heart, inward!" was the sharp response from the fifteen throats.

Again the gang broke the stillness. And the company cried:

"On the cross we swear it!"

"What do you swear?" the Emperor[4] asked.

"Loyalty to the Emperor and the Invisible State!"

As the echo of their voices died away, the gong once more rang out and the members of the council rigidly dropped into their seats, sitting immovable like a ghostly company.

The Emperor smote the table with his gavel to command attention. "What," he demanded, "is the penalty for traitors within our ranks?"

"Death, death, death!" was the sonorous response from the assembly.

"Certain of our jealously guarded secrets have found their way to Hatbry and his band of howling niggers! You say the penalty of such betrayal is death?"

"Death death, death!"

"We are still agreed upon this matter?"

The company rose instantly to its feet and each member stretched forth his bared right hand to the flaming cross: "On the cross, we swear!" they once more cried in chorus.

The Emperor struck the table and the company again sat down.

For a short space of time silence ensued. Then the Emperor said: "Now, to our business. Clouds are gathering and the hour has struck for us to show our power. The Soviets have joined the yellow hordes of Nippon. The niggers have been approached by them, and we must first deal with the danger nearest home. A membership campaign must be launched at once. The heads of industry throughout the land must be forced into our ranks. They must be shown that we are in grave danger from within as well as from without. We have the most important sections of the press linked with us. We'll use this weapon with effect. Each of you present will return without delay to your several communities and liven-up the work. No time is to be lost. The employers of nigger Labour must discharge such men and women as they employ—gradually, so as to avoid panic. They will riot when they have no food. The militia and the police must wipe them out completely. Every possible excuse must be used to root out this curse, this blight, upon our civilization. Warn the heads of industry that the yellow enemy and the Soviet is at the gate. Urge them, intimidate them! Those who are not with us are against us. Japanese and Chinese must be driven from the Land. Then

---

4   At some point, Ali stops including quotation marks around the Emperor's self-appointed title. It is unclear whether this was intentional.

must Jew and Catholic be dealt with. This is the white man's country. The East Indians and Filipinos must also go. The former plot against our English brothers using this land as an asylum. No Asiatic must remain in these United States. This is a white man's country!" And the assembled white-robed figures rose suddenly to their feet and cried aloud, "This is a white man's country!"

The Emperor stood up and raised his right hand on high.

"The Black, the Yellow and the Brown must be exterminated!" he exclaimed.

And the ghostly company repeated: "The Black, the Yellow and the Brown must be exterminated!"

The Emperor smote the table with his gavel and the ghoulish council resumed its seats.

Then, indicating the first figure on the right, he said "Has Number One any statement or report to make?"

The number addressed raised his right hand.

"Speak," the Emperor commanded.

"The Emperor knows my loyalty and diligence," he cried rising slowly from his seat. "Under my command we have lynched seventy niggers and driven five hundred of their prosperous farmers from our State. Three hundred others have been marked for like treatment." He then resumed his seat.

"Number One has spoken well," the Emperor said. "What of Number Two?" This member raised his hand and rose to his feet.

"In my State we had but fifty nigger families two months ago. We have none now." With this brief statement he resumed his seat.

The Emperor then called upon each in turn and they individually reported some similar corrective measure upon the defenceless Negroes until the Company was wrought to a pitch of vengeful frenzy, each vowing to excel himself in his future efforts.

The Emperor appeared quite satisfied with the reports of his henchmen. And having once more charged them to speed up the policy he had outlined he rose to his feet. The opening oath was repeated by this precious group. The gong once more sounded and the Triumvirate departed as silently as it had come.

The other figures one after another, slowly and mysteriously melted into the surrounding gloom.

The electric cross surrendered its brilliance with a click and the still silence of the tomb pervaded the apartment which had so recently been the scene of an unusual recital of human tragedy and intolerance.

CHAPTER IX.

Napoleon Hatbry sat at his desk dreaming of Empire. If Colonel Blood "Emperor" of the Invisible State dreamed of the day when the world would be "all white" Napoleon Hatbry was not only dreaming but endeavouring to evolve a plan which would at least make Africa "all black" for he had successfully selected the slogan—"Africa for the Africans!" It is indeed true that the average Afro-American denied having lost anything in Africa, and that Dr. Reginald Bologne De Woode, the special champion of the educated group, was fighting tooth-and-nail for the political and social recognition of the American people of colour; but each of these leaders represented ideals which although diametrically opposed, were equally difficult of accomplishment. Prior to the advent of Hatbry, the real black of America had no champion. As a rule Afro-American leaders, who were of mixed blood, were mainly political, selected and employed by the white political bosses to do their bidding without being allowed to enter the secret conclaves or caucuses of the dominant group. It therefore followed that these hireling "Leaders," whether preachers or laymen, were for the most part, using their people as pawns in the political game of the whites.

The circumstances attendant upon the selection of leaders of mixed blood by the white politicians was to be found in the fact that the whites always discredited the mental capabilities of the simon-pure black. Rightly or wrongly, they believed that the admixture of "superior" blood was an unfailing index to a high criterion of mentality. Beside this conclusion was the outstanding fact that the mulattoes or near-whites did in a large-measure procure educational advantages in pre-emancipation days which were denied the blacks. Not a few independent or philanthropic-minded planters and slave owners were known to take a personal interest in their offspring. Many of their coloured children were sent to the North, freed and educated. Others were granted special privileges in the "great houses," received preferential consideration and were taught by their master-fathers to despise the black feminine stock from which they sprung. And this resulted in a division between the two coloured elements, which is only now being healed by segregation and intermarriages which are mainly due to economic conditions. The black man when marrying a mullato woman not only secures a thrill, but at the same time satisfies his vanity when walking abroad with a "high yaller" on his arm. And the "high yaller," who has become an expensive luxury, marries the black man because he invariably proves a better provider than the male of her own complexion. The men of mixed blood, usually marry a black, or what is termed a brown skin, by courtesy, because being a worker she will assist in building up his fortunes should he be industriously inclined. The Afro-American 'brown skin," it should be noted in passing, is far less haughty than her "high yaller" sister.

The advent of Hatbry was, therefore, hailed by the blacks as a distinct evidence of the intervention of an ever-watchful Creator who sent to the real Afro-American a real black leader who, Moses-like, would lead them back to the land of their forefathers.

In the case of Dr. De Woode, the political forces believed that he aimed at the attainment of Afro-American social and political equality. And inasmuch as he always saw white and thought white, they, the Caucasians, would by a system of attrition, wear him down on the one hand, and by extending some slight show of social recognition on the other, effectively reduce him to a condition of enslavement. Thus, his "policy" remained wobbly and uncertain with a consequent diminution in the volume of his following. This condition of affairs continued until Hatbry's appearance, whose success was instantaneous because of his racial ideas and the fire those ideas contained, which was absent in the mild academic propaganda of the much-learned Doctor. The self-educated Hatbry aimed to build an industrial group. Dr. De Woode stressed the 'intellectual' at the expense of the industrial. He seemed unable to understand that Doctors, Lawyers and Preachers, although a necessary evil, were mere parasites who, as a class, contributed comparatively nothing in the way of group advancement or enrichment and that a race possessing no material foundation was doomed to ultimate extinction. Hatbry went to the other extreme in his fantastic effort to produce an African empire from an industrious but illiterate proletariat.

Hatbry's dreams were suddenly interrupted by a visit from "Mr Smith," who followed close upon the heels of the attendant who announced him.

"Ah, Mr Smith!" exclaimed Hatbry, rising and extending his hand. "This is an unexpected pleasure." He pulled a chair forward. "Please be seated." Smith, having shook Hatbry's hand cordially, accepted the proffered chair and proceeded to puff vigorously at his black cigar.

Hatbry regained his seat and thrusting his hands in his pockets, eyed his well-groomed visitor, carefully taking in every detail of dress and figure.

"Beg pardon!" cried Smith, producing his cigar case, "you smoke of course."

"No," Hatbry answered apologetically. "I neither smoke nor drink."

"No chance of breaking the eighteenth amendment, then," laughed Smith. He looked about cautiously and leaning across the desk that divided them, asked: "Any likelihood of our being overheard?"

"None whatever," Hatbry answered as he rose and went to the door, opened it and looked out, then closed and locked it. "We will not be disturbed," he said, as he resumed his seat.

"Good. I'm glad I found you in, matters are developing quickly. A secret order has gone forth from the "Emperor" to gradually eliminate all Negro workers from factories, workshops, and domestic employment."

"Good God!" cried Hatbry, "they mean to starve us out."

"That's the idea."

"But they can't do that—they dare not do it!" was Hatbry's rejoinder.

"They dare do anything they are big enough to do. We—they—are twelve million strong. Fear of the Japanese has brought in a large number of manufacturers, and not a few legislators from the North, East and West, have taken the oath."

"The devil, they have!" exclaimed Hatbry. "Looks as though they mean business."

"They mean business alright," said Smith as he stroked his blond head reflectively. "And the Negro is still sleeping. You see Hatbry, fear of the Japanese brought this thing to a head. The Emperor thinks that the Negroes will join the Japanese in the event of invasion. De Woode is reported to have had secret correspondence with their agents and you have been notorious for your outspoken advocacy of an alliance between the two groups."

Hatbry was anxious and he looked it. Beads of perspiration stood upon his receding forehead. "Why should they pick on me?" he asked. "I have only done my duty to our people. I am not afraid. Let them try to starve us out. Let them try it!" he exclaimed, pounding the desk with his fist. "They'll get more than they bargained for! This country owes us a living for three hundred years of slavery—three hundred years of free service—and by God, we're going to have it!"

"Don't raise your voice," admonished Smith. "This is a time for a deep thinking, not loud talking. I have come to see whether it is possible for us to devise a plan. Something must be done and that quickly. The 'Emperor' is working in darkness, you must do likewise. The thing he is attempting is possible, nay probable. Here in America, a man's soul is touched when you reach out for his gold. Everybody in business has the jumps. They have been scared stiff by Hitchell's 'Unprepared in the Air' stuff in the papers. The

"Emperor" saw his opportunity and took it. I have brought you some of the most recent news. The employers are to do the work assigned to them gradually, so as not to cause alarm or panic. You have time to formulate a plan, but you must get busy!—I mean busy!—but you must also be secret. Don't let the other fellow see your 'whole[5] card,' or you're lost!"

"Have you any suggestion?" asked Hatbry.

"Well, I have, and I haven't. You have been talking about industries for your followers, but you have fallen down on performance. You had time to deliver the goods, but you didn't. This is a time for straight talking. I don't talk much and I don't flatter anybody. If you can find a real man, a real organizer, I'll put half a million dollars at your disposal to create a real live industry that will give work to ten or twelve thousand people; that will help some. And in three months, if I see you have got in your stride, I'll find another half million—if the 'Emperor' don't get me before then."

"Get you?" asked Hatbry anxiously. "Do they know you have been seeing me?"

"I don't know, and I don't give a damn! But I'll tell you this. Very little of importance is going on that the "Emperor" doesn't know. He's got spies everywhere—coloured and white—and even I, who am near the throne, don't know all that is going on. Our membership is increasing at such a rate that the 'Emperor' himself can only keep track of some of the big names. The Invisible Throne Warmer trusts nobody. And I daresay they have been watching my movements. So, if I am to help you, you've got to work fast or my hour might strike before I can be of any assistance. Now, it's up to you!"

Smith threw the butt of his cigar in the cuspidor, rose to his feet, stuck a fresh cigar jauntily in his jaw, and grasping Hatbry's hand, he concluded. "See you as soon as I can… But get busy!—so long!" Smith flew out of the room, and as he descended to the street, a coloured man as well-groomed as himself, looked at him searchingly and then turned on his heel, walking slowly toward Seventh Avenue

CHAPTER X

Once more the Smithsons were entertaining at Norman Towers. Colonel Blood and Doctor Detritcher were invited for the week and a few other

---

5 The original text is partially obscured. It is possible to make out "hole" as the word preceding "card" ("hole card"). Most likely this was an error. We have substituted "whole" for "hole."

guests had come over from New York to dinner on Saturday evening. They were succeeded by a Connecticut group for lunch on Sunday and Hillyarde had put in an appearance with the hope of capturing a young heiress or an unchartered dowager with an attractive bank account.

The news of Hillyarde's Boston adventure had reached the Towers to the chagrin of his sister and the disgust of Smithson who never entertained a special admiration for the pedigreed degenerate. Possessing, as he did, the superiority complex of the one hundred per-centers, it was only natural that Hillyarde should become a member of the Invisible State and he subsequently became an active recruiting officer. The commission obtained as a reward for his efforts enabled him to indulge his passions to the full. And although the Colonel practised an austerity which was rigidly Puritanical, condemning the frailties of his opponents, he was careful to overlook the moral lapses of his immediate followers. Possessing no special claim to ancestral distinction, he was flattered to have men of Hillyarde's social antecedents actively identified with his movement, because they supplied the aristocratic background so sadly lacking in his own person. His frequent visits to the Towers were actuated by the acquisition of social contacts that could not be obtained elsewhere. His snobbish outlook caused him to regard Smithson with some outward show of tolerance. He had raised Virginia's husband to an exalted position in the Invisible State because of Smithson's wealth and connections, but the mystery of his origin was ever present in the mind of the Emperor, resulting in an undefined distrust of the man who was indirectly responsible for these very social contracts which he valued so highly. Having used Smithson's frequent invitations to the Towers to draw Hillyarde into his political net and having there-by successfully won Virginia over to his intolerant views, he believed that he could well afford to dispense with the services of the man whom he secretly held in contempt.

The Emperor had long sought some means of removing Smithson from the eminent position he held by virtue of the Colonel's support. When, therefore, he discovered him in Harlem, by putting Jones on the scene to ferret out his movements, he felt that he would somehow by this means be supplied with the weapon he hoped to use to remove Smithson. He had stated at the Supreme Council meeting that secrets of the inner circle had been divulged to the coloured people and the Council had declared the penalty to be death. Jones had reported that Smithson had direct contacts with Hatbry, but his ingrained prejudice caused him to hesitate over the acceptance of a Negro's evidence against a white man's. He required what he termed more reliable information and that information had to be supplied by a white man. He had therefore commissioned a detective member of his organization to shadow and report upon Smithson's movements. The statement he had made to the Council was intended to betray Smithson into resignation, or some other overt act which would assist him in placing the guilt upon the shoulders of the man he meant to ruin. As it chanced, Smithson having carefully studied the Emperor's character and methods, although cognizant of the intentions of his chief, carefully avoided betraying himself in any way. Smithson's demeanor therefore left the Colonel sorely puzzled, causing him to doubt the accuracy of Jones' information. He considered it probable that Smithson had seen Hatbry, but although he did not refer to such visits, he might have been seeking information which would be useful to the Invisible State. Moreover, he could not credit the possibility of a white man betraying his people to Negroes. There was, therefore, nothing left to him but to await the report of the detective. On the other hand, Smithson read all that was passing in the Emperor's mind and he secretly gloated over the fact that his chief was puzzled; nevertheless, he did not minimize the danger that threatened. He had expressed his fears to Hatbry on his last visit to that agitator, and he was fully prepared for any eventuality.

Meanwhile, the invigorating weather had induced the party at the Towers to seek its spacious gardens. As was natural they wandered off in pairs and Doctor Detritcher, who was glad of the opportunity to combat the wild theories of the Emperor, took him by the arm and led him out among the flowering plants in the bright autumn sunshine. A short walk brought them to a secluded spot where they sat on a rustic bench.

"How goes the affairs of the Invisible State?" the Doctor asked, as he lit a cigar. There was a merry twinkle in his eye as he put the question. The Colonel squared his shoulders, cleared his throat, and countered: "Why don't you join us?—You'll know all about it then."

"As a rational man, you could not expect me to join a movement I know nothing about."

"What do you particularly wish to know?" the Colonel drawled somewhat irritably. "The last time we talked, you told us we were niggers, or some other absurd statement."

"I only tried to impart a little necessary information which you were not disposed to accept," the Doctor answered.

"If you hold such views how could our activities possibly interest you?"

"Well," said the Doctor, knocking the ash from the end of his cigar, "I have an open mind. I am sixty-five, and at sixty-five I have discovered that I know much less than I thought I knew at twenty-five."

"So you have begun a voyage of discovery at sixty-five? You haven't much time left. You'd better get busy," was the Colonel's sarcastic rejoinder

"Some of us never learn anything," the Doctor answered. "We become too fossilized—too wrapped up in our own conceits—our pet aversions. In fact, most of us call, or miscall ourselves, Christians without practising one of the cardinal principles of the Christ."

"What is the implication?" the Colonel asked.

"I imply nothing. I merely voiced fact."

"The dividing line between fact and fiction is so faint and blurred that one is often mistaken for the other," the Colonel replied with a slight show of irritation.

"In this we are agreed," was the suave rejoinder of the Doctor.

"What cardinal principle have you in mind?" the Colonel asked.

"Love your neighbour as yourself" was the prompt response.

"Who is my neighbour?" inquired the Colonel.

"All humans!"

"Including niggers?"

"Of course—there was no reservation in the injunction!" asserted the Doctor.

"I don't see it that way. Christ didn't have savages in mind."

"I beg to differ," replied the Doctor "Go ye into all the world and preach the gospel to every creature."

"We've done that: don't we send missionaries out to the heathen, and didn't we preach Christ to the niggers in slave-time?"

"Of course you did, but isn't something lacking?—the spirit for instance. Christ further stated: "Little children love one another." You, as I understand would exclude Jews and Catholics as well as Negroes from participating in the Government of the United States. This is a free country. Christ was a Jew and our religion in its entirety comes from the Jews. The Catholics may not believe as we do but they are Christians and have a perfect right to worship God according to the dictates of their own consciences. You claim that the Pope would dominate American affairs through American Catholics. He would not do so. I know many American Catholics, both clergy and laity and they only accept the Pope's ruling in Spiritual matters."

"What more would you have us do?" the Colonel asked. "Take Catholics to our hearts and the niggers to our homes, and marry them and the Jews to our daughters?"

"I fear you lose your sense of proportion, Colonel. You're doing it in Oklahoma. Out there you have a number of half-caste Negro-Indians, whom you style Indians for social convenience. They possess valuable oil lands and their wealth seems to eradicate the Negro blood. Hence, the proud Nordic in that section finds no barrier to a union of his son or daughter with these Negroes. As for the Jews, you also inter-marry with them if they possess a large bank account."

The Colonel was silent. Here was a phase of the situation that he had overlooked.

"Well," he answered lamely, "out in Oklahoma they have their own views in these matters. In any case, it's a bit doubtful whether the half castes out there can be called Negroes."

"What of that small percentage of Negro blood in an otherwise white person south of the Mason and Dixon line, which makes him Negro according to your theory."

"We can't mix our blood with known niggers," the Colonel answered.

"But you have done it, otherwise there would only be black and white and Indian in America."

The Colonel was being too closely pressed by the Doctor, so he endeavoured to change the subject by saying: "You were enquiring about success of our movement."

"Yes," the Doctor answered, smiling. He had demonstrated the illogical position to the Colonel, he could therefore afford him the relief he desired by returning to a question which had been previously evaded.

"Yes", he repeated: "I'd like to learn a little more."

"I don't suppose you'll fall in line with our aims," began the Colonel. "We are out to make the country safe for the white man—in fact, for all white men. The Black, the Brown, and the Yellow outnumber us about three to one. If we don't stir ourselves we shall be overwhelmed. It's a case of self-preservation." He hesitated, not knowing quite how to proceed with the antagonist by whom he had already been cornered.

"Yes, yes, I grasp your objective," said the Doctor encouragingly.

"No white man" the Colonel proceeded, "could wish to be dominated by the groups I mentioned. They'd undo all that we have done in the way of civilization and we should become their slaves." He paused again, looking across the rosebushes for inspiration.

"That's very nice and proper," commented the Doctor thoughtfully—"very proper indeed."

Mistaking the Doctor's comment for acquiescence, the Colonel proceeded. "We have lined up all industrial heads and we are making a clean up of the Negroes."

"You don't mean to say that you are going to murder them all!" exclaimed the Doctor in alarm.

"I don't like the term murder—I prefer to say remove them."

"Oh, I see," replied the Doctor. "Rather a nasty, messy term. But that's what I call it. How do you expect to accomplish this without discrediting America among the Nations?"

"America is capable of standing alone, we need no foreign approbation and we are self-sustaining."

"We are self-sustaining today, but how long do you expect this to last with our increasing population? Besides, no country is independent of another in these days of our complicated civilization."

"If the other white groups will not join us," cried the Colonel, "so much the worse for them."

"That may be so," the Doctor answered. "But remember Russia threatens and Japan is in an angry mood. This is a time for national unity. The Negroes you speak of exterminating have always been loyal to this Government. They saved the Union—"

"Saved the Union?—preposterous!" exclaimed the Colonel.

"I said, 'saved the Union'—this might not please your Southern ideas, but you are an American after all. The Civil war was very much in favour of the South until General Butler incorporated his Negro camp followers into his army and Massachusetts could only supply Lincoln with two Black regiments when he applied to that State for additional troops. Crispus Attucks the Negro Freeman was the first to fall at Boston in the War of Independence. When we entered the late war, the Negroes were among the first to volunteer for service. They fought for the Flag in Cuba and the Philippines and to attempt any form of extermination after all this loyalty and their three hundred years of slavery and free labour deserve a retribution to be visited upon us, such as the world has never seen." The Doctor was indignant at the proposed injustice of the Colonel and his followers to a defenceless and inoffensive group of Americans. He rose from the seat, threw his cigar butt away, brushed the ash from his clothes, and strode off to the house.

The Colonel felt somehow crushed. He was however too greatly obsessed with his "all white America" idea to be turned from his purpose. He was about to rise from his seat when he saw Jones approaching across the lawn. He was in no mood to be bothered with Jones. Moreover, he considered Jones' encroachment on his privacy an unwarranted impertinence. He had supplied his address to the man in order that he might be communicated with should any important matter arise; but to have him call was in his opinion an unpardonable outrage.

"Afternoon, Colonel," grinned Jones, removing his hat.

"What the devil do you mean by coming here—who sent you?"

"Beg pardon Colonel, I got bad news," Jones answered humbly.

"Come on, out with it!"

"Well it's this way, Colonel. The niggers have got my measure and they is aftah me, hot foot!"

"What have I to do with that?" the Colonel asked irritably.

"Ain't I your servant, Colonel? And ain't I done your bidding, and you wouldn't see me in trouble—would you, Colonel?"

"I'm not sure about that. However, what do you want?—be quick about it!"

"Well, Colonel, I've got to get out of America. Those niggers are on my track—and they are bad niggers, Colonel, real bad!" Jones looked about him in fear. His enemies might be hiding in the surrounding shrubs for all he knew.

The Colonel paced the lawn in thought for a few moments. Jones had served his purpose, he was no longer useful to the Invisible State. Here, perhaps, was an opportunity to be rid of him for all time. This Negro who had done his bidding might divulge any stray information he may have picked up and he was in no mood, after Detritcher's peroration, to have the Negro killed. "Well Jones," he said, "you'll find a letter of instruction at your Harlem address in the morning."

"Oh God, Colonel, not there!"

"Where then in God's name—hurry up, I have no time to waste."

Jones drew a soiled envelope from his pocket and handed it to the Colonel. "This is my address Colonel. Please, please! Don't throw me down or I'm a dead man!" He fell on his knees at the Colonel's feet. "I beg you! Colonel," he pleaded. "I beg you! Don't leave me to them hell-hounds!" The Colonel was touched in spite of himself. "Have you any money?" he asked.

"Not a thin dime, Colonel."

The Colonel took a hundred-dollar bill from his pocketbook and threw it to the groveling wretch. "There!" he cried. "Take that. There'll be no more money for you. Tomorrow you'll have a letter you will take to a Captain at Galveston, who will take you to Honolulu. You'll have to fight your own battle after he puts you ashore. Now go!"

"Oh, thank you Colonel, God bless you! You won't forget the letter?"

"No!" exclaimed the enraged Colonel. "Get out of here, quick!"

"Yes, Colonel; thank you, sir! Thank you!" Jones glanced about him furtively, and dashed madly off across the lawn.

CHAPTER XI.

Jones hastened direct from his visit to the Colonel at the Tower's to the Hell's Kitchen district of New York and hid himself in one of those low dives with which he was so familiar, there to await the promised communication from the Emperor. That he hastened to take cover is a very mild suggestion of the speed he adopted to negotiate the intervening distance.

He had told the Emperor that the Negroes were after him, and they were on his heels in very truth, for he had barely left the Towers when two rather desperate and wild-eyed men of colour were observed to approach the gates in the opposite direction from that taken by Jones. They hung about until late into the night and might have watched the place until daybreak but for the appearance of a guardian of the peace who eyed them suspiciously as they slowly slunk away in the darkness.

On the following morning the Colonel's anxiously awaited communication arrived. Jones read the instructions carefully and tucked them away safely in his undergarments. Then he instructed his temporary paramour to take his suitcase to the Express Office and forward it to Galveston. Upon her departure, he rubbed a little dust into his face, disguised himself in a suit of torn and dirty overalls, and hiding himself in the remote recesses of the cellar abode, he stretched his limbs upon a dilapidated straw mattress and anxiously awaited the woman's return and the enshrouding darkness of the night.

Jones, who had fallen asleep, was suddenly aroused by a loud knocking at the door. He started up and looked about; carefully he lit a match and drawing forth his watch, he discovered the hour to be three o'clock. Fearing that his paramour had forgotten to take her key, his first impulse was to open the door of his room. He removed his shoes and stole silently to the outer door and looked through the keyhole. A man whose face he could not see, was standing outside. He was in the act of retreating to his lair, when the man banged the door more loudly than before.

The sudden noise brought the sweat of fear to Jones's countenance. He trembled violently as he sneaked back to his hiding-place as silently as his trembling limbs permitted. He sat, his head between his hands, upon the mattress and listened intently. He heard the noisy children returning from school as they yelled at each other, their uproar prevented him from hearing whether the unwelcome visitor had departed. He raised his head, cursed the children under his breath, reached in a dark corner for a bottle of vile spirit and took a copious draught to give him courage. A rat scurrying along the uneven floor caused him to jump to his feet in affright, beads of perspiration standing thick upon his forehead.

Once more he crept to the door and listened. He heard a man's footstep. The pedestrian passed on. He peeped through the keyhole. There was no one there. Did the caller go away or was he waiting on the pavement until he should issue forth?

"You fool" he hissed under his breath; "do you think I'd take a chance like that?"

A drunkard passed disjointedly singing a ribald song as he unsteadily wended his way down the street to the speakeasy on the corner. Evidently, thought Jones, there is no one about or the drunkards he knew!

He turned and crept back to his hiding place, struck a match and looked at his watch. It was five o'clock; where could the woman have got to? Had she joined the conspiracy against him? "Damn these women!" he mumbled. "You never know when you have them!" He took another drink and coughed as he was almost strangled by its potency. The noise caused a rat to scamper across the floor. He reached down for his shoe to hurl at the rat, lost his balance and, still clutching the bottle, fell across the mattress with a "damn!" He indulged in a perfect fury of profanity. Then sitting up he poured the remaining fluid down his throat.

The darkness began to affect him. He feared to light the lamp, it would attract notice. What had become of the woman? An hour, which seemed an eternity, passed. Footsteps were heard descending the basement steps. A key was thrust in the door which was opened and quickly closed. He heard the blinds drawn and the rustle of paper packages as they were thrown upon the table. A match was struck, the gas turned on and a faint light pierced the gloom of his hideout.

"Where is yo' hon?" came from the other room. Jones breathed with relief, crept to the door and cautiously peeped into the room.

"Where is yo hon?" the voice repeated.

He entered the room.

"Where in hell has yo been all dis while?"

"I had such a time hon', getting dat ole bag o'your'n off." She removed her hat and cast it on a chair, going up to Jones and putting her arms around him. "Has yo' been lonesom' widout yo' sugah?" She kissed him.

He roughly thrust her aside.

"Gimmie something to eat—don't you know I'm hungry, after all de hours yo been away!"

"Alrite hon." She smiled and busied herself with dinner. "I'll soon fix yo' up."

The woman was about thirty-five years of age and quite corpulent, brown of skin with large sensuous eyes, full ripe lips, even white teeth and marked traces of youthful beauty.

Jones looked at her searchingly for a while, as she silently prepared the meal of pork chops and biscuits. Taking a packet of cigarettes from the table he lit one and threw himself on the couch. At length he spoke.

"Some rough nigger knocked on the door to-day—I had a doggone fright, I can tell yo."

"Huh! did yo' see him—what did he look like?" The chops were sizzling in the pan. Fork in hand she turned and looked enquiringly at Jones.

"Du'd'nt yo' see him through the keyhole?"

"Wundah who it cu'dah been?" She pulled the pan of biscuits from the oven.

"Lawd, Lawd! A minute longer an' ah wud hah to make a fresh pan ah biscuits, an' yo' so hungry, sugah!" She turned her head and looked at him alluringly over her shoulder.

"Cut the sugah! Get on with the eats!"

"Alright, hon; ah show will." She hastily set the table using newspaper to cover the black tablecloth produced the food and set it out exclaiming with finality: "Dere's yo pork chops, Hon!"

Jones threw his cigarette away, pulled a threelegged chair across the room, and sat down to his pork chops and biscuits, washing them down with hot coffee. Obviously his desperate situation had not affected his appetite. He pushed his chair back and fell over as the woman jumped to her feet.

"Is yo hurt, hon?" She assisted him to rise, which he did to the accompaniment of some rather unchaste language.

"I aint hurt—why in hell don't yo' get some chairs people kin sit on?" He limped to the couch and lay down with an oath, produced a cigarette and lit it.

The woman knelt beside the couch and put her arms around him. "Hope yo' didn't hurt yo' self, hon; I'se real sorry—"

"Cut that out!" he cried gruffly, pushing her away. "Go get me some 'white mule'—quick!"

She got up and put on her hat and coat. "I'll be back in a minute, sugah!" The woman turned and quickly departed on her errand.

As the door closed upon her, a grim smile flitted across her face.

"Yes, yo got to treat' 'em rough if yo hopes to make em like you. Lucky I got to beat it soon—couldn't a stood much more o' that sweet stuff o' her's." He lay on his back in deep reflection. "Dog-gone!" he exclaimed as he jumped to his feet. "Why in hell didn't I think o' that before?" He went to the table drawer and drew forth a miscellaneous collection of oddments, turned them over and extracted a needle, thread and scissors. Then cutting a corner from the black waterproof of tablecloth, he shaped a blinker. A strip of the cloth supplied the fastener, and having sewed it in place, he proceeded to adjust it over his eye before the broken mirror on the wall. "Hot-dam! Some one-eyed man; the hounds won't recognise me like this—I ask yo'?" A rumbling motor van deadened the sound of footsteps descending to the basement. A sharp knock at the door put a period to his reflective admiration. He stood all but transfixed trembling in every limb. There was another, more peremptory knock.

Carefully, Jones got down upon his hands and knees. Keeping in the shadow of the dimly lighted room, he crawled quickly back to his hiding place.

"Helen!" came a masculine voice from without. "Helen! I knows yo' indoo's—wat's matter wid yo'?" He knocked again. "Open dis dooh-O, dere yo' is—bin heah two times befor'. Whar is yo' bin—runnin' round?"

"No, I aint been runnin' roun'—bin too busy heah." There was irritation in her tone.

"How come yo bin busy heah, when I done tell yo' I'se bin heah two times befo'; a-knockin' on this heah dooh?"

The key was thrust in the door and Helen entered, followed by six feet of muscular black humanity.

"Wot yo' seekin' me for, Joe?"

"Why shudden' I look fo' ma ole sweetie; tell me dat?" He put his arms around her resisting form and kissed her.

"Wat's de mattah wid yo' Joe: stop? Ah doan feel like messin' roun' tonite." she disengaged herself. "Sit down an' doan act de fool." Placing the bottle of "white mule" on the table.

Joe sat down on the couch. "So yo's havin' a party and yo' doan ask yo' sweetie?"

"Says which?"

"Ahm says, yo' doan ask yo' sweetie to yo' party,"

"Wot party?" removing her hat and coat.

"Yo' aint gwine to drink all dat dey 'white mule' by yo self—is yo'?"

"Search me, sister! yo' is real uppish tonite."

"Scuse me, if ah is, but ah want to be let alone tonite."

"How come?"

"Ah doan want to be bothered wid no man." She began to clear away the dishes.

"Ah see yo' had company to dinnah—ah see his cigarette ends—doan wondah yo' doan want to be bothered wid no man." He laughed heartily. "Doan yo' go signin' me dem kind o' blues."

Helen turned from the sink and looked disdainfully at Joe. "Since when has yo' bin payin' ma rent? Lemme tell yo' niggah; I pay's ma own rent an' has who I damn well please to dinnah! Get me?"

"O, hell! Looks like yo's in a bad tempah." Rising, he went to the table and took the bottle of white mule.

"Doan yo' touch datta likkar, niggah! doan yo' touch it!" He moved to the table and seized the bottle, there was a struggle. She bit his hand.

He brutally knocked her down to the accompaniment of a vile epithet. Three shots rang out in quick succession and Joe slumped on the floor with a groan.

Jones rushed out pistol in hand as Helen rose from the floor, her mouth covered with blood.[6]

"My Gawd! wot's happened? Did yo' kill him?"

"Sh—sh!" warned Jones. "Wot in hell he wanted wid the likkar I paid for?"

"My Gawd! wot shall we do?" wailed Helen in a half whisper. "Wot did yo' do dat for? Aint yo' got enuf trouble?"

Jones stood over the prostrate man. The woman knelt beside him, placing her hand upon his heart. "My Gawd—he's dead!" She slowly rose to her feet, wringing her hands. "My Gawd, my Gawd!"

"Shut up! It's all your fault; why in hell did yo' let him in?"

"C'uld I help it? He pushed his way in."

The undamaged bottle lay on the floor beside the dead man; Jones reached for it and swallowed almost all of its contents.

"Get yo' dishes washed up while I think——hurry up!"

The weeping woman went shudderingly to the sink and began to cleanse the dishes. Jones, still clutching the bottle, sat on the couch and gazed

---

6   In the original, serial version of the novel, this chapter was published across two installments, one printed in The Comet's May 12, 1934, issue, the other on May 19, 1934. Though, for the most part, the novel's chapter endings corresponded to the breaks in serial installments, in this instance, they did not.

vacantly at the dead man. He took another drink. "So yo'd steal other people's likkar, mistah niggah?" Jones spoke sneeringly to the stiffening corpse. The woman, still sobbing, turned to look at him.

"Wot's wrong wid yo' eye?" she asked.

"Why in hell don't yo' get them dishes cleaned up, and let's decide what we'll do with this guy?"

"I'se done dem!" She exclaimed.

"Well, come over here——put that light out! Some of yo' sugah babies might be calling on you!"

She attempted to turn out the gas. "O! O! I kant! I just kant be in de dark wit dat dead man in de room. O, Lawdy, Lawdy!"

"Cut it out! this aint no wailing wall. Come over here——will you?"

He fingered his gun and that bloodshot uncovered eye gazed balefully at her. Gingerly, she made a circuit of the corpse and stood before Jones.

"Listen here!—stop that sobbing! Do you want people running in here to find out what the row's about." She bit her lips and choked down her sobs nervously wringing her hands the while.

"We got to get this guy out o' here, somehow—"

"O! I cuddent touch him...."

"Couldn't you? Didn't you bring him here?"

"He forced his way in, I telled yo'!"

"To hell wid that stuff! Listen!" He looked at his watch. "Doggone—it, one o'clock, and I should ah been on my way two hours ago. Turn out the light. Put your hat and coat on. Go in the street and see if there is anybody about!" She proceeded to do his bidding, only too glad to escape the proximity of the dead man.

Jones followed her to the door and stood there listening while she walked leisurely up the street. Upon reaching the speakeasy on the corner, she saw the policeman coming down the block striking the pavement with his nightstick as he came toward her. She stood in the shadow, holding her apron to her mouth until he came near.

"That you Helen?" What you hanging about here for?"

"Waitin' for somebody to buy me a drink."

"Wish you luck." He passed on down the street and Helen watched him until he turned the corner. Then she walked slowly back to her basement hovel. She stopped at the door and whispered: "Dere's nobody around; quick!—Wat you going to do?"

"Jones who had learned the art of carrying inert and limp comrades from No Man's Land while in France, quickly lay down beside the dead man, got him on his back and tottered to the door.

"Is all clear?" he whispered.

"Yes."

He stumbled up the broken steps and carried the corpse to the corner and set him down in the shadow, against the speakeasy wall, scurrying back quickly to the dive.

"Well?" she asked as he was admitted.

"He's O.K. Now I got to get quick—and I mean quick!"

"Wot is I gwine to do?"

"Stay right here to cover up. Clean up the blood. If they ask anything about it, show your battered mouth—they'll know you been bleeding. If they ask: "Who did it," tell them a man beat you up and run away because you wouldn't pay for his likkar! Hear?" She nodded, being too full to speak. He put his arm about her waist and kissed her twice upon the cheek.

"Cheer up, sugah! I'll send you your fare when I get set—goodbye!" In a few moments he was swallowed up by the darkness.

Meanwhile, as Jones had truly said, the dogs were after him. His photograph had been published by the Negro newspapers and the arrangements of the several vigilance committees of the Protective League were at once comprehensive and complete. At every possible point, in every State where there was a large Negro population, watchers were placed to be on the lookout for Jones. In many communities he was personally known, which made potential identification easy; in all other cases his photograph and complete description were circulated, not only among the vigilance committee, but also among Negro travellers who might encounter him. Thus, the net was carefully spread for the successful landing of Jones. And a thousand-dollar reward was offered to anyone who would accurately report his whereabouts to any committee.

When he left Hell's Kitchen, he made his way to Thirty Third Street Station, boarding a Journal Square Transfer he took a train for Jersey City. He changed at Manhattan Transfer and boarded a train to Elizabeth, intending to "Jump a freight" train at that point and beat his way to the Pacific Coast.

Arriving at Elizabeth in the early morning, it was too late for him to board a freight train safely, so he hid in a boxcar where another tramp of colour had already taken up his quarters.

Jones did not see the man at first because of the darkness of the car's interior, but upon making his entry the tramp's snore made investigation necessary with the assistance of a match.

The luminant aroused the sleeper who with an oath demanded who the intruder was. There was a scuffle in the darkness, a short was fired, a knife flashed, the man went down with a groan and Jones jumped to the rails with blood gushing from the knife thrust in his side. Here indeed was a difficulty. Jones could neither go to the hospital nor the police. In either case he might be detected. He could not count on Helen's silence should she be put to the third-degree test by the police. The wound had covered his clothes with blood and that caused him to keep out of sight. So, he sought quiet in a secluded section of the freight yard, where he boarded another box-car into which he fell exhausted.

A few hours after he was discovered unconscious by one of the yardmen. The police were called in and he was taken to the hospital where he lay for several days. The Colonel's letter had been found upon him, but that worthy denied all knowledge of Jones, in fact he contended that the wounded man was not the Jones he knew. In the meantime, his photograph was circulated in the press, his fingerprints were taken and the coloured vigilance committee in that section of New Jersey started a secret conspiracy to capture him.

His gradual recovery being reported, the day before he was to be brought up on a charge of vagrancy, the New Jersey Negro Vigilance Committee entered the hospital at dead of night, gagged and bound him, and took him off in an automobile to the woods before the sleeping police guard, watching his bed, realised what had happened.

Jones was hanged, dying without uttering a word. And the small crowd officiating at his execution, after fastening a sign on his breast which read: "A TRAITOR TO HIS PEOPLE!" quietly dispersed in the four directions of the compass, leaving Jones dangling from a tree limb.

And as the dawn approached, the measured throbbing of an automobile was heard approaching the scene of the tragedy. And afterwards, a tall gaunt figure enveloped in a cloak was observed to cautiously emerge from the surrounding shrubs, gazing approvingly upon the stiffening form of Jones, like a human vulture gloating on its prey which gently swayed in the morning breeze.

CHAPTER XII.

The American Negro Press flashed the news throughout the country that Napoleon Hatbry had secured a clothes factory in which he intended to employ one thousand Negro workers, and further, that he was about to close a contract for a laundry which would employ another hundred or more. De

Woode, while heaping ridicule upon the pretensions of Hatbry, was caustically critical of his rival, pointing out among other things that an enterprise such as that outlined by Hatbry would require a vast amount of capital as well as trained executives, and that Hatbry possessed neither of those two vital qualifications without which, one being dependent upon the other, this newest sensation of Hatbry's would pass into the realm of those nightmares which he had so frequently administered to his credulous followers. He, however, qualified this criticism by stating that the money question might not be an insuperable difficulty because of the vast sums which were at the disposal of Soviet and Japanese agents operating in the United States.

Hatbry rebutted that he was neither in the pay of Russia nor Japan, and that if De Woode knew of the existence of such money, he had evidently been approached and paid off; that being the case it was curious that this leader had not used such funds for the benefit of his people. The controversy was long and bitter with a resulting recrimination which hugely amused that section of the whites which read the Negro Press while the Emperor and his following felt that this division among the Negroes would materially aid in blinding the two factions to their proposed suppression or extermination by the Invisible State, which after all was the main point at issue.

Over in Boston, Hewitt Browne had gradually arrived at Ette's view of the situation and his first move was to obtain all possible information from the Communists which he handed over to the United States Government from time to time. He was offered highly remunerative employment and financial reward. To the former he replied that his law practice was sufficiently remunerative and as for accepting money for his services, he was an American Citizen performing such duty to his country as was within his power, and further, while he did not know what the future held for him, he had not yet become a professional spy. Thus, despite the independence of his bitter report, his sincerity and integrity could not be questioned.

Upon reading the criticisms of Hatbry and De Woode, he wrote privately to those gentlemen pointing out that this was no time for washing dirty linen in public for the edification of the dominant group, but a period when a solid front should be shown to the common enemy with unswerving loyalty to the Flag as was the duty of every American irrespective of race, creed or colour, because of the danger which seemed to threaten from without.

De Woode treated Browne's communication with superior disdain and Hatbry, anxious to escape De Woode's criticism for a time, seized the occasion to publish Browne's letter with an accompanying editorial in which he ridiculed the pretensions of the "Black American Lawyer" who boasted a non-existing Citizenship, thereby "Licking the boots of the white man and placing the yoke of inferiority more firmly about the black man's neck." He further suggested that Browne should reassume his discarded headkerchief and return to his native Southland where his "yes sah, Colonel, boss," would quickly secure him those smiles of condescending approbation from his white masters for which he so earnestly yearned.

Browne's friends of both groups were highly incensed at Hatbry's editorial and his indiscreet publication of a confidential communication. Those of his group were anxious to take up the cudgels on Browne's behalf, but he wisely dissuaded them from any such impolitic action. For his part, while regretting Hatbry's indiscretion, he considered the incident closed, his silence causing him to rise considerably in the estimation of his associates and well-wishers.

Ette who had not seen Browne since the interview in her sick room and who had now recovered, read the editorial at the bookshop where she had resumed her employment. Hatbry's broadside greatly annoyed her and she was immensely relieved when informed by mutual friends that Browne declined to enter into a discussion with Hatbry or permit his friends to take up the matter in his defence.

She had received several telephone calls from him enquiring about her health, but he had not written her, nor had he disregarded her injunction not to see her. On many occasions, when faced by the political situation which had arisen, he was tempted to go to her for counsel and advice, but he refrained because he not only wished to avoid displeasing her in any way, but she had become so necessary to him that he feared to lose her by perpetrating any indiscretion.

On the other hand, the promptings of her heart coupled with her loneliness caused her to make frequent attempts to shorten the period of her self-imposed separation. Many letters were written him only to be destroyed. Now, however, the Hatbry editorial gave her the excuse she needed. So, she wrote reprehensively upon the subject and added a postscript suggesting that Browne might call, "if he cared to do so," in order that she could be granted the opportunity to express herself at greater length.

The perusal of Ette's letter supplied Browne with a much-needed consignment of joy, and the discreetly-worded postscript filled his heart with gladness. "If I cared to come," he repeated, not alone upon receiving the letter but also throughout that day which seemed the longest in his experience. So engrossed was he at the prospect of seeing Ette, that he almost lost a very important case which had engaged his attention for several months.

The evening at length arrived, and impatiently watching the hands of the slowly moving clock until he concluded Ette would be at home from business, he called her up on the phone, thanked her for the letter, and invited her to dine with him. Knowing that in a public place they could not indulge in that long deferred tete-a-tete for which her soul had longed, Ette suggested that he should have dinner with her, which she volunteered to prepare with her own hands. Her invitation was accepted with alacrity and while she indulged in the delicate occupation of preparing a delectable repast, poor Browne was finding it extremely difficult to decide upon a sartorial ensemble befitting the momentous occasion.

Finally, after considerable perturbation and the increase of his laundry bill by the perspiring destruction of three stiff collars and a shirt, his common-sense returned and he decided to present himself in the serviceable business suit he had worn that day.

"You are late" was Ette's greeting when Browne entered. "Dinner was ready twenty minutes ago—I'm afraid it's utterly spoiled."

"What matters if the dinner is spoiled? You at least remain unspoiled, for which I offer thanks."

"Pray don't flatter me Hewitt; I set great store upon my cooking and being all but reduced to a grease spot in the process, I'm naturally aggrieved at your lack of appreciation."

They entered the dining-room where the handywoman had already placed the steaming dishes on the table.

"What detained you?" she asked, as they took their seats.

"Where is the Bear?" This reference to Ette's aunt.

"She is indisposed, I sent up her dinner while waiting for you: but you avoid my question,—what detained you?"

There was a twinkle in Browne's eye. "Shall we proceed with the meal? I'm as hungry as a bear."

"Shall I help you to a portion of the national bird?"

"Is it an eagle?"

"No, just an alleged barn-yard strutter." She carved the fowl. "This should be your job."

"Never was any good at surgery."

"You like white meat?"

"No, black—all black!" they laughed. This was a slap at the all-white organization. "Even Hatbry recognized my colour scheme in his attack."

"It seems you're getting away from my question. Was there a woman in the case?"

"What case?"

"You should know what I mean—your detention."

"Woman detains and retains, my dear. No, I'm not avoiding your question. I was debating in my mind whether I should tell the joke against myself."

"Out with it!"

"It was this way your honor—"

"You're not in court."

"Yes I am; courtship."

"That pun is too poor. Go on with your sad story."

"I was debating what suit I should wear on this momentous occasion—"

"Momentous occasion! That's rather good."

"Don't interrupt—" Hewitt attempted the difficult task of carving a chicken wing whilst looking at Ette, and the protesting joint skated from the plate and skied across the table into Ette's lap. "Damn!—I beg your pardon!—Have I ruined your dress?"

"No, don't get up, it's alright," wiping her dress with a serviette. "If it's ruined, you'll have to buy me another one. That's that! She helped him to another portion. Sorry to interrupt your story."

"Well, as I was about to say, I got so excited over the prospect of seeing you that I decided to don holiday attire in celebration of the momentous—"

"No—no! You said that once!" they laughed.

"Well, the sweet occasion."

"I'm not surprised that lawyers charge such large fees. I suppose you work it out at so much per word."

"No, I think not—why?"

"You're so long coming to the point."

"Is that so? We'll see about that. Anyway! I tried on five suits and didn't like either of them. Got so excited about it that three collars and a shirt were ruined with perspiration."

"Then sanity returned and you wore the suit you wore in court today."

"How did you know?"

"Aha! woman's intuition."

"Then you know what I had in mind—what I still have in mind?" He leaned across the table a little nervously.

"Of course I do." She was serious and gazed at him with those large lustrous eyes of hers.

"If you know all about it, I shall not find it necessary to make any statement."

"I said a month."

"I kept my promise to stay away. You called me and I naturally thought—"

"That you would jump to inconclusive conclusions."

"Faint heart never won fair lady."

"I wish you would be original." She rose, and Hewitt went over and took her arm leading her to the living-room. "Is there anything original?" he asked as they crossed the room.

"Some things are; many things, I should say, that are not original seem new to us in the telling of them."

"For instance!" They sat together on the divan, Browne holding Ette's hand.

"I'll instance you no instances, kind sir." She looked up smiling, there was an inviting coyness in her tones.

"What then?"

"Yes, what?" He put his arms about her waist and drew her to him kissing her tenderly on the neck.

"Don't do that," she said quietly. "The woman is clearing the table." He did not answer but held her more tightly.

"When will you marry me?" he whispered.

"How do I know?"

"You'll be a party to the contract."

"First or second party?" she questioned with a laugh.

"First part—first part!"

"Does it matter?"

"Of course it does—in this case, shall we say a month hence?"

"The party of the second part seems to do all the arranging."

"No, no! I was merely suggesting. I'm in your hands—tell me?"

"I hardly know what to say." She thought for a moment, then, disengaging herself, she got up and taking a chair placed it before Browne and sat down before him with her face between her palms. "It is necessary that we understand each other at the start. You have known me for many years and I think you know that I neither indulge in falsehood nor subterfuge."

Hewitt nodded assent and Ette proceeded.

"You know the views of my people regarding colour. I do not hold those views, but frequent discussions upon the same subject, no doubt, subconsciously affected the views I held. As you know I am employed with a firm whose clientele is almost exclusively white. This doubtless also affected me subconsciously. I am very sensitive. I did not accept you although I must admit that I admired you immensely."

"Very sweet of you, Ette."

"Not at all. One night we were together and two Frenchmen we encountered, rudely referred to us as: "cafe au lait.""

"Yes, yes, I remember the incident."

"From that night I avoided going about with you, as much on your account
as my own."

"Why on my account?"

"I did not enjoy any unpleasant reference to you. Well, a man called at
the bookshop one day—a white man—he appeared to be a gentleman. He
offered marriage and took me to the home of his sister and introduced me—"

"Did he know you were coloured?"

"Not then, I never thought much about it; although I must admit, I was
somewhat flattered—taken off my feet, as it were. At his sister's house, the
colour question was discussed and I somehow got into the discussion, airing
my views rather boldly, I fear. They were Southerners—Virginians—and he
did not like my statements. Subsequently he met me by appointment at the
Commonwealth Hotel for dinner. After dinner he suggested adjournment to
a private room where we could discuss our differences. To my astonishment,
I was ushered into a bedroom before I realized what had happened. He made
an attempt upon me, which I resisted with superhuman effort, reaching the
phone I succeeded in giving the alarm."

"The brute! That's the sort of thing they want to do with all of our women!"
Browne stood up, visibly affected. He placed his hands to his head, and made
a circuit of the room.

"My God, how long must this thing continue! I'm sorry Ette." He returned
and took his seat on the divan.

"I was rescued by the hotel staff and a lady customer of ours who happened
to be visiting friends on the same floor. That was the cause of my illness.
During that illness I had time to reflect and work out a true estimate of racial
values. That is the story. I esteem you very highly. It is possible I love you, or I
would not have sent for you tonight. I am not damaged goods; but such as I am,
if you think we can be happy, my answer to your proposal of marriage is, yes!"

Browne sighed. He leaned forward and drew Ette to him on the divan,
kissing her gently, reverently. "You have made me supremely happy," he said
simply. "You are necessary to me, my happiness, my work—my career—
our—career! Kiss me." She nestled in his arms and held her lips to his, and in
that moment she knew that she was his for all eternity.

The doorbell rang. Ette went to the door and admitted Mrs Weatherall
and Doctor Detritcher. Browne stood up.

"Mrs Weatherall! Doctor Detritcher! What a surprise! I mentioned you not five minutes ago. Allow me. This is my attorney Hewitt Browne, Mrs Weatherall, my future husband! Doctor Detritcher, Mr Browne.

"Congratulations to both!" exclaimed Mrs Weatherall enthusiastically. "I'm so glad, Mr Browne; you have made a wise selection—a noble girl! One whom I do not blush to call my friend."

"It seems that I have tumbled into and disturbed a cupid's bower!" laughed Doctor Detritcher. "Congratulations, my young friend. You have secured a pearl of great price."

"Thank you, Mrs Weatherall. Thank you Doctor Detritcher. I'm sure I value Miss Swanson at least as highly as you do, and, well, I shall do my utmost to make her happy."

"I'm sure you will," interjected the Doctor. "I'm sure you will. I like your face, my young friend. As for my dear child, Ette—you see I have adopted you!—I know you will make your husband happy. If you ever have any differences," patting Ette on the cheek, "bring them to me; I'm reputed to be a sort of joy-dispenser."

Ette went over to the radio and tuned-in. The sweet sad notes of "Love's old Sweet Song," filled the room and its four occupants quietly seated themselves, each delving into a sheaf of treasured memories, until the strains dreamily passed on into the ether.

CHAPTER XIII

The four sat silently for some moments after the music ceased. The announcement of the next Radio item was unheeded until the air was rent by an ear-splitting jazz selection that rudely awakened the friends from their reverie.

The Doctor, living up to his reputation as a dispenser of joy, looked over the faces of the others and broke forth into a hearty laugh.

"Why," he said, "we all look as solemn as a funeral party, when we should be joyfully celebrating a betrothal!"

"They all joined the Doctor's laugh and Ette said: "Perhaps my future life partner is reflecting upon the rashness of his plunge."

"I have been informed," replied the Doctor, "that the matrimonial sea is deep and beset with many perils."

"Which accounts for your inclusion among the Benedicts," was the comment of Mrs Weatherall.

"That is hardly correct, Mrs Weatherall. You are my ideal woman, and as Weatherall refuses to die—an elopement being out of the question—I have been forced to worship my divinity from afar." There was a mischievous twinkle in the Doctor's eye as he gazed at Mrs. Weatherall.

"Obviously, judging by your increasing waist-line and rubicund countenance, you have not enlisted in the slender army of 'piners." Which sally of Mrs Weatherall provoked general laughter. "Look at Ette; look at Mr Browne. The most casual observer can see that they are not only deeply in love with each other, but that they have both grown thin with pining."

Ette smilingly blushed. Browne laughingly replied: "I'm afraid, Mrs Weatherall, that I belong to that lean and hungry tribe which Shakespeare calls dangerous."

"Ette, beware! You have heard the confession." was Mrs Weatherall's mock-serious admonition, as she raised a warning finger.

"I'm not disturbed." Ette smiled back at her friend. "I said, Ette was a pearl," came from the Doctor, as he combed his white beard with his fingers. "Now it appears, she is mineral as well—a diamond."

"I'm not as hard as that."

"Now, pray be careful what you say, my child: your future victim is a lawyer, and your statements may be brought forward in evidence against you."

"I'll chance it," laughed Ette, glancing slyly at Browne. Then, changing the subject. "It was very nice of Mrs Weatherall, and you Doctor, to treat me—us—to this pleasant surprise."

"Yes we were glad to come. The Doctor mentioned you at dinner, saying he had not seen you since the night he took you away from the Hillyardes. I told him I had not seen you myself for three weeks and he suggested we should drive over after dinner; and here we are."

"Yes," the Doctor returned. "I heard from Mrs Weatherall about your unfortunate encounter with that brute——" he hesitated, looking in Browne's direction, fearing he had unwittingly said too much, and Ette quickly interjected. "It's quite alright, Doctor, Mr Browne knows all about it. I related the affair to him just before your arrival. I can have no secrets which may not be shared by my future husband."

"I said you were a pearl; that's the way my dear child: start right, and avoid subsequent suspicions and probable bickerings."

"That's the trait I admire in Ette; frankness, truth, is always best," said Mr Weatherall.

"I read Hatbry's unjust criticism of you, Mr Browne; I'm glad you did not reply. I commend your restraint—your straight thinking. You do more good to your people by this method than by useless antagonisms. An unjust minority can always win friends for itself by sane methods and avoidance of hysteria. I had no idea, when Mrs Weatherall suggested this visit, that I should enjoy the pleasure of seeing and conversing with you."

"As for Hatbry, Doctor Detritcher, I can well afford to forget him. I must, however, plead guilty to the possession of some of the emotionalism of my race—hysteria, if you prefer the term. That this emotionalism, this hysteria, is under control, is entirely due to Miss Swanson."

Mrs Weatherall and the Doctor clapped their hands approvingly. "Bravo!" the lady exclaimed. "What a manly confession! I'm sure the two of you will be happy." Mrs. Weatherall who was seated beside Ette on the divan gave that young person an enthusiastic hug and planted a kiss upon each of her cheeks. "So glad, my dear, that you are helping to mould the character of this worthy man and that he is willing to be moulded."

"You ladies have the making or marring of us weak men," was Browne's calm answer. "Whatever I am is due to the encouragement and sacrifices of my dear mother, and now, I have Ette, who has taken up where my mother left off."

"Is she dead-your mother, I mean?"

"Yes, Mrs Weatherall. She died while I was in the trenches."

"Fighting for the self-determination of small nationalities," was the Doctor's sarcastic comment. "And after all the sacrifices the American Negro has made for the country of his birth, his payment is meted out in lynchings, and burnings, and worse in the interest of the establishment of an all-white insanity. I marvel that he remains so passive."

"They call us children, Doctor, do they not?"

"Yes, my young friend. It is fortunate that you still possess religious enthusiasms. These enthusiasms have bought you safely through three hundred years of serfdom. They aid and comfort you in your perils of to-day. Am I right?

"Well," responded Browne. "We of the new generation have largely lost the religious enthusiasms of our parents. We are more material. With the acquisition of the higher education and the wider outlook, our aspirations are whetted. We find ourselves in this whirlpool of civilization with its complexities and its cursed ostracism; but we are in the fight believing—not as our parents did in Divine Miracles—but, while appreciating the probability of Divine intervention, we accept the dictum that 'God helps those who help themselves.'"

"That is wisely spoken, my young friend, as I have said, sane thinking and acting will win you friends. Not all white—or so-called white—people despise the Negro. Many of us are trying to find a way out. The interracial groups in the South as well as in the North, although academic in thought and action, must produce understanding. We have no knowledge—no worth-while knowledge—of the Negro in our midst. We must possess understanding if we hope to solve this vexed problem. We are as great a problem to the Negro as we claim the Negro is to us. Many of our pre-conceived ideas must be scrapped. Not a few of us have watched Hatbry's efforts with interest, because we felt that the solution might be found in economic endeavour. Some of us were prepared to help financially—we were watching events. The hatreds he has fostered have alienated many sincere well-wishers. Nevertheless, the fire he had put into his movement might smoulder when he has gone, but it will not be quenched entirely. We have the case of Egypt as an example of this. The patriotism first kindled in the breasts of the ignorant Egyptian peasants by Arabi Pasha in 1882, has borne fruit in the today's Egyptian march to complete freedom. As Booker Washington sagely said; "If you keep the Negro down, you must sit in the ditch with him to keep him there." But, I'm afraid I have silenced the ladies by my conversational monopoly, and I see Ette, literally exploding to get a word in."

"No, I won't explode, Doctor, some of my sex can listen. We must listen if we hope to learn."

"Yes, but do you not agree, that in voicing our opinions we frequently arrive at those correctives resulting from the expressed views of others."

"Oh yes, interchange of thought, to my mind, does broaden the outlook, causing re-adjustments of opinion, where opinion has not become perversely stagnant as a result of egotism. But, I still contend that one of my years and inexperience must listen if one would learn?"

"That is very nicely put, little pearl. What says my young friend?"

"I'm in full agreement with Miss Swanson," responded Browne. "For example, I came to this very room some four weeks ago with a rebellious urge against the troubles that beset us. Ette—Miss Swanson—immediately set me right. I admit my ego was slightly jarred, but I gradually recovered my mental equilibrium and—well, you saw her influence in my letter to Hatbry."

"I admit that your position—I mean the position of your race—is extremely difficult; and you appear supersensitive on the point, especially on the question of inferiority. To go further back; from the time of Moses, if we are to credit all that has been attributed to him, we have had this question of inferiority—I speak of Moses because he first advertised the idea of a specially selected people, chosen by God to the exclusion of the remainder of the human family. But, the Romans called all other people barbarians, and when they conquered the more cultured Greeks and enslaved them, the Greeks were treated as an inferior group although Rome owed any culture she possessed to the Greeks. The whole question of inferiority is due to power, domination and the glorification of nationality. Nationals pay greater reverence to their flag than they do to the Godhead. Few, if any remove their hats at the mention of God, yet the appearance of a piece of coloured bunting accompanied by a band, will provoke the greatest enthusiasm and respect. It is a form of insanity, this national idea, and was the direct cause of the late war."

"Have you seen the Emperor of the Invisible State since my visit to the Towers?" Ette asked, breaking the silence which had followed the Doctor's recital.

"Yes, I saw him a few Sundays ago."

"I suppose he is responsible for this new outbreak of lynching and burning of our people?"

"I fear he is."

"What do you think Doctor, the end of all this will be?" Browne enquired.

"It's very difficult to say. I fear there will be more bloodshed. It seems that all our boasted civilization has not eliminated the savage from within us. We must fight; even the pacifist are at it, not with violence perhaps, but it might come to that."

"I hold the opinion," remarked Mrs Weatherall, "that we women must take this matter into our hands."

"Exactly my opinion," exclaimed Browne.

"You are a prejudiced party," the Doctor answered dryly.

"I may be prejudiced, but please bear in mind Doctor, that women have the rearing of us, men or women, and our training for good or ill, is all we have to look forward to. Our race would be much less than it is today, but for our women."

"With this statement I'm forced to agree," said Mrs Weatherall. "I think the coloured women of America the grandest women in the whole world. They came out from the plantation on their emancipation, with little on their backs and nothing in their hands, but their naked children, for few of them had husbands. They went to work in kitchen, washtub, and farm to educate those children and make something worthwhile of them. In the church, the coloured women have been the mainstay of that institution, and they have been, and are, the backbone of all worthwhile Negro enterprise."

"I'm delighted to hear you speak like that, Mrs Weatherall!" exclaimed Browne with enthusiasm. "You have said a thing which few of our group realize. I admit not to have thought of it quite in that way—familiarity breeds contempt."

The Doctor looked at his watch. "Good heavens Do you know it's after twelve?"

"Is it really? We must be going," said Mrs Weatherall.

"Please don't go yet," pleaded Ette rising, "you must have a cup of coffee or something. It'll be ready in a moment."

She was in the act of leaving the room when Mrs Weatherall got up saying.

"Can I help you Ette?—Oh, I know I had forgotten something! I never asked about your Aunt—how is she?"

"Upstairs in bed—asleep, I think."

The two women left the room arm in arm. While coffee cups clattered without there was a short silence in the room.

Then the Doctor said: "A leader of your people is badly needed, Browne; why don't you do something? You possess all the needed qualifications, good common sense and a remarkable restraint. Have you thought about it?"

"I can't say I have, Doctor. I have always felt—and I still feel—that the job should seek the man. I'm prepared to serve, but rather be a follower than a leader."

"I admire your modesty, which proves your deserving. Think it over. You'll do some—considerable—good, I am certain."

"Whom the Gods would destroy they first make leaders."

The Doctor laughed at this statement. "So you think destruction is the reward for leadership?"

"History tells us so."

Mrs Weatherall, Ette and the woman helper returned with steaming coffee and cakes.

"Your future husband is exceptionally gifted, Ette," was the Doctor's statement as he took a cup of coffee from her hands.

"I'm delighted to hear you say so, Doctor."

"Yes, my child," sipping his coffee reflectively. "Exceptionally gifted. No, thank you, no cakes; this coffee is excellent. I always enjoy a good cup of coffee; so few people know how to make it. I suppose this was your work, Ette?"

"Of course she did it," said Mrs Weatherall, "you don't know how clever our Ette is. She told me she cooked your dinner tonight, Mr Browne."

"Yes, Mrs Weatherall, and a fine dinner it was!"

"Ah, Ah!" The Doctor exclaimed, "they say you reach a man's heart by way of his stomach! woman, woman!"

"We do not appear to have reached your heart", said Mrs Weatherall.

The Doctor rested his cup. "Well, you see, my corpulence is responsible for that. The food has to go down to come up; in my case, it takes such a long time to circulate through my system that it only reaches my heart after I have left the lady. Besides," with a twinkle in his eye, "you have never cooked a dinner for me."

There was a general laugh at this and the Doctor rose. "Shall we go Mrs Weatherall?"

"Yes I think we must. Ette, Mr Browne, I've enjoyed my evening hugely—I would not have missed it for worlds." She kissed Ette. "So glad to have come."

"You must come again soon, when you can spare a moment. And of course, you'll come again, Doctor?"

CHAPTER XIV.

Once more the hooded Triumvirate met in the holy of holies to discuss its more intimate affairs. Once more the mummery of the skeleton and the flaming cross was enacted and the discussion hinged upon present and future activities of the all-embracing Invisible State.

As Smithson had informed Hatbry, the spies of the Emperor were present at every political or social gathering, not only collecting evidence pertaining to the activities of the members of that far-flung body, but were also collecting the views of the people for and against that organization. Those who were in sympathy with the views of the all-white organization, were quietly, but insistently, importuned to link their fate and fortunes with what was termed the only "true" American Organisation in existence. Those who declined the honour were marked, their business or social prestige ruined, and disloyal members, with the co-operation and active assistance of judicial affiliations, whether Judges, Sheriffs or Police, were sent to long terms of imprisonment and where the offence was regarded of so serious a nature as to impede the activities of the Invisible State, such members were unceremoniously removed. A deputation without warning, suddenly descended upon them at the dead of night and the following dawn found them dead in a ditch or dangling from a tree limb with the legend: "A Traitor's End," flanked by two flaming crosses.

Thus, a reign of terror ensued. Members went about with anxious faces and were exceedingly cautious and correct in their deportment, both public and private, never under any circumstances permitting the name of the Invisible State or its designs to pass their lips. And the general public which half suspected the source of the executions, only referred to these mysterious happenings in whispers. Smithson, who was well aware of the danger that threatened him, had carefully made his preparation. In his office safe he had deposited a complete history of his antecedents and his connections with the Invisible State, together with a full account of the inner working of that organization and its secret intention to seize the reins of Government. He had instructed his private secretary to deliver this sealed document to the American Press, should his absence be unaccounted for during any three consecutive day period. He was therefore prepared for any eventuality in so far as the Invisible State and himself were concerned.

He had kept faith with Hatbry by anonymously depositing five hundred thousand dollars to the credit of that leader's organization in cash, and a further half million dollars in a special account which he had instructed his executors to pay Hatbry on condition that he carried out the provisions previously outlined to that individual.

Smithson, having set his house in order, continued to meet the Emperor without the slightest outward show of anxiety, which caused that worthy an unlimited amount of perplexity.

The Emperor could not conceive it possible that one of Smithson's intelligence and position should adopt such a care-free demeanour, well knowing that the penalty of "death to traitors" had been announced by the Grand Council and that the Grim Reaper might overtake him at any moment.

The facts of Smithson's guilt were however before him. Apart from the report of the unlamented Jones, Colonel Blood's most trusted spies had confirmed all that Jones had reported. Yet he feared to act. Smithson was well known, so was his important position in the financial world. It would be difficult to hide the source of his "taking off" and that action might lead to defection among some of the better placed members who, for the most part, had been cajoled and threatened into affiliating themselves with the organization. Fear of a Japanese and Soviet invasion had prompted many of the new adherents to embrace the cause; others again were obsessed by the "all-white" idea, but in the main, they felt ashamed of their connections and not a few would have gracefully retired, but for the fear of the consequences and the assassinations which were of frequent occurrence were by no means reassuring, but were extremely disconcerting.

Thus, when the Triumvirate assembled on this fateful occasion, the Emperor was perplexed. Smithson was quite unconcerned about his future, and the Third Member was in complete ignorance as to the actual trend of events in so far as they affected Smithson. Various matters had been discussed, reports had been read with regard to the destruction of Negro life and property, and the rather violent attacks made upon Jews and Catholics in many States.

The Jews were maltreated because of their wealth, and the Catholics were attacked under the pretext that the resumption of Temporal Power by His Holiness at Rome and the creation of an independent State, the Roman See, was secretly undermining the religious liberties of the American Nation by using American Organizations to send a Catholic to the White House and to elect a Catholic majority to the two legislative bodies at Washington. These wanton and baseless attacks resulted in a combination of Catholic and Jew, and these two groups were actively importuning the Negroes to join a defensive alliance. All Negro Leaders, however, both laity and clergy, united in their opposition to any such union on the assumption that the Negro would only be used as a temporary instrument to advance the interests of Jews and Catholics, and, the three factions being recognized white groups, when the differences of the contending parties were adjusted, they would then turn their attention to the extermination of the defenceless minority.

Naturally, the Emperor was by no[7] means delighted at this condition of affairs, because such a projected combination among these groups, with the potential adherence of the Communists, would result in a majority which would easily nullify the activities on the Invisible State. Consequently, at the instigation of the Emperor, many of his spies had become temporary Catholics, the better to promote dissension in the Catholic ranks, and at the same time report on their activities.

The Emperor, therefore, had created an organization which was as complete an instrument for the destruction of those very liberties he claimed to safeguard, as it was possible for any human agency to construct. The rank and file of his fanatical following did his bidding blindly and with the influx of wealthy members, unlimited funds were at his disposal to purchase the

---

7   In the serial edition, "no" has been omitted. We inserted it here based on grammatical and contextual clues.

services of gunmen and gangsters to assist in his policy of ruthlessness and violence which was intended to intimidate the Nation at large.

All things being considered satisfactory without, it was now necessary, notwithstanding his perplexity, to adjust the immediate internal affairs of the "State". Three members of the Grand Council who had secretly, but sincerely gone over to the Catholic faith, had recently joined the royal army of martyrs at the Emperor's express command. And now Smithson remained to be dealt with as a proof that the nearer the throne, the more unsafe the head, which would, in his opinion, prove a signal warning to intending transgressors.

There was now an interregnum in the proceedings which suggested the imminent close of the session, when the Emperor nervously cleared his throat, rapped the table, and delivered himself of the burden of anxiety.

"We have all heard the decree of the Grand Council of the Invisible State wherein it was stated, without dissent, that Death should be the portion of the traitor."

Smithson remained immovable and the Third Member of the Triumvirate, who suddenly recalled that he had appropriated several thousand dollars of the organization's money to his own use, moved uneasily in his seat, nervously twining and untwining his fingers beneath the shadow of his voluminous sleeves.

"I relate with grief," continued the Colonel, "that a highly placed and greatly trusted member of this Triumvirate has betrayed our most closely guarded secrets to the niggers."

Number Three breathed a sigh of relief as the Emperor paused and his shrouded eyes danced with glee, at the respite which Colonel Blood's words conveyed; he secretly vowed to make restitution on the following day ere Nemesis should overtake him.

"I have before me reports of unimpeachable veracity that prove Number Two to be the culprit and traitor, not only to the Invisible State, but to every red-blooded white man in the United States and the world at large!"

As the Emperor warmed up to his subject, he completely lost his nervousness, hurling his accusation at Smithson with the violence of an accusing angel.

"It is unthinkable that one so highly placed could stoop so low as to consort with niggers! That was bad enough, but to deliver us into the hands of these vile savages to supply them with the most carefully guarded secrets of the State—secrets which we have withheld from the rank and file of our vast membership—I repeat, is unworthy of any all-white-hundred-percent-American!"

The Emperor paused, turning his hooded head in the direction of Smithson, who he expected would vouchsafe a suitable reply. As Number Two declined to be drawn, Number Three, who had now fully recovered his composure, asked; "What are the Proofs, oh, Emperor, against the accused?"

"Proofs!" exclaimed the irate Emperor. "Proofs! We have an abundance of them!" He held up a sheaf of papers to confirm his statement.

"But, should not the accused be given a chance to defend himself, Oh, Emperor?"

"Chance? He shall have a chance," (sarcastically).[8] "Is not his guilt fully established by his silence?"

"These charges are serious, Number Two; can you say nothing in your defence? The Emperor surely will hear you."

"What shall I say?" Smithson enquired. "The proofs he talks about, or some of them, come from one of the niggers he claims to despise—the nigger Jones, you got out of prison to serve the Emperor. I saw him following me about. He even came to my house to plead with our Emperor to get him out of the country, so that he might escape his people who were after him. And when the police found our precious Emperor's papers on the man, he denied all knowledge, claiming that the Jones he knew was not the felon who had been arrested. The Newspapers carried the story."

Smithson spoke without the slightest emotion. The Emperor was astonished that he knew so much. How much more did he know, the Colonel wondered. It seemed to him that Smithson had adroitly turned accuser.

Number Three, hoping to protect himself by defending Smithson, ventured the remark. "I can't believe the Emperor would hire my ex-convict, nigger Jones, to spy upon one of us. I didn't know I was getting him for that!"

"You don't know many things" the Emperor sarcastically rejoined. "If you did, your little brain would hardly bear them. I'm the Emperor! My word is law! Get that, and get it straight, from now on!"

"O, I get you alright," answered Number Three. "It looks as though we've turned from destroying niggers to destroy ourselves. I've always been obedient, but I draw the line at our men being accused to you by niggers and ex-convicts. We poor saps may not boast your massive brain, but I warn

---

8   This is how the sentence appears in the original. We have placed it in parentheses. It is likely that some text was omitted in *The Comet*'s printing.

you Colonel, this kind of thing has got to stop or someone else will have to warm your seat!"

"What is this?—a threat?" The Colonel rose in rage. "Who made you counsel in defence of Number Two? You forget yourself! I'll have no rebels here. I say, I have the proofs on Number Two and he must defend himself before the Grand Council of the State, which shall have these proofs. I use what instrument I please to serve our ends. Death is our reward for treachery! As for my seat, I'll take good care that you shall never warm it while I live!"

"Just a minute—just a minute! We three rule this organization." Number Three was on his feet. "The Grand Council does our bidding! Understand?— our bidding! You've taken a lot upon yourself, without consulting us, and I'm damned if I'll stand for it! You're just a man like either of us, in spite of your massive brain! But from now on we have got a voice and we are going to use it; What say, Number Two?"

The Colonel shrugged his shoulders and resumed his seat.

"Chance is a necessity, Number Three. I for one don't care a tinker's damn what happens! This Colonel, this Emperor, has used me and my house to push the organization. I let him use me—it suited my purpose. I did tell Hatbry of the Emperor's intentions. There is a vast difference between dominance and extermination. If the organization believes it can dominate twenty million Negroes, let it do so by all means, but I'll not be a party to their extermination! I sat at the Council board and heard the Colonel's plans, even as you did "Number Three," but neither you nor I had a single word to say—had we been allowed! The Emperor did all the talking and the planning, we were just voting machines. Who in hell is the Grand Council, that I should give an account of my actions to it? The Colonel forgets that the Grand Council takes its orders from the Triumvirate, which he isn't, unless the rules of the organization are scraps of paper! I know that our great man has the power and the means to order my death at the hands of his hired gangsters and gunmen; let him go to it! Does he think I have been asleep all this time? He pretends to be a Negro-hater—yes, he hates the men! ask him, Number Three, how many negro women he has ruined in his youth and manhood—ask him?"

The Emperor jumped to his feet. "I've heard enough, I've said, I'm master here!"

"The hell you are!" cried Number Three, also springing to his feet. "When did you purchase me or Number Two? You've got to drop this high-hatting, Mister—and quick, or else"—

"Else what?" The Emperor asked, calming himself with effort. "So, you threaten me?"

"The conclusion is yours!"

"This, ah, conference is at an end," said the Emperor. He stepped on the spring and the skeleton and the flaming cross appeared.

"All-white!" he exclaimed extending his right hand.

"Oh, hell!" was the retort of Number Three, who began to tear off his robe as he strode from the room.

Smithson lay back on his chair and roared with mirth; and the Emperor, releasing the spring, caused the skeleton and cross to swing back to their appointed place then, turning from the table, he left the room with such spurious dignity as he had at his command.

CHAPTER XV.

The Negro Protective League met in secret and solemn convention in the City of Louisville. Delegates from every State arrived by diverse paths decked in the most fearful and wonderful disguises. The professional element pressed pigs and chickens into its service to heighten effective disguise, thereby rendering the noisome surroundings of the Jim-Crow cars more natural and home-like.

Doctors and Lawyers who had quietly disappeared from their homes at dead of night, disguised as farmers and tramps, took the precaution to leave their assistants in charge, having previously circulated the report among their clientele that they were either very sick men, or were compelled to visit some outlying section of their district on urgent business.

The eternal vigilance of the minions of the Invisible State compelled both secrecy and disguise on the part of those Negroes who were actively engaged in stemming the tide of racial aggression which threatened to overwhelm them.

To save their skins and their properties, several members of their group had become spies and informers to Colonel Blood's organization. Even the preachers whose Churches were being gradually deserted by the followers upon whom they battened, were guilty of betraying their brethren in return for small weekly doles and promises of freedom from molestation by the agents of the Emperor. These men were more greatly enamored of worldly advantage than they were of celestial preferment. Before the advent of the Invisible State, they unctuously preached a gospel on Sundays which was completely forgotten on Mondays, especially when they sold out to the highest political bidder; turning their Churches into places for questionable political propaganda in their frantic endeavours to capture a few elusive electioneering dollars. Such were the perplexities confronting this momentous League Convention. Secrecy being the chief requisite to the success of this remarkable gathering, a local member had succeeded in enlisting the kindly cooperation of a friendly Jew who loaned the convention a dilapidated and abandoned machine shop which he used as a junk emporium, principally devoted to breaking up condemned automobiles. It was in this junk-shop that the convention was held, and as the premises contained neither electricity nor gas, the delegates were compelled to supply their own illumination in the form of candles.

With the approach of darkness, one by one, they wended their way to this rendezvous in the all but deserted quarter of the city, where they parked themselves on decayed cushions, skeletons of dismantled cars, and heaps of springs or other stray mounds of metal in which the place abounded. Empty bottles were pressed into service as candlesticks, all of which combined to produce a most weird effect.

Someone moved that a member be voted to the chair, and the selection unanimously fell to Hewitt Browne, who had turned up in a sewer cleaners outfit complete with long rubber boots. Without fuss of any kind, Attorney Browne declared the meeting open. Custom caused the assembly to hesitate for the usual opening prayer, and an aged preacher rose in his place and delivered himself a few words of thanks and a request that the Creator would confer His blessing and guidance upon the convention.

The preacher having concluded his remarks, a member rose to offer a vote of thanks, and at the same time availed himself of the opportunity to castigate the entire preaching fraternity. There were loud protests against this wholesale condemnation until Browne silenced the malcontents with the warning that the loud noise they were creating was calculated to draw the common enemy to their meeting place.

The preacher rose to his feet and begged permission to say a few words which he thought would clear the situation. "For," said he, "although I've been a preacher for over fifty years, I must admit that my fellow preachers of latter-days have done more harm to our race than the Invisible State." There was considerable applause at this statement which Browne quickly silenced. The old preacher continued: "For the past twenty years, I've found it difficult to get bread because I preached the word of Christ and warned my congregation of the wrath to come. The Bishops said my preaching was too old fashioned. The congregation left the Church because I condemned the women for overdressing—or wearing hardly any clothes at all. I condemned the school teachers for setting a bad example to their pupils by turning up to school like Jay Gould's or Rockfeller's daughter, bound for a wedding. I blamed the parents for joinin' their gals to the silk-stocking brigade, instead of learning them to cook and wash and iron, so's to make them useful members of the race; and a whole lot o' things. They turned against me for that, and the Bishops and the new-day preachers at the Conference, supported them in their lawlessness—I don't wonder Russia has turned Godless, if the priests out there had no more to offer the people than our preachers have to offer us. And I don't confine my remarks to our preachers alone. Whoever heard a white preacher North or South condemn lynching in this land?"

He sat down amid the noisy plaudits of the convention.

Browne experienced considerable difficulty in restoring order. It became necessary for him to inform the delegates that they had met to discuss important and secret matters affecting the race, and that he found it expedient to warn them again that they were in the enemy's country, where loud demonstrations would attract unwelcome attention, resulting in possible trouble, which should be avoided at all costs. Ultimately, the meeting was brought to order, and the delegates, realizing the truth of Browne's statement, continued their deliberations in subdued tones.

Those from the far South reported the lynchings, burnings and forcible evictions that had befallen their fellows. Those from the North and East demonstrated how, in the past, their group were the first to be discharged when unemployment began, and when factories or workshops were fully staffed, they were the last to be employed, their main opportunity coming during periods of unrest, when, at the risk of their lives they were forced to become strikebreakers in order to find bread for their half-starved families. And now that the Invisible State had dominated the labour situation, starvation was rife because there was no employment to be had for Negroes. Even the women, who in the past were enabled through domestic employment to help their men, were now supplanted in the homes by white women domestics.

One after another, delegates pointed out that lack of unity had largely contributed to their perilous condition and their disposition to think in terms of white men which tended to produce an inferiority complex.

At this point, a delegate rose to his feet and condemned both institutions.

Said he: "What have they done to improve our lot? Their funds now in the banks of the white man may never be used for industrial purposes. Whereas they have been employed against us. Our deposits, earning two and a half or three per cent, have been used by white speculators on short loans carrying enormous interest, to buy out the cotton crops and watermelon crops of coloured producers. Whereas, rightly employed, we could have brought up these crops ourselves applying the profits to mechanical industry to assist the coloured city dwellers whose women have been dependent upon their earnings from domestic service or sweatshop labour in Jew factories, while the men represent the flotsam and jetsam of casual labour."

Another delegate, with an unmistakable Hatbry leaning, while admitting the justice of the previous speaker's remarks averred that Hatbry was working on those identical industrial lines to which the brother referred, but had failed to receive support from either the Churches or the fraternal organizations, and that that leader was their only hope at this critical period.

The mention of Hatbry's name resulted in general protest. The convention was in an uproar; delegates jumped to their feet and, forgetful of Browne's previous admonition proceeded to yell their threats and imprecations against the absent leader, ignoring in their wrath the cries of "order" and the vigorous efforts of the chair to restore the convention to a condition of comparative sanity. As they failed in their futile efforts to out-talk each other, one by one they resumed their seats completely exhausted by the consuming violence of their vocal exhibition of vituperative eloquence.

It was now well past the midnight hour. There had been complaints and suggestions but nothing constructive had resulted from the deliberations of the convention.

Browne had vainly tried to suggest a line of action, but his every suggestion was lost in a torrent of discussion which he found it impossible to stem.

Finally, during a momentary lull, a native African of stately mien caught the eye of the discouraged chairman, and upon being granted the floor, he pointed out that much valuable time had been consumed in talk, but no action had been taken toward the betterment of the race's condition.

"There is no place in all this world for the blackman" he exclaimed.

"I've sailed the seven seas. I left my home to seek education among the so-called civilized to assist my people. I got that education and returned to the homeland to find myself a misfit in the land of my fathers—a Europeanized African! Every worthwhile job was in the hands of our masters, and while they played golf and tennis and gambled in their clubs, my people did their work on starvation pay. I saw my people ill treated because their skins were black! They called us savages or half-civilized monkeys because we wore the clothes of civilization. I stood up to defend my people! I was jailed as an agitator. I left the homeland in disgust and went to Europe. I starved and walked the streets of Christendom at night because I had no bed to lay upon. Then, I got a chance to go to sea, working in the bowels of the ship—a stoker: I, the descendent of a thousand kings, tended fires till the pains of my hands and strained muscles, bereft my eyes of sleep. My sorry plight made me weep tears of blood and I became the butt and ridicule of those unfeeling brutes dressed in the trappings of a brief authority! I travelled far and was hardened in the process. There was no place for me in Europe, for I am black! There was no place for me in Africa, for I was black! In East Africa, where the Portuguese are lords, they jailed me because I wore a chain of gold and dared to trod the pavements where the white men walked. In South Africa, it was the same. On board ship, I was brutalized by the Nordics in command. I came to America. Someone was killed in Harlem. I was taken to the Police Station on suspicion, where I was unmercifully beaten upon the head with rubber hose to wrest a false confession from me for a crime I had no knowledge of. God of my fathers! Is there indeed a God who sees and knows these things and yet permits this suffering to a defenceless people, because their skins are black? In the days of my misery, I've prayed earnestly to the white man's God for help—He did not hear, for I am black! I who am descended from a line of Kings whose frighting men went forth to battle in the days of long ago, have fallen to the vile condition of a brute because I'm black! I say you black men talk, you do not act! Better to die free men, than be forever slaves; the black Haitians threw off the Frenchmen's yoke! The half-caste Cubans bravely won their liberty! The Basutos of Africa stood up well-armed against the invaders of their lands, and they are free! Are we men? Nature demands the sacrifice of blood—the fittest only can survive! kill or be killed is Nature's unalterable law! If we are men—true men—and worthy of our noble heritage, let us awake and strike! If we must die, let us die sword in hand—our faces to the foe—covering ourselves with glory as we fall; so shall our names be graven eternally upon the hearts of mother Africa's sons!"

There was a moment's silence as the African resumed his seat. Then thunderous applause broke forth which Browne found it difficult to still. And as the assembly jumped to its feet springing upon the broken metal to loudly voice its approval of the African's appeal, the doors were broken down by an armed group of hooded men whose weapons vomited a hail of death.

The convention was taken by surprise but quickly recovered itself when companions were observed to fall on every side. Unhesitatingly each man drew his gun taking cover behind the broken metal seats they had occupied. Instantly candles were extinguished. The African whose towering form overtopped his fellows was one of the first to fall. The side of his face being almost blown away. The white-robed invaders became an easy mark as they stumbled about the tangled junk that impeded progress.

The weapons belched their death-dealing fire and the hooded brethren of the Invisible State, finding their ranks diminishing, turned and fled followed by the thoroughly aroused delegates, some of whom remained to collect their dead and wounded.

And the morning dawned upon a holocaust of intolerance and hate, with white-robed corpses piled on every side, whose sightless eyes gazed fixedly at the morning sun that glanced furtively through the interstices of the battered roof. And the fallen African, gathering up the remnants of his fast-departing strength, rose up among the dead like an accusing angel, his clothing mantled in his crimson blood.

Wildly he gazed about him, laughing triumphantly as he pointed accusingly with a bleeding hand to the inert bodies.

"Behold my bodyguards, who bear me company to the throne of my ancestors! The blood sacrifice! the blood sacrifice!" he cried. "It is written that blood must flow to appease the God's—even your Son-God, O, Nordics—had to die! The ancestors demanded sacrifice for the untold sufferings of their royal son!"

He gazed fixedly before him. "Ah, you have come to escort me home?" A smile of triumph lighted up his battered countenance.

"Ah, my father! You have come to lead the way? Behold my escort! Ah, I see your father standing by your side, and your father's father! and a noble company of our great forebears who went before. It is well—it is—well——"

Feebly he sank down upon a motor seat behind him and his body stiffened as he sat erect, a King among the dead. And a shaft of sunlight pierced a broken pane covering the African with glory.

CHAPTER XVI.

Smithson locked himself in his library, placed "Sentinel," his police dog, on watch without the door to ward off intruders, and was only available to his valet. Even Virginia was not allowed to enter the sacred precincts of his sanctum during the self-imposed three weeks he remained incarcerated while being engaged in the task of setting his house in order while awaiting the next move of the Emperor of the Invisible State.

Smithson was not afraid of the Colonel, but he had not underestimated the potential danger which threatened. He was in close telephonic communication with his office where business proceeded uninterruptedly in his absence, and he had instructed his secretary to hold the documents intended for the press until further notice of upon his possible disappearance.

Meanwhile, Virginia, who was at first alarmed, subsequently became annoyed at his mysterious behaviour, finally taking herself off to "The Towers" in high dudgeon, where she remained two weeks. At the end of that time her anxiety returned and she motored back to New York only to discover that Smithson's seclusion was as persistent as before and her exclusion from his presence as rigid as when she retreated to Long Island.

Two days had passed since her return to their spacious River-side mansion; days of suspense and chagrin; and Virginia, denying herself to all visitors, parked herself and son in the ample sun parlour just across the hall from Smithson's library. The morning of the second day after her arrival found her seated with an open book upon her knees which failed to engage her attention. Her unseeing eyes were fixed upon the wide window that opened on a small Spanish garden flanked by a blank wall. Virginia had requested the valet to inform her husband that it was imperative that she should see him, and now she awaited his summons. Her boy romped around the room. He was beautiful, blue-eyed, with short golden curls that clung in diminutive rings about his well-formed scalp like circlets of burnished metal catching the beams of sun-light that flowed from the windows, as he gleefully pranced about in semi-nudity, a veritable reborn Eros.

Occasionally, Virginia returned to the consciousness of her surroundings and smiled at the antics of her boy. There was pride in her smile, but instantly her thoughts would wander off again and the open book remained unread. Across the hall, the watch dog, "Sentinel", barked aggressively. The boy paused in his play and looking up at his mother, asked: "Mother, may I play with Sentinel?"

"No, darling," she replied. "Father, does not wish it."

The child came to his mother's side and nestled his head against her breast. "Where is daddy?" he asked, "and why doesn't he come home?"

"Daddy is at home, my darling—he is busy and cannot be disturbed."

"Will he always be busy?"

"I cannot say, my dear; it may be a long time, a very long time." Her chin twitched, she sighed and bit her lips to regain her composure.

"Now, run along and play." She pressed the child to her breast for a moment, then pushed him away gently. "Go and play with nice horsey, sweetheart."

The child looked up into his mother's face, put his arms around her neck and kissed her. She held him tightly for an instant, kissed his ruby lips, sighed once more, and then released him. "Now run along, dearest, mother wants to be quiet."

The boy silently turned away, his head bowed and slowly mounted his wooden horse on wheels. Puzzled, he watched his mother as he listlessly pedaled his wooden mount backward and forward. From time to time, Virginia smiled wanly at the boy, crying out encouragingly at intervals: "That's right, darling; ride the good little horsey."

In due course, a light luncheon was served, of which Virginia partook sparingly, and the boy was taken to his room by the governess for his afternoon nap. After the departure of her son, she passed out into the little garden, book in hand, and strode swiftly up and down the narrow path to calm the inward turmoil that burned and surged like the fires of a restless volcano which threatened to erupt.

Virginia admired her husband detachedly. His strength of character and executive ability had brought the wealth so necessary to her existence, and these factors compelled admiration. But, she was completely obsessed by the mystery surrounding his antecedents. Her own birth, social standing and ancestral background, notwithstanding the bar sinister previously noted, caused her to look askance at anyone, possessing a doubtful pedigree, and when that one happened to be her own husband, her pride was jarred despite the material benefits abundantly bestowed upon her. Although moving in a gay circle where moral lapses supplied the thrills which seemed so compelling to a life of indolence, Virginia by reason of her sense of moral values, was voted an incorrigible prude by her associates. Philanderers were kept at a respectful distance, and while she smiled good-naturedly upon the foibles of her friends, she studiously avoided the moral indiscretion of a personal intrigue. Her brother's loose character and libertine extravagances had caused many heartaches, humbling her pride in the estimation of her husband, for Algernon, found it convenient to extract frequent loans which were relegated by Smithson to his tale of uncollectable debts.

As already inferred, Virginia married Smithson for his wealth. She was not in love with him; in fact it was unquestionable whether she was capable of experiencing the grand passion for any man. When, however, a child was born to the union, her deportment became less imperious, and on rare occasions her habitual iciness thawed to the extent of spontaneous embraces which invariably came in the nature of a surprise to Smithson.

Smithson was proud of his wife, admiring her immensely, and there were times when he felt like throwing himself at her feet to proclaim his devotion, but that chilling barrier which Virginia erected about herself seemed unsurmountable. Hence, he suppressed his tender impulses, swallowed his emotion, and retreated into his shell.

Her husband's reasons for denying himself to her were rather mystifying to Virginia. At first, she thought his fortune had been lost in some financial undertaking, but that thought had to be abandoned in view of the fact that taxes and other domestic obligations were promptly met and he had deposited five hundred thousand dollars to her personal credit just prior to his self-imprisonment. Other and wilder thoughts crowded her brain only to be dispatched leaving her more greatly perplexed than ever. Having exhausted every possible contingency for his strange and unexampled behaviour, she finally determined to have the matter definitively settled by demanding immediate admission to his presence. When, therefore, she had recovered her mental poise by hasty perambulation around the narrow confines of the garden, she re-entered the house and arriving at the library door, tapped lightly for admission, Sentinel barked furiously and the door was opened by the valet, whom she pushed aside, and entered the room with all the regal hauteur of a descendant of the Plantagenets. Smithson, who sat in an easy chair reading Marcus Aurelius, looked up in surprise; a shade of annoyance passed across his face.

"This is a distinguished pleasure," he smiled, rising from his seat.

"Did you not understand that I wished to be alone?"

The valet had closed the door upon Virginia's entrance. He stood holding the door-knob uncertain what to do.

"Kindly send your man away," she commanded. "I desire to speak with you alone."

Smithson shrugged his shoulders, and with a nod, indicated that his valet should leave the room.

Virginia watched the man depart closing the door after him. Then she turned her questioning gaze upon her husband.

"Well?" he asked. "Won't you be seated?"

She hesitated a moment, then drawing a chair forward she sat down.

Smithson threw the book upon the table and resumed his seat.

"Well?" he repeated, after observing with surprise how much thinner Virginia had become during the two weeks since he had seen her. She did not answer, so he continued: "Did you not understand that I wanted to be alone? It is a very rare thing to have you manifest such touching solicitude for my well-being—I suppose it is my well-being that prompts your insistence to see me?"

"I'm not sure that it is" she answered dryly.

"Is it money then?"

"No, it is not money! I wanted you to explain the mystery of your imprisonment."

"Oh, is that all?" There is no mystery. You know quite well that I have never bored you with my personal troubles."

"Then, there is trouble."

"I never said there was trouble, did I?"

"You imply as much."

"Let us get to the point. What do you wish to learn?"

"Don't be so fearfully irritating!"

"Am I?"—

"Of course, you are. I'm still your wife, and naturally, I want to know things."

"What is it, mere feminine curiosity or wifely solicitude?"

"Please don't trifle!"

"I'm not trifling. Your friend, the Colonel, has made it necessary for me to remain in hiding"—

"Why—what Colonel?"

"Colonel Blood—"

"Colonel Blood?" Virginia was puzzled.

"Yes, the Emperor of the Invisible State."

"But why?" She rose to her feet and paced the room. Smithson shrugged his shoulders, reached for the book, and returned to his reading. Standing for a moment at the window looking out upon the garden, Virginia tried to disentangle the mystery.

Colonel Blood had been a close friend of the family and a frequent visitor. Why should Smithson hide from him? Past experience had taught her that her husband could be stubbornly non-committal on occasion. His unwillingness to see her suggested to her mind that he was in one of his stubborn moods. Nevertheless, she felt herself unable to bear any suspense. Her thoughts flew to her infant son. How would he be affected by this mystery? She must know at all costs, even should her importunity provoke an unwelcome scene. She hated scenes, but the difficulty had to be faced. Quickly turning from the window, she said: "Do you think it fair to me, to my—our—child, to withhold a secret,—or whatever holds you prisoner?"

Virginia's correction from "my," to "our child", caused Smithson to raise his eyes from his book in surprise. It was the first time she had spoken of the boy as joint property. Heretofore it had been "my child" or "my boy." Virginia sat down and Smithson laid the book aside, an amused smile flitting across his countenance.

"This is no laughing matter," she cried irritably, "you surely did not suffer voluntary imprisonment for the fun of the thing?"

"No," he replied, stretching his legs out, stifling a yawn meanwhile. "I told you why I am a prisoner. Your precious Emperor seeks my life—"

"Your life?"

"Yes, my life, I await the summons in my own house, as I had no desire to be bumped off by the roadside as had been the recent fate of many another of his dupes. I prefer a more decent and orderly exit?"

"Why, this is terrible—terrible!—why did you not go away?"

"Go away! Run?" he laughed. "Incredible! I never was guilty of being what is termed "yellow". The Colonel knows where I'm to be found. I supplied him with the necessary information."

Virginia's chin trembled and a vagrant tear dimmed her eye as she sat silently gazing at her husband. "What are we going to do about it?" she finally asked.

"Do? Why, nothing."

"Nothing? why should Colonel Blood desire your death?"

"Because I knew too much—because I told the Negroes about the designs of the Invisible State—"

"You told the Negroes?" she interrupted in surprise.

"Why not?"

"You don't mean to say, you sought out the Negroes to do so?"

"Of course I did—why shouldn't I do so?"

"Why should you?"

"Because my mother was a Negress!—"

"What! She rose to her feet, there was terror—loathing in her eyes.

"You—you! a Negro?"

"Many of us are Negroes, or Negroid, without knowing it," he replied calmly.

"Then my child—my boy—oh, it is horrible! too horrible!" she jumped to her feet and strode to the chair where Smithson sat and stood over him with clenched fists—"you brute!—you beast!" she hissed! "And you knew this terrible thing and dared to marry me!—"

"Just a moment—Lady Macbeth!—Just a moment. Let us calmly consider things in their true perspective. You married me because you wanted wealth. I married you because I could buy you with that wealth—"

"Buy me!"

"I said, buy you! Pray be calm!—"

"Be calm! a Nigger to dictate to me!—"

"Oh yes; The grand Lady of the descendant of Plantagenets by way of a lady Hillyarde's indiscreet penchant for royalty——"

"Do you dare insult to injury? You brute—you beast! And to think that I—oh, I loathe you!" She wrung her hands and strode up and down the room.

"You forgot that the Nigger is the father of your child you spoke of our child a short time ago—what can you do about that?"

"Do you taunt me with that, too? I said you were a brute. It shows plainly the low bred stock——"

"Stop!" He rose to his feet. "Please do not let us look carefully into the family closet. We both have our skeletons. It was one of your own blue-bloods who ruined my mother and murdered her when he was threatened to expose the dastardly wrong he did her. I escaped to be revenged upon your entire cursed group, through you—"

"Through me?"

"I said through you! 'An eye for an eye, a tooth for tooth!' My mother was ruined by your people, as her mother and grandmother had been ruined! We were the weaker group—we had no defence—no remedy! My God! My poor dear mother was murdered in the bloom of youth—before my very eyes! You, you! have set the example and—I—I—have bettered the instruction; for I did at least, beast, brute, as I am, make an honest woman of you!"

"An honest woman!" she cried sneeringly. "An honest woman! Good God!—that I should have descended to this! I degrade myself by discussing the matter." She drew herself up and looked at Smithson, and with withering contempt turned and left the room.

Smithson smiled, took up his book, and resumed reading. There was a knock on the door and the valet entered.

"A gentleman to see you, sir."

"Did he give his name?"

"He told me to say: 'Number Three' would like to have a word with you."

"Alright, let him enter."

CHAPTER XVII.

"Have you come to perform the final rite?" was Smithson's greeting to Number Three. The other, seating himself, laughed immoderately.

"Perform the final rite? I've come to convey important information, which is a right, not a rite."

"Well?" Smithson ventured encouragingly. "Has the Invisible State blown-up, or has the Soviet invaded us?"

"Neither has occurred so far. But things are happening. The Colonel called the Grand Council and a vote of censure was taken on you together with a sentence of death."

Smithson laughed uproariously. "I should worry about his sentence of death, I could expect no less. I have been awaiting the executioner for the past three weeks—"

"Stop a moment! There won't be any executioner. The Council didn't know upon whom they were passing the death sentence until I spilled the beans and told them who you were and what you had done personally for the Emperor. He got mad as hell when I told them and tried to link me with what he called your plot. He was madder still when they refused to draw lots as to who would do the dirty job."

"That's all very well," replied Smithson, "but the Emperor won't be turned from his purpose. No doubt I'll be quietly bumped off by some of his gangster friends when I least expect it—that is if I am caught napping,"

"I'm sure you won't be caught like that."

"Well, one never knows. You can't be too cautious with that bird. I'm not worried, however; I've set my house in order and it will be all the worse for him if he tries anything. Your defense of me was very nice. Then the Council is in rebellion?"

"Well, it looks that way. We've got him in a tangle. They told him flat that enough blood had been shed lately. That it was alright killing niggers, but when we set out killing each other we were heading for destruction; and besides, yours was too big a head to be lopped off. The meeting broke up in confusion with the Colonel vowing vengeance on everybody. We're not all fools. But why did you tell the niggers about our doings?" he concluded.

"There were many reasons, some of a private nature, which I won't discuss just now. One of them was the fact that I don't agree with the slaughter of the innocents. The Negroes have laboured for three hundred years helping to build this Great Republic of ours. The only wrong they appear to have done is, their skins are black, and when they are not black, white men have been responsible for lightening their complexions because their women are helpless. I'm prepared to gamble that this very Emperor of yours has been responsible for some of these light complexions. I have always found that the negro-hater and negro-baiter is one who is ashamed to own up to his part in American miscegenation."

Number Three was puzzled for a moment. He glanced searchingly at Smithson, then he said: "Well, I must admit that I don't like niggers, but I can't say that I have ever mixed my blood with theirs. In fact, I know I haven't. But I don't see why I should defend them."

"Perhaps not, but I don't know why you should persecute them. They never wronged you, did they?"

"Well, I can't say they have, that is, not directly: but my family lost all the property we had, consisting mainly of slaves, in the Civil War, and—well, the niggers have become too chesty since they've got education and a little money."

"Suppose they have? We made them citizens, and as such, they are entitled to such rights as we accord other citizens."

"I don't quite get you," responded Number Three. "We can't class them with our white stock—can we?"

"I never suggested that. But, they are at least as good as some of the foreigners who have sought these shores. But, we wander from the main point."

Smithson discovered that he was treading on dangerous ground. He desired to extract information from his auditor. It would never do to antagonize the man who was disposed to be friendly and who had taken the trouble to bring him valuable news. "My opinion," he continued, "is of little importance to you, which after all is quite personal, and although I may not agree with you on certain points, I respect your views, which you have a perfect right to express. There are always two points of view, and one has to be tolerant of the views of others."

"Surely, surely," Number Three answered, delighted to escape from a disagreeable subject. "By the way, I forgot to mention that our friend Hatbry has gotten into trouble with the Government."

"Oh, when did that happen?"

"This morning."

"What is the charge?"

"Plotting with the Soviet."

"That's bad."

"I think our Emperor had a hand in that business."

"No doubt, no doubt!" Smithson nursed his chin and reflected for a moment, then reaching for 'The New York Times' he turned to the front page and indicating the first column, he asked: "Did you see this?"

Number Three took the paper and replied: "No, I seldom read 'The Times.' I read 'The World' to see what the enemy has to say." They both laughed.

"This is serious for the Colonel," said Number Three. I didn't think Doctor Detritcher was a politician. If he goes to the Senate to fill the unexpired term of Senator Long as 'The Times' says here, he'll kick up a hell of a rumpus."

"I don't think there is much doubt about his going if he accepts the Governor's nomination," was Smithson's answer. "From what I know of the Doctor, I believe he will accept. Privately, he has always opposed the pretensions of the Invisible State as being un-American, and lately, he has aired his views in public rather strongly. The Governor is to the Doctor's way of thinking. He belongs to the old Colonial stock, not to mention the abolitionist leaning of his family long before the Civil War. Both the Governor and the Doctor are solidly behind political equality and justice for all citizens irrespective of race, creed or colour."

"Guess the 'Emperor' is in for a warm time", commented Number Three. I'll have to ease out of this mess, or—" He paused reflectively and laid down the paper.

"There's death in your cards, as the fortunetellers say, in any event." Smithson quickly interrupted, completing Number Three's unfinished comment.

Number Three looked up with a start, "How did you know what I was thinking?"

"Well," answered Smithson, "the thing is quite plain. If you quit, the Emperor will get you as a traitor. If you remain, you'll be doomed anyway, being a party to what the Emperor calls my plot; The way I see it, you're between the devil and the deep sea.[9]

"Hell-of-a-fix—hell-of-a-fix," was the anxious and reflective cogitation of Number Three, as he nodded his head in agreement. "What'll I do?"

"I'd suggest, you stand pat and observe events. I'm out of it. The Colonel can't throw you out just now and disrupt things. The Grand Council appears to be with you. Apologize privately to the 'Emperor.' Erupt bushels of baloney and bluff. He is vain and will fall for flattery. Tell him you defended me because you thought my taking-off would wreck the plans of the organization—you know he'll fall for some of that stuff. I know I've got him guessing—"

"You surely have," was Number Three's interruption. "I can vouch for that; and for that very reason, you've got to watch your step. So have I. I guess he knows I'm here to tell you all the news—I've chanced that. I just don't care a

---

9 The original copy of this sentence is partly indecipherable. We have edited with our best approximation.

damn about it. I've got my wife and children to think about: but what's done is done—should have thought about that before. Seems like these niggers got the devil or somebody looking after them; just as soon as we whites start something against them, we get all bawled up. We were winning the Civil War, then up they came and butted in, and we lost. We sought to make shock troops of them before Verdan in the big war, to get them blown up by the mines we knew were there; and the Germans called an armistice instead of blowing up the niggers, as they could have done. I guess they've stowed away a bigger rabbit's foot—or some other kind of Juju—than we have."

"I don't think they have a rabbit's foot, as you term it. I do believe, however, that it is a case of retributive justice. The law of cause and effect is always operating, what we sow we usually reap. The whites have committed rape on their women—and worse. The white women—well, the Negroes have been accused of rape, and you as a Christian must have read in your Bible of the celebrated case of Potiphar's wife and the slave boy Joseph—"

"No, no!" hastily interjected Number Three. "Our women are not like that! It's these black brutes who take advantage of their unprotected condition when our men are away from home. You have never lived in the South; you don't know what happens down there."

"I do know a bit about what happens down South, my friend. The men you talk of as being away from home, are often busy with some coloured paramour and the Negro men are only imitating the example set by their superiors, if they do not follow in the footsteps of the Hebrew Joseph. Besides it has been a remarkable fact that none of these men you accuse of rape has ever been allowed to face their accusers."

"You, as a red-blooded white man, couldn't think that our women should be brought into court to proclaim their degradation to the world? It's unthinkable from my point of view."

"If you don't mind," Smithson answered calmly, "we'll not pursue this subject further. We are not likely to agree as we see things from two points, as opposite as the poles."

Number Three was somewhat nettled at Smithson's criticism, but finding him unwilling to continue the discussion, this member of the Triumvirate shrugged his shoulders and lapsed into a sulky silence.

"Have a cigar," cried Smithson, breaking the silence. He passed his cigar box to Number Three who helped himself and returned the box. Smithson then opened a nearby filing cabinet and producing a bottle and two glasses, continued: "Here is some pre-Prohibition beverage. You must pardon my forgetfulness, I suppose you are as dry as I am, with our profitless discussion." He passed over the bottle, Number Three helped himself copiously and returned the bottle to Smithson who poured out a stiff dose and raised his glass. "Here's to the Invisible State," was his ironical toast. "To hell with the Emperor!" was the exclamation of the other, as he swallowed his portion at a gulp. They laughed and harmony was once more restored. They filled their glasses again and were in the act of raising them to their lips when Sentinel barked loudly, scratching at the door, as a peculiar grating sound was distinctly heard against the outer wall of the apartment.

Number Three leaned over and looked fixedly in the direction of the window overlooking the garden. Smithson was about to turn in his chair when a volley echoed through the room causing him to jump to his feet and then topple inertly to the floor.

"They've got me!" was his exclamation as his form contracted and he pressed his hand to his side, and Number Three hastily took cover by falling flat upon his face, there to await developments.

The fusillade ceased as quickly as it started, six shots having simultaneously rang out in succession from the neighboring sun parlor and scampering feet were heard escaping over the garden wall.

Meanwhile, Sentinel continued his barking as he rushed up and down the passage outside the door which was hastily opened by the valet, who was thrust aside by Virginia, as she hurried into the room carrying a smoking revolver in her hand.

CHAPTER XVIII.

After Virginia's irate argument with her husband, she caused the boy to be dressed, ordered her car, and drove away, intending to shut herself up in The Towers until she could think out her position with clarity. There was no doubt about her agitated condition of mind and the staggering blow she considered herself to have received at the hands of her husband had wounded her pride. Her head throbbed and her brain seemed about to burst. From the moment she left Smithson's library her one thought was to get as far away from him as possible and from the hateful place of her humiliation.

She felt she had arrived at the most perplexing moment of her life. Upon leaving the mansion the words: "Tied to a nigger! Tied to a nigger!" seemed to be the refrain to which the monotonous throbbing of the engine maddeningly beat a nerve-racking accompaniment. She was gazing straight before her as the car winged its way to her Long Island home. Her handbag slipped from her knees. She leaned over forward and as she picked it up her hand came in contact with the revolver she always carried in the receptacle when travelling between Manhattan and Long Island. Opening the bag she removed the weapon and began to toy with it aimlessly. A sudden thought seized her.

Why not? Better death than eternal disgrace! And the maddening throb of the motor seemed to urge her on: "Tied to a nigger! Tied to a nigger!" She raised the gun to her temple, her finger on the trigger. "Mother dear," lisped the boy at her side. "Mother dear," he repeated. She paused and turned to look at the child who nestled against her breast looking up into her face with a winning smile. "Mother dear, I do love you—you are so sweet and beautiful."

In a moment her proud heart melted. She leaned down and kissed the boy, tears dimmed her eyes. Reopening her bag she replaced the gun. Then holding him tightly to her breast she kissed him wildly, madly, and in that moment her pride fell away from her. This was her own child, flesh of her flesh, bone of her bone. Her blood flowed in his veins. Was it his fault that he was a nigger child? After all, why should this poor innocent child suffer? No one need know of his parentage. Besides, if he did have the Negro taint, no one would suspect it. If he possessed African blood he could also boast the blood of the Plantagenets. He was so fair, so sweet: her darling! She drew him closer to her breast as the tears coursed down her cheeks.

"Does mother love her baby boy?" he asked in concern.

"Yes, my darling. I do love you with all my heart!" And she held him closer and kissed him again and again.

"Why does mother cry? Is it for daddy?" She released him suddenly, a pain at her heart, and sat bolt upright. There was a sneer on her face as her chin shot up. "Daddy indeed!" she thought, "A nigger!" Virginia laughed contemptuously.

"I know why mother laughed," cried the boy joyfully.

She turned, placed her arms around the child, and looked down smilingly upon him, all her pent-up love was in that smile. "Tell me, darling, why did mother laugh?"

"Because you thought of daddy," was his prompt reply. Once more she released him and averted her gaze. She did not smile on this occasion, she was merely thoughtful. They approached a filling station. The chauffeur slowed down and stopped. "Need more gas, madam," he said, and descended. Two men were deep in a religious discussion. "Ah," one answered, "I've got you now! It was said: 'a little child shall lead them.'"

"Where?" asked the other.

"To Peace and Love and Righteousness. He also said: 'These things have been hidden from the wise and prudent and has been revealed unto babes.'"

"A little child shall lead them," the other repeated reflectively. And Virginia, whose thoughts had been interrupted by the stopping of the car and who had listened somewhat detachedly to the discussion, caught the words: "A little child shall lead them!" She turned and looked down at her boy who had quietly curled himself up in the corner of the seat and was almost asleep. An angelic smile suffused his countenance, and the wind blowing through the open window recklessly blew the ringlets from his brow.

"A little child shall lead them," she whispered. Her thoughts flew back to the lonely man she had left behind in his New York library awaiting death. Whatever, or whoever he was, he was her husband whom she swore to love and honour, if not to obey. Was it his fault she reflected, as he had inferred, that he had revenged himself on her because she was what she was? That was not her fault either. Then she thought she recalled his statement that he had seen his white father murder his mother. "How horrible!" she thought, was it surprising that he thirsted for revenge? Had she treated him fairly? After all, was he not the father of her child—the beautiful boy who now lay fast asleep unconscious of the tragedy that impended? "My God!" she cried almost aloud. "I may be too late." The chauffeur re-entered the car. "Return to New York as quickly as you can!" she exclaimed breathlessly. "New York, New York,!" She repeated almost frantically as he hesitated. "Hurry, hurry!"

The car was turned. There was anxiety, terror in her eyes. What if she should be too late? The car seemed to crawl although the speedometer was registering seventy-five miles an hour. The car speeded on! A Traffic Cop was passed. He stepped on the gas and gave chase. After they had covered a mile or so he drew up alongside, but the chauffeur did not slow down. "What's the new racket?" he asked breathlessly, holding on to the car as they both sped onward. "Please, please, officer! A case of life and death! The policeman turned his head and caught that look of terror in her eyes. He knew her.

"A doctor?" he asked. She nodded her head. He grunted, "Why didn't ye say so" and, releasing the car, slowed down, turned around, and rode back to the nearest booth, phoning in to look out for Smithson's car and give it right-of-way.

On, on, they sped. The road was clear until they reached Williamsburg Bridge. The car was jammed in the traffic. Virginia, who by this time had completely lost her accustomed poise, cried to the driver: "Can't you get through? Do, please, hurry!" she pleaded. The man looked back in surprise.

Could this be haughty Virginia Smithson? "I'll get through, madam," he answered apologetically. "The traffic is a bit tough about here—I'll get through." He manouvered for an opening and shot through, turning off the end of the bridge on three wheels to the amazement of a traffic policeman who stood speechless as the car disappeared in a cloud of dust. Virginia wrung her hands in agony as the car sped on. She prayed as she had never prayed before. It was barely two hours since her departure from New York, yet it seemed an eternity to her. Would she be in time was the thought that now obsessed her. At length, the car drew up before the door followed by two traffic policemen. The chauffeur sprang from his seat and opened the door almost before the car had stopped. Virginia seized her child and hurried up the steps. Sentinel was barking furiously as she rushed into the hall, depositing her sleeping child in the arms of the butler who had opened the door. Sentinel, still barking, hurried before her to the sun parlor. She sensed danger and followed. Opening the door quickly she heard the shots. She opened her bag, drew the revolver, and fired at random.

The assailants scampered off in the gathering darkness leaving a trail of blood on the garden path. The household was aroused. The frantic servants dashed about the house hysterically. The handyman rushed from the basement, shovel in hand, followed by the stately English butler who, although trembling at the knees, could not shed his studied dignity. This worthy was armed with a lady's umbrella seized from the hall stand in a moment of determined daring and doubtful bravery. The handyman hastily led the timorous servants to the garden in time to see two intruders escape over the garden wall, disappearing in the darkness. In the meantime Virginia, arriving in the library, where she observed her husband writhing on the floor, completely divested herself of her accustomed dignity, and falling upon her knees beside his prostrate form, cried out in anguish: "My dear! My dear! Are you badly hurt?" as she fell fainting across the body of her husband.

Number Three, who had by this recovered his senses, sprang to his feet and turning towards the door encountered the hesitant valet who stood irresolute in the doorway. "Don't you see your master is wounded?" he asked. "Call up the nearest Doctor!" The valent hurried to the telephone and the servants crowded about the passage. Number Three stepped out and called the butler whom he requested to send in Virginia's personal maid. He then turned and administered a dose of whisky and water to the mistress of the house, which gradually revived her. Number Three then lifted the inert woman and deposited her on a couch. The maid hurried in with smelling salts and pleaded with Virginia to go to her room. Although distraught by the day's events, she refused to leave the library until the arrival of the Doctor. Meanwhile, her tired eyes exuded tears. Number Three shrugged his shoulders helplessly and quickly effaced himself, leaving Virginia to the ministrations of her maid. "Did they call the Doctor?" Virginia asked weakly.

"Yes, madam."

Drying her tears, Virginia pulled herself together, slowly resuming her accustomed poise. On attempting to review the happenings of the day, her thoughts were suddenly arrested by the voices of the servants in the passage.

"What is the meaning of the uproar?" she asked a shade of her former hauteur in her tones.

"The servants have been upset by the shooting," replied the maid.

"Upset by the shooting? What shooting—did anyone get shot?—the servants, I mean?"

"No, madam."

"Why the excitement, then? Order them back to their duties at once!"

"Yes, madam." The maid departed on her errand. After a few moments, the valet knocked and entered followed by the Doctor.

"The Doctor, madam," announced the valet.

Virginia rose quickly to her feet. "So glad you came so promptly, Doctor." She was very pale and the strained expression of her face mirrored the pent-up agony of her soul. The Doctor eyed her critically. "You are not well, Mrs Smithson. Where is the patient?"

"Here," she answered pointing to Smithson on the floor. "I thought it unwise to move him until you came."

"That was quite right," he replied, as he bent over Smithson and began a hasty examination. As the Doctor turned him over he emitted an agonized groan.

"Tell me, Doctor, is he badly hurt?"

"I fear he is—cannot say with certainty." Then to the valet, "call up Belle-View!—an ambulance—quick!" The valet hurried away. The maid re-entered as Virginia fainted and quickly caught her ere she fell.

"Better get her to her room," the Doctor advised. "This is no place for her. Get some man to help—the butler."

"She would not go, Doctor."

They laid her on the couch. The maid departed for help and the Doctor proceeded to administer a restorative. She opened her eyes wanly at the Doctor.

"You must not remain here," he admonished. "I cannot have you both ill upon my hands." The Doctor removed his coat. The maid returned with the butler.

"Take her feet! Turn yourself around man! You can't see behind you. I'll take her head." Then to the maid. "Hurry on and have her bed ready! Tell the valet as you go, to call the hospital for a nurse."

The maid hurried away and the two men bore Virginia off. As they passed out of the door she shrieked: "My boy, My, boy! My darling boy! Don't take my husband away, don't take him away!"

Smithson heard her shrieks and tried to rise. He, somehow, managed to lift himself on his elbows and fell back with a groan, lapsing once more into unconsciousness. The ambulance arrived. The valet re-entered. The Doctor hurried in accompanied by the ambulance surgeon and a nurse.

"Not a moment to be lost," the Doctor said. "Stretcher ready?" The attendants brought the stretcher in and quickly removed the wounded man. Before departing the Doctor took the valet aside. "I'll return in an hour or two. Should anything serious transpire," he pointed upward, "call me up at the hospital. I'll hurry back as soon as I can, in any case."

"Very serious with Mr Smithson?" enquired the valet gloomily.

"Don't know just yet, you'll have some news shortly. Cheer up! Keep near the phone." He slapped the valet encouragingly on the back and bustled out to the ambulance.

Up in Virginia's room, the nurse had arrived and was installed at the bedside. In the next room, the boy was crying for his mother and would not be comforted. Virginia had been overcome by the shock and strain which had been so suddenly thrust upon her. In her delirium, she pleaded for her boy and these pleas were blended with agonized demands that her husband should be saved. A love that lay secreted in her inmost soul, hidden from herself and all who knew her, was at length revealed in these frequent periods of delirium. The Doctor returned from the hospital to report that Smithson, who had been operated upon, was in grave danger. A bullet had passed through the chest just above the heart and—well, he possessed a strong constitution. That represented his only chance of survival. But Smithson always had luck, they said. Even a large dose of gas in the World War, which had wrecked the lives of other stronger men, had left him scatheless. He had started as a poor unknown boy in Modern Babylon, reaching the pinnacle of financial success at thirty-eight. He had captured the reigning Beauty of her time with a pedigree reaching back to the Plantagenet Kings of England, out-distancing all rivals in the race. The proverbial Smithson luck should pull him through they said—but, the Doctor, finding it difficult to cure a mind diseased, tried every known expedient on Virginia. At length, he assented to the importunities of the nurse and had the boy brought in. The child who cried all night was only stilled when placed by his mother's side. He was soothed by her loving though unconscious touch. The nurse was right, in a moment of returning consciousness she saw and recognized the boy beside her. She smiled sadly. "My darling, my darling," she whispered, gently drawing him to her breast. He cooed "Mother Dear," nestling closely to her. And mother and child passed gently into a soothing dreamless sleep.

CHAPTER XIX.

As Number Three had reported, Napoleon Bonaparte Hatbry had been arrested on a charge of treason against the United States and thrown into jail there to await trial. His protesting followers had rioted and were shot down in hundreds, and their ringleaders were cast into prison where they languished like their leader, without bail, inasmuch as they were considered dangerous to be at large.

Hatbry's clothing factory, like his laundry and printery, had gone up in smoke with the half million Smithson had supplied. But notwithstanding his many failures, he possessed such a magnetic hold upon his followers that they regarded him as a martyr who had been sacrificed to the cause of Negro uplift which had for its ultimate objective the creation of an Independent African State where Negroes the world over would be permitted to enjoy that freedom which was denied them under Nordic domination. Carried away by his eloquence, his followers failed to realize that his alluring dream could not be effectively accomplished without the cooperation of the very Nordics he had unremittingly vilified. The Emperor, who was using every means at his command to create an all-white State, was not unmindful of the value of Hatbry's propaganda in the fulfilment of his own pet theories. He, however, refused to believe that the Negroes, because of Hatbry's anti-white agitation, would not get out of control, and in those Southern States where they were in the majority, they might conceivably exterminate the whites before the latter had fully mastered the situation. Hence, his policy of Negro eviction from their farms, or complete extermination where they resisted was intended as an intimidating agency to demonstrate Nordic superiority and power, thereby proving the futility of Negro pretensions. Smithson being deposed, Algernon Hillyarde was appointed to take his place as the second member of the Triumvirate. The Colonel knew that the Hillyarde's name would have considerable influence in the American Southland, where the old families were still held in high esteem. He was also mindful of Algernon's dissolute habits, and that so long as adequate funds were supplied him, he would be a willing instrument in the hands of the Invisible State. Furthermore, his dash and daring coupled with his notorious distaste for the Negroes, made him a highly valuable Lieutenant. The fact that he despised Smithson while accepting his hospitality and his loans, was also known to the Emperor. He had also observed that Virginia was not particularly enthusiastic about her husband. It therefore followed that the Ruler of the Invisible State had a two-fold reason for elevating Smithson's brother-in-law to a position second only to himself.

When, therefore, Smithson's removal was ordered, Hillyarde had been selected to supply the means and method of his taking-off. The Colonel counted upon Hillyarde's cupidity as well as his contempt for his sister's husband to bring his plot to a successful consummation, inasmuch as Virginia would succeed to her husband's wealth, and through her, Algernon would be liberally supplied with those funds that were so necessary to his life of debauchery.

Now, therefore, that Smithson was reported to be at the point of death, Hillyarde called to offer his hypocritical condolences to his sister. He had absented himself from the home of his brother-in-law for several months because his sister had forbidden him the house until he had liquidated some of his financial obligations to her husband. Now that Smithson was well out of the way, he believed himself capable of convincing Virginia that he had paid off some of his loans to her husband. She had always loved her only brother, although she knew him to be a ne'er-do-well; but he was her brother. He did not know of her illness, nor did he know that Smithson had divulged the plot of the Emperor against his life, and that she had not only caused a watch to be placed about his hospital room to prevent further mischief but, for upward of a week, sick as she was, she had also sat by his bedside as an additional protection. She had also caused bulletins to be published daily, which indicated Smithson's early demise, although his private physician whom she had taken into her confidence and to whom she had communicated her fears had informed her that the crisis had passed and that Smithson would recover. Hillyarde had read the discouraging bulletins with inward satisfaction and he and the Colonel, having gloated over the prospect of Smithson's speedy departure, it was with an air of nonchalance that he rang the doorbell and was admitted to the presence of his sister.

"So you have come at last?" she asked, after indulging in an affectionate embrace.

"Yes," he replied. "I have been rather busy with our friend, the Colonel. Too bad about Smithson; you'll be glad to be rid of him, I guess."

CHAPTER XX.

"Why glad?"

"You know quite well, Sis, that he didn't quite measure up to your—our—standard—did he?" He tickled her under the chin, which was a little affectation of his when he wanted her to confer a favour of some kind. She knew this quite well and his mention of Colonel coupled with his disparaging standards of social comparisons placed her on her guard.

"So, you are in the Colonel's confidence?" she asked innocently, as she sat beside him.

"Oh, yes," he replied boastfully. "I've got Smithson's place. He got what was coming to him by giving us away to the niggers."

She winced a bit at the term niggers, answering lamely: "I suppose he did."

"Pity you had that brat by him—"

"Brat!" she was in the act of voicing a few unpleasant truths but restraining herself with an effort, she smiled sweetly and continued, "Oh yes, you mean the boy. Pity isn't it?"

"Damn, pity, to mix the Hillyarde blood with a colossal Unknown!"

"Not to mention the Plantagenet blood," she smiled cryptically. He glanced up at her, but her lids were half closed and the smile was disarming.

"And the Plantagenet blood," he said reflectively. "I could kill the brat to remove the taint—"

"You could do what?"

"If it were not yours, Sis."

"That does make a difference." Suddenly the thought took possession of her. Could it be that Algernon, her own brother, had a hand in the attempted assassination of her husband? "Well," she ventured, "he'll soon be out of the way."

"Who, the brat or Smithson?"

"Smithson, of course. Who else should I mean?"

"I hope he will be, or—"

"Or what?"

"Oh, he'll have to be removed somehow; but he can't recover—he must not! You are still young! What a grand thing it will be with the wealth you'd have at your disposal to go to Europe and marry in your—our—class!" He jumped to his feet and paced the room. "Yes, yes, it would be grand! We could do the Grand Tour together—"

"On the wealth of the man you claim to despise! Why did you come here Algernon?" Rising to her feet she stood before him looking him straight between the eyes. "Do the grand tour—the two of us on the gold of a murdered man! I despise you, my brother—you who boast the blood of the ,Plantagenets! This man whose death you seek is my husband, whom I swore to love at the altar. And you, a parasite, who was not ashamed to borrow from this man—"

"A parasite!" he interrupted passionately.

"Yes, I said a parasite!—he, at least, made good by his own unaided effort. What have you done, with all your boasted Plantagenet blood? Borrowed to gamble—gambling with other people's money, which you never repaid! A life of questionable ease at the expense of others! You say you could kill my child!—My child! The child of your only sister who has stood by you, believing there was some good somewhere in your contemptible body. You are nothing but a common thief and murderer at heart; if you have not been guilty of murder! I half suspect you had some hand in the attempt upon my husband's life!—you and your precious Colonel! Go tell him I've taken his measure, even as I have taken yours—my brother! You think to spend his wealth? I'll see to that. If there is any spending, I can attend to that alone. I have perhaps failed to appreciate my husband as fully as I should, but I'll have you understand that while he lives he is still my husband! I despise and pity you, Algernon; you have dared to enter a dying man's home to traduce his wife!" She moved to the door and opened it. "Algernon Hillyarde, your presence pollutes this house. Go! I never wish to see your face again—Go! or I'll call my servants to throw you out!"

"Sis!"

"Go! I'm no sister of yours. Go!" She held the door open and Algernon, stepping across the threshold, turned, and hissed: "You defy me, do you?—You threaten? I'll take care that your damn adventurer-husband shall awake in hell before the dawn."

"We shall see," she cried, as she banged the street door after him.

Meanwhile, Doctor Detritcher who had now become a full-fledged Senator had taken his seat and entered the fray in support of the Constitution with particular reference to the Thirteenth, Fourteenth, and Fifteenth

Amendments. In his maiden speech, he forcefully attacked the un-American activities of the Invisible State and sponsored a Resolution for the impeachment of that organization and the prosecution of its Leader for High Treason against the United States. He pointed out that if Hatbry could be jailed without being allowed bail because he rose in defense of his people whose rights were not respected under the Constitution and had plotted with a foreign power to enable him to secure those rights, an organization whose avowed purpose and whose chief object for existence was intended to create a State within a State, which would be more powerful than the State itself, because of its secret agitation against honourable citizens of the State by underground methods, wherein all men were guaranteed equal liberty and the pursuit of happiness, where, and by whom, the inalienable rights and liberties of Citizens were suppressed, and where resistance was attempted, these Citizens were ruthlessly murdered, and their properties destroyed. Such a condition of lawlessness, prejudice, and intimidation, should not be allowed to go unpunished. If it were, the Constitution would become a noxious sham, lawlessness would supplant order, and the United States would become the sport and byword of the civilised world. He further pointed out that Japan had ever been a friendly nation, even when greatly provoked by our ill-advised immigration bar, that, that friendly nation, from unconfirmed reports had now become our secret enemy. The Soviet government, while debarred diplomatic representation, had seized upon the occasion of internal disorder to ferment agitation within our borders, because a section of our press by its sensational criticism had unwisely provoked reprisals which might result in far-reaching consequences of a disastrous nature.

The Doctor's speech was charged with the righteous fire of indignation, and his peroration contained the warning that the War debts had already fomented enmity abroad and our tinkering tariffs having also done incalculable harm to our foreign trade, would ultimately lead to our commercial isolation. "For", said he in conclusion; "from a Debtor Nation we have become a Creditor Nation; we have failed to accept our prowess with becoming modesty: we have become intoxicated with our new-found wealth—a wealth which was acquired in blood and tears, the blood of those millions who now lie beneath the crosses that mark their honoured graves, blacks and whites, rich and poor, in the bivouac of the dead; and the tears of the widows and orphans of those who patriotically went forth to make a "world safe for democracy" and of those maimed unfortunates who yet survive, eking out a miserable existence: living, yet dead to us! Marking a halting time until the Grim Reaper shall make his final call. Through these have come our newfound wealth and pride, which God grant, may not prove to be our ruin!" The Doctor's Resolution was lost. The Invisible State was too strongly entrenched. But there were those, however, who heard that speech and, touched by the Doctor's sincerity of purpose, knew that the first gun had belched forth its devastating fire in the war against prejudice and intolerance.

CHAPTER XXI.

The press had barely reported Doctor Detritcher's Senatorial broadside against the Invisible State when Smithson's secretary, believing the bulletins issued from the hospital, felt that the moment had arrived to launch the exposé she had been commissioned by Smithson to forward to the press in the event of his absence or death. This secretary was a very prime person of precise habits and a decided leaning towards the dramatic, who always followed the advice of her employers to the letter. And, fearing that she might delay the matter too long which would result in an anti-climax, she decided to act without further delay in view of the fact that the Senator-Doctor had unexpectedly found himself on the front page of the morning papers. Feeling that he had usurped the place which indubitably belonged to her employer, she rushed to the office, called a messenger, and sent him post haste to the New York papers with Smithson's statement which had been typed by her and carefully sealed in their respective envelopes. If Doctor Detritcher's speech in the Senate had caused a sensation, the publication of Smithson's inside information, regarding the Emperor and his organization, was reputed to be a riot. Every detail of importance was reported with the names of the leading conspirators, his own connection with the Invisible State, together with the information with which he had supplied Hatbry. No single item of moment was withheld, and the individual papers, not to be outdone by each other, published the report in full. The Departments of State, honeycombed as they were by the minions of the Emperor, stood revealed in all the nakedness of their double-dealing. The less sensational section of the press which possessed no Invisible State leanings was warm in their praise of Smithson's manly stand, pointing out that the ex-member of the Triumvirate, speaking as he did with authority, had abundantly substantiated Doctor Detritcher's accusations.

Thus, the country was divided into two camps, those who defended the Nordic supremacy idea, and the others who contended that an organization which tended to divide a Nation by secret means should be immediately suppressed. While the nation was disturbed by Smithson's revelations, rumours were filtering through that Japan was making additional active war preparations.

Speculation was rife as to the real cause of Japan's activities and her ultimate objective. There were those who claimed to have the necessary knowledge, but if they did, they were as uncommunicative as the Sphinx. Meanwhile, Attorney Browne, by reason of the secret information at his disposal, secured a body of fifty University men, formed them into a prospective flying corps, and slipped off to Tulsa, Oklahoma, where a rich member of his race had bought a plane, taught himself to fly, and constructed a flying field of his own. The owner of the field supplied six planes at his own expense, teaching the young men such knowledge of flying as he had acquired and an experienced pilot and navigator who had seen service in the late War, was engaged to complete that technical instruction which the Oklahoman lacked. Quickly the news of the coloured aeroplane corps was broadcasted by the Negro press and applications for inclusion in the corps poured in from all parts of the United States. In less than two months some three hundred young men had passed through a rigid and intensive training proving themselves as efficient as any pilots in America. The Negro press, because of the novelty of the experiment, without an inner knowledge of Browne's objective, successfully solicited subscriptions to purchase a full complement of machines, and Browne, in order to allay the growing jealousy and alarm of the Southern whites introduced a passenger service between North and South "For Coloured" people, and the drone of the ALL BLACK planes were heard throughout the land rhythmically proclaiming a symphony of praise to the rising tide of Negro enterprise. In the meantime, the Emperor became alarmed at what he termed "a new phase of nigger arrogance." At first, when the news filtered through that the Negroes were attempting to fly, he regarded their effort in the light of a sensational joke, but when he heard that they were actually flying and had engaged a white pilot to complete their instruction, he began to fear that they might assist the unemployed Negro rioters or take reprisals from the air on his lynching parties.

If the Emperor possessed his spies, the Negro Protective League was equally vigilant. There were still Negroes engaged in domestic employment, many of them in the service of members of the Invisible State. And they, for the most part, were directly or indirectly affiliated with the League or some allied organization. Hence, these Negro employees were enabled to gather stray bits of information dropped from time to time by their employers. Always pursuing the line of least resistance in their contact with the dominant group, their "yes Colonel" or "yes sir, boss," successfully deluded their white contacts into a confirmed belief in Negro unsophistication. Moreover, the white women, some from a sense of ethical values and others from pride of race coupled with the reputed loquaciousness of their sex, supplied highly valuable information at odd moments which was promptly reported to the League. Letters lying about carelessly, and partially destroyed correspondence consigned to wastepaper baskets, yielded their quota of illuminating data. There was also a group of near-whites, like Smithson and Ette, who had been pressed into the service of the League to mix with the Nordics in social and public gatherings where highly valuable information matter could be collected. Under Browne's advice, a thoroughly comprehensive system of espionage had been introduced with Ette installed Chief of the clearing-house Bureau. It therefore followed that the League was more familiar with the moves of the Emperor than he was with the intentions of the Negroes. The latter procured their information firsthand, from within. The Colonel secured his second hand from without, even his venal Negro spies did not always supply him with accurate information. Hence, his alarm at the progress of the ALL BLACK AIR LINE, and the methods he intended to adopt to smash the enterprise were known to the Negro League before he could put his plans into execution. They, therefore, sent Ette post-haste to Washington to see Doctor Detritcher, with the object of enlisting his support in approaching the Government to obtain the desired permission to legally operate their airline. The Doctor stepped into the breach with his accustomed enthusiasm, and in twenty-four hours the necessary powers were granted, to the great chagrin of the Emperor who arrived in Washington for obstructive purposes twelve hours late. To add to the Colonel's discomfiture and annoyance, the information was brought him that Smithson was not only convalescent but had recently passed through Washington, with his wife in attendance, on his way to Hillyarde's Country seat at Culpeper County, Virginia. Smithson's recovery represented a greater and more pressing danger to the Colonel's plans than a corps of Negro flyers. The latter, he felt, could be easily exterminated directly and[10] he could spare the time to give that matter his undivided attention. The Smithson affair, however, presented a question of extreme gravity requiring his immediate action. Why had this man been permitted to live in order to be a perpetual thorn in his side? Why had his minions permitted themselves to be deluded

---

10   The editors have inserted the conjunction "and" here based on grammatical and contextual clues.

by false bulletins, allowing the enemy he held in his grasp to escape to that County in Virginia, where, like the English Barons under the feudal system, the Hillyardes ruled for three hundred years, and where, even in these democratic days, there was but one man who could encompass the death of the culprit in the Hillyarde stronghold. Truly, Virginia Smithson who had been apparently a willing disciple, outmaneouvered him. Had beaten him at his own game successfully setting her wit against his, and that exposure in the press had almost ruined everything. Such were the Emperor's unpleasant reflections as he sat alone in his hotel room overlooking Pennsylvania Avenue. "Damn these women!" he exclaimed, rising from his chair.

"My sentiments exactly," agreed Algernon Hillyarde, as he sauntered in unannounced.

"The very man I want to see! How the devil did you let Smithson slip through your fingers? You told me he only needed an undertaker!"

"That's O. K. Virginia wrecked all our plans—damn her!"

"You must have bungled, some."

"I guessed I counted too much on her dislike for Smithson. The hussy laid a trap for me but I'll get even—I'll get even!"

"Don't be too sure young man. Virginia has brains. Do you know she has escaped to Virginia with Smithson?"

"Yes, I just heard it," was Algernon's petulant answer.

"What are you going to do about it?"

"Don't quite know—I guess I'll have to go to Culpeper! Damn thing is, I've had so many love affairs in that quarter, I'm hated, whereas Virginia is loved and obeyed without question by the whole County."

"Well," drawled the Colonel, "you've made a damn mess of the first important commission I entrusted you with. Damn brilliant member of the Triumvirate, you are, and no mistake."

"What in hell do you mean Colonel? And who in hell are you to dare to speak to a Hillyarde like that?"

"I'll speak to a Hillyarde or hillbilly, as and how I damn well please! don't you know I'm your master?"

"Master be damned! Since when has a Georgia cracker become the master of a Virginian Hillyarde, tell me that? You may lord it over the pack of asses who believe in your bogus pretensions, but you're rather a bad guesser if you think you can bully me or lead me around by the nose!"

The Colonel became livid with passion and that passion was so overwhelming that he was bereft of speech. Hillyarde glared at him contemptuously, took a seat, crossed his legs, and nonchalantly stuck a cigarette in the corner of his mouth and lit it.

"Who in the hell do you think you are?" the Emperor asked lamely as he faced Hillyarde.

"Are you deaf?" was the rejoinder, as he blew a cloud of smoke in the Colonel's face.

"I'm damned!" exclaimed the irate Emperor, as he turned and paced the room. The Colonel paused and turning stood once more over Hillyarde.

"You dirty little rat!" he began venomously. "Don't you know I can have you killed—that I have only to raise my finger to have you removed from my path? Even as I have made you what you are, I can destroy you!"

"Any more jokes?" Hillyarde lit another cigarette. "See here, Colonel, let's stop this fool talk. You know you can't afford to remove me. You've got your graveyard pretty full—there isn't much room left for me: besides, what'd you do without the dirty little rat? By the way, I'll make you eat that remark some day. Let's get down to brass tacks, you want Smithson removed—the term is yours—sounds better than murdered. You hate Smithson because he gave you a dirty deal. I hate him because he has been so damned successful, even to the extent of turning my sister against me, while I have been a complete failure. Had I not been, I would not have mixed myself up in your dirty business—"

"Dirty business?"

"Stop a minute! I haven't finished yet. You can bleat when I'm done if you have anything worthwhile to say. The fools you run have let you run away with them. The only man outside myself, who told you a thing or two was Smithson. You might as well face the facts. You'll never recover from that black eye he gave you in the press. You see, you're not as smart as you think you are. Do you mind sitting down Colonel? You'll digest what I have to say in a greater comfort, that way." Reluctantly, the Colonel sat down.

"That's real nice of you," Hillyarde commented, "now that you are comfortable, I'll proceed with my little story."

"You're wasting valuable time," the Emperor heatedly rejoined.

"I know time is slipping for you, Colonel, but I have lots of it to burn. Please keep still and don't interrupt. What was I saying? O, yes—that black eye in the press; well, the number's up, Colonel. I'll get Smithson somehow, but you'd better find another job—we both have to do that thing. Detritcher is in the Senate. Elections are pending all over the country, and they won't be in favor of the Invisible State. Many of your friends in Congress and the Senate are selling out—lost cause, Colonel! Ship sinking; everybody worth

—while is taking to the boats. The majority of your friends must face about or trim, if they want to be re-elected. Their wives and daughters will see to that—Washington Society is more alluring for the wives and daughters of back-woods legislators, than the mouldy society back home. You know that, Colonel. That was a great speech the Doctor made—you must admit that."

"I don't agree."

"I don't suppose you do. He hit right from the shoulder. None of your clap-trap stuff—the Constitution was his line. It's a great line, Colonel. You're older than I am, and should know that our people worship the Constitution first and God afterwards—maybe. Well, the Doctor got us licked there, and Smithson's wallop coming on the top of that was a clean-cut knock-out. We're counted out, Colonel. On the top of all this—you haven't been to head-quarters lately?—telegrams and Special Deliveries and Air Mails containing resignations from the monied groups have been pouring in during the past few days—there's a perfect monument of them to your greatness! They're all taking cover, Colonel. Take a fool's advice and quit while quitting is good and healthy."

During Hillyarde's recital, the Colonel's naturally pale face became ashen. The beads of perspiration stood out on his forehead like a dew-covered lawn. Too late, he realized his grave error in crossing swords with Smithson, whose powers he had foolishly underrated. What was to be done? He hated to admit the correctness of Hillyarde's deductions, yet what could he do?

"I cannot desert my loyal friends," he said with calmness. "While one remains true to the cause, we must keep the flag flying." He rose from his seat. "Algernon Hillyarde, here we part company. I was damn rude to you; I'm sorry." His cloak was resting on the chair. He took it up and wrapped it about him and pulling his black slouched hat over his eyes, departed without uttering another word. Hillyarde watched his every movement, an amused smile on his debauched countenance. "Well," he reflected, rising to his feet, "that's that!" Thrusting his hands in his pockets, he drew forth and counted his remaining wealth. "Fifty-two dollars and seventy cents! Not much for a new start in life. Well, I hear the Soviets and Japanese are casting wealth about. I think they can be persuaded to part with some. And, lighting another cigarette, he set his hat jauntily on his head at a rakish angle and went forth into the night.

CHAPTER XXII.

When Hillyarde left the hotel, he leisurely strolled down Pennsylvania Avenue somewhat unsettled as to his future movements. The limited wealth at his disposal was insufficient to do any worthwhile thing. He could not take a distant journey from the Capital because wherever he landed his available cash would almost be exhausted in travelling expenses. His luxurious habits made it impossible for him to travel any other way than in a Pullman where he occupied a drawing room, to occupy an upper or lower berth being quite beneath his dignity. Then the porters who knew him in view of his well-known liberality always expected handsome tips which the present state of his finances would not allow. He could not think of lowering his accustomed prestige, thereby causing the Negro porters to guess the true condition of his exchequer. He knew those porters! On many occasions, they had gossiped with him about some unfortunate "regular" who had conveniently forgotten to donate to his customary largesse and had reduced his previous liberality to an all-but-vanishing quantity. Travel for the time being was, therefore, out of the question. Several friends passed him on the Avenue. Some saluted him as they went on their way; others engaged in thinking out their own affairs hurried by without speaking. Ordinarily, such minor happenings would have passed unnoticed. But, in his then condition of mind, he believed that his friends avoided him because they either knew or sensed his unfortunate plight. He was about to pass a well-known hostelry where he had spent many a gay evening when an acquaintance came up from behind and slapped him on the back. He turned and was greeted cordially, and the warm greeting instantly revived his drooping spirits.

"Well, well, Algy! I haven't seen you for ages. Where have you been keeping yourself?"

"O, Bobby, old top; I've been wandering up and down in the earth—"

"Like the devil seeking whom you might devour—especially the girls!" They both laughed as they halted outside the restaurant.

"What say?—some east?" was Bobby's next remark, "just arrived in Washington—hungry as a hunter! Had dinner?"

"No, hadn't thought much about it, lunched late on the train."

"Oh, I guess you can manage something light, not to mention some of that pre-Volstead, within," indicating the restaurant with his thumb.

"Lower your voice", admonished Hillyarde. "Tell it not in Gath! Guess, I will have some of the vintage you mention."

They entered the restaurant arm-in-arm. Both being frequent guests and notorious spenders, they were ushered to a table which although secluded, enabled Bobby to obtain a good view of all who entered, Hillyarde's back being toward the entrance. They indulged in the usual petty gossip of their kind until dinner was served and the liquor began its merry round, when tongues were loosened, and jokes regarding amorous experiences were exchanged without stint. Gradually the room filled with many friends and acquaintances of the two jolly diners from whom they received bows and smiles of recognition. The Orchestra opened up and as though tuned to the occasion, a small Japanese wearing a flaming carnation entered to the strains of the "Star-Spangled Banner" and was obsequiously ushered to the table next to that at which Algernon and his friend were seated.

"How matters going with you?" enquired Bobby.

"Not as well as I look like," Hillyarde answered with a laugh. "Just had a damned unpleasant row with my people because I wanted some cash. Been spending rather recklessly of late—you know how it is?—white lights, red lips, and the rest of it! Don't let's talk about it."

"So sorry, old top, I've had some of the same medicine. I've managed pretty well lately without my people—shown them, I could get along without their damn help."

"Got yourself a job?"

"Yes, guess you could do the same if you've got guts."

"Tell me!" Bobby leaned over and whispered in Hillyarde's ear.

"I'm on, if you can fix me up," rejoined Hillyarde.

The Japanese who overheard the dialogue, raised his glass to his lips and in doing so looked steadily at Bobby, pointed his forefinger of the hand that held the glass meaningly at Hillyarde's back, which was turned to him. Bobby nodded quickly as though in recognition of a toast and lifted his glass.

"Your health!" he said aloud. Hillyarde turned and looked covertly at the Japanese, then filled his glass. "I suppose I'm in this?" he asked.

"O, surely!" Bobby exclaimed. They clinked their glasses.

"Happy days!" cried Hillyarde.

"Happy days!" echoed Bobby, as they emptied their glasses.

The music, general laughter, and buzz of conversation flowed on to the joy-inspiring accompaniment of ambulant hip-flasks and clinking glasses as the night wore on. Some of the groups moved on to dances or other social engagements, their places being quickly occupied by a few arrivals from the theaters. Doctor Detritcher arrived with a party which included three former partisan Senators of the Emperor's, who had thrown over the Invisible State and joined themselves to the Doctor. As Hillyarde had told the Colonel, these men's wives and daughters wanted to return to Washington, and they were forced to seek re-election according to the trend of the times and the insistent demands of their female connections. The Doctor was the life of the party. The backwoods legislators, as they were named by Hillyarde, did their best to be comfortable, at home, and well-behaved, and failed dismally. The Japanese gentleman eyed them with curiosity, wearing that static Nipponese smile which expressed pleasure or contempt, according to the concept of the beholder.

A man of commanding figure and obvious Muscovite origin entered and was escorted to a seat at the extreme end of the room. He was immaculately dressed, sported a monocle and a beard which was parted in the very centre of the chin with painful precision. The Russian ordered his meal and while awaiting service adjusted his monocle and looked the company over. Finally, his eye rested on the Japanese who had also been a quiet observer of the proceedings. As their eyes met, the Russian smiled and the Japanese raised his glass by way of recognition, subsequently turning his attention to Hillyarde's back and Bobby's inconsequent chatter. A male member of Doctor Detritcher's party excused himself and left the restaurant. Immediately upon his departure the Japanese scribbled a few words on a leaf of his notebook, called the waiter, and requested him to deliver it into the hands of the Russian. He then examined his bill, took out his wallet, and unobtrusively extracted three notes, two of five hundred dollars each and one of twenty. The latter he placed on the table beside his bill, carefully folding the two five-hundred-dollar notes under his serviette, placed them on his knee. Then, once more taking his notebook he wrote again, extracted the page in which he enveloped the two notes. The entire operation being deftly accomplished with speed and dexterity under cover of that cryptic smile. The waiter returned and, with a nod, the Japanese indicated the twenty dollar note and his bill.

"Will his Excellency have something more?" the waiter asked, as he removed the small metal tray on which the money rested. The Japanese shook his head negatively and the waiter departed. He then stood up, crossed to Bobby's table, bent low, and shook Bobby by the hand, leaving the folded note in the young man's palm; he was then introduced to Hillyarde. The waiter rushed up with his hat and the man from Japan bowed himself out of the restaurant with that ineffaceable smile and hesitant deportment, which suggested an apology for leaving such honourable company. As he passed out into Pennsylvania Avenue and gained the shadows, he removed the red carnation from his coat substituting a white rose which he took from an inner pocket. On the opposite side of the Avenue, the diner who had left the Doctor's table stepped out of a dark doorway, leisurely crossed over, and followed the Japanese as he slowly wended his way in the direction of the Capital. The Nipponese had barely departed when Bobby leaned across the table and whispered: "I have some 'spinach' (American dollar bills) for you, and an appointment for tomorrow morning at seven."

"The hell you have!" Hillyarde exclaimed excitedly.

"Sh-h-h! Not so loud," the other whispered, "we must remain here a little longer. I have a date—"

"One girl or two?"

"Two, old top!—blondes, they are!"

"Great Caesar's ghost! You're a benefactor," cried Hillyarde.

"No, just a pal."

"A pal in need is a pal indeed! Let's have some more vintage."

The waiter arrived. A signal was given and he bustled off, returning with a bottle of fluid which certainly possessed greater potency than water. The orchestra closed down and Doctor Detritcher paid his bill and left in conversation with his party. The restaurant was now all but deserted. The Russian, who had consumed several bottles of mineral water and a few dozen cigarettes to kill time, now came to Bobby's table. "I hope I do not intrude," he said in perfect English.

"Not at all," Bobby replied winking at his companion. "Sit down, won't you?" The Muscovite took a seat beside Hillyarde and adjusting his monocle smilingly gazed at Bobby and then at Hillyarde.

"You young gentlemen appear to be hugely enjoying yourselves."

"Well," Bobby replied, "there's nothing else to do. Have a drink?"

"No, thank you. I never drink—or rather, not intoxicants. I should add, not in your glorious country."

"We wish we could exercise your restraint; don't we, Hillyarde? O, I forgot; this is Algernon Hillyarde, and I am Bobby—no, not Jones the Golfer—they always connect us when I say, Bobby! Smythe's my name; spelled with a "y" and a terminal 'e.'" The Russian bowed to each of the young men in turn. "I am honoured. My name is Stylykoff. My card, gentlemen—have a cigarette?" He displayed a huge gold cigarette case of chaste design. "These are genuine Turkish" he said, touching the spring. Hillyarde helped himself and Bobby exclaimed, as he took one from the proffered case. "What a lovely cigarette case! Quite antique too." He examined the case critically and returned it.

"Yes", reflected Stylykoff, "it was one of the late Czar's treasures. Quite a history. A present from one of the Turkish Sultans, when the two countries were friendly."

"Very interesting," commented Hillyarde.

The two expected blondes entered and made a dash for Bobby whom they embraced effusively, leaving rouge on his cheeks and powder on his coat.

The Russian and Hillyarde were introduced to the girls, and after a couple of rounds of doubtful whisky at Stylykoff's expense, he suggested a Cabaret, which was hilariously approved by the girls. There were more drinks, then the four led by the Russian walked rather unsteadily to the pavement amid the laughing banter of the flappers. Upon reaching the sidewalk, the Muscovite hailed a couple of taxis and the gay party hurried away to a barbaric orgy of questionable pleasure.

CHAPTER XXIII.

When the Colonel left Washington, he went direct to the headquarters of the Invisible State. Early next morning he proceeded to examine the alarming communications of which he had been informed by Hillyarde, and to answer them by long-distance phone and telegram. Many of his former adherents, particularly those in the North, either declined to listen to him or referred him to their resignations. His effort in the South were, however, more successful because of the fear and hatred of the Negroes in that quarter. Upon checking up his efforts of that day he found the outlook more encouraging than he had reason to expect from Hillyarde's alarming report. In the circumstances, he felt it incumbent upon him to attempt something spectacular in order to prove to his delinquent followers that he was not only very much alive but that he was also up and doing. He therefore promptly issued orders for a concentrated raid, on the ground and from the air, on the ALL BLACK AIR LINE, and the immediate destruction of their planes and hangers in Oklahoma, Georgia and Louisiana. These orders were barely issued when the Negroes were informed of the Colonel's expected intentions and they at once provided themselves with all the means of protection at their command. When, therefore, their observers saw the gathering storm below and the small groups of strange planes manoeuvering above their landing fields, they unhesitatingly gave battle to the invading aerial forces with the machine guns which they always carried for eventualities. The hired planes of the Invisible State being taken by surprise, were quickly shot down or driven off, and the incendiary parties on foot, who in every case were permitted to invade the property of Negroes before being attacked, upon being sprayed with machine gunfire by the low-flying planes of the ALL BLACK LINE, turned and fled, leaving their dead and wounded behind them. Well knowing that the Emperor and his adherents would use every illegal means to destroy their undertaking, the planes were supplied with cameras. Consequently, upon the dispersal of the enemy, they quickly landed and photographed the demolished planes and their occupants, as well as the fallen invaders in order to establish the fact that they were being attacked by armed aggressors and not by peaceful excursionists. The result of this aerial battle was fraught with far-reaching consequences, both for the Negro and the Invisible State. The Southern press, ignoring the abortive raid pointed to the permission granted to a group of lawless niggers with a smattering of education, to become skilled in the use of the most valuable weapons scientific man had invented for his protection. And further, "to allow these semi-savages to shoot down our unarmed people would not alone provoke reprisals but might conceivably end in a general massacre in the South which the Federal and State Governments should take immediate action to make impossible, and should begin by putting the entire ALL BLACK AIR LINE out of commission."

The Northern press, for the most part, while condemning the action of the Negroes as being likely to add to the prevailing riots resulting from unemployment contended that the pictures in their possession, taken on the spot, amply demonstrated that the intentions of the whites were far from peaceful. But no remedy was suggested. In the Senate, Doctor Detritcher stoutly defended the prompt action of the Negroes in protecting their lives and properties, pointing out that they had every reason to adopt any means at their disposal to protect their rights and liberties inasmuch as they could not rely upon either military or civil authorities to do so. He also produced the photographs with which he had been supplied to prove the aggressive intentions of the raiders. In his manly stand, he was supported by a large majority of his colleagues from the East, West and North, but the Southern Senators solidly opposed his views, creating quite a scene which almost led to a near riot. Congress would have been disturbed in a similar manner, but for the action of a Congressman from Virginia, who took the wind out of the debate by moving a resolution to appoint a special committee composed of both legislative bodies, who would make an immediate investigation on the spot and report their findings as to what action should be taken to avoid like occurrences in the future. Naturally, feelings ran high throughout the country, resulting in minor clashes between black and white, but these never assumed major proportions for very obvious reasons, although the Communists did unsuccessfully endeavour to capitalize on the incident. For the time being the question was allowed to fall into the limbo of forgotten incidents because of more disquieting news from the Pacific which engaged the attention of Government, press and public. The Colonel, finding his plans wrecked by his recklessly abortive efforts, began to take stock of his position.

His Southern adherents had not deserted, but they had become lukewarm and discouraged by the turn recent happenings had taken, and they began to doubt the wisdom of their executive head whom they considered to be out of touch with his followers, and the actual conditions prevailing in the South. On his part, he bitterly complained that his instructions had not been carried out with intelligence, and the Invisible State's defections from the North, where the Emperor had found his chief financial support, were by no means encouraging. His headquarters, heretofore a veritable hive of activity, had now become all but deserted, and the majority of his visitors were mainly critics of his policy. He, therefore, deemed it highly expedient to devise some scheme whereby a dramatic "comeback" could be staged, which would confound his enemies and hearten his friends. Hillyarde had told him to quit, but he was inordinately ambitious and egotistical. That being the case, inasmuch as he had tasted the sweets of dictatorial power, the Colonel determined to go to any length to prove himself right, even to that of joining up with a foreign nation that would advance his mad enterprise. He knew that the Soviet Government as well as the Japanese were unfriendly to his country. One, because it had been previously denied diplomatic representation and had been attacked by the American Press; and the other, because it laboured under a natural grievance, as Doctor Detritcher had declared. An alliance with Japan was out of the question because it was Asiatic and belonged to the darker section of humanity which the Colonel utterly despised. He was not in sympathy with the Soviet form of government, but after all the Russians were a Nordic group, and as long as they helped him to the dictatorship which he craved, he believed himself quite capable of throwing them out should they become too aggressive when he was once master in the United States. Meanwhile, his ex-henchman, Hillyarde, had unconsciously paved the path to his desires. When the group left the Washington restaurant for the cabaret, Stylykoff, who had carefully observed the little comedy between the Japanese, Bobby and Hillyarde, rightly concluded that Hillyarde was in desperate financial straits.[11] When, therefore, they entered the taxicabs the Russian attached himself to Hillyarde by courteously helping the two girls into one of the vehicles with Bobby Smythe, while adroitly steering Hillyarde with him into the other, where they were tête-à-tête for the short journey. The Muscovite having made excellent use of his time while they rode to the rendezvous, the two were inseparable during the

---

11   In the original text, Ali spells this word as "straights," but contextual clues indicate that it should be its homonym "straits."

short period they remained with their companions. And Stylykoff seized the opportunity when the girls, Bobby and his friend they encountered in the cabaret, were engaged in a terpsichorean melee of syncopation to detach Hillyarde from his friends and carry him off to his own hotel apartment.

It will have been concluded from the foregoing that Hillyarde was a man of independent views, and being also possessed of an overweening vanity, he could not see himself playing second fiddle to a chance acquaintance of Bobby Smythe's calibre. He knew the Japanese had given Smythe money which was intended for him, but when that money was given to another to whom he would be placed under an obligation, he regretted the haste with which he had confided his impecuniousness to Bobby. Had the Japanese entered into personal touch, the matter would have assumed an entirely different aspect. Stylykoff, who saw his chance stepped into the breach in so far as it affected Hillyarde, at the opportune moment, making faster time than the slothful Japanese or the ebullient Smythe. Thus, the latter was richer by one thousand dollars and Hillyarde retained both his independence and his freedom of action.

On arriving at the hotel, Stylykoff had coffee and cigarettes served to his guest and as soon as they were alone, without more ado he proceeded to the business in hand. To the intense surprise of Hillyarde he bluntly told him about the money the Japanese intended for him via Bobby; outlined his connection with the Invisible State and his break with the "Emperor," together with his present financial circumstances and his need for immediate funds. Hillyarde who marvelled inwardly at the Russian's fund of information was non-committal and waited. He had not long to wait for Stylykoff was engagingly direct. He quickly and deftly laid his plan before Hillyarde, pointing out that he was prepared to pay handsomely for good and faithful service. His Government urgently needed information as to the number of planes at the disposal of the United States Government that could be put into immediate service. The present preparedness of the American Army and any other useful information he could obtain regarding poison gas, as well as the number and names of bribable legislators who could be depended upon to delay the military activities of the Nation. If Hillyarde could and would procure this information, ten thousand dollars would be at his disposal at once. A half million at the conclusion of his mission. And suiting the action to the word he unlocked the drawer of his dressing table, produced a strong box opened it, and displayed a huge bundle of crisp American gold certificates before the covetous eyes of Hillyarde who extended his trembling hand to the Russian.

"You will accomplish?"

"I will!"

Without another word, Stylykoff counted ten thousand dollars into Hillyarde's shaking palm. Then he said: "Remember! No tricks. The arm of Russia is long. She rewards her friends liberally, but traitors are exterminated without mercy or remorse. I expect you to report in three days. Meanwhile, the ever-wakeful eye of Russia is upon you!"

Hillyarde rose to his feet and took the extended hand of the Russian.

"Have no fear," he said, "what do the legislators get?"

"We will pay five million for a strong group of talkers who can really obstruct."

"Good! My pay will be half a million net—do I understand correctly?"

"You are correct. Half a million for the entire job as outlined by me."

Hillyarde carefully stowed the twenty notes in his breast pocket and taking his hat said: "I report in three days," and turning on his heel he moved to the door which the Russian opened.

"Good morning!" he cried as he stepped out.

"A pleasant day to you!" Stylykoff replied.

The Russian closed the door after Hillyarde and went to his dressing table, returned the strong box to the open drawer, closed and locked it. Then he took a comb and hair brush, brushed his hair, and combed his beard with meticulous care. Completing the performance with a smile of satisfaction, he turned from the dressing table and exclaimed: "And now for the Emperor of the Invisible State!"

CHAPTER XXIV.

On the spacious verandah of the old colonial country Manor House of the Hillyardes Smithson convalescently basked in the health-giving rays of a Southern sun. He was stretched full length among luxurious pillows on a reclining chair: Sentinel lay curled up at his feet, and Virginia sat beside him reading "The Nation's" editorial comment on the recent events connected with the ALL BLACK AIR LINE.

"What do you think of it?" she asked laying down in review.

"I think it a blot on our civilization that a group of black people cannot be permitted to peacefully pursue a legitimate undertaking without undue interference from a pack of envious scoundrels. Only wish I were well enough to get into the fight—"

"On which side?"

"Can you ask such a question? where could Smithson find himself, other than on the side of the weak!"

"All of which is very heroic and quixotic, and all that sort of thing, but does not aid your recovery. On his last visit, the Doctor recommended complete rest and freedom from excitement. I'm afraid I was at fault to read the editorial."

"But you read at my request."

"O, yes, I know, but I could have purposely mislaid the paper."

"It was good of you to read to me; I appreciate it very much." He yawned. "I'm sorry; I'm not tired of your companionship; you've been so good—so good to me, more than I deserve."

"Please do not mention it. I'm your wife, and it is my duty—"

"Duty?" a pained expression flitted across his face."

"Now dear, please take a little rest," she said, rising and shaking up the pillows to make her husband comfortable. "Now, go to sleep like a nice obedient child." After straightening out his dressing gown, she concluded: "There! I think you'll have your morning nap in comfort. I'll go and cut some flowers for you. Keep your eyes and ears open, Sentinel!" The dog wagged his tail, and with a smile she descended the steps to the garden and was soon out of view among the abounding shrubs and towering trees. For a while, Smithson lay thinking of the several incidents connected with the attempt upon his life, trying to piece them together as best as he could. He was unable to understand why the Colonel had not succeeded in finishing him off. He believed himself to be doomed in any event; the Colonel never forgave, and he wondered how he had escaped thus far. His thoughts then passed to Number Three. What had become of him? Had he also been sacrificed, or was it the Emperor's plan that he should be the decoy for the assassins? He was troubled and perplexed. He then thought of Virginia— her devotion to him was inexplicable, especially after the bitter interview that had ensued before the shooting. He remembered that she bent over him after he was shot, and that he next recalled her seated by his bedside in the hospital when he returned to consciousness, and how she afterwards sat with him away into the night. It seemed to him that she was never absent from his side. Could it be that she had become reconciled to her fate as the wife of a "nigger", as she had termed him? Or was it the child who supplied the missing link to this puzzle? Perhaps her pride and her love for the boy had combined to cause her to avoid a scandal. It was all too intricate for his poor brain, helpless as he was. Wearied with thinking, he fell asleep.

Out in the garden, Virginia had wandered aimlessly among the flowers, smelling a rose here and a carnation there, until she came to a bed of lilies standing up against the heated onslaught of the Southern sun. Pausing to pluck one, she hesitated, sighed, and turning sat upon a nearby rustic seat. She was very tired. For the past eight weeks, she had been in active attendance upon her husband. There were two trained nurses in the house but, there was little they were allowed to do for the patient except to keep watch, principally at night, when Virginia permitted herself a few moments of much-needed sleep. Then, at the slightest movement in Smithson's room, which was next to her own, she would instantly don her dressing gown and be in his room ready for action. She had passed through much mental anguish and soul-examination during these trying weeks. By easy stages, she had arrived at the conclusion that no good purpose could be served by washing her dirty linen in public. She knew her friends and the empty-headedness of her social circle. To go into the divorce court would make it impossible for her to hold her head up among them again. Besides, the knowledge of her husband's antecedents, such as he had communicated in that sad moment of bitterness, was their own affair. When she rushed back from Long Island, her main thought was to save the father of her child and if possible, remedy an injustice.

During those weeks of anxiety and suspense, she suddenly realized that she was really in love with him and that his loss would be irreparable. She always admired him for his accomplishments and his indulgement of her whims, but she never believed herself capable of giving way to the weakness of a grand passion. She considered herself too proud for that. But here she was head and ears in love with the very man she had told how wholeheart-edly she loathed him because of the blood taint for which he was in no way responsible. Miss Swanson had said to marry a Negro was not such a terrible thing after all. At that time she considered such a prospect absolutely out of the question. In fact, it was her own brother's threat that quickened her understanding as to the true state of her affection for her husband. Fortu-nately, that worthless brother did not know all, or he might have provoked a lynching. Yet, she could not tell Smithson of her changed feeling. She knew that he loved her, his actions proved that, and the barrier between them was entirely of her making. She had noted, by the peculiar look in his eyes, how on many occasions, he wanted to take her in his arms while she had always frozen him with her rudeness and austerity. What was she to do? To fall at his feet and declare her love would be ludicrous in the extreme. On the other hand, her devotion to him during the period of his illness must have proved that she possessed a deeper feeling than mere wifely duty. While she sat on the rustic seat, that statement of "wifely duty" recurred to her. She had said it quite unthinkingly but his repetition of the word "duty," the emphasis he laid upon it, and that pained expression of his face, were not lost upon her. Why would this senseless pride always stand in the path of her happiness? Could she not have said wifely devotion or something of that sort, to give him a little insight into her real emotion? It is true that during his moments of unconsciousness, she had kissed him on the cheek and lips, and on one occasion, he had opened his eyes and smiled and causing her to blush with that shame which attended an emotional admission. But she afterwards discovered that he had been unconscious all the while and had no recollection of the happening. With feminine inconstancy, she was rather annoyed that he was unconscious of her act. Had he known, it would have made matters much easier for her. Virginia was suddenly aroused from her reverie by the loud barking of Sentinel. There was an unmistakable snarl and a yell of pain. Hurriedly she ran back to the verandah where she found Smithson sitting up in his chair; the two terrified nurses holding their faces and Sentinel's fangs sunk deep in the throat of the stranger. Quickly calling Sentinel off, she bade the nurses attend the man, call a Doctor and the police. She dashed up the steps, while issuing her orders, to the side of Smithson who was unnerved but quite unharmed.

"Have you been hurt, my dear?" was her anxious enquiry. She was not conscious of the heartbeat she had expressed in the last two words. Smithson heard and was amazed. Could he believe his own ears, or was he still dreaming as he had been doing when Sentinel's bark aroused him? "No", he answered, recovering his self-possession with difficulty, "Sentinels bark woke me up."

Virginia breathed a sigh of relief. "You're sure you're alright?"

"O, yes, quite alright."

Meanwhile, the house servants gathered at a respectful distance as the man holding his throat was receiving first-aid from one of the nurses.

"Is he much hurt?" Virginia asked.

"No, Mrs Smithson, I don't think so."

The gardener now arrived on the scene, shears in hand.

"Search that man for weapon!" commanded Virginia from the verandah.

The gardener went through the stranger's pockets and found a loaded revolver and a knot of cord tied up in his coat. Virginia leaned over the rail and asked. "Can he talk, do you think, nurse?"

"I am not sure," came the answer. "Bring a pail of water somebody, to wash this blood from his face."

A housemaid dashed away returning quickly with a pail of water and a towel. The nurse got busy and Sentinel stood by observant and watchful as the man groaned under the ministrations of the nurse.

"Ah!" exclaimed Virginia as the man's face appeared from beneath its mask of blood. "So, it is you, Red Robb?"

"Who is Red Robb?" asked Smithson.

"O, one of the loafers of the district, who always went with Algy on his hunting trips. O, I see; how stupid of me not to have thought of this." Then to the gardener: "Go through his pockets again and bring the contents here." The gardener did as he was ordered and brought Virginia a fifty-dollar bill, some silver coins, a newly typed note of instructions in an envelope, and a few fragments of soiled paper. Virginia examined the envelope, noted the Washington postmark and address. She then removed the typed sheet and read: "Get Smithson alive or dead, truss him with up a rope if alive, and bring him to Washington. Wire me when you get him. Act quickly. The bill enclosed pays expenses. An automobile will call for you and take you to the place, it will also bring you and your captive to Washington. Destroy this note. Hunter."

"P.S. five hundred for you when you have done the job."

She turned the sheet over and over, then returned it to the envelope. "What's it all about?" enquired Smithson.

"Another plot—to kidnap you, this time."

"O, that's interesting!"

The Doctor's car drove up with two policemen and the Inspector from Culpeper Court House.

"How-do, Mrs Smithson." The Inspector saluted and mounted the steps with the Doctor. To the policemen, he turned when half way up, saying: "Watch that man! What's wrong here, madam?"

Virginia handed the contents of Red Robb's pockets to the Inspector. "These were found in his pockets, also a cord and a gun which the gardener found on him."

"How are you feeling, Smithson?" enquired the Doctor.

"I'm O.K, Doc."

"Better give Red Robb some attention Doctor," suggested Virginia.

The Doctor went to the man and examined him quickly, asking a few questions of the nurse. "We'll have to take him back to the hospital," he said. "The dog got him in a bad spot." He bandaged up Robb's neck. "There!"

The Inspector was reading the typed sheet. "Can Red Robb talk?" he looked up and asked the Doctor. "Not just now, perhaps, not at all."

"I'll keep these papers," said the Inspector. "Put him in the car," he commanded his men. "This looks pretty serious." He flicked the envelope with his fingers as he turned to Virginia. "My two men had better hang about here for a while. I'll send in a relief at six. Let's get back, Doc. We passed a strange auto on the road, fortunately, I took the number. Good day, Mrs Smithson. Quick recovery to you, Sir. We'll keep a close eye on things hereafter. Sorry you had all this trouble. Good job you had this dog."

Sentinel growled ominously as the man was lifted into the car.

"Come here, Sentinel!" called Virginia. The dog reluctantly mounted the steps and lay at Smithson's feet. The car moved on, the Doctor waving a goodbye, and the two policemen walked off into the grounds with the gardener, and the house servants and nurses left the Smithsons together. "What was really the matter?" Smithson asked. "And what did the letter say?"

"That they wanted to take you away from me and—"

"Well, would that matter so much to you if they did?" he asked insinuatingly.

"Perhaps," was her tantalizing answer.

"Hang it all! I can't stand this any longer!' he said, rising unaided from the chair.

"My dear—my dear! Do be careful; the Doctor ordered."

"Hang the Doctor! I've got to get up!" He struggled to his feet, his hand on her shoulder. "I must be up and doing." He put both hands on her shoulders and looked searchingly into her steadfast eyes.

"You've done lots for me. Was it for me, or the boy—our boy! I wonder."

"I wonder," she repeated cryptically. Smithson sighed, turned, took her arm, and entered the mansion.

CHAPTER XXV.

When Hillyarde left Stylykoff, fortified as he was with ten thousand dollars, his first impulse was to call up some of his friends and indulge in an orgy of drink and lust. It was a long time since he had so large a sum at his disposal, and the ease with which the money was acquired had gone to his head. As there were no conveyances about, he was forced to walk some ten blocks to his hotel. The early morning air, however, assisted to clear his brain causing him to change his mind regarding those anticipated carnal indulgences because he bethought him of Stylykoff's warning and the latter's uncanny knowledge of his personal affairs. The Russian knew too much. Even now, he might be shadowed. He turned around cautiously while hastily covering the intervening distance, then, another thought took possession of him. The thoroughfare was deserted; what if he were held up and relieved of his ill-gotten wealth? He saw a policeman approaching. Suppose he should be challenged as a suspicious character and taken to the police station? He would be searched, and it would be rather difficult for him to account for having so large a sum of money on his person. He slackened his pace and boldly accosted the officer. How could he account to Stylykoff for the loss, and he had but three days to report progress. He would enquire his way to the hotel. That would be a capital ruse; in this way, he would also have an escort.

"Say officer," he called, "where in hell am I? I want to get to the Capitol Hotel and it looks as though I've been walking in a circle. Had a few drinks with some friends. Guess, I'm lost, somehow."

The policeman eyed him suspiciously. "Want to go to the Capitol Hotel, do you?

"Yes!" swaying unsteadily. "Is it far from here?—could you help me out?"

"It's just two blocks away—you stay there?"

"Yes; if you'll come with me, you can have the piece of some cigars.'

"Come on," said the officer glancing around. "Been in Washington long?"

"Four weeks, in and out. They know me at the hotel." The officer grunted, and they walked on in silence. Arriving at the hotel, Hillyarde put his hand in his pocket and passed a five-dollar bill to the policeman. "Could you come inside to my room and have a drink?" he whispered. The officer looked around. "Nearly time for the Inspector; guess I'll take a chance."

They entered together, Hillyarde secured his key, and the pair ascended to his room. He produced a bottle of whiskey; they both drank and the policeman remarked:

"Damn good whiskey, this."

"Have another shot?"

"No, I guess not. Perhaps, another time."

"Sure, anytime! Ask for Hillyarde—my name."

"Alritey: I must be going, Mr Hillyarde, thank you."

"Sorry you must, but duty is duty." He escorted the officer to the elevator and dispatched him, returned to his room, locked the door, and fell into a chair with a sigh of relief. "That's that!" he exclaimed. "Oh yes, almost forgot, the Cop's number. He might be useful." He took out his notebook. "N.3378,

I forgot to ask his name." After making the notation, he returned the book to his pocket, went to the door, and looked into the passage, locked the door again, and proceeded to count his newly-acquired wealth. "Well," he soliloquised, "Ten thousand dollars sets me on my feet again. How fortunate I dodged Bobby Smythe and his Japanese friend." The phone rang. "Talk of the devil!—bet that's Bobby!"

Carefully stowing the notes in his wallet, he went to the phone. "Hello!— O, that you, Bobby?—O! my appointment? It's past seven thirty now, can't go—too sleepy—only got home a few minutes ago. What! Japanese arrested? Poor beggar! He was too slow. Appointment off? Quite alright with me. No, I don't want any of that kind of money. Found my people relented and wired a remittance. Everything O.K., see you later in the day. Shall be very busy and goodbye!"

He hung up the receiver. "My luck's in! Guess, I'll capture the half million. I must get busy and play it up. O, boy!"

He went to his desk, turned over some papers, and found Smithson's name on a duplicate promissory note. "I promise to pay!" He laughed. "Like hell! What a joke! Won't Virginia squirm when she learns that I'm travelling to Europe without her husband's money? Hope the Emperor fixed him up. I'm too busy to attend to the job myself. All the same, I hate the upstart."

He phoned down for breakfast, taking his bath in the interim of waiting. Then hastily swallowing his ham, eggs, and coffee, he hurried off to the bank to deposit the ten thousand. Afterwards, he leisurely strolled to the Capitol to "lobby" for his venal legislators.

After Hillyarde departed from Stylykoff's hotel, the latter ordered coffee and entrained for the headquarters of the Invisible State. On his arrival, he experienced little difficulty in obtaining an audience with the Emperor.

"Glad to know you!" he exclaimed effusively, as he shook Stylykoff by the hand and led him into his private office.

"Have a seat! Have a seat!" cried the Emperor, drawing up a chair for his guest beside the enormous desk that stood in the centre of the room.

"Thank you, sir," said the Russian, seating himself. He took his cigarette case from his pocket. "Will you smoke?"

"No, I never smoke; nor do I drink, Sir."

Stylykoff lit a cigarette, returned the case to his pocket with studied deliberation, adjusted his monocle and gazed curiously at Colonel Blood, as though he inspected a rare biological specimen.

"Quite a warm day," ventured the Emperor, to break the embarrassing silence.

"Do you think so? I have failed to notice it, too busy with my work, I suppose."

"Yes," drawled the Colonel, "I suppose you are, I suppose you are. I'm rather busy myself; perhaps that makes me feel the heat."

"No doubt, no doubt," responded the Russian. "Shall we proceed to business? I presume we are alone and cannot be overheard?"

"We're quite alone, Mr er—ah—"

"O, I beg your pardon! Stylykoff—General Stylykoff—my card." He passed his card to the Colonel.

"Yes, you called me long distance this morning, but I didn't quite get the name. General, ah, Stylykoff. These foreign names get me sometimes."

"I understand. So silly of me not to have announced myself properly. My business was of a confidential nature, however, which accounts for my extreme reticence."

"Well, General, tell me all about it. I'm all attention."

"I think you find your following a rather disappearing quantity?"

"Disappointing would sound better, General."

"Disappearing or disappointing means the same in your case. I had a very interesting chat with your former lieutenant, Algernon "Hillyarde."

"Hillyarde!" interrupted the Colonel with a start.

"Yes, I talked with him last night."

"What did he say?"

"He said perhaps you would like to discuss matters with me."

"O, he did, did he? Where did you meet him?"

"In Washington."

"O, I see."

Stylykoff took out his watch and noted the time. I fear we are wasting precious time, Colonel. I must catch the two-thirty back to—well, it does not matter where. Can you listen to me for five minutes without interruption?"

"Surely, surely, General."

"You cannot carry on your work without adequate funds. You desire to make yourself master of these United States. Suppose I could supply you with these funds and lend you sufficient support to attain your end, would you accept?

"That would depend upon the extent of the financial aid and the amount of, and quality of the support."

"I speak of support from without," replied the Russian.

"If it could be contributed in a manner acceptable to my followers—"

"Pardon my interruption; your followers, such as they are, have no voice in the matter. You are the organization—the dictator is a better term, I think. We are prepared to help you to a throne or any other title you may like to give your dictatorship. I say a throne for convenience because you are styled Emperor. We need trade relations and greater recognition. We have the money and the means to satisfy your ambition, provided you unite with us."

"But I am in the dark," the Colonel answered, "as to with whom I am dealing.

"I am a Russian Citizen!" Stylykoff answered proudly.

"And I am a Citizen of this great Republic!" was the Colonel's rejoinder.

"And Emperor of the Invisible State!" the Russian added: "rather a contradiction in terms—is it not?"

The Colonel was non-plussed by the subtlety of the Russian, and he passed over the irony of Stylykoff in silence. Though a boasted Citizen of the Great Republic, he was forced to admit to himself that this was a very remarkable paradoxical position. But he was narrow, stubborn, ambitious and egotistical, utterly lacking a true sense of values. He lusted for power in order that it would enable him to trample upon the rights and liberties of others, and the method employed to obtain that power, however questionable, was no special concern of his. The Russian who was a keen observer, not only knew the psychology of the man with whom he dealt, but he also possessed the advantage of a complete knowledge of the Colonel's background. Thus, the Colonel being no match for his adversary, the negotiation resolved itself into a game between the cat and the mouse, and the poor bombastic mouse never had the most shadowy chance of escape.

As the Colonel remained silent, Stylykoff continued.

"Shall I proceed?" The Colonel bowed his assent.

"Now you understand who and what I am. I think we may come to the point without further skirmishes. We have settled the question of your disappointing and disappearing followers. The matter of your being dictator of your organization, which after all is the child of your own brain, is also settled. Now we come to the question of fulfilment of pledges and guarantees. You can give no guarantees otherwise your desk would not be littered with a pile of resignations from your most prominent and promising— promising to pay, I should say—following—"

The Emperor was aghast. "How did you know all this? That damn Hillyarde, I guess!"

"Your conclusion is wrong, Emperor. Hillyarde never discussed the inner workings of your organization with me. I know these things. We have a most perfect secret service, Emperor. Little transpires of importance in any part of the world with which we are not familiar. For example, your first act on arriving here from Washington was to order the kidnapping of Smithson, your former aid, by Red Robb." The Colonel started and turned pale.

Stylykoff re-adjusted his monocle, lit another cigarette, and beat a tattoo with his fingers on the corner of his desk while watching the effect of his revelation upon the Colonel.

"What manner of man are you?" the Colonel asked.

"Merely an observer of events, my dear Emperor. You see, we arm ourselves with knowledge, and this gives us power. Power to reward our friends and to crush our enemies."

The Russian spoke in soft even tones without the slightest trace of bitterness or resentment, which caused the Colonel to register the impression of a steel glove beneath a velvet covering. He shivered visibly as he sat gazing in awe at the unruffled Muscovite.

"Would the Emperor have me impart any further information which would be regarded by him as being of a strictly confidential nature?"

"No, no!" cried the Colonel desperately, raising his hands in alarm. "That's quite enough—quite enough!"

"Now, my dear Emperor," purred Stylykoff in soothing tones. "It would never do to have Smithson learn that you were the 'Hunter' who treated him to an unexpected and unpleasant visit from Red Robb. His wife, Madam Virginia has influence and might be impelled to request the Court to put some rather pertinent questions to you. And there was that little matter of the Negro, Jones"—

"For God's sake, General no more!" interrupted the Colonel, in appeal. He gazed about him in affright as though the room were filled with Russian spies. It suddenly dawned upon him that at length, he had found his master, and it would be no easy matter to dislodge the Russians, as he had contemplated, once they got a foothold in the country. But this Russian knew too much. There was no time for retreat now.

"As you will, my dear Emperor; as you will." The Russian answered suavely. "I crave your pardon for wantonly—shall I say, indiscreetly—trespassing within the holy of holies of your most jealously guarded secrets. Had you been less skeptical, I would have been less communicative. However, let us forget these little impertinences of mine and return to the point at issue. We can aid your ambitions by supplying money. You can help us with information and men. Your present following consists of those men who will be drafted into the army in case of invasion. You must so arrange your affairs that should we require the use of these men, they will cross over to our forces or those of Japan, should they be the sole invaders."

"I could not think of joining up our white brothers with those yellow monkeys! exclaimed the Colonel hotly. "With you, it would be different, you are Nordics! Our object is to impose Nordic rule upon the black, brown and yellow hordes that threaten to overwhelm us!"

"We in Russia hold no such views, my dear Emperor. Neither colour nor creed matters to us. In fact, the lesser the creed or the absence of it is the most acceptable to us. Therefore, unpalatable, as it may be to you, should we order you"—

"Order!" exclaimed the Colonel.

"I beg your pardon, Emperor! I should have said request. Should we request you to join an invading Japanese army, we would naturally expect you to do so, or be responsible for the consequences." The Colonel breathed heavily. Could he be expected to reverse his own divinely inspired policy? He must temporize. Perhaps a way out would be found when the occasion arose.

"I am afraid there is no way out, my dear Emperor," said Stylykoff, disturbing the Colonel's train of thought, causing him to start guiltily.

"How did you guess my thoughts?" he enquired unthinkingly.

"Did I guess your thoughts, Emperor? Again, I crave your indulgence. How inquisitive of me. Well, time is passing, are you in accord with our views?"

"Yes," the Colonel answered hesitatingly.

"Very well then, up to what sum would you require for your work?"

"I guess I should have to make calculations, General."

"Now, come; give a rough idea, Emperor."

"How would five million strike you?"

"Suppose we say ten?"

"Ten million! That's a lot of money!"

"Not in these times. I'll book you for ten. And remember, we demand loyalty!" He rose and bowed. "A messenger will call upon you at noon to-morrow with the first instalment of two millions in cash. You will give him your receipt. The balance will be paid to you from time to time on demand. Good day, my dear, Emperor. Pray accept my sincere thanks for receiving me." And before the Colonel could recover from the financial surprise to which Stylykoff had treated him, the Russian had boarded a taxi, and was on his way to the railroad station.

CHAPTER XXVI.

Events were now moving with startling rapidity. India was in a turmoil over the question of complete independence. The Soviet Government had supplied arms and expert technicians to Afghanistan, the technical native Soviet Indian experts in aeronautics were making raids in India, numerous Indians were crossing the border into Afghanistan to assist the Afghans with their projected invasion of India under Soviet tutelage. While the eyes of the world were fixed on India, where the Russian government had created a successful diversion in Asia to mask its real aims, the Soviets were massing troops in Siberia for their contemplated attack upon America. Japan, while actively engaging in arming, was still negotiating with Russia and at the same time vigorously protesting to the Washington government on the question of the imprisonment, detention and deportation of her nationals. The Japanese Ambassador asked for and received his passports and the American Ambassador at Tokyo had been recalled by cable.

Over in Mexico, the Japanese settlers were awaiting the action of their government, and the entire South American Confederation, which by this time had become restive over the encroachments of the United States of America was not only looking on, but was also making military preparations for any eventuality. America, which was vigorously protesting over the military activities of Japan in Mexico had placed a fully equipped army in Mexico, Texas, Arizona and California, on the Mexican border. The United States Fleet on the China Station was watching Japan's fleet. The American press was urging the government to invade Mexico without further delay; the American army was being recruited to war strength, and Canada, caught as she was in the prevailing panic began feverish war preparations to protect her territory. The American ammunition and aeroplane factories were being obstructed for lack of adequate appropriations and the Communists were rioting all over the country where they were constantly coming into armed conflict with the militia and police.

Now that the Emperor was supplied with adequate funds, he began to terrorize the employers of labour, causing the various industries of the country to gradually continue the discharge of their Negro employees in accordance with his previous commands which were being disregarded at the time of the resignations of these leaders of industry. And Hatbry's distracted followers, in the absence of their imprisoned leader, were to be found agitating in all of the Northern and Eastern cities wherever there were large Negro populations. In Chicago, Washington and New York, important Negro deputations had been dispatched to the governments, state and federal, and those Negroes who were actively identified with Hatbry's movement were secretly arming themselves for the purpose of assisting the anticipated Soviet invasion as well as to assist riot and looting among their unemployed fellow workers. DeWoode, who had been approached by the Japanese and Soviet agents, was on the fence hoping that something would turn up to enable him to arrive at a decision in regard to his future action. In Boston, the more conservative Negroes, being unable to force DeWoode into a decision, had elected Hewitt Browne to the Presidency of the Negro Protective League. He not only counselled patience, but got into the thick of the fight in the defense of America, showing his followers and their opponents that their duty lay in the direction of loyalty to the flag and the country of their birth, and to this end, he toured the country in the interest of the ALL BLACK AIR LINE accumulating planes, for which the Negroes subscribed liberally, and which were being armed for bombing purpose to aid the United States against the prospective invasion. In this connection, ALL BLACK AIR LINE planes and pontoons were dispatched along the coast to San Francisco and along the borders of Canada to the Alaska Peninsula to establish bases at Nome and on the Seward Peninsula, as Browne had obtained secret information from soviet agents that Russian bombing planes were being massed on the Chukchee Peninsula with concealed bases at Capes Olyutorsk and Navarin.[12] In order to carry forward Browne's plans with success, Ette, who by this time was in the thick of the propaganda the League was conducting in the interest of the United States, had made frequent trips to Washington to interview her friend, Doctor Detritcher, on behalf of the League and of Browne's efforts in defence of the country. This had become vitally necessary in view of the fact that Soviet bribery had materially obstructed war appropriations at Washington for aerial protection, where Hillyarde's "lobbying" for Stylykoff had been eminently successful. Browne had, however, succeeded in arousing the Negroes to a sense of their responsibilities as citizens of the republic. All of this occurred in the midst of a presidential election in which Doctor Detritcher found himself the unwilling presidential candidate of the Republican Party with the Emperor's Democratic nominee, secretly supported with Russian gold, as his opponent.

Added to Browne's war activities and his loyalist propaganda, he was also touring the country by aeroplane making speeches in the interest of Doctor Detritcher's election. Never in the whole history of the United States had

---

12   Original corrected to read "ALL BLACK AIR LINE" consistently.

there been such unrest, potential anarchy and division of opinion within the nation. There were Wall Street crashes, gilt-edged stocks and securities tumbled, trade languished and many of the wealthy migrated to the continental cities of Europe taking such available wealth with them as could be hurriedly collected from the wreck. Gang warfare was openly practised in the streets of the cities, homes were invaded and sacked, millionaires were held at ransom, state governments were shaken to their foundations and the judiciary was utterly paralyzed. The country was flooded with drugs from Japanese sources and the agents of the country assisted to finance dope rings which had increased a thousand fold and the distracted populace found its only solace from its manifold sufferings in "snow-sniffing" parties in the pernicious drug-dispensing dives that flourished openly in every city.

Meanwhile, Smithson, who was rapidly recovering realizing the Nation's danger and gallant efforts of the Negroes, hurried to Boston and placed his services at the disposal of Browne. Having obtained a short period of training in aeronautics towards the end of the World War, he was selected by Browne to assist in establishing bases on the Pacific Coast and he volunteered to cross the Behring Strait into Siberia to discover the true disposition and extent of the Russian land and air forces. Ette, with the aid of Mrs Weatherall, who had done Red Cross work in France, was recruiting and training a staff of coloured nurses and Virginia, not to be outdone by her husband volunteered for services with Ette. Thus the Negroes aided as they were by their Nordic friends were not only making headway in their war preparations but were also commanding the respect and admiration of all patriotically inclined Americans by their infectious enthusiasm and self-abnegation in the face of persecution by their enemies. Browne had not only fired them with a newborn enthusiasm which, by employing their hands and minds gave them an entirely new outlook, but had also awakened a new concept of their duty to the state whereby it was hoped their political and industrial condition might be materially ameliorated. The Emperor, by his acceptance of Soviet assistance had now become the tool of Russia, and the communist group was mainly composed of the lawless section of his following, who were too ill-informed to weigh the niceties of the political situation or to determine in what direction their unthinking efforts would lead them. These, being incapable of making any distinction between communism and democracy, together with the Southern members of the Invisible State were breaking up Republican mass meetings, wrecking Republican clubs and maltreating Negroes despite the warning the Emperor had received from Stylykoff as to the international character of Russia's political outlook. The treatment therefore that the Negroes received at the hands of the Emperor's communist adherents resulted in the Negroes studiously avoiding any political propaganda that carried the Russian hallmark. Hatbry's demoralized and fast diminishing group being the only Negroes in America to regard the communists with any degree of seriousness. This political condition resulted in an overwhelming Negro Republican vote which assisted to send Doctor Detritcher to the White House with a plurality that was regarded in the nature of a political landslide. And the doctor's defense of the constitution during his short term in the senate had produced a revulsion of feeling throughout the country in favour of stable government and the suppression of the Invisible State, thereby enabling the Republican party to elect a crop of twenty-five Governors of State, many of them in the reputed Democratic strongholds of the South and Southwest.

Colonel Blood's followers being therefore outed at the polls and his most formidable opponent elected, the political situation assumed an entirely new and unexpected phase and the Emperor found himself in an exceedingly desperate condition. The following he had depended upon to raise him to the dictatorship upon which he had staked his all, had, for the most part, either taken cover after the electioneering debacle or completely deserted. And now in his moment of peril the only solution which presented itself was to throw himself unreservedly into the arms of the Soviet, doing their bidding without question, in hope that their invasion of the United States would free him from his perplexing difficulties, and perchance, raise him to that position of political eminence which would enable him to crush his enemies and punish those who had lacked the high degree of enthusiasm so necessary to the success of his questionable designs. Much as he despised the Japanese, it gradually dawned upon him that political expediency frequently made it necessary to cooperate with those one despised in order to successfully accomplish the desired aim. Political manipulation in the interest of national advantage had created political friendship between two such opposing forces such as Russia and Japan. Russia needed Japanese assistance to dethrone those very political ideals upon which the Nipponese government was based. Japan expected or countenanced such a temporary union because her enormously increasing population required and immediate outlet, and there were not only nearby islands in the Pacific Ocean that were necessary to Japan's economic salvation, but there was also the rich and flourishing State of California which her nationals had largely cultivated only to be dispossessed after they had made its arid wastes to blossom like a veritable Eden. This latter phase of the situation, in so far as it concerned

Japan, did not appeal to Colonel Blood. If the Japanese had been excluded from America, he considered that they got no more than they deserved. Yet he held the conviction should they succeed in occupying California, even as the Spaniards had been ejected from the New World, he counted upon his ability to ultimately create enmity between Russia and Japan in order to secure the assistance of the former for the purpose of ridding America of the hated Asiatics he so uncompromisingly loathed. Then, unfortunately, his insular outlook, his egotism, caused him to over-estimate his diplomatic powers, leaving him floundering in a morass of unsurmountable difficulties, to which his insane dream of power produced a blindness so complete that he was unable to see the disastrous potentialities of his situation. "Whom the Gods would destroy they first make mad." This insanity of the Colonel was speedily carrying him over the precipice to complete destruction.

Over in Abyssinia, where the Soviet had been teaching people to construct aeroplanes and other instruments of modern warfare, Abyssinians were embarrassing the French in Somaliland by their frequent raids. The Arabs of the Yemen were also on the warpath, seizing outlying portions of Transjordania while making warlike gestures in the direction of Palestine to the utter consternation of the Hebrew population. With Indian unrest demanding Britain's undivided attention and a pacifist labour government in power, both in England and Australia, the cry for help coming from Canada and other outlying sections of the Empire remained unheeded, and the Canadian government entered into serious negotiations with the United States to obtain military support in the event of a Soviet invasion. While these negotiations were pending the Japanese fleet quietly slipped into the Pacific and seized Borneo, Guinea and Sumatra to the utter consternation of the British and Dutch governments, and the intense joy of America, where it was believed that the seizure of possessions so remote from the United States established a prima facie case that after all, Japan contemplated no unfriendly designs upon California. Thus the path was supposedly clear for America to deal with Russia should she attempt to cross over from Siberia into Alaska. But the Japanese, Abyssinians and the Arabs had thrown down the gauntlet creating a serious situation in both Near, and Far East.

CHAPTER XXVII.

The war was on.

It will have been recalled that the Negroes under the leadership of Attorney Browne had carefully laid their plans to take care of an invasion by the Soviet, and this before adequate and effective measures had been outlined by the government. Browne's friend now being elected to the Presidency, possessing as he did a complete knowledge of the lawyer's plans, there was not only no likelihood of obstruction, but every prospect of active assistance and cooperation from the Washington Administration.

Smithson had made an exhaustive survey of the Russian bases, and having taken an aero-photographer along, they were furnished with pictures of the Soviet positions and the disposition of their forces, including a powerful wireless station which was partially hidden among enormous trees. Quickly these pictures were being developed and forwarded to Washington with a confidential request to Doctor Detritcher to obtain permission from the War Department to allow the ALL BLACK AIR LINE corps to raid and destroy the enemy's bases without further delay. The country being uninformed as to the true condition of affairs, the War Department hesitated to take action until it had been properly authorized by Congress. Meanwhile, the Secret Service men had uncovered another wireless station in the wild Klondyke[13] region which was the undoubted transmitting point from the United States. These men, disguised as miners, hung about the district on the pretext of prospecting while quietly pursuing their investigations. In the meantime, code messages had been intercepted and the experts at the Capitol were kept busy in their fruitless endeavour to discover the key. They were in the act of abandoning their labours when information arrived that the secret service men had arrested and detained Stylykoff and Colonel Blood with the code in their possession, thus making it possible to decode the messages which, upon investigation, proved that members of the Invisible State to the number of 50,000, were to be gradually filtering through into Alaska in small numbers disguised as miners, distributing themselves in that territory as near the Seaward Peninsula as possible in order to destroy the ALL BLACK AIR LINE bases as far as practicable, then to wait for a supply of arms which would be landed by aeroplane at nightfall somewhere between the Seaward and Alaska Peninsulas.

The Secret Service, being now in charge of the wireless station, with the Colonel Blood and Stylykoff closely guarded prisoners, proceeded to relay messages from Washington tending to deny the dispatch of arms until the Cabinet met and a plan formulated. Browne, having at length arrived upon

---

13 In the original text, Ali writes of the "wild Klonklyke region." It should read "Klondyke" instead. When, on the next page, he refers to this same location, he used the correct spelling ("Klondyke").

the scene he, in consultation with Smithson, decided upon immediate action especially as a message purporting to be from the President-elect had been received by Browne advising him to cross the Strait if he cared to take the risk. Neither Browne nor Smithson required urging. Like bloodhounds straining at the leash they were rearing to be up and at the enemy. On the evening of the day the message arrived, Browne assembled his squadron at Seaward Peninsula addressing his men in the following words.

"Brothers! This night we undertake a mad and unauthorized adventure. We are not commissioned by the War Department at Washington to raid the country of a supposedly friendly nation. Our commandant here and our Brother Smithson, have reconnoitered and photographed the bases of the enemy—I say enemy because we hold undisputed proof of their armed intention. It means that we strike them or they strike us. I'll take the liberty of paraphrasing England's most foremost poet by saying: 'Thrice armed is he who knows his cause is just but four times armed is he, who gets his blow in fust!' We, some of us at least, want to strike that blow first. The enemy are about to attack across the Strait and have unsuccessfully tried to sap our loyalty to the only country we know anything about. Our treatment has been hard, even brutal at times; in these United States we still have a host of friends and well-wishers. Many of them would wish us luck if they knew our mission. Some of them would say it was not our business. But remember men, whatever anyone shall say, we are Citizens of this Great Republic!—" Here he was interrupted by wild and vociferous cheers. He raised his hand to enjoy silence. "Men," he continued, "I understand our emotional nature. This is no time for applause. Some of the actors are present, but the curtain has not yet risen on the first act of this drama—I was about to say, tragedy. God grant that there be no tragedy—to us at least!"

"Amen, amen and amen!" they cried in chorus.

"I join in the amens, men, but let me continue. Time is passing, the stars look down upon us. This night means death to all our hopes or a glorious hereafter in this land of ours!"

Again, the squadron broke forth in cheers. When these subsided, Browne once more took up the burden of his discourse. "Have your pilots and mechanics examined your planes with care?"

"We have! We have! Captain Browne!" They replied in chorus, standing to attention and saluting.

"I put this serious question because there will be no landing. Our job's to get there and back. It won't be an easy job nor a picnic. Our pontoons might cause trouble if any landing is attempted. How's fuel?"

"Fuel, O.K." one responded.

"Good! Most of your men were in school when we were Over There in that hell, where we were made shock troops of, and would have been blown to— well, I don't know where, if the Germans had wanted to solve the problem of our race for America by blowing us all up. Some of us have been saved for a more glorious fate. We hadn't a voice over there! Here at last is our chance. It all means, just this. From the time of the Revolution until now, we have been in every worthwhile American war, and we have always won although we were led by the other group. Nobody ever found any bullets in our backs, get that? And we never got much thanks. On this occasion, we are doing this thing ourselves. ALL BLACK! Hear me? ALL BLACK!"

Once more enthusiastic cheers rent the evening air, and the cry: "ALL BLACK!" was repeated until the echo died away in the distance.

"Is any man here afraid to die?" Browne asked.

"No! No! No!" was the instantaneous exclamation.

"Good! This night, men, brothers, no man must allow himself to be taken prisoner! Shoot, shoot, shoot! But keep a few bullets for yourselves; if you are cornered, die like men!"

"We will! We will! We will!" they shouted.

"You fight for your freedom tonight, my men! This night's work must be gravened in letters of brass in that future generations may read! To your planes; men! To your planes! Let our watchword be; Death or Glory!"

And the men broke ranks rushing to the water to regain their planes, crying as they went: "Death or Glory!" They hurried to the waiting boats and were rowed out to their machines on the cold waters of the Behring Sea. Each man took his appointed place and determination was written large on every face.

The motors were started, the propellers moved in circuitous unison, and in a moment, five and twenty planes like unto a flock of black swans moved gracefully across the face of the water rising swiftly to the starlit sky until the V-shaped battle formation was complete. Commandant Smithson gave the signal and the plane moved on gathering momentum as they went. And the crooning measure: "Death or Glory! Death or Glory!" kept time with the throbbing motors passing onward and upward through the ether until it seemingly merged itself into one long soul cry of appeal and supplication. "Death or Glory! Death or Glory!"

They crossed the sea, the Siberian coast, and divided, travelling at a high altitude. Smithson led eight planes on the Chukchee Peninsula, Browne went on to Cape Obyutorsk leading seven planes and Captain Jackson, the old Oklahomain who had taught himself to fly, and was named "Father of the ALL BLACK AIR LINE," piloted the remainder to Cape Navarin. Like black specks against the star-sprinkled azure canopy, they hastened onward to their destiny. The Russians were taken by surprise. Having been informed by the Secret Service men in the Klondyke that the only active air group was the ALL BLACK AIR LINE, which the government had forbidden to commit any overt act, the Soviet bird-men were not only enjoying a false security but they were actively celebrating their intended raid upon Alaska which was scheduled for the following dawn. When, therefore, the bombs began to fall thick and fast upon their bases, the exploding ammunition dumps threw them in a panic causing great loss of life. Those of them who collected their wits rushed to the hangers only to find their planes in flames. Their position was not alone hopeless but extremely perilous. An additional squadron to augment their intended raid which had been expected in the early evening had failed to arrive. To add to their peril, the Black Liners encountering no opposition, having exhausted their bombs descended and practically wiped out the demoralized Soviet airmen with machine-gun fire. Meanwhile, the expected squadron was simultaneously sighted by the three raiding parties. The wireless signal was given by Smithson to close up, fly high, move toward the Strait, and wait an attack. The squadron came on at a high rate of speed and, sighting the explosions which were devasting their base, they gave chase to THE BLACK squadron. They maneuvered about and then separated, each plane choosing his opponent. Then they went on to the attack over that strip of water diving the two continents. The Negroes got behind their foes and drove them over Alaska. Both attackers and attacked were desperate. Success by the attackers meant the liberation of a race from political and economic bondage. Failure on the part of the attacked meant utter annihilation. Neither would or could give quarter. "Death or Glory!" was the watchword.

An enemy plane fell like a flashing torch on the Seaward Peninsula. Another fell burning in the Bearing Sea. Smithson's plane with a wing flapping, came down. Captain Jackson's plane, was being attacked from above and below. The machine gunner somehow got the pilot in the lower plane, which got out of control and went down. Twenty enemy planes were brought down. Six escaped into Canada and were interned. The Negroes lost four planes, twelve men wounded, and two dead. Smithson escaped with a broken collar bone, Browne with a broken arm, and Captain Jackson had both legs broken when his machine crashed. The flight concluded over American territory establishing the diplomatic presumption that the Soviet were the invaders. Browne immediately transmitted the news to the delighted Doctor Detritcher. Washington considered the situation grave but had accumulated sufficient evidence that Russia intended war on the United States and had made preparations to that end. Now that Japan had deserted Russia, U.S. planes and troops were instantly rushed from the Mexican border through Canada to Alaska and the Pacific squadron was ordered to the Behring Sea. Newspaper correspondents were quickly on the spot and the Negroes were enthusiastically lauded in the press as the heroes of the moment for taking the initiative from the War Department and saving the United States from invasion. Death had claimed a few but glory had covered them all with its imperishable mantle. Naturally, Negroes, whose enthusiasm knew no bounds, celebrated this remarkable event throughout the world. For the thing that they had done was trumpeted over the earth, and although the memory of man is short, the act of this noble band of despised men would be written on the brazen tablets of enduring fame to the eternal glory of the Negro whom, henceforth, men might vilify, but could no more despise.

CHAPTER XXVIII.

With the arrival of troops in Alaska, which included coloured cavalry regiments, came Ette, Virginia, and Mrs Weatherall, with their Red Cross volunteer nurses and a detachment of these headed by Ette, Virginia, and a doctor, took planes to the Seaward Peninsula to render such aid as the occasion demanded.

The unexpected defeat of the Soviet airmen had shed consternation in the ranks of the Colonel's hundred percenters and on the approach of the army, these disgruntled unarmed followers of the Emperor scattered, for the most part, vanishing so completely from Alaska as to suggest that they had been caught up in one of those cyclones so frequent in that region. Over at the private Soviet wireless station in the Klondyke, Stylykoff and Colonel Blood, who were still held prisoners under heavily armed Secret Service guard, awaiting instructions from Washington as to their ultimate disposition, were enjoying anything but a comfortable incarceration. The Colonel, wrapped in his accustomed cloak, not only felt his condition keenly but also began to realize the futility of his bid for power which resulted in sleepless nights and a soul-searching which was by no means a pleasing occupation. He had bartered his honour in his insensate lust for a dictatorship only to be caught in the toils of his own vainglory. The Secret Service men had taken care to report the triumph of the Negro aviators which added to his bitterness. For while he, a boasted red-blooded-hundred-percent-American, had betrayed his country to the enemy. The despised Negroes had saved it from invasion, thus proving themselves more worthy of citizenship than himself or his deluded Nordic followers. He did not believe the Negroes capable of accomplishing so gigantic a task single-handed, browbeating his captors with arguments as to the impossibility of the Negro possessing the imagination and executive ability necessary to so daring an enterprise. Even when shown copies of prominent American newspapers in which the heroic undertaking was lauded, so obsessed was he with his prejudices that he stubbornly contended the news was manufactured at the instigation of the Republican Party to placate the Negroes who assisted to send their College Professor to the White House.

Stylykoff, on the other hand, accepted his detention philosophically, and while the Colonel sulked, the Russian, who utterly despised the Colonel, regarding him with as much contempt as the Emperor was wont to regard the Negroes, entertained his captors with amusing anecdotes of his travels while secretly planning a means of escape.

Algernon Hillyarde's sudden acquisition of wealth having prompted him to return to his old haunts of pleasure, he succeeded in creating jealousy and enmity among his associates because of his ostentatious expenditure and his overbearing manner; and that jealousy, by reason of his notorious impecuniosity, led to suspicion resulting in a secret investigation of the source of his finances by the government. Hillyarde, like many other aristocratic but impoverished idlers who had suddenly come into the possession of mysterious wealth, because their social connections brought them in close contact with highly placed government officials, from whom they could extract secret information for which they were generously paid by the spies of foreign governments, and who were being constantly shadowed by Secret Service agents, could not fail in coming under government surveillance. He had, however, cultivated the acquaintance of Police Officer "N.3878", to some purpose. By entertaining that officer with liquid refreshment in his hotel suite, coupled with an occasional bottle to take home for the enjoyment of his family, added to liberal cash donations. "N.3878", had become his willing tool. The officer had been assigned to detective duty. Coming as he did in contact with Government investigators he was in a position to impart information to Hillyarde about those who were under observation. In this way, he was enabled to advise this precious descendant of the Plantagenets of his approaching peril and Hillyarde not only paid handsomely for the information but lost no time in shaking the dust of Washington from his aristocratic feet. Knowing that Stylykoff had almost completed his work, arriving in Alaska on his way to Russia, Hillyarde was quickly on his trail, getting into the Klondyke twenty-four hours after Stylykoff's arrest. He was, however, too clever to be caught napping, so he hung about until he obtained the requisite information, and, having discovered that his employer was completely in the toils, he made his way to the Seaward Peninsula arriving there in time to witness the defeat of the Soviet air squadron by the Negroes.

When, therefore, the howling victors appeared on the scene bearing Captain Jackson, and led by his brother-in-law, who he believed to be safely housed in their Virginian country home, his surprise took on the nature of a minor panic by reason of his lack of knowledge as to what information his sister had imparted to her husband regarding that final interview he had with her in New York. In his miner's disguise, he was not recognized by Smithson, so he slunk away to the hut of a miner, where he had temporarily settled himself with some of the Emperor's followers until the expected Soviet invasion was an accomplished fact. The Doctor having set Browne's arm and Jackson's leg, fixed up Smithson's shoulder in a plaster cast and ordered him to bed, with Virginia once more in attendance as his nurse. He was delightedly surprised at her unexpected advent, being quite unaware of her affiliation with the coloured nursing outfit. Moreover, on account of her engrained prejudices against the Negroes, he would have been less surprised had the Colonel appeared in their midst as an army drug dispenser. As it was, he manifested his delight in a manner pleasing to Virginia, although she found it difficult to completely divest herself of her cold hauteur and reserve. When they were at length alone, Smithson, having successfully applied a most vigorous assault of warm embraces with his uninjured arm, Virginia proved herself as pregnable as any member of her sex by gradually melting away in her husband's arms. Ette, who had unexpectedly broken in upon one of these affectionate interludes was filled with delightful wonder at the miracle, especially in view of Browne's statement to her regarding Smithson's blood affinity with the Negroes and her own recollection of the discussion on that question on the occasion of her solitary visit to The Towers.

On the evening of her arrival at Seaward Peninsula, Ette suggested a walk with Browne to obtain a little much-needed exercise before her final round of inspection for the night. Being an alluring night with a bright moon overhead and the two lovers having much to discuss, they wandered several miles from the base of operations encountering small groups of miners on the way who regarded them with glances that were by no means friendly. Some of these glances were accompanied by uncomplimentary remarks in which the phrase, "nigger men and white women," was applied to them with threatening frequency. Fearing an unwelcome altercation they hurriedly retraced their steps and were but a stone's throw from the base when they passed Hillyarde in an advanced stage of intoxication lurching along on the arm of his miner-landlord who was assisting him home with difficulty. The encounter greatly disturbed Ette, who recognized Hillyarde in spite of his strange appearance, being apprehensive that his presence in the vicinity in disguise boded ill. She not only communicated her fears to Browne but hurried off to Virginia's tent to impart the news. Smithson, who was present at Ette's recital, noted the inexplicable alarm manifested by his wife. Upon inquiring the cause she told him all about her brother's last interview and his threats against their boy's life and his own. Recalling her own experience, Ette related her encounter with Hillyarde at the hotel, explaining to Virginia for the first time the full details of her relations with him. A general discussion then ensued as to the best method to be adopted to prevent Hillyarde from creating a disturbance or any attempt at revenge upon either member of the quartette. It was obvious that he would endeavour to injure either or both of them. Hillyarde hated Smithson, and his sister's defense of her husband would cause Ette to be included in any attempt at revenge. They were quartered in a wild and sparsely settled district with a lawless group of miners outnumbering their little band by more than a hundred to one. What defense could they put up should Hillyarde surround himself with a gang of drink-crazed miners to rush their ill-conditioned encampment? They possessed machine guns and an adequate supply of ammunition but in the event of a concentrated attack the little band would be subdued by sheer weight of numbers. Virginia and Ette both counselled flight. Browne and Smithson were disposed to hold their ground and fight it out if necessity arose. The two women reminded them of the nurses and the wounded who should receive prime consideration. They argued until dawn approached, and with the dawn came the half-sobered Hillyarde and a half dozen miners on a tour of investigation. They were challenged by the guard outside Smithson's tent. Shots were exchanged as well as oaths and imprecations. Hillyarde fell wounded as the quartette rushed to the opening of the tent to discover the cause of the disturbance. Virginia, seeing her brother writhing in agony on the ground, flew to his aid. As she knelt beside him, he looked up and recognized her. "Virginia," he cried weakly, "what are you doing here?"

"The Doctor, quick!," she called to Browne. "Come Ette, help me, here—hold his head up!"

"Ette,—Ette! you here too?" he asked with difficulty.

"Yes," she answered simply. "I'm here, you must not speak until the Doctor comes."

The blood gushed from his mouth and ears as the half-dressed Doctor arrived who, after a hasty examination, shook his head. "No hope, here," he said. "Shot in the chest and mouth. It'll soon be over, poor chap," and turned his attention to the other wounded men.

Hillyarde smiled grimly as his eyes began to glaze with the film of death. "Smithson—here—too? Well, they've—all—come. Sorry—I—did'nt get—you." The last words trailed off in a whisper. He was seized with a sudden spasm. He raised himself to a sitting position in the arms of the two women. He tried to speak, his breathing was difficult. He uttered the two syllables in a whisper. "Sor—Et—" His head fell forward and he passed to his reckoning.

With tear-dimmed eyes, Virginia and Ette looked at each other across the crumpled figure of Hillyarde. Silently they laid him out on mother earth. Smithson hurried away returning with two bearers and a stretcher on which they bore him off, while fifty arriving relief planes circled over Seaward Peninsula. Browne took five bombing aeroplanes under his command and once more crossed the Behring Strait, flying swiftly until they came to the Soviet wireless station which they completely demolished. Their adventure being accomplished they returned, collected their women and wounded and flew back to California to perform their interrupted avocations. And when the full report of their doings reached Washington, Doctor Detritcher smiled genially and remarked to his secretary: "Such are our heroes. Humans are humans. God made us all of one blood, black, white, brown, or yellow. All of us do the same old things, in the same old way."

CHAPTER XXIX.

While Hillyarde remained in the vicinity of the Secret wireless station where the Colonel and Stylykoff were detained, he came in contact with many of the Emperor's followers who were hanging about awaiting orders. It was from this group that he learned of the arrest of the Russian and his former chief. In order to divert suspicion of himself by keeping the Secret Service men busy, he suggested to the members of the Invisible State that they should rescue the Emperor and Stylykoff. The success of the BLACK AIR squadron had dashed their hopes of an invasion and they were at a loose end with ample time on their hands to engage in any mischievous adventure. Some of the more lawless, therefore, determined on the daring plan of carrying off the Colonel and his companion in adversity. The evening before the return of the Negro squadron was chosen as the most suitable, inasmuch as the United States troops were on their way to Alaska through Canadian territory, and the relief planes had passed over on their flight to Seaward Peninsula. A quantity of dynamite was collected and a mine laid near the wireless station which was operated from a low surrounding outhouse constructed of concrete blocks with a corrugated iron roof. The two prisoners were loaded in this outhouse manacled to each other's wrists by a single handcuff and a connecting chain six feet long. This chain permitted Stylykoff and the Colonel to move about as far as the confined space permitted without unduly disturbing each other. The eight Secret Service men, two of them wireless operators, were divided into two shifts with one man at the instrument in each relief. One man was always on duty outside while inside two kept guard over the prisoners with drawn guns. The men off duty either slept or lounged about to be handy in case of need. On the evening in question, a poker game was in session to break the monotony. The players were Stylykoff and the four men off duty, with the Colonel, the two guards and the wireless man looking on. The outside man was observing the game through the window. Suddenly there was a loud explosion then a second and a third causing the wireless outfit to sway and fall with a crash across the hut which went down in ruins. There was a rush by the raiders on the debris. The outside man was blown to the winds. Five of the servicemen were killed by the falling metal and two were slightly injured along with the Colonel. Stylykoff, who somehow escaped with a few bruises, disappeared in the confusion and was not heard of again, but the two surviving Secret Service men who gradually disentangled themselves from the wreckage held on to the Colonel who was too stunned to escape and stayed the on-rush of the raiders with drawn guns. In the meanwhile, the moon rose and six aeroplanes scouting over Alaska were attracted to the scene by the explosion. Flying at a low altitude they discovered the plight of the attacked. Descending quickly they swept the raiders with their machine guns and one of the planes landed and "took off" with two men and their captive while others circled overhead until rejoined by their companions when they flew to the Pacific on the return to California.

THE BLACK AIR squadron was now once more in California where the populace taking its lead from the Executive Mansion which had proclaimed a general holiday, went wild with excitement. Receptions, public and private were not only the order of the day but the magnificent appreciation accorded the squadron heralded in an event previously unknown in the annals of that state where the Negroes, although for the most part prosperous, were not specially regarded with favour. Captain Jackson was carried on a float at the head of the procession as the prime factor. For it was universally recognized that only through his pioneer work in Negro aeronautics could the achievement of the BLACK SQUADRON been possible. Neither Browne nor Smithson were neglected. The latter, who had not publicly declared himself because of the annoyance such a declaration might cause for Virginia, was still regarded as a Nordic, positively refused to take personal credit for his work or to accept any recognition whatever which did not include the other members of the squadron.

After the festivities, Captain Jackson was taken to a private nursing home where Virginia and her husband were constant visitors. In fact, Virginia, who had sent for the child to be with her in California, spent much of her time by Jackson's bedside reading to him or listening to his recollections of the South. On one of these occasions, he was telling her of the terrible moral conditions under which the coloured women were compelled to live.

"Why," said he, "I have known cases where Southern men would not stop at murder if they were obstructed in their immoral designs upon our women."

"Murder!" she exclaimed. "Surely, you overstate your case. I cannot conceive that any civilized man would proceed to that extremity because of being balked in the satisfaction of his passion."

In a moment, however, she recalled the recital of her own husband's experience and she added: "That at least should not apply to the educated classes."

"My dear kind lady, your upbringing, your connections would shield you from knowing these things. Why, I have known an executive of the state where I lived, to murder his coloured mistress—"

"A Governor of a State?—impossible!"

Smithson suddenly entered the room, "Who wants to make me Governor of a State?" he asked jokingly. "And why should it be impossible? What do you think of it, 'Cap?'"

"I was just telling your lady that the men in the South don't stop at the murder of our women if they can't have their way with them."

The horror of that night Smithson experienced when a child, which was burnt into his memory, came back to him and he turned aside to suppress his emotion. Virginia understood but was puzzled as to what action she should take in the circumstances. She shook her head vigorously at Jackson, endeavouring to put a period to his recital, but he warmed up to his subject and misinterpreted her sign as a denial of his statement.

"Well," he continued, "I was all but an eyewitness of one of these events and the man was a Governor down home. I was eighteen or nineteen then and was then his chauffeur. One night I took my boss to the outskirts of town where he had built a nice snug bungalow for his Octoroon mistress, who he visited three times a week. Shortly after we got there I heard a rumpus inside and the woman screaming. I went up the verandah on my toes and peeped in I saw my master with my own eyes knock the woman down as she was getting up with the blood streaming from her mouth. My boss took out his knife and cut her throat. That was enough for me. I got down those steps and back to the car faster than I came, trembling in every limb. It wasn't safe for me to know the white folks' secrets, particularly the Boss of the State, so after a while when he came out to go home, I pretended to be asleep, and I can tell you I gave my boss a lot of trouble to wake me up."

"Yes, yes!" cried Smithson excitedly, who had become pale as death. "What happened next?"

"I'm comin' to that. 'Quick!' said my boss, 'turn round and drive out to the country, I want fresh air, when you get to the Headly Farm, turn along the dirt road and go home the other way.' After a while, he leaned forward and asked me: 'Did you hear any noise in the house while you were waiting?' No; I answered, not a sound. You know, Colonel, we been out in the car most of the day, and I went fast asleep just as soon as this car stop. I hope you aint cross because you had to wake me up? He said he wasn't cross, but it took a dam long time to bring me back to life. I thought of that poor woman there on the floor who most likely would never come back to life, poor gal."

"Did this—Colonel—and the woman have any children?" asked Smithson with difficulty. A lump had risen to his throat which almost impeded utterance.

"Well, yes, there was only one child, a boy," was Jackson's answer.

"How old?" was Smithson's hasty interruption.

"I should say he was about, maybe, ten years old. I used to play with him a little, when I took messages to the house from my boss."

Smithson paced the room in perturbed reflection. He wanted to know more. He wished his wife were absent during the recital. Ere he could frame the next question that was taking form in his brain, Jackson proceeded. So he took a chair beside his wife, his head in his hands, and Virginia placed her arms around him comfortingly.

"Well, I drove the Colonel home, and day was breaking when I got there. When we got out of the car he said to me, 'Say, niggers who talk too much about white men's affairs don't live long to do more talking. If anyone should ask you where you were last night and where I went, tell them you drove me to Athens. But it's better for you if you give them no satisfactory answer.' He turned to go indoors, but before I could start the car, he turned back and said: 'Better you don't talk to anybody till I see you in the morning. Put up the car and go to bed. When I am ready for you I'll call you,' and he went indoors. That morning at eleven o'clock he called me. I went into his private office; I could see he hadn't slept a wink. 'Look here,' he says. 'You got to get out of this State, as far away as you can. You must not be found. Change your name; you must vanish. Better not take anything with you in the way of luggage. Forget you ever saw me or heard my name; get that?' He opened a drawer of his desk and took out a bundle of bills, a thousand dollars of them. 'Here,' he says, 'take this, and make yourself scarce, and don't waste no time. Don't flash your money about you might have to tell where you get it, and I can't know anything about it, or you—understand? I know nothing about you when you leave here. Now, hit the trail and be quick about it; a train leaves here for the North at eleven forty. You've just got time to make it. Goodbye, and good luck.' I went out a bit dazed, I can' tell you. I had a thousand dollars that I'd be afraid to spend. I had been warned not to flash that roll so I made Chicago and kept going West till I got to Frisco. One day I happened to be in the Post Office saying I was wanted for murder! I went cold all over—was just naturally paralyzed, didn't know what to do. I turned and went out not knowing if I should run or walk. I decided to walk; wouldn't create suspicion that way. Was thinking what I should do when I run into a tattoo artist shop, with a lot of pictures outside. It struck me all of a sudden that I might get some help here; I had to change my face somehow. See this scar down the bridge of my nose? Well, when I went West, at different times I ran into some black men with blue tattoo marks down the bridge of their nose. I found out they were Africans and that was their tribe marks. I decided from then on I was going to be an African and have one of those blue marks, and here was my man to do the job! So I walked in and jollied him along and got that mark down the bridge of my nose. When it healed up, it got me a lot of respect in this country. I was African, and an African wasn't a United States Negro; that got me a lot of help in out-of-the-way places with my messed up American language and all that. I changed my name to Alamazoo, and changed back to my own name when I came to Oklahoma. I was a bit too light for that mark and it nearly got me into a serious jam. You see, I didn't know what I meant, and one day I ran into one of those real honest-to-goodness Africans with a mark like mine—or almost. He stopped and looked at me as though I was a zoological curiosity. Then he said some words that sounded like a chimpanzee in pain. I answered him back in some manufactured jargon of my own invention that he didn't understand anymore than I understood him. He tried it again, then shook his head in despair and went his way. You see, I was another kind of African that didn't belong to his tribe, because when I looked at him, I discovered his mark started higher up the nose than mine. It was well for me that that African didn't carry on the discussion." Captain Jackson lay back with a reminiscent smile of that encounter. Virginia was amused in spite of her concern for her husband, who, although smiling occasionally at Jackson's story, was greatly perturbed. There was a short silence. Then Smithson asked: "Can you describe the boy—the boy you played with, Jackson?"

"Well, let me see, let me see? Strange, I never thought of it before! Holysmoke! That boy was the very picture of your kid, as like as two peas." He looked at Smithson inquiringly, critically. "If that boy was alive he'd be about your age—by gum! Were you born in the South?"

"Yes, I was, but don't you know just where. My own story is somewhat like the one related by you. My mother was killed by my own father in the same way, and I saw it!"

Jackson sat up in his bed excitedly. "Can you remember what the room looked like?"

"Yes, the room was blue, my mother wore a rose-coloured robe—"

"Yes, yes! And your father – the Governor—what did he wear?—"

"A dark suit and a Panama hat—"

"That's it, that's it!" exclaimed Jackson in excitement. "That was the Governor—your father! My God to think that I should see you again after all these years? And I held you in my arms! how small the world is after all!—don't you remember I used to call you Blue 'Eyes?'"

"Blue Eyes, Blue Eyes? I seem to remember, vaguely—"

Browne entered hastily. "Sorry to interrupt," he cried breathlessly, "the matter's urgent, Colonel Blood—"

"Colonel Blood!" exclaimed Jackson in affright. "Colonel Blood! Why that's your father!"

"My father?"

"Yes, your own father—"

"Stop!" Smithson cried. "What of Colonel Blood, Jones?"

"Escaped; they suspect he's hiding in your hotel suite. Better come on at once. They don't want to break the door unless you are present."

"Come," cried Virginia, rising and taking her husband by the arm. "Come, we must see what has happened."

"That villain, my father?—My God! My God!" Smithson, Virginia and Browne entered the waiting car and hurried to the hotel where they found an army of detectives awaiting their arrival.

"Glad you have come, Commandant Smithson," said the Inspector of police. "We believe the Colonel is in your suite. Be careful, we think he's armed."

"Oh," replied Smithson, opening the door. "I have no fear."

"Please be careful, dear!" was the anxious exclamation of Virginia. Smithson opened the door and entered the apartment. He turned the place inside out assisted by the detectives, but they could not locate the Colonel.

"He could not have entered without my key, or without breaking the door," said Smithson. "The nurse is out with our boy and won't return for an hour. There was no one here to let him in."

"He might have come by the fire escape," the inspector remarked, going to the window which he opened. He stepped out on the fire escape and looked around but there was no sign of anyone in the vicinity. Virginia took a seat and sighed. Browne and Smithson also sat down.

"So the Colonel made his get away?" the latter remarked.

"Vanished," said Browne.

"Most exciting and unnerving. So glad the child was out," came from Virginia. There was a movement in an oaken linen chest that stood near the entrance. "A rat!" exclaimed Virginia rising quickly to her feet.

"I think not—where?" asked Smithson.

"In that chest."

Browne jumped up followed by Smithson, went over to the chest, and opened it. They pulled out the linen as Virginia hastily climbed on a chair.

"The Escaped Emperor of the Invisible State as God lives!" Browne exclaimed.

"Be careful," Virginia cried anxiously.

"Come out of it," called Smithson.

"I can't," came a weak voice from the chest, "I'm wounded."

The two men pulled the Colonel out. "For God's sake," he cried as they sat him on a chair."

"For God's sake, don't hand me over to the police. Mrs Smithson, I plead to you—your woman's sympathy. Don't let them take me away!" He fell on his knees before Virginia. Smithson pulled him to his feet and threw him roughly on a chair. The Colonel gasped for breath. The months of mental torture and the physical pain he now suffered had set their mark upon him. No longer was he the tall, gaunt, cynical, masterful Emperor before whom a crowd of sycophantic followers were wont to bow in terror at his stern behest, but a wizened, broken old man who knew that even now, the Grim Reaper stood beside him, ready to deliver that unescapable summons.

"Would you mind taking my wife out to the car?" was Smithson's request to Browne. "She knows where the nurse and boy have gone. Find them and take them with you." Turning to Virginia he said, "You don't mind, dear? I wish to talk to him alone."

"I don't mind, dear; we'll return in an hour." There were tears in her eyes as she kissed him affectionately and passed out with Browne.

"Now that we are alone," Smithson began, "I have much to say to you—"

"For God's sake, don't hand me over to the law!' the Colonel pleaded. "I'm wounded in the chest and can't last much longer. Have mercy on a broken old man, or I'll be forced to end it all here and now." He drew a revolver, which Smithson instantly seized. "Not here!" he exclaimed. "If you must end your miserable existence, do it elsewhere. But before you do so, I have a few pointed remarks to make. Refresh your memory; perhaps you will recall a blue room of a well-appointed cottage on the outskirts of a Southern town." The Colonel grew deathly pale but remained silent.

"You do not answer?" Smithson continued coldly. "I didn't think you would. Perhaps you remember also there was a woman—a young coloured woman, dressed in a rose—pink negligee, brutally thrown to the floor of that blue room while a white man stands over her. Again and again, he knocked her to the floor—"

"For God's sake, man, have a little mercy!—"

"Mercy? did you show mercy to that poor, lone woman when you drew your pocket knife and thrust it in her throat? I hate you. I did not think it possible I could loath you as I do!" Smithson paced the room, the loaded revolver in his unbandaged arm. The Colonel groaned in anguish.

"You may groan, you dirty cur-murderer! That woman was my mother!"

"Your mother?" gasped the Colonel half rising from his seat, his eyes starting from their sockets in terror. "Your mother?"

"I said, my mother, who had been ruined by you because she was a helpless Negro woman, and you were a Governor of the State! My God! And to think that you—a bestial thing like you, should be my father. It's too horrible to contemplate—too horrible!"

The old man slid back limply in his chair, a baleful look of hate in his eyes. Smithson paced the length of the room and, returning stood before the Colonel. "What shall I do to you? You are my father. I cannot shoot you as you deserve, and I cannot have you hanged." Smithson paused reflectively. "No, I cannot do either thing."

The Colonel laughed sardonically. "So you are cornered," he cried with a languid show of triumph.

"No, I'm not cornered," Smithson answered. "Not cornered."

"What'll you do?" the old man leered mockingly. "My precious son, couldn't send his father to the hangman and ruin his own boy's life, not to mention the disgrace to the boy's mother. Then: where are your proofs?— your imagination is running away with you—my dear, precious son—if you are my son."

"I expected no less from a dirty murderer like you! After killing my mother, you would now disown her son!—Your own child! My God, to think that you—you!—you! should be my father?" Smithson stood over the old man with blazing eyes and hand upraised like an accusing Angel. "And to think that I cannot avenge my mother's death! My poor mother!" Smithson could not restrain his tears, and the Colonel, seeing his son's anguish, laughed sardonically.

"Yes, laugh, laugh, laugh! Are you man or devil?" He raised the gun to the old man's head.

"Shoot!" exclaimed the Colonel, "Shoot if you dare!" And again, he laughed wish bitter irony. "Nice sort of son you are!" he continued tauntingly. "Threaten to kill your old father—eh? Can't believe you are my son, somehow."

"Stop!" commanded Smithson. "I've had enough of that! Your servant who drove you to the house on the night of the murder still lives—"

"What! Jackson alive?—God!—"

"Yes, Jackson's very much alive, and ready to testify against you. You thought him asleep in the car, but he saw the murder, even as I did. Now this is my decision. You'll go through that window to the fire escape and blow your brains out. I can't accuse you of my mother's murder, although I have the proofs, because of the others. But I can hand you over to the police, and I have enough influence to prevent you from talking too much. You told Jackson, niggers who talked too much didn't live long, when you sent him away with that thousand dollars and then had him accused of the murder which you had committed! If you had any decency left in your worthless carcass, you'll empty this revolver in your head. I'd do it, but I wouldn't stain my hands with the blood of so contemptible a cur as you are. Get up!"

Smithson held the gun in his injured hand and pulled the Colonel to his feet with the other, "See? The window is open! Here is your gun. Do the only honourable thing you have ever done in your worthless life!" He pushed the Colonel to the window and roughly assisted him to mount the fire escape. Thrusting the gun in his father's hand; he turned and went to the telephone and took up the receiver. "I give you two minutes to make peace with your God! I hope He will forgive you—I can't! Damn you!"

The Colonel gathered his remaining strength and turned, levelled the pistol at his son, and drew the trigger. Smithson saw the old man's movement in time to drop the receiver and step aside as the shot struck the telephone box. Three shots were discharged at Smithson, but the Colonel's energy was spent. Groaning with suppressed rage, he emptied the remaining bullets in his head, and tightly grasping the revolver, fell headlong down the fire escape to the floor below. The shots were heard through the telephone and the hotel manager rushed to the room with a few bellboys in his wake. They entered as Smithson rose from the floor.

"What's happened?" the manager asked.

"Oh, nothing much. The Colonel was hiding in that chest. I discovered him, and he tried to shoot me as I was about to call the office. I fell on the floor to get out of range. I think you'll find him somewhere on the fire escape." The Inspector, who had not left the hotel, now entered with two detectives. They descended the fire escape and found the fugitive dead.

When the ambulance arrived, they wrapped him in his cloak and bore him off. And he who had recklessly gambled with fate to satisfy his vanity, passed on amid his blighted ambitions to an unnamed grave with no man to do honour to his ashes.

CHAPTER XXX

President Detritcher was now established in the White House with an over-whelming majority in Congress and the Senate pledged to drastic reform with an absence of freak legislation. The President, being a bachelor, the Weatheralls were invited to take up their residence in Washington, and Mrs Weatherall was appointed official hostess.

The Inauguration had passed off with great éclat. The ALL BLACK AIR Squadron was accorded a premier place in the procession, its members being enthusiastically acclaimed the heroes of the hour. The President, in his message to Congress pointed out that true administration of justice and equity is the most enduring pillar of government. That the judiciary had

failed to discharge its functions, and that a tidying brush was to be immediately brought into active operations so that the country would be a safe
place for its citizens to dwell in. He pointed out that the facts had to be
faced. Prohibition had failed, and there must be immediate alteration in
the law which was intended to operate in the highest interest of the people,
but which, in this case, had been an active instrument in promoting crime
and the general demoralization of the country. That the Negroes, by their
brave and timely act in the face of discouragement and opposition, had
saved the United States from the devastation and ruin attendant upon a war
of invasion, and that heroic act of loyalty, bravery and self-abnegation had
indisputably proved their worthiness to all rights and privileges of citizens
granted them by the Constitution, and that while he had no desire to infringe
upon the rights or the independence of States, the several provisions of the
Constitution must be respected henceforth, with particular reference to
the Thirteenth, Fourteenth and Fifteenth Amendments, and such respect
must be enforced even to the extent of reintroducing the military methods
of President Grant to command that respect. That, whereas the Eighteenth
Amendment had encroached upon the rights of both citizens and States,
the Thirteenth, Fourteenth and Fifteenth Amendments were added to the
Constitution to safeguard the rights and liberties of all citizens of the United
States, especially those weaker citizens who, by virtue of their three hundred
years of service were entitled to every consideration and protection at the
hands of the Government for which they were ever willing to sacrifice their
lives. Lives which had been patriotically sacrificed from the War of Independence to the present time. That the appalling lawlessness following in the
wake of an ill-considered experiment in moral legislation must be crushed
and immediate action should be taken to that end. He said that many of the
enactments on the Statute Book were useless and unwieldly instruments,
and that the entire laws of the United States needed overhauling and revision
to suit present-day conditions. The first step of the new administration was
to call a Conference of all the Governors of States for the purpose of devising
means to accord adequate rights to the coloured citizens of the Republic.
This was followed by a Congress of all Commissioners of Police, whereby
a plan was adopted to effectively deal with gang rule, the narcotic peril and
racketeering. The heads of the United States Bar were convened to institute
machinery to control and recommend appointments to the judiciary and to
limit election expenditure to a minimum so as to eliminate bribery, corrup-
tion and the purchase of judicial appointments from political wire-pullers,
until a more satisfactory method could be evolved to remove the judicial

system from the realm of politics. The line of policy undertaken by the new Government proved its determination to abandon the lethargic policy of its predecessor to boldly face the facts and usher in a new and comprehensive regime. Diplomatic relations with Japan were restored, and a closer union with Canada and Mexico was established. Negotiations were opened with Russia to iron out the war differences between the two nations with the ultimate object of entering into more effective diplomatic relations upon Russia's guarantee to abandon Soviet propaganda in any form whatsoever in the United States of America. Hatbry was placed on trial for High Treason against the United States and was sentenced to ten years imprisonment with five years deportation to the Virgin Islands under police supervision. The followers of the leader, with a few stubborn exceptions, had gradually merged themselves into the ranks of the Negro Protective League and they were followed by the majority of DeWoode's adherents. Congressional Medals were conferred upon the members of the BLACK AIR Squadron and each member was promoted to Commission rank on the Reserve Air Force of the country. Browne was appointed Solicitor-General of the United States, and Smithson was made Registrar of the Treasury. The firm action of the Detritcher Administration had restored the confidence of the Nation. There were mutterings south of the Mason and Dixon Line, but on the whole, truth, righteousness and justice were once more taking their rightful places to the honour of the South, where evicted farmers were being reinstated, and many of the most flagrant violators of the law were severely punished for their ruthless campaign against the Negroes.

The Emperor of the Invisible State being dead, his wild scheme of partisan government departed with him, and many of his most ardent followers were vigorous in their denunciation of his policy, strenuously denying any affiliation with his defunct organization, and the distracted Nation was gradually returning to a condition of peace, prosperity and sanity.

The Weatheralls, the Smithsons and Browne were now all quartered in Washington, where Ette's marriage to Browne was to be consummated. It was the President's desire to be present at the wedding, hence the change of the ceremony from Boston to Washington. There were only a few select invited guests to the wedding, which took place at the home of the Smithsons and was of a semi-private character. Mrs Weatherall had made the wedding cake with her own hands, and the Smithsons had loaned their New York home for the honeymoon. The President, who was to give Ette away, arrived late, keeping the party waiting fifteen minutes, which all but unnerved the future bride, causing Mrs Weatherall to do a little fuming on her own account to the intense amusement of her husband, who remarked to the President on his arrival, that since his wife had been appointed the Official Wife to the Chief Executive of the Nation, he had found her exceedingly difficult to manage because she had somehow conceived the idea that she was the entire Administration. Whereupon the Official "First Lady" replied that it was news to her that she had ever been managed by her husband or any other man, and it was now too late in life for her to submit to masculine management of any kind. And turning to Ette, she said: "Watch out, my dear, these men have always tried to dominate us poor, weak women—"

The lady's indictment was cut short by the uproarious laughter of the President and Mr Weatherall, in which the entire party joined. When the laughter subsided, Mrs Weatherall returned to the attack with renewed vigour, pointing out that all the worthwhile things done by men were all influenced directly or indirectly by women, at which statement the women enthusiastically cheered. Browne remarked that he was quite in accord with Mrs Weatherall. He modestly said he could only speak from his personal knowledge and such limited observation as came his way. "If I have had any ambitions in the past," he said, "those ambitions were due to my mother's training and encouragement. If I have accomplished anything at present, I must confess that Mrs Browne has successfully galvanized me into that achievement."

"Now, Ette," exclaimed Mrs Weatherall, "you have heard his confession. Please keep him trained in the right path! If you let him slip one inch, you'll never be able to bring him back to an admission of his inestimable obligation."

"I shall remember your sage advice," responded Ette. "By the way, Mr President, I have to offer you my warm and sincere thanks for—"

"Giving you away?" President Detritcher quickly interposed in order to forestall the statement he knew Ette was about to make. "You may live to regret it, young lady! You've heard Mrs Weatherall's indictment of us poor, defenceless men—what more can I say?"

"That I thank you for my husband's excellent and unexpected appointment."

"You had to get that out or burst!" the President exclaimed. "Don't you realize that it was intended to be your wedding present?" There was a mischievous twinkle in his eyes. "Mrs Smithson has outwitted you; however, she consigned her thanks to the tender mercies of the mail box so as to save my blushes. Both Smithson and Browne tendered their rather nervous thanks in person. You should have seen them standing before my august presence, like two overgrown school boys who had been given an unexpected holiday that they didn't know how to use up adequately." He whispered to his Secretary who passed him a small package under the table. "I shall now be forced to leave of the bride and groom because of official business. I wish you a long life, in the fullest enjoyment of unalloyed happiness!" Rising from the table he concluded. "And now, as is the custom at such gatherings, because I shall be unable to see you off on your honeymoon, I have a farewell offering to make." Breaking open the package, he filled his hands with rice, and before anyone realized what he was about to do, he sprinkled the rice over the bride and groom, reserving a handful for Mr Weatherall and her husband who subsequently declared that they were shedding grains of rice for over a month. The President then took his leave, departing amid the unsuppressed merriment of the assembled guests.

In due course, Browne and Ette departed for New York. Smithson and Virginia, who had escorted them to the car, returned to the drawing room and faced each other. "Well?" was Smithson's query.

"Well?" Virginia answered.

"At last, we are alone."

Virginia turned, sighed, and seated herself in an armchair. "I think there is enough room here for two—don't you think so?"

Smithson came over to the chair, sat on the arm, leaned over, and embraced his wife.

"Do you forgive me for all the ill I have brought you?" he asked.

"Forgive you? There is nothing to forgive. I have understanding and sympathy."

"Only sympathy?"

"Is not sympathy akin to love?" she asked coyly.

"Have you then succeeded in breaking down the barrier that has stood between us?"

"My dear, I learned my lesson on the day you were shot in New York. Did I not return to be by your side in your hour of peril—to nurse you back to life?"

"Yes, but—"

"But me no buts, sir! Just kiss me, and, no—"

Her further utterance was smothered in the warmth of her husband's embraces.

"How blind I have been—how blind!"

"It was natural, darling—entirely my fault," she said. "Kiss me again!" The first gong summoned them to dinner. They rose reluctantly and left the room entwined in each other's arms.

THE END

Appendices

Appendix 1: Cover of Saturday, May 12, 1934 issue of *The Comet*.

Appendix 2: Cover of Saturday, July 21, 1934 issue of *The Comet*.

Appendix 3: Cover of Saturday, August 19, 1933 issue of *The Comet*.

Appendix 4: "Hear America Round the World Radio," Advertisement for Philips Superhet Receiver published in *The Comet*.

Appendix 5

KA-TE-BET THE PRIESTESS.

a short story by Duse Mohamed Ali

[*The Comet*, Nigeria. XMAS, 1934.]

"Say Bill! Wot price the Bloke's toe rags?"

"Don't be silly, Emma; it ain't a bloke, it's a lady."

"Lady! I don't think."

"That's it," rejoined Bill, "Show yer ign'rence, Emma Smith. Can't yer read wot it says? 'Six-six-six-five. Mummy-Ka-te Bet, Priestess of the Temple of Amen-Ra at Theebees."

"O!" exclaimed Emma, "It looks jus' like a guy wot they burns on 'Amstead 'Earth on the Fifth o' November—it does straight! An' it's numbered like a convick."

"Well, it ain't a bloke," insisted Bill, "and it ain't a guy; it's just a laidy wot lived in Egypt, years an' years ago—afore we was born—she was a kind of nun in them times, she was."

"O!" ejaculated Emma, walking around the case which contained all that remained of Ka-te-Bet, whose fame lay buried for a full 3,000 years beneath the ancient ruins of the Theban Temple of Ra, until rescued from oblivion to be exposed to the vulgar jest of the thoughtless multitude, ticked like some felon with the number "6665."

"Wot a funny little kid she got a'tween her knees," continued Emma, pointing to the ushabti figure. "An' look at the big cockroach on her stummuck." Indicating the hawk-headed pectoral containing a scarab, which rested on the mummy's breast, "Ain't it funny, Bill?" And Emma giggled nervously.

"I shouldn't laugh if I was you, Emm'; after all it's a dead-body, an' you oughter respect the dead."

"It is a bit creepy, Bill—not half! They must o' thought somethink o' 'er by the way they churked the gold ab out 'er coffing. Wot price the little dickey birds!" And Emma giggled hysterically as she pointed to the inscriptions on the mummy of Peta-Amen, door-keeper of the Temple of Ra.

"Them there ain't dicky birds," rejoined Bill. "Them's hierglyphics. That's the only kind o' writing they had in them times."

"O!" exclaimed Emma, digesting Bill's crumbs of Egyptology, as with awakened interest she made a further detour around the cases. 'I, say, Bill! Look at 'er rings! An' the precious stones—not half! Wot price the immitashun bracelets!" And Emma broke forth into renewed merriment.

"Don't do that, Emm', it ain't right!" cried Bill, irritably. "How'd you like it? Besides I told yer afore, it ain't decent to mock the dead."

"All right, Bill! keep yer hair on, old cock; wot's it to do wi' you?"

"Never you mind," interjected Bill, "I don't like it."

"You take on as though she was a relative o' your'n." And tossing her head in the air Emma moved towards the walls to contemplate the gilded cartonages and coffins of the dead that stand like impassive sentinels lined in single file behind their earthy tenements of glass.

The cheerless gloom of that Christmas Bank-holiday, with its snow and sleet had all but plunged the British Museum in darkness; and these two lovers impelled by some supernatural agency, or being more morbidly curious than their fellows, had detached themselves from the holiday throng, wandering into the Egyptian Room, ONE, to steep themselves in the eternal mysteries of mummied Egypt.

Emma Smith was a pickle-packer, "walking out" with William Adulphus Brown—commonly called Bill—whose occupation was that of a handy-man to a large book-printing firm.

Emma was pleasure-loving and facetious whilst Bill's sobriety and studious habits served as an antidote to the somewhat flamboyant levity of his chosen partner.

For whereas during the dinner hour Emma could be seen parading Soho Square arm in arm with some three or four boon companions singing at the top of their voices "Let's all go down the Strand" or some other of London's "classical" ditties, Bill could always be found curled up under a printing machine with a fearsome sandwich in one hand which he devoured leisurely, while in the other hand he held the pages of some printed book with which the establishment abounded, from which he absorbed wisdom and from which he could not be detached even by the boisterous excitement produced in the neighboring Court by his fellow-workers who earnestly kicked a huge lump of paper about with an energy that would have done credit to a team of international footballers.

Bill's work-mate sarcastically called him "the scholar," and Emma, who was rarely serious for five minutes at a time, looked-up to her 'boy' because of the "book learning" she believed him to possess.

The gloomy day and doleful environment having depressingly affected her sunny spirits, Emma was anxious to depart to some more gay surroundings. Therefore, having passed along the walls glancing curiously at the mummy cases she reached the door, and pausing, shot a furtive glance from the corner of her eye at Bill who still remained in his original position contemplating the swaddled feet of Kat-te-Bet.

"Ain't you coming Bill?" she cried. But as Bill made no sign of life or movement, Emma continued banteringly, "P'raps you're tryin' to sneak her toe-rags to wear to work in the morning! I am hoppin' it, anyhow" she concluded, and hurried from the room.

Without, the snow and sleet was succeeded by a dense fog that suddenly descended on the place enveloping the room in an eerie mantle of blackness, blotting out all the sharp angels of the cases, leaving only here and there the shadowy shapes that seemed suspended on the air within this grim Valhalla of the Dead.

Then a nebulous light appeared to the shroud the bier of Ka-te-Bet from whence her form immerged in all the grand simplicity of her pure white vestments. And Bill, with eyes starting from their sockets, remained transfixed before this wonderous apparition of a mystic past.

The air seemed laden with the scent of frankincense and myrrh, as though an hundred tripods gave forth their perfumed fires and a thousand censers wafted their sweet-smelling vapors to the enthroned Osiris, who sits enshrined upon the walls, accepting the justification of Ani, the Scribe.

The lips of Ka-te-Bet moved in articulate utterance.

"Tothmes," she cried, "Tothmes, whom the men of later days call "Bill," harken to my words. In that long buried day, ere Menes or great Thebes was; when man skipped forth joyously on the Dawn of Time, we met. Then did my soul go forth to thee, but Nes-Khensu—whom now thou callest Emma—thrust her laughing eyes between mine and thine and thou wert dazzled, so that thou couldst not see the light of the love and the life and hope that faded from mine own.

"She became thy wife, and in despair I sought oblivion in the calm mysterious bosom of the placid Nile. And ere the waters wrapped me in their cold embrace, the mocking laugh of Nes-Khensu pierced my sere and withered heart, bearing my soul unwelcome company along the ceaseless journey through the Realm of Shades.

"Three cycles passed, and my purification being then complete, I once more trod the earth. We were in Upper Egypt. Thou wert then known as Khati the Scribe—behold thy bones devoid of flesh in yonder case that flanks the portal." Ka-te-Bet pointed to a skeleton near the entrance to the room. Bill groaned in anguish as he gazed in the direction indicated by the Priestess, and the dew of fear stood forth like beads of crystal on his trembling brow.

"Behold," the priestess cried, "the bones of Heni on the farther side, like thine, bereft of flesh. Canst thou recall how that the laughing face of Nes-Khensu crossed our paths once more, bringing woe and desolation? She then was a daughter of the Royal House. She lured thee from my side—for I was but a hand-maiden. Heni the Chamberlain she also snared, causing Heni and thee to meet in mortal combat for her hand. The Pharoah learned these tidings and had ye slain, stripping thy flesh and Heni's flesh away, before your bones were taken to their resting place. I wept for thee, beloved; but Nes-Khensu mocked my grief. Once more I passed unto the underworld and then again returned to Thebes to feed the altars at the Shrine of Ra.

"At Thebes we three met once more. The eternal Nes-Khensu was at thy side. She saw the love light beaming on thee from mine eyes. She bade me tend the fires of Amen-Ra, mocking the priestess who dared to gaze on thee with eyes of love.

"And so a-down the ages, from cycle to cycle, we three have met, and for aye 'twas my portion to be crossed and mocked by Nes-Khensu. Even in death she must needs come with witless jests upon her lips to mock the crumbling tenement which once held my soul.

"For thou shouldst know 'tis here on earth the soul, whether encased in men, birds, or beasts, must work its penitence. The baser soul in bird and beast, the higher in the trunks of men.

"Thus do the gods but typify the transitory stages of the soul. The lesser-gods, bearing the heads of birds or beasts move upward to the higher pinnacle of divinity, as embodied in the manly form of our Dread Lord Osiris.

"Therefore, shalt thou learn the fate of Nes-Khensu, and thine own. Nes-Khensu, whom Amen-Ra divinely dowered with a sunny smile to thaw the frozen miseries of mortal hearts, hath debased and turned the noble current of that god-like gift, replacing the smile of pity with the ribald jest, the joyful smile, with wanton mirth and mockery.

"But as I would not have thee think that malice drives me to pronounce her fate, I call on those with whom the gods commune and who like me return to earth no more.

"Arit-Heru-Ru," she cried, "Priest of Horus, Anubis and Isis, prophet of the diving Seker—I call thee from thy place before Osiris' throne!

"And thou, Penta-Heru-Pa-Khorat! sometime official in the sanctuary of Amen-Ra at Thebes—I call on thee!

"Step forth, Amen-Ari-Arit! overseer in the palace of Queen Amenartes; come forth from thy bandaged tenement with those reposing here, whose souls return to earth no more.

"And thou, also, Heni! whose bones bereft of flesh have stood the test of time—stand forth!"

And, as Arit-Heru-Ru, the prophet, forsook his mortal tenement and stood forth, he said: "'Tis meet that Tothmes shall see himself even as he was known in Upper Egypt. So shall mortal blindness quit his eyes and memory of the hidden past return to him again."

Khati, come forth!" the prophet cried, "and let thy soul inhabit thee once more!"

And Khati stood forth, and all the shades stood forth, lining themselves along the corridor. And the form of Bill sank out of sight upon a seat for his soul hovered over the shade of Khati. The windows of a divine understanding were open, and the soul of Bill saw the whole course of human destiny spread out before his eyes, even from the Dawn of Time.

"Speak, O, Prophet of the Gods," cried Ka-te-Bet, "Speak of the fixed decree of our Lord Osiris, touching the woman Nes-Khensu."

Then the prophet moved forward to his place above the line of shades, and Khati took his place below.

"Thus it is decreed," the prophet cried. "The woman Nes-Khensu, though bearing the form divine of our holy mother Isis, hath trailed her soul's divine promptings in the dust, causing the gods to unleash the floodgates of their wrath against her. Therefore must she descend unto the underworld engulfed in the Womb of Time till full three cycles shall run their course. Then shall she pass the lower transmutations of beast and bird for yet again three cycles. The seventh cycle shall see her in the underworld once more; so shall she be purified. dwelling again amongst the daughters of the earth, till Isis calls her to her abode on high."

Then the voices of the shades were lifted up—like unto a mighty eastwind that wafts the unwary mariner to his doom.

"All hail to our Lord Osiris, the maker of gods, the King of the South and North, the Lord of Heaven! Thy decrees are Truth!"

Again the prophet spoke. "As for thee, Kahti—Bill!"

And Bill's spirit returned to him once more and he stood upon his feet, being unafraid. For the divine spark which lies dormant in the human breast was lit directly from the sacred fires of Ra. The veil of fear, that hides futurity from mortal eyes whereof his bred despair, was utterly consumed.

"Ever hast thou shown nobleness of soul", the prophet cried. "The gods take pleasure in thee. Therefore it is decreed that after seven years thou'lt join the gods and us, uniting thy soul at length with that of the faithful Ka-te-Bet, for she hath waited long, and the gods have taken pity on her patience. Such is the will of our Lord Osiris."

One by one the shades blended themselves with the surrounding fog and their voices seemed to whisper like a passing zephyr of the night:—"The will of our Lord Osiris is Truth." And as the shades gradually faded from Bill's sight he heard the solemn chant of monks in supplication for departed souls. He looked up timidly to the wall where the pictured Osiris sat enthroned, and the "Lord of Heaven and Earth" appeared to smile benignly on his humble servant Bill, who bowed himself before the bandaged form of Ka-te-Bet.

Out from the vast silences of the Museum the voices came: "All Out!"

"All Out!" returned the sonorous echo through the deserted halls. And Bill, awakening as from a trance, dashed blindly from the room into the arms of Emma who stood crouching at the door, white to the lips.

"Nes-Khensu—Emma!" her lover cried, "My Emma!" And folding his arms about her as though to shield her from the impending doom, he kissed her tenderly on the forehead and, as in a dream, he led her homeward.

The End

This story was published in *The Comet*'s special 1934 Christmas number. It was previously featured in Ali's London-based Pan-African journal, *ATOR*

Appendix 6

ABDUL

A TALE OF A CORONATION TRIP—AND WHAT BEFELL

By DUSE MOHAMED ALI

[The Comet, Nigeria. Saturday, February 17, 1934]

"ALL Ashore! [S]trangers leave the ship! All ashore! Shouted the boat-swain. "All ashore!" shrieked the steward, as he elbowed his way through the seething mass of humanity that crowded the decks of the S.S. "Royal George" as she lay moored in the quay of Alexandria. The ship clanged its final warning to those who had no desire to be taken to sea. The "Royal George" strained at her lines like a dog on the leash and her anxiety to take herself off to the port of London seemed as keen as the anxiety shown by the tanned and sunburnt Englishmen and Englishwomen passenger to once more set foot on English soil after a long sojourn in the torrid East; or of the mixed nationalities, Hindu, Egyptian Turk and Levantine, who jabbered excitedly, a veritable babel of tongues—over the prospect of seeing England, and what was more important, viewing King Edward of Britain and his Consort in their coronation robes, seated in their gilded coach, surrounded with all the pride, pomp, and circumstance of glorious state.

At length, amid a deluge of farewell kisses and admonitory remarks from suspicious wives who were leaving their males to the dismal prospect of an Egyptian summer and the tender mercies of the female harpies who infest the "Ostend of Egypt," the "Royal George" began to cast off her moorings. The last visitor had made a frantic dash for the quay with a rather coquett-ish and quite unnecessary display of lace and silken hose. The gangway was unshipped, peparatory to being thrust ashore, when Lord Loam, a very effeminate and much monocled youth, apologetically elbowed his way through the crowd on the quay-side followed by Abdul, an extremely dark Sudanese, who falteringly struggled beneath a some-what cumbersome and weighty kit-bag and a bundle of golf-sticks.

Abdul's tarbush surmounted a very weather-beaten and battle-scarred countenance which, being tilted at a painfully acute angel, seemed in momentary danger of falling on to the quay. Perspiration literally poured down the furrows of his aged face and his breath came in spasmodic gasps.

The owner of the bag had safely reached the deck and the gangway was ominously moving shoreward, when the boatswain leaning over the ship's side pulled man and bag aboard where they both fell upon the deck. The bag bursting open with the impact, the Sudanese was buried beneath the golf-sticks and the miscellaneous eruption of articles so necessary to the comfort and respectability of a touring aristocrat.

"Bai Jove" exclaimed Lord Loam in dismay, as he carefully adjusted his monocle. "You've ruined my dinner things and I don't suppose there's a tailor fellah on boad. I say, steward, steward!" "Yessir, yessir!" cried the steward pushing his way through the giggling throng as he touched the peak of his cap.

"Will you collect my traps and take them—ah to Number 5?" "Yes sir," replied the steward who immediately proceeded to gather up the somewhat tangled mass of clothes, toilet necessaries and golf-sticks

"Here, fellah," cried Lord Loam. He took a gold coin to the fallen Abdul and turning on his heel, his Lordship passed on to his state-room amidst the blessings and salaams of the Sudanese, the fluttering of numerous lace and cambric trifles and the waving of hats, as the majestic floating palace gracefully glided down the Mediterranean to the measured pulsation of her engine. And the "Good-bye" "Bon voyage" "Write soon!" were wafted to the retreating ship in a gradually modulated medley of subdued sound.

II.

MALTA was in sight. Those unfortunate mortals who were unable to come to a settlement with the artistic productions of the ship's chef had long since settled down—to bed, with stewards and stewardess in active attendance.

The Captain paced the bridge, and those hardy persons comprising the human freight of the "Royal George" assembled in groups about the decks, debating whether the ship would remain at Malta long enough for them to tour the island and make purchases and return to the ship, and other inconsequent small talk.

Without "Number five" state-room, Abdul sat curled up in a state of coma. Within the stateroom Lord Loam manfully wrestled with a severe attack of mal-do-mere, the steward being in frequent attendance.

"Have you a ticket for your servant my Lord?" deferentially inquired the steward.

"I have no bally servant," irritably wailed his Lordship. "Please go away", he weakly cried, turning his face to the side of the ship with an awesome groan.

The steward slipped from the state-room and, grasping Abdul by the shoulder, shook him violently. "Where's your ticket?"

"Me have not the ticket," wearily replied Abdul.

"Well, you've got to see the Old Man" growled the steward. "Come along", and pulling Abdul to his feet, he dragged the old Sudanese up the steps of the bridge into the presence of the Captain.

"This man's got no [no] ticket, sir": exclaimed the steward, smartly raising his fore-finger in the direction of his cap.

"How did he come aboard?" inquired the Captain.

"Brought Lord Loam's luggage aboard, sir."

"Now then, my man, we'll have to put you ashore at Malta"; cried the Captain.

"No Malta, Captain; London—me see great White Sultan—him crown."

"You wish to see the King crowned, do you?"

"Yes, please, Captain."

"A very laudable desire, no doubt. But the owners object to the carriage of unpaid human freight, so you'll have to go ashore at Malta."

"No Malta, Captain—no Malta; Please, please, London!" pleaded Abdul. "Me see Sultan Edward! You good Engleese, mooch good Engleese— me servant Gordon Pasha;" and he stood on his feet and smote his breast proudly.

"You, Gordan Pasha's servant?"

"Yes, Captain-pasha. Long, ago, Gordon Pasha come Khartoum. He, Sudan Khedive, very good Pasha—mooch pray Allah—God! Allah Akbar!' And the devout Sudanese bowed himself. "Gordon Pasha tell me God very good for all mans. Me love great Pasha very mooch. After he go me very lonely, me cry, me pray mooch. Mahdi come. Osman Digna come, kill, kill, kill! Allah no like. Good Khartoum mans no like. Dis no good. All good mans pray Allah: 'Send Gordon Pasha: Send Gordon Pasha!' Allah hear good mans pray. Allah send Gordon. All good mans say mooch good— Allah Akbar;—Gordon Pasha come, Mahdi mafeesh, wipe out"!

"Ebry day Gordon Pasha go house-top. He watch Korosko Desert. Me go sit on house-top. Gordon pray mooch. Me mooch pray—very mooch! Me un'stand Gordon Pasha mooch hurt here—here!" and the old man indicated the region of his heart.

"Gordon Pasha put de hand on my head. He say: 'Good Abdul, faithful Abdul, blessings from Allah on thee! If Allah will, one day I go England I tak' you see great White Sultana. Very good Sultana Victoria! Me say: 'T'ank you bery mooch, O great Pasha!' He say: 'Me no great—man no great— God great—Allah Akbar'; Me say: 'Allah Akbar!' Gordon Pasha say: 'Good Abdul!'

"Mahdi sit down outside Khartoum. Mooch, Mooch, very Mooch Dervish come outside Khartoum. Pasha go house-top: look long time to Korosko Desert. He speak with Allah. He say: Dey will come. De troops must some; surely they no desert me?"

"Nothing to eat. All Khartoum only leteel bread. Gordon give all mans leteel bread. He no eat, me no eat. Everyday he go house-top. Plenty bad mans Khartoum. He say bad mans; 'Today Engleese come. Engleese soldier come—Mahdi mafeesh!" Engleese no come. Gordon Pasha no sleep; no— no—sleep. He write, write, write. Afta he sigh, den he sit on him knees. He say: 'God help me for dis peopeel sake!' He cry, me cry. Me love Gordon Pasha! He say me: 'what you cry?' Me tell him so: 'What time great Pasha cry, inside here (pointing to his stomach) all turn over.' Me too mooch love Gordon Pasha—too mooch, too mooch—Gordon Pasha! Gordon Pasha!" exclaimed the aged servitor, bursting into tears. "Look down from the breast of Allah on thy servant Abdul. Speak in de heart of de good Captin, so he take on de great steamer of mooch smoke to see de son of de great White Sultana!" And Abdul lifted his tear-stained face in supplication to Heaven.

The steward turned and looked at the surging billows, and a big crystal tear fell on the beard of the Captain, who said, with the suspicion of a sob in his throat. "We'll see what can be done."

"Ah, Captin, good Engleese Pasha!" cried Abdul and, folding his hands across his breast, he bowed himself, saying: "To Allah be all praise and to his servant Gordon."

"Were you with Gordan when he died?" queried the Captain.

"Yes, long time: no eat, no drink. Bad Khartoum mans say: "Gordon Pasha, we no eat, open all gate to Mahdi."

"No!' say Gordon: 'dis thing no good.'

"Bad Khartoum mans berry cross, he go open gate All Dervish come. Kill, kill, kill! All house blood all street mooch blood—so!" And he pointed to the surrounding waters.

"Plenty Dervish come palace. All servant, all soldier, run 'way—me no run! Gordon stand. Him fight. Den plenty Dervish come kill him—ooh!" and he put his hands to his face as though he would blot out the memory of that dreadful sight. "Me take sword, me fight Dervish. Dervish cut me head with big sword—look!" and he pointed to an old scar reaching from his forehead to his chin. "Me see nothing—before, all black—me fall. After mooch time, me better, me strong. Me come Wadi Halfa. Me show Engleese Pasha Khartoum way. Engleese Pasha take mooch soldier. Kill Dervish! kill, kill, kill. Den Khartoum. Mahdi mafeesh—Osman Digna mafeesh."

"Engleese soldier. Khedive soldier. Sudan soldier. Kill, kill, kill, for Gordon Pasha in Paradise." And the ancient Sudanese with uplifted head, heaving breast, and the lust of the battle blazing from his eyes, shrieked the words: "Kill, kill, kill," for Gordon Pasha in Paradise!" with such energy that the passengers were magnetically drawn up the steps of the bridge by the fervid accents of martial fire.

"Ladies and gentlemen," hurriedly cried the Captain, "you see before you a man who was with Gordon in Khartoum during his terrible siege—a faithful servant of the martyred General. He wants to see his Majesty, King Edward the Seventh, on his way to the Coronation. He had no money to pay his passage. Unless he has the money, according to regulations I must put him ashore at Malta. Who'll help? I'll start with two guineas."

"I'll give five," shouted an old weather-beaten Colonel from the fringe of the crowd.

"Ten guineas me," came the tremulous announcement from a lady on the bridge.

"Hang it all, Captain," exclaimed Lord Loam, who had dashed forth from his cabin at the words, "Kill, kill, kill," dressed in rose-pink pyjamas with a lilac stripe, armed with his monocle and a lady's hair-brush.

"Hang it all, he cried, brandishing the hair-brush, "I'll pay the passage-money for the poor old beggah".

The passengers turned their glances on his Lord-ship. A chorus of "Oh's!" was voiced by the ladies on beholding the shameless attire of the young noble, who beat a hasty retreat covered by the blushes of the ladies which mingled with his own and the laughter of the men, accelerated his dash for the stateroom, and the anchor dropped form the davits with a splash, bringing up the "Royal George" to her anchorage in Malta Harbour.

III.

"Program! Full program o'the Royal proceshun! Buy a program, sir?" "Souveneer of the King an Queen!" "Who wants a program? Only a penny!" "Program!" "Souveneer!"

Such were the cries and counter-cries of the street-hawkers who plied their precarious trade along the embankment into Parliament Street on the morning of the Coronation.

It was but 3 a.m. yet the crowd had assembled in its thousands, taking up all the available positions along the short route long before midnight. Abdul had duly arrived in London at the end of May, and great was his disappointment at the postponement of the ceremonial, but with the fatalistic instinct of the Oriental, on learning of the King's illness, he reverently bowed himself remarking that it was the will of Allah, "To Whom Be All Praise!"

His kind friends of the "Royal George" had taken care that his return passage to Egypt was secured, the money for that purpose being logded with the steamship company, and he was safely housed at the London Home for Asiatics. And now that the long expected day had at length arrived he stood among the surging mass awaiting the coming of the King.

A kindly policeman who had seen service in the Sudan had entered into conversation with him and having heard his disjointed story, promised to help Abdul to a good view of the procession. The guardian of the peace, however, found his hands rather full keeping the crowd within bounds until the arrival of the troops and poor Abdul got lost in the human maze.

The troops duly arrived taking up their positions in front of the crowd, which formed a densely packed mass from the House Guards, stretching itself away into Trafalgar Square, where it hung itself upon the lions around the base of Nelson's Column, and overflowed to the National Gallery even to the steps of St. Martin's Church.

A space was cleared at the base of Gordon's statue for the St. John's Ambulance Corps, who were kept busy from early morning until far into the afternoon.

The sound of distant music was heard, the bells rang out their gladsome warning and the local but unseeing populace shouted: "Here they come! Here they come!"

The people in Whitehall and Charing Cross begin to press forward all endeavouring to get a glimpse of the procession. There was a fearful crash. A few ladies fainted, and Abdul went down with a cry, almost crushed to death by the crowd.

The policeman heard his cry, got into the crowd, and rescued him as the procession entered Whitehall.

"Are you hurt?" he asked.

"Yes—me—die! Quick—me see Sultan Edward?" he painfully inquired. The policeman, despite regulations, lifted the old man in his arms as the King and Queen passed into Whitehall.

With a super-human effort he raised his head and cried aloud: "Allah save King Edward!" And the populace took up the cry: "Long live the King!"

The King saw Abdul, bowed, smiled, and saluted.

"Great—Sultan—Allah Akbar, was the broken exclamation of the old Sudanese as his head sank on the shoulder of the policeman.

Somebody blew a whistle. An ambulance arrived and Abdul was borne away to Trafalgar Square to the base of Gordon's Statue.

"He cannot live," said the surgeon in attendance.

With closed lids the old man muttered: "Me see great White Sultan—Abdul—happy! He laugh with Abdul!" His face twitched with pain. A tremor passed through his aged frame. He tried to rise, and opening his eyes, he caught the calm benign countenance of Gordon Pasha gazing down upon him.

"Gordon Pasha!" he exclaimed. "Good master! Abdul come with thee—to Allah!"

Abdul fell back, his face illuminated by a smile of peace. His soul passed on to join the martyred Gordon amid the pealing of bells, and huzzas of the multitude, the blare of trumpets and the martial strains of "God Save The King"

THE END

This story was published in *The Comet* on February 17, 1934. It was previously featured in Ali's London journal, *ATOR*

"About It and About - - -"

BY THE EDITOR.

Dictators, Colonies and Disarmament.

I learn that Sir Oswald Mosley has been " stating the case " for British Fascism at the Royal Albert Hall, London. The BLACK SHIRT of the British Fascist is a badge of despair rather than an emblem of hope.

The electorial figures in Germany prove that in 1928, a period of booming trade, the Nazis had only twelve members in the Reichstag. In 1932, when there were six million unemployed in Germany, they had 228 seats in the Reichstag. In like manner the British Fascists would very probably benefit by an economic crash.

But would the British people benefit ? There would be no Parliament as we know it. Parliament would become a mere voting machine which would meet to register the decrees of the Government. The Press would possess no liberty whatever. No freedom of speech. And such organizations as the Labour Party would be snuffed out of existence with potential riot and bloodshed similar to the recent happenings in Austria.

Apart from Sir Oswald Mosley there is another possible dictator in the person of Sir Stafford Cripps, ex-Solicitor General, who has darkly hinted he would use the forces of the Crown to carry out his programme which he would attempt to do within the statutory period of five years, failing this he would raise a private army to dragoon Parliament and the Nation into a Crippsonian angle of mind. A Socialist League being his particular obsession.

Sir Stafford Cripps appears to possess a fighting chance on account of his Socialist Labour affiliations. Sir Oswald Mosley's success would depend largely on the reaction of a Socialist League Dictatorship in the direction of Fascist constitutional revolution resulting from unemployment. The Cripps scheme would very probably provoke anger, resistence, and national disaster occasioned by unemployment admitting of Mosley's intervention to readjust economic condition on Germanic lines.

Such a readjustment would unfailingly lead to Jewish persecution and probable expulsion. Although the BLACK SHIRTS contend that they are not anti-Jewish, their headquarters are reported to have been plastered with anti-Jewish posters. Such are the straws which show the direction of the wind.

Meanwhile Franz Von Papen, former Chancellor of Germany, has been urging the return of the German Colonies as a necessity to German commercial existence. He points out that after considerable effort-"the new German Empire eventually acquired 1,000 000, square miles of Colonial territory, as against more than 800,000 for Portugal, 3,500,000 for France, 900,000 for Belgium, a n d 12,000,000 for Great Britain."

"When the German Empire crumbled under the onslaught of 23 nations, Germany's Colonial Empire was sunk without a trace. At Versailles, Germany lost her place in the tropical sun. The Allies stripped her of all her colonies."

He contends that while some Germans previously regarded their colonies as white elephants, today the majority have learned that every great industrial state must have colonies as a reservoir from which to draw its raw materials. And that Germany must expand or explode.

These statements are quite logical, but while this writer has always contended that present world unrest can be traced directly to the diplomatic bungling at Versailles, the German hot-heads who plunged the world into war in 1914 should have been mindful of its potentialities in the event of defeat.

On the other hand Sir Philip Gibbs, who has been discussing disarmament, very wisely says: "There cannot be a complete abandonment of force. An abandon of all force, a complete disarmament of all weapons would result in rivers of human blood amongst the innocent and the most helpless of the world's populations . . . . There are bandit minds and bandit nations not a thousand miles away from London, Paris, or Berlin."

He also tells us: "The position of the extreme pacifists is impossible until human nature changes more than a little, and until the ideals of civilisation are worldwide." Man is a fighting animal. An acquisitive animal. The bandit mind seems impossible of eradication. Almost every one covets his neighbour's possessions, "civilisation and ' progress " notwithstanding. Ambition is too rampant.

The abandonment of force is an impossible dream so are the "ideals" of international law. Both Germany and Japan have quitted the League of Nations. The former demands the restoration her colonies and equality of armaments. The latter demands economic expansion and the entire "progressive" world is arming. The utter destruction of civilisation appears to be the ultimate result of this insane armament race.

Appendix 7: Ali discusses "Dictators, Colonies and Disarmament" in his weekly column, "About It and About….," *The Comet*, May 26, 1934.

ERE ROOSEVET CAME.

a Record of the adventures of
The Man In The Cloak

By DUSE MOHAMED ALI

————:o:————

The characters in this story are entirely fictitious and do not represent any living persons.

Chapter XIII.

The American Negro Press flashed the news throughout the country that Napoleon Hatbry had secured a clothes factory in which he intended to employ one thousand Negro workers, and further that he was about to close a contract for a laundry which would employ another hundred or more. De Woode, while heaping ridicule upon the pretensions of Hatbry, was caustically critical of his rival, pointing out among other things that an enterprise such as that outlined by Hatbry would require a vast amount of capital as well as trained executives, and that Hatbry possessed neither of those two vital qualifications without which, one being dependent upon the other, this newest sensation of Hatbry's would pass into the realm of those nightmares which he had so frequently administered to his credulous followers. He, however, qualified this criticism by stating that the money question might not be an insuperable difficulty because of the vast sums which were at the disposal of Soviet and Japanese agents operating in the United States.

Hatbry rebutted that he was neither in the pay of Russia nor Japan and that if De Woode knew of the existence of such money, he had evidently been approached and paid off; that being the case it was curious that this leader had not used such funds for the benefit of his people. The controversy was long and bitter with a resulting recrimination which hugely amused that section of the whites which read the Negro Press while the Emperor and his following felt that this division among the Negroes would materially aid in blinding the two factions to their proposed suppression or extermination by the Invisible State, which after all was the main point at issue.

Over in Boston, Hewitt Browne had gradually arrived at Ette's view of the situation and his first move was to obtain all possible information from the Communists which he handed over to the United States Government from time to time. He was offered highly remunerative employment and financial reward. To the former he replied that his law practice was sufficiently remunerative and as for accepting money for his services, he was an American Citizen performing such duty to his country as was with-

in his power, and further, while he did not know what the future held for him, he had not yet become a professional spy. Thus, despite the independence of his bitter retort, his sincerity and integrity could not be questioned.

Upon reading the criticisms of Hatbry and De Woode, he wrote privately to those gentlemen pointing out that this was no time for washing dirty linen in public for the edification of the dominant group, but a period when a solid front should be shown to the common enemy with unswerving loyalty to the Flag as was the duty of every American irrespective of race, creed or colour, because of the danger which seemed to threaten from without.

De Woode treated Browne's communication with superior disdain and Hatbry, anxious to escape De Woode's criticism for a time, seized the occasion to publish Browne's letter with an accompanying editorial in which he ridiculed the pretensions of the "Black American Lawyer" who boasted a non-existing Citizenship, thereby "Licking the boots of the white man and placing the yoke of inferiority more firmly about the black man's neck" He further suggested that Browne should reassume his discarded headkerchief and return to his native Southland where his "yes sah, Colonel boss", would quickly secure him those smiles of condescending approbation from his white masters for which he so earnestly yearned.

Browne's friends of both groups were highly incensed at Hatbry's editorial and his indiscreet publication of a confidential communication. Those of his group were anxious to take up the cudgels on Browne's behalf, but he wisely dissuaded them from any such impolitic action. For his part, while regretting Hatbry's indiscretion, he considered the incident closed, his silence causing him to rise considerably in the estimation of his associates and well wishers.

Ette who had not seen Browne since his interview in her sick room and who had now recovered, read the editorial at the Book-Shop where she had resumed her employment. Hatbry's broadside greatly annoyed her and she was immensely relieved when informed by mutual friends that Browne declined to enter into a discussion with Hatbry or permit his friends to take up the matter in his defence.

She had received several telephone calls from him enquiring about her health, but he had not written

"About It and About - - -"

By The Editor.

PRESIDENT ROOSEVELT'S "VERY NEW DEAL."

On another page we publis a letter from "Buckeye" every word of which I unreservedly endorse. It is quite correct to tate that lynchings in the nited tates of America have not been confined to egroe although they have been the greatest suff rer from that form of rough and ready "justice." everthele , lynching of whatever group, must remain a blot on any civilised nation.

Obviously the Wagner-Costigan Federal Anti-lynching bill, which was favourably reported by the nate Judiciary Committee, has received the personal interest of the President who ha. brought pressure to bear upon Congress to pass a bill which is intended to aboli h lynchings in those States where lynching of egroes ha been regarded as an exciting diversion.

Curiously, the Democratic Party of America has proved itself anything but democratic in o far as the egro wa concerned. And the so-called "Grand Old Party" (Republican) after emancipating the egroes under Lincoln, has gradually departed from the concepts of the anti-slavery group which controlled that party during the administrations of Lincoln and Grant.

As "Buckeye" states there were several Senators and Congressmen elected to the Federal Legislature, but such elections occurred during those Republican administrations which immediately succeeded the emancipation, and Oscar De Priest of Chicago, is at present the single coloured representative in the United tates Congress.

It is uncontrovertable that no group can effectively represent the aims and desires of another group especially when the unrepresented group is both segregated and voiceless. The American Constitution unquestionably the most equitable and comprehensive Bill of Rights which the civilis d world can boast. But racial prejudice has caused that instrument to be largely ineffective in so far as it affects the status of the American egro.

At the same time it must be admitted that the American egro, notwithstanding all his political disadvantage , possesses great material opportunities than any other coloured group in the world. Even in the Southern tates, where lynching has been most prevalent, there are many prominent egroes, pro fe onal and industrial, who are accorded consideration and respect at the hands of the dominant group provided they "know their place" in the social scheme.

The Roosevelt family has ever been noted for its equitable views regarding t h e rights and liberties of the Negroes. Theodore Roo evelt, for example, political showman though he was, created a storm of protest during hi Presidential term of office by inviting B oker T. Washington of Tuskegee fame, to dine at the White House. And that President did not consider it beneath his dignity to seek the advice of Washington on important matters that affected the egroes.

The present head of the United States Government although a democrat, or because he possesses a more intimate knowledge of the meaning of democracy than the majority of Democratic Presidents, together with his wife, have proved that they both considered the Negro to be entitled to those political rights which the American Constitution awards and which cannot be legally alienated.

President Roosevelt demonstrated this while Governor of New York State when he made it possible for two coloured lawyers to become municipal judges. And since his election to the Presidency he has insisted that the Negroes should receive adequa e recognition under the National Recovery Act. For the first time, under a Democratic Administration, a coloured man in the person of Dr. William J. Thompkins of Kansas City, Missouri, has b n appointed Recorder of Deeds of the District Columbia. And the U.S. Senate, knowing the will of the President, confirmed the appointment without a dissenting vote.

More than half the White House employees are coloured men and women. The President's personal body guard is Gus Grenich, and his constant attendant i Irvin Henry McDuffie, incorrectly designated by a newspaper writer as a Scotsman, but both of these men are coloured. The Steward and director of the White House cuisine is a Mrs. Allen, a coloured woman.

Mrs. Franklin Delano Roosevelt, the President's wife, addressing a group of educators recently, declared: "The day of really working together has come. We must learn to work together regardless of race, creed, or colour." She said she advocated educational opportunities or every child in the land. "We can have no group beaten do n, under-privileged, without reaction on the r st, where the standard of education is low, the standard of living is low."

(Continued on page 16)

Appendix 9: Discussion of Roosevelt's New Deal in *The Comet*, September 22, 1934.

Appendix 10: Cover art for Duse Mohamed Ali's first journal, the London-based *African Times and Orient Review* Cover [Artist: Walter Crane].

Appendix 11: October 12, 1921
US Intelligence Report on Duse Mohamed Ali's
activities in the US

New York,
Oct. 12, 1921

Mr. Geo. F. Ruch,
Dept. of Justice
Washington D.C.

Sir:

I will report that yesterday Duse Mohamed editor of the African Oriental Review arrived in New York. This publication was stopped before the war and again during the war and I think there is still a ban on it because of its radical expressions. About seven years ago Garvey worked in Duse Mohamed's office in London but they had a falling out over Garvey seducing a young girl. I have been told that only through Mohammed's influence was Garvey kept out of prison. Mohammed was at the office yesterday looking for John Bruce who is Garvey's secretary and whom he knew before coming to this country. It seems that Mohammed had not intended seeing Garvey while here but Bruce had Mohammed at his house last night and succeeded in getting Mohammed to call on Garvey this morning. Mohammed is here in the interest of some newly formed corporation. I understand that he is going to travel through the country trying to get negroes interested in this corporation, especially negro bankers, but he doesn't want the negro public to know that he has had an interview with Garvey, in fact he doesn't want anyone to know it. It seems as if Garvey got his idea of Africa for the Africans, from this man Mohammed.

I learned that the Morse Shipbuilding Co. has attached the money of the Black Star Line in the bank for debt and at the present time they can't touch a dollar.

I am enclosing a form letter that Garvey is flooding the mails with in order to get money. He is sending one of these to every member of the association, and no doubt, will receive thousands of dollars.

Duse Mohammed's address while in New York will be 238 West 136th St. I would advise that a close check be kept on this man while in this country as I understand that England has made some compromise with him for stopping his magazine. Am enclosing clipping of his arrival, from a New York Daily.

Respectfully,
"800"

Appendix 12: October 14, 1921
US Intelligence Report on Duse Mohamed Ali's
Relationship to Marcus Garvey and the U.N.I.A

New York,
Oct. 14, 1921

Mr. Geo. F. Ruch,
Dept. of Justice,
Washington, D. C.

Sir:

I will report that Duse Mohammed was in conference with Garvey to-day for an hour, the greater time of which Garvey excluded his secretary from the office. I do know that Garvey offered Mohammed a room in his house while in New York which Mohammed refused, saying, he was very well located and did not wish to change. I had supper with Mohammed last night and we had a two hour talk, mostly about Garvey. To me he referred to Garvey as "the beggar". He seemed to be hostile towards Garvey; told me all about the trouble he had had with Garvey and the girl in his office in London, how Garvey had come to him "down and out", and how he finally discharged Garvey. It seems that John Bruce who is a very good friend of Mohammed and was an agent for Mohammed's magazine when it was being published, is now a confidential secretary for Garvey. Through Bruce's efforts he has brought these two together. Garvey is more than anxious to make friends with Mohammed because of Mohammed's influence in Africa. From Mohammed's talk with me I learned that he is in touch with a great many African Chiefs. It seems that Mohammed runs a commission house in London in connection with his other business, to which these African Chief's ship their goods for him to sell. Mohammed became very friendly with me during our talk showing me his passport or a paper that answered for a passport. It seems that he had some trouble in getting papers to come to this country and the paper that he has was issued in lieu of a passport. It has his picture attached but no description, only his age. It says, with permission to visit the United States. He has been in communication with President King of Liberia about the loan that King is trying to get from this country, and he told me that he had advised King not to accept the loan because if he did Liberia would be in the same position that Haiti is now in, governed by U. S. Marines. He said that he was going to send a telegram to King and let him know that he was in the country. I tried to draw out of him just what his business was in this country but he evaded an answer and soon changed the subject. I understand that he is to speak in Liberty Hall here Sunday night for Garvey. His address is 230 West 136th street instead of 238 as I reported.

I learned today that a Mr. Barnett of the Chrichlow Coal Co. has put Garvey in touch with a Portuguese (could not learn his name) who is willing to go Garvey's bond for $200,000 (two hundred thousand dollars) so that Garvey can purchase the ship that he is after. I think this transaction ought to be investigated as it doesn't sound very good to me. I understand that this Portuguese is to do all of this gratis.

I learned today that the Dept. of Justice has been in communication with the Faramount Novelty Co. of New York asking them not to advertise the sale of guns in the Negro World; that the department had sent them one of Garvey's speeches in which Garvey had said "we must protect ourselves" I report this to let you know what class of people this Faramount Co. is.

Will go more into details of my interview with Mohammed when I see you Sunday.

Respectfully,
"800"

Appendix 13: November 5, 1921 US Intelligence Memorandum on Marcus Garvey's Activities Addressed to J. Edgar Hoover

November 5, 1921

MEMORANDUM FOR MR. HOOVER

In discussing the general situation of Garvey's movements with confidential informant #800 last Sunday, I was advised by him that he, Garvey, was very much worried over the action which Cyril Briggs had brought against him for slander. Garvey feels that the local state authorities in New York are receiving the assistance of the Department of Justice in this case.

800 suggests that Edgar Gray, a well known character in Harlem be checked up by our New York office to ascertain the nature of his employment.

It is further suggested by this informant that the New York office ascertain from the Chelsa Bank, 135th Street and 7th Avenue, the extent of the bank account of Briggs. According to informant, the money which he is receiving from the "Crusader" is certainly not sufficient to warrant the publication of same. In all probability he is receiving some outside financial assistance.

This informant further suggests that Duse Mohammed Ali, who resides at 230 West 136th Street, be covered to ascertain the nature of his activities. According to 800, Ali is in this country as a representative of some British concern and is endeavoring to interest Garvey and other negroes at Harlem in some business proposition.

According to this informant Briggs is making every possible effort to have the Post Office Inspectors take motion against Garvey for the publication in the "Negro World" of an advertisement showing a picture of the "Phyllis Wheatly" which, according to the statements of Garvey, had been purchased by the Black Star Line. As a matter of fact, this was an ordinary steamboat with the name "Phyllis Wheatly" placed on same and used for a "out" for the advertisement and used for the purpose of securing further purchase for Black Star Line stock.

It is suggested that Mr. Grimes give this matter particular attention.

According to 800, the circulation of the "Negro World" (Garvey's paper) in the past four weeks has decreased from 35,000 to 25,000. 800 advises that this decrease is due to Briggs' action in sending a copy of his magazine to all important centers where Garvey's paper is distributed.

The above is for your information.

Respectfully,

[name redacted]

Appendix 14: November 12, 1921
US Intelligence Report on the Activities of
Marcus Garvey and Duse Mohamed Ali

New York
Nov. 12, 1921

Mr. Geo. F. Ruch,
Box 1822
Washington, D. C.

Sir:

Enclose you will find a copy of a release that Garvey sent to all the dailies on the Disarmament Conference. Am also enclosing a letter that will probably [be] of some interest to you on conditions in Africa among the natives.

I have just learned that will be a conference tomorrow (Saturday) in the rooms of President King of Liberia, at the Commodore Hotel 40th Street and Lexington Ave. at ten oc with Duse Mohamed Ali (whose card I am enclosing) and J.[?]. Austin of Tacoma Wash. Both of these will see King, but [with] different missions. I was present when Austin made arrangements to take Duse Mohamed down town in his car. Mohamed said that when he was through talking with King, King wouldn't take the loan from this country. I don't think that Mohamed will allow Austin to hear what he has to say to King, but I don't know about all that Austin will say. Mohamed is not very ative, but I will try and get the results of this conference. I have been unable to learn anymore about the Japanese, but the next time he gives talk up here, I am to meet [?] have arranged that.

Will report to Washington Sunday as per instructions.

Respectfully,

"800"

Appendix 15: May 10, 1922
US Intelligence Report on Duse Mohamed's work at *The Negro World*

New York
May 10, 1922

Mr. Geo F. Ruch
P. O. Box 1822,
Washington, D. C.

Sir:

Enclosed you will find the front page of this weeks issue of the paper. From this article one would infer that the U.N.I.A. is going to help Liberia pay back this loan. Just another one of Garvey's ideas of getting money from the poor illiterate negroes.

I am also enclosing you Duse Mohamed's article under the caption "Foreign Affairs". In these articles you will find both anti British and Mohammedan propaganda. Each week Duse Mohamed sends twenty copies of the paper to the officials of the Turkish and Egyptian governments. It is purely a case of Garvey useing Mohamed, and Mohamed useing Garvey paper to spread his propaganda. Garvey makes use of Mohamed's acquaintances in securing delegates to his convention in August. This fact I have reported before.

Other than these few facts, everything seems to be going on in the usual manner.

Garvey is at present in Milwaukee, Wis.

Respectfully,

"800"

P.S. Am enclosing under separate cover this weeks issue of the paper.

Appendix 16: March 21, 1922
US Intelligence Report on Duse Mohamed's
Anti-British writings for *The Negro World*

New York,
March 21, 1922

Mr. Geo. F. Ruch,
P. O. Box 1822
Washington, D. C.

Sir:

There seems to be very little to report. Everything seems to be at a stand still waiting for Garvey's trial.

Duse Mohamed is now editing a section of the paper under the title 'Foreign Affairs'. You will notice that this section is very Anti-British.

Miss Jacques told me, that Duse Mohamed, was visiting Miss Lamos' (Garvey's new secretary) at night, trying to get a line on Garvey's confidential communication. I found this was not true, but only propaganda of Jacques trying to put both Miss Lamos and Mohamed in bad light, knowing that should Mohamed run the organization after Garvey is sent up, she would be put out. Jacques is doing everything that she can to bring about a break between Garvey and Mohamed. Jacques told some one in my office that Garvey had beaten her, and that she was tired of his beatings. If there is ever a break between Garvey and Jacques you need never worry about the out come of the case as she knows enough to hang him. You can rest assure that anything that I can do to bring about this condition will be done.

Mr. Ruch I have not received my check for the 15th of March, I notify you for fear that it may have been lost in the mails.

Respectfully,

"800"

Appendix 17: Special Agent J.G. Tucker's November 19, 1921 Report on Duse Mohamed Ali's Activities in New York

It is understood that the Negro named Major York, who has recently been operating in Philadelphia, has arrived in New York during the last few days with a new Liberian scheme. His idea, however, is different from that of Garvey's as it is his intention to g[a]ther together as many business men as possible and proceed by steamship to Liberia and there point out to the party the advantages to be had in the country by business men who will establish enterprises there.

Duse Mohammed Ali, who resides at 230 West 136th St., New York, has recently been having conferences with Marcus Garvey, the subject of which, however, being at this time unknown. This man is described as being very highly cultured and about fifty-two years of age, and is said to have been in this country several weeks, arriving here from London. He is Director of the Inter-colonial Corporation, Ltd., of 180 Fleet St., London, and publisher in that city of the "African-Oriental Review." The publication of the Review is said to have been forbidden by the British Government during the war owing to the periodical's extreme radicalism. The American correspondent for the Review is John E. Bruce who is associated on the "Negro World" with Marcus Garvey and writes under the nom-de-plume "Bruce Grit." It is understood that Bruce has been friendly with Mohammed Ali for upwards of twenty years and that it is quite possible he has been responsible for Ali and Garvey getting together at this time, as it was known that Garvey and Ali had been enemies for several years. The person who furnished the above information stated, that he had been told Garvey was once employed by Mohammed Ali in London as a porter and general worker around the former's office and that the "back to African scheme" was at that time engaging all of Ali's attention. Garvey is said to have gathered all information possible and suddenly left Ali's employ and come to this country where he immediately started the first of his many schemes which was based on the idea which he stole from Ali.

The affairs of the Black Star Line are still in very bad financial condition, a number of suits having been brought against the Line by the creditors.

The Universal Negro Improvement Association is also said to be in bad financial condition.

J.G. Tucker

DJ-FBI, file 61. TC

Published in Robert Hill, ed., *The Marcus Garvey and Universal Negro Improvement Association Papers, Vol. IV, September 1921-September 1922* (Berkeley: University of California Press, 1983), 203.

Appendix 18: American Consul General's March 24, 1921
Memorandum on Duse Mohamed Ali's Inter-Colonial
Corporation, Limited Business Venture

No. 11034.

AMERICAN CONSULATE GENERAL
LONDON: ENGLAND

March 24, 1921

Subject: LIBERIA – THE INTER-COLONIAL CORPORATION –
PROJECTS OF DUSE MAHAMAD ALI

The Honorable
The Secretary of State
Washington

Sir:

I have the honor to report as of probable interest in connection with
Liberian matters, that Mr. Duse Mahamad Ali Editor of the Africa and
Orient Review, of 158 Fleet Street, London, E.C.4. is shortly proceeding to
the United States. He expects to meet President King of Liberia, with whom
he has been in communication, either in New York or Washington, and
while there, to further the commercial prospects of the Inter-Colonial Corporation, Limited.

Mr. Duse Mahamad Ali is a native Egyptian himself and the Inter-Colonial
Corporation, Limited, which he is promoting, is primarily a business undertaking, whose founders hope will succeed in handling the raw products of
West Africa upon a very large scale and will be instrumental in constructing
a railway system in Liberia, and otherwise in developing that country.

So much for the commercial aspects of his enterprise. Mr. Duse Mahamad
Ali is also very greatly interested in preventing West Africa generally, and
Liberia particularly, from falling under the domination of European political and commercial interest to the exclusion of the native element. He has
observed the rising power of Lever Brothers Limited who, through a series
of interlocking corporations, practically control the gathering, forwarding

and ultimate manufacture and sale of the staple crops of the West Coast, and he is persuaded that intimately associated with this actual commercial control, there is an expectation of fastening political control as well. He has especially in mind the hazardous situation of Liberia which maintains a precarious independence due to the benevolent attitude of the United States towards that Republic, and according to his own statements, has discussed the future of the country with Mr. King, from whom apparently he has obtained encouragement.

I enclose one copy of the prospectus of the Inter-Colonial Corporation, Limited, from which it will be observed that its powers are practically unlimited. Mr. Duse Mahamad Ali, on his arrival in the United States hopes very much to obtain American capital for this undertaking, and I judge that it would suit his purposes if all the necessary capital might be furnished from within the United States.

I made special point of enquiring of Mr. Duse Mahamad Ali about the position of the Liberian International Corporation, Limited. This is the overriding corporation representing the shadowy Liberian understandings of Mr. James E. Dunning and his friends. Mr. Duse Mahamad Ali does not think this concern has any prospects whatever. Although undoubtedly its Directors have, or have had, some hope that Lever Brothers, Limited, might furnish the funds which they have not been able to raise among themselves. I also made enquiries about the group represented by Sir Alfred Sharp, who broke away from Mr. Dunning, and his associates, and started another corporation, the object of which is to build a railway in Liberia. Sir Alfred Sharp is now in Liberia in the interest of this concern. Mr. Duse Mahamad Ali considers that Alfred Sharp has no prospects whatever of securing a concession from the Liberian Government, and seems inclined to doubt whether any money could be raised for the undertaking, even if the concession were forthcoming. He says quite frankly that both of these enterprises contemplate the commercial absorption of Liberia by British interests to be followed eventually by political absorption as well.

My informant is an Egyptian of good appearance, very intelligent, who talks well about West African matters. I have no information as to the actual capital of which he disposes, if any.

I have the honor to be, Sir,
Your obedient Servant,
[can't read name]
American Consul General

Appendix 19: Front page of *The Negro World*, June 17, 1922

VOL. XII. No. 18   NEW YORK, SATURDAY, JUNE 17, 1922

CHRISTIAN BOERS OF SOUTH AFRICA USE AEROPLANES TO BOMB HOTTENTOTS

FELLOW MEN OF THE NEGRO RACE, *Greeting:*

So the Hottentots have risen in rebellion in South West Africa, and the English are about to use their aeroplanes in bombing them into submission! Not very long ago the natives of Kenya, South East Africa, rebelled, and they also were put down by organized military force. This reveals to us an unhealthy state of affairs. The natives of Kenya were able to fight only with sticks and stones; the Hottentots in this their new rebellion are fighting with wooden spears and leather shields. Surely they cannot put up much resistance against aeroplanes bombing them from the sky and mounted forces charging them with bayonets and shooting them down with the latest model rifles. The spirit of the people, according to these two rebellions, has arisen to the sense of liberty, but they do not know how to get it. They believe that they can successfully use their sticks, stones, and wooden spears to repel and expel the "vicious alien enemy." It is not practicable. Those of us who have mixed with modern civilization know that the natives of Africa will never be able to redeem their country in this way. If they must expel the invader, and that is expected, then they will have to do so on modern, scientific lines. We cannot fight for our liberty nowadays with sticks and stones; we must have the latest model machine guns, the most deadly gas, and those weapons that have stood the test of modern combat.

A Bit of Advice

Instead of so many of us wasting our time in pool rooms, cabarets and places of evil repute around these modern American cities and the progressive countries of the West Indies, why not put in our time developing ourselves scientifically, learning how to manufacture chemicals that can be applied for useful purposes in such conflicts as do take place in Kenya and in South West Africa? Surely the introduction of chemical gas among the Hottentots and the natives of Kenya would place them in a better position to handle "the alien disturbers of African peace." Surely Smuts and other Boers would not have such an easy time subduing black men if our brothers knew how to apply a little chemical fire to some of these "cold and frigid disturbers of human liberty." Surely the chemical heat would warm them up a bit, and they would get to realize that the whole world is not an iceberg, and that certain parts in Africa can be made as warm even as the borders of Hades!

Opportunity at Our Door!

It strikes me, with all the civilization that America and this Western World affords, Negroes ought to take better advantage of the course of higher education. In any city we can find institutions of learning where we can develop ourselves technically and otherwise. We could make of ourselves better mechanics, better scientists, better artisans, and if we have no use for the knowledge today, surely we could apply it in the days to come, and in cases where we can help our brothers in Africa by making use of the knowledge we possess, it would be but our duty. If Africa is to be redeemed the Western Negro will have to make a valuable contribution, and there can be no better contribution to African liberty made by us than that which is technical and scientific.

Aeroplanes in Africa

The Hottentots have no aeroplanes, and because of that the Boers and the British can bomb them out of their holes and huts and ultimately subdue them. But around these American cities and this Western World we have many Negroes who can fly in aeroplanes. Why not build some, and when the Hottentots need aeroplanes to combat aeroplanes, why not give them of our technical ability and help them to put over the big job that all of us want done? It is true that we cannot get our aeroplanes from America to Africa; but, after all, we can build aeroplanes anywhere for that matter, even in South West Africa, and it does not take such a long time to build them after all. But first of all we must get the knowledge; we must have the skill by which we can do these things when the time comes.

The Duel of Brains

This may sound very harsh and cold-blooded, but it is for me to let the world know, it is for me to let all the members of the Negro race know, that nobody is going to listen to you if you pray, if you sing, or if you shout. Nowadays God only being that listens to prayers is our Heavenly

NATIVES ONLY HAVE STICKS AND LEATHER SHIELDS WITH WHICH TO FIGHT

IF AFRICA IS TO BE REDEEMED THE WESTERN NEGRO MUST HELP WITH SCIENTIFIC AND MECHANICAL SKILL

MAN DOESN'T LISTEN TO PRAYERS OR HARKEN TO PETITIONS, BUT HE FEELS

THIRD ANNUAL INTERNATIONAL CONVENTION OF NEGRO PEOPLE OF THE WORLD PROMISES SOLUTION TO PROBLEM

Father, and He is quite away in Heaven. We hope to meet Him one day, because, as Christians and believers in the one true and living God, all of us hope to see our judgment; but today we are on earth, and I repeat that man does not listen to prayers; he does not hearken to petitions, and you may hold as many mass meetings as there are days in the year, he is not going to listen to you. Man only feels. If you can drop a bomb further than he can, and even more deadly, then he is going to listen to your complaint. If you can make some chemical and produce some explosive by which you can put him out of commission easier than he can you, he is going to listen to you; so we must not expect our brothers in Africa to save Africa by prayers, petitions and mass meetings; Africa can only be redeemed by the scientific skill of the Negro himself. We will have to match fire with hell-fire; he will have to match science with higher science; he will have to match brains with greater brains. It is well we understand this now.

The great white man that held sovereignty over the world through his power in science, in art, and in industry. Negroes, my advice to you is to get that kind of power that will place you on a par with the great white man. If you think that you can stand on Mother Earth with a bow and arrow in your hand and shoot the man from the plane five miles above you, you make a tremendous mistake, because in two seconds he will put you out of commission by dropping a bomb on your head, and the next thing you know you are on a long trip across Jordan. If you want to meet the other fellow and he has his aeroplane, get one. If you want to hold that which is your own, you have to get the kind of protection that is necessary. If the other fellow has a long-range gun, you cannot use a bow and arrow, because he will blow you to pieces—you have simply to go and get a long range gun, and one that can fire at least ten yards further than his. These are cold facts, and it is well the Negro realized that now. We are living in a material age, the age when power rules—not sentiment, not emotion, but power, and the best thing you can do is to get it.

The Negro Tradition

We are not disappointed, however, because the Hottentots have lost in their effort for freedom, or because the natives of Kenya have lost their chance of liberty. The reverses they have suffered only tend to open our eyes, to make us realize that the age of sticks and stones is past, and the age of scientific combat is here.

I trust Negroes nowhere will try to start anything unless they are well prepared, because this is an age of preparedness on the part of all peoples. We want a better system of world organization. We want that common sympathy going on as a race that will cause us to feel over the reverses of the Hottentots as they do themselves. Surely the Hottentots are not related to the Boers or to the Alexander Bond, or even the Englishman; but the Hottentot is flesh of our flesh and blood of our blood. We can hardly distinguish the Hottentot from an American Negro, or the Kenya native from a West Indian Negro. We feel our own can do by subscribing to the same cause, because we are of the same race.

While may are so loyal to their tribes that Romans are suffering from a famine, American white men will still

Lafayette

Lafayette came to this country and helped in the founding of this grand nation...

MARCUS GARVEY, President-General, UNIVERSAL NEGRO IMPROVEMENT ASSOCIATION

Appendix 20: Article on Marcus Garvey's meeting with the K.K.K, published in *The Negro World*, July 1, 1922

THE NEGRO WORLD, SATURDAY, JULY 1, 1922

GARVEY INTERVIEWS WIZARD OF KU KLUX KLAN

Appendix 21: Hon. Marcus Garvey Tells of Interview with the Ku Klux Klan," *The Negro World*, July 15, 1922

Appendix 22: "The White Man's Civilization a Splendid Example to Negroes," Leader article of *The Negro World*, June 10, 1922

The indispensable Weekly — *The Voice of the Awakened Negro*

Negro World

A Newspaper Devoted Solely to the Interests of the Negro Race

VOL. XII. No. 17   NEW YORK, SATURDAY, JUNE 10, 1922

THE WHITE MAN'S CIVILIZATION A SPLENDID EXAMPLE TO NEGROES

FELLOW MEN OF THE NEGRO RACE, *Greeting:*

As one journeys through the great United States of America he is bound to come in contact with the white man's progress in industry, science and education. On every side you see evidence of his great work. He has built a civilization upon the surface of a wild and neglected country. He has planted city life where only a desert existence was once manifest.

The Early Colonists

Whether you live in New York or in Los Angeles you are sure to come in contact with the civilization that the white man has wrought by his labor, sacrifice and endurance. I am left to think whether the Negro of this twentieth century is able to rise to the heights of the white man. When we contemplate America a few hundred years ago, we see a vast wilderness, a forest, a prairie country, unkept, undeveloped, rude in every element of Nature's make-up. Then suddenly we see a ship crossing the tempestuous Atlantic. It makes port, it anchors off the New England coast, the passengers disembark, they settle at Plymouth. From there I see the beginning of a mighty colonization. I see these colonists land, I see them suffer, I see them die. Their numbers diminish, and yet they are not discouraged. On and on they go, until gradually they become acclimatized. Steadily they made their encroachments upon the rights of an aboriginal race; yes, I see them strengthened in their courage and determination to colonize a new country, to develop a new land. Years passed, decades came and went, and still on and on they go. One hundred years have rolled by, two hundred years have rolled by, three hundred years have gone, and today we see a great civilization standing to the credit of an ancestry most grand, most noble. Can I lay claim to that ancestry? Unfortunately, no! The men and the women who laid the foundation of American nationality and American progress and American civilization were not my forebears. They were the ancestors of another race; yes, the white race. Do you wonder, therefore, that the white man boasts that America is a white man's country? Do you wonder that he takes pride in the development of his own nation? Do you wonder that he Jim-crows, segregates, murders, burns and lynches the black man when the black man shows a disposition to rival him in industry, in politics, in social life in the country that he, the white man, has suffered for, has died for, has built for his own convenience? You may argue that my ancestors worked as slaves to build up alongside of the white man the great American nation. But, ah, when the circumstances under which we were brought here as slaves are taken into consideration we will immediately realize the fact that the white man owes no obligation to the Negro. But because I employ the bricklayer or the carpenter to build my house should I in turn give over my apartments to him as his property. If he was paid for his work or the building is erected, he goes; I take possession. I will say that the slave was not paid for his work. The man believes that the slave has been well paid for whatsoever service he gave, even though not of his free will for the building up of the great United States of America that the white man claims that he has given the civilization and Christianity; the white man claims he rescued the Negro from the jungles of Africa, otherwise would still have been a barbarian, a savage, a cannibal. The white man claims that he has within the twentieth century given the Negro every opportunity to do for himself, as he, the white man, has done; therefore, he argues, is not reward do you want for the labor that you for 250 years did as a slave?" If we are to admit the truth we must come to the conclusion that the white man cannot be touched even with the soot that devout prayer, in asking him to share America's lights with the black man. It is not going to help the black man to tell him how to run the city, by run the nation. Nor after he has suffered ...

WHITE MAN HAS PLANTED CITY LIFE WHERE ONLY DESERT EXISTED

WHITE MAN WILL NOT YIELD UP AMERICA OR EUROPE TO NEGROES

NEGROES MUST CREATE UNITED STATES OF AFRICA

APPEAL FOR SUPPORT FOR THIRD INTERNATIONAL RACE CONVENTION

much for the building of this nation, for the founding of this great republic. The white man who has built New York, who has built Boston, who has built Philadelphia, who has built Chicago, who has built Milwaukee, who has built Kansas City, who has built Washington, who has built Portland, who has built Los Angeles and San Francisco, who has built New Orleans and Atlanta, is not going to yield up to the black man that which he has worked for, suffered for, and died for.

A Temporal Age

Tell me that a better time will come when there will be an amicable settlement between black and white as far as the life politic, economic and social goes, and I laugh at you in derision, because no sensible student of political economy, sociology or economics could come to any such conclusion.

As one studies the country and the people the more, one is bound to realize that this great white man is going to make a death struggle to maintain the civilization that he has founded for his own convenience. If any Negro in America or anywhere thinks that the white man is going to lay down the railroad tracks, put on his Pullman and other cars for the purpose of conveying himself from one part of the country to the other, to his own comfort and convenience; that he is going to establish his own government, and divide them up into various departments to suit his own convenience and comfort; that he is going to build his own homes, palatial homes, hotels, theatres and playhouses and adorn them to his own comfort and convenience and allow the Negro to monopolize them, he makes a big mistake. The white man is not thinking about the Negro or any other race but himself, and no sensible human being will blame him in an age so material, in an age so human as this twentieth century. We are not living in a spiritual age; we are living in a temporal, material age, and it is unreasonable for any set of human beings to expect another set to give up to them what they themselves would not give up. It is well we return to reason and thereby understand and know ourselves as a people and as a race. If the Negro wants the comforts of modern civilization, if he wants the happiness of city life, if he wants the privilege of governmental control, then he must create these things for himself. If he wants to ride in Pullman cars from New Orleans to New York, from New York to San Francisco; if he wants to occupy the orchestra seat in the Metropolitan Opera House; if he wants to sit in the front seats of a trolley car; if he wants the first job on the industrial list; if he wants the opportunity to represent his district in the House of Congress or in the Senate; if he wants to sit in the White House as President of the nation; if he wants to sit in the Department of Justice as Attorney General, he will not expect these things in the United States of America. He shall go and will create for himself the United States of Africa. America is not going to yield these things to the Negro! Great Britain is not going to yield these things to the Negro; neither is France, Italy or Germany, so there is no use trying, there is no use

/aggravating this great white chief, however he is not going to do it, simply because it is unreasonable. It is not going ...

The Japanese Empire

Negroes, let us take inspiration from the white man's achievement in America and in Europe. If we do not desire to pattern the white man's civilization of Europe and America, then to have a fair and splendid example of what man can do, take the achievement of the great yellow man in Japan. In the space of seventy years a few million Japanese have built up a mighty empire that occupies today not a second place, but is numbered among the first rate powers of the world. England in the space of a few centuries has built up a vast empire where she was but an island kingdom, and if forty-five million Anglo-Saxons could have done that to their own honor and glory, four hundred million Negroes, united under the leadership of the Universal Negro Improvement Association, can do it for themselves in another hundred years.

An Appeal to Africa's Sons

I am appealing to the manhood of the race everywhere, in America, the West Indies, South and Central America and Africa to let us get together now and put over this great program of the Universal Negro Improvement Association. Let us take inspiration from the white man's civilization. Let us look at the West Indian and the manhood of the race in North America, South and Central America can do the same. Let us unitedly then apply our knowledge of western civilization to the development of Africa. Africa needs her mechanics, her scientists, her industrial captains, her teachers, her ministers, her business men, her statesmen. Scattered as we have been for the last three hundred years, and educated as we have been in the different schools of adversity, can we not rise with this higher education to save ourselves and our country? Surely we can, and that is why I am this week appealing to every Negro to support the work of the Universal Negro Improvement Association. You can support it morally and financially. Those of you who have the education, it is for you to throw yourselves in body and soul and contribute the little you can mentally to the putting over of the program. Those of you who have no ability educationally, you can help with your money; yes, you can help by donating $1, $2, $5, $10, $50, $100 to help us in the great work. Do so now by subscribing to the African Redemption Fund by writing to the Secretary-General, Universal Negro Improvement Association, 56 West 135th Street, New York City, N. Y., U. S. A., or help us in subscribing to the Convention Fund of 1922. A large sum of money is needed to successfully put over the program of the forthcoming convention. You can help with your $2, $5, $10, $50, $100 by writing to the Registrar, Universal Negro Improvement Association, 56 West 135th Street, New York City, N. Y., U. S. A.

With very best wishes for your success, I have the honor to be

Your obedient servant,

MARCUS GARVEY, *President-General*

UNIVERSAL NEGRO IMPROVEMENT ASSOCIATION,

Los Angeles, Cal., June 5, 1922.

Appendix 23: Duse Mohamed Ali's August 9, 1919 Petition to A.J. Balfour, Secretary of State for Foreign Affairs for a Declaration of Nationality

August 9th 1919.

Rt. Hon. A.J. Balfour, P.C. O.M.,
Secretary of State for Foreign Affairs,
Foreign Office.
Whitehall, S.W.

Sir,

I take the liberty of infringing upon your valuable time for the purpose of drawing your attention to my anomalous position in this country regarding the question of nationality.

I arrived in this country from Egypt in 1876, and the particulars of my life since that time are in the Home Office and the New Scotland Yard. Consequently, I find it unnecessary to waste your time with these details. Suffice it to say that I am known not only in London but in the Provinces having a reputation of sorts as the Historian of Modern Egypt, Journalist and Newspaper Proprietor.

Up to the present time I have never been in a Police Court as defendant in any action whatever, nor for that matter in any other court of law. On the outbreak of hostilities I was visited by the Police and investigations were made by the Special Branch of the C.I.D. into my antecedents. Obviously the Police were satisfied with my bona fides, or proceedings of some kind would have taken place eventually because it was claimed that I was pro-Turkish.

Like all other Egyptians resident in England, I registered as an Egyptian subject when the order for such registration was issued by the Government. Although I received visits from the Police for one reason or another of a political nature the matter of my nationality was not questioned until I applied for a Passport for the purpose of visiting Africa in 1917 in the interest of Messrs. Jules Karpeles of 21, Minding Lane, E.C. on the one hand, and on the other in connection with the West African Directory upon which I have been engaged and which is intended to benefit the British Manufacturer and Trader.

Upon making this application for Passport, I was called before Mr. Stafford of the Passport Office who had a lengthy interview with me concerning my antecedents and my reason for visiting Africa. At the end of the interview he told me that as far as he could see he had every reason to believe that a Passport would be granted to me. A period of some three months elapsed, and hearing nothing from the Passport Office, in the interim I sent to enquire at the Passport Office whether the Passport would be granted or witheld. I received a vague reply to this enquiry, and on the following morning the Brixton Police sent for me. I was told by them that they had instructions from the Home Office to demand that I should re-register as a Turkish subject, inasmuch as the Egyptian Government knew nothing about me. Meanwhile, I must draw your attention to the fact that a photographic copy of my birth certificate was in the possession of the New Scotland Yard authorities. This certificate was obtained for me from Alexandria, my birthplace, by Abushady Bey, Advocate of Cairo, on information supplied by me. It should be known to you that to procure an Egyptian birth certificate one must not only know the full name of one's father, but one must also know the name of the midwife by whom one was delivered, and who is responsible for the registration of all births with which one is directly concerned. My reasons for stating these facts should be obvious to you.

I therefore respectfully ask that you, as His Britannic Majesty's Secretary of State for Foreign Affairs, should issue to me a declaration of nationality, as I find myself at present politically suspended between Egypt and Turkey. Egypt is now under the protection of Great Britain. No one can dispute that I am an Egyptian, consequently, I have the right to demand British protection, inasmuch as I have never accepted Turkish rule for my country or myself. The unenviable position in which I find myself makes it absolutely impossible to carry on my business, because neither the people with whom I have business relations nor myself are able to determine whether I am an Egyptian, Turkish or British. As this is a manifest injustice to which I am sure you will not be a party I most respectfully beg to ask that you will comply with my request for this declaration of my nationality which I hereby make.

Awaiting the favour of your early reply,

I have the honour to be,

Sir,

Your obedient servant,

Duse Mohamed Ali

Appendix 24: Aubrey Herbert's Inquiry about Duse Mohamed Ali's Nationality

28 Bruton Street, W.1

16th May 1918

Dear Sir William,

I should be very grateful if you would have a question looked into. There is a negro called Duse Mohamed. He is by way of being an Ottoman subject, though actually I believe he is American born and does not talk either Turkish or Arabic, but he is, or calls himself Mohameddan. In the past he was quite useful at Moslem meetings, when a number of people used always to try and make anti-Government speeches. I don't think that there is any harm in the man. He is anxious to go to West Africa for trade purposes, and has been refused a passport. I should be very grateful if you would look into this.

I am &c.,
(SD.) AUBREY HERBERT.

Thanks to our Patreon subscriber:

Ciaran Kane

Who has shown generosity and
comradeship in support of our publishing.

Check out the other perks you get by subscribing
to our Patreon – visit patreon.com/plutopress.

Subscriptions start from £3 a month.

The Pluto Press Newsletter

Hello friend of Pluto!

Want to stay on top of the best radical books we publish?

Then sign up to be the first to hear about our new books, as well as special events, podcasts and videos.

You'll also get 50% off your first order with us when you sign up.

Come and join us!

Go to bit.ly/PlutoNewsletter